FROM THE THE SHADOWS

NEIL WHITE

ZAFFRE

First published in Great Britain in 2017 by
Zaffre Publishing
80-81 Wimpole St,
London W1G 9RE
www.zaffrebooks.co.uk

A CIP catalogue record for this book is
available from the British Library.

Trade Paperback ISBN: 978-1-78576-095-2
Paperback ISBN: 978-1-78576-092-1
Ebook ISBN: 978-1-78576-094-5

1 3 5 7 9 10 8 6 4 2

Typeset by IDSUK (Data Connection) Ltd
Printed and bound by Clays Ltd, St Ives Plc

MIX
Paper from
responsible sources
FSC
www.fsc.org   FSC® C018072

Zaffre Publishing is an imprint of Bonnier Publishing UK,
a Bonnier Publishing company
www.bonnierpublishing.co.uk

FROM
THE
SHADOWS

Neil White was born and brought up around West Yorkshire. He left school at sixteen but returned to education in his twenties, when he studied for a law degree. He started writing in 1994, and is now a criminal lawyer by day, crime fiction writer by night. He lives in the north of England with his wife and three children.

Also by Neil White

Fallen Idols
Lost Souls
Last Rites
Dead Silent
Cold Kill
Beyond Evil
Next to Die
The Death Collector
The Domino Killer
Lost in Nashville

One Year Earlier

It was almost one in the morning. The house was in darkness, the curtains closed. He was wearing just a light sweatshirt and jogging bottoms but he didn't feel the cold. His nights were about silence, not warmth, and the more he wore, the more noise he made.

He waited. He wasn't sure what for at first, because he'd stood there before, long hours as he waited for a sign that the time was right, but it had been too still.

This time, it was different. He felt them. A light ruffle of wind through his hair, and movement under his feet like soft rumbles in the ground. Whispers behind him. He whirled round but there was no one there, just a fence that shielded him from the houses behind.

He closed his eyes, just to make sure, because sometimes there were false alarms, small teases that made him move too soon. It felt right, though. His breaths were shorter and his arousal made his tongue flick to his lip.

She had her routines to keep herself safe, but they were her weakness, because all he had to do was keep watch. He slipped into her stride as she'd walked home, or he was the man sitting three rows behind her on the bus, or in the queue in the local shop with that bottle of wine to get her through the evening. She loved her Thursday nights; he'd seen her relief as she clutched the bottle and a long week at work became just one more day to get through. He knew what sandwiches she bought at lunchtime and how she would sit outside if she could, when the weather was good enough.

Habits made her feel safe, because then she'd never forget to do something, like checking that everything was turned off or locked up. It was just the opposite, because all he had to do was learn her patterns.

Her lights gave her away, the same order each night. The television went off first, and then the flickering candles. The light for the stairs went on and then her face would appear at the back door, distorted through the glass, checking the door was locked. He was watching and waiting, just a shadow amongst the leaves.

Patience brought its rewards. There was always a way. Some people are casual about their keys. Others forget to lock their doors when they go to bed, or fall asleep drunk on the sofa. All he ever had to know was how to get in.

She never left the key in the back door. Always the front. He'd guessed why: so she could open the front door quickly if she had a delivery or something, rather than rush round for the keys. People are forgetful though, and she kept a spare back door key under a flowerpot.

Habits are dangerous.

The stair light first, followed by the landing light. Her bedroom was next, although that was harder to see, because the bedroom was at the front, so the light was not much more than a glow. There was always a delay, when he imagined her getting undressed and slipping into her nightclothes. Usually pyjamas, but in summer it was just knickers and an old T-shirt.

The bathroom came next. It was the middle window at the back of the house, frosted, with a blind she didn't always close.

He'd watched the movement of her arm as she brushed her teeth. Two minutes. Always two minutes, as if she timed herself. Then it was the toilet. Her back to the window, bending over as she pulled down her knickers, before disappearing from sight. Such a private thing but it was his view. Her secrets became his secrets.

Her garden was long and dark. He'd been in the undergrowth for an hour. Dressed in black, he was invisible. The cloth mask moved in and out as he breathed. Black and made from thin nylon, eyeholes the only bright spots. He'd passed her in the street and she hadn't known him.

He'd waited a long time for a dry, moonless night. The winds got faster, the tremors under his feet made him unsteady. The whispers were small words of encouragement. It was time to move.

He pulled the branches of the laurel bush that grew in a corner to one side. His footsteps were light. No rustles, no noise.

There was no security light as he stepped on to the patio. He reached under the flowerpot for her spare key. The pot scraped on the paving slab. He paused as he looked out for a light in one of the windows, but they stayed dark.

The key was there.

He crept to the back door, staring through the glass as he hunted for a sign of movement inside, but it stayed dark and still. He turned the key slowly, letting out a breath at the slight clunk of the lock. The door opened silently, as he knew it would. She didn't know that he'd oiled the hinges. The back door, and all the rooms in the house, so that he could move silently He'd been in there before, when she'd gone out, learning his way around the house. He knew the weak points, the creaks and the groans. Avoid the third step.

He moved quickly, his breaths getting faster under the hood. He tried to concentrate but the ground moved beneath his feet, the whispers in his head like chants. He passed the doorways to the other rooms, the streetlight at the front providing a half-light in the hallway until he reached the bottom of the stairs.

He stared upwards. It seemed darker up there. A droplet of sweat ran into his eye, making him blink.

He kept to the edge of each step, striding over the third one, his clothes brushing the wall. He paused at the top. The voices stopped as if holding their breath. The earth stayed still. Now he was in control.

Her bedroom was large, with the streetlight outside the window. Her bed faced the door, so this was the most dangerous time. If she heard a noise, or just sensed his presence, she'd see him, but only as a shadow, a vague outline. Darkness was his friend, but he couldn't afford to be caught.

He listened out for the creak of the mattress as she moved, or the sound of her feet on the carpet, investigating the noise. Nothing. Her bedroom door was ajar and the only sound was the steady tick of a clock.

He pushed at the door. It opened slowly, silently. He remained still, to see whether she moved or opened her eyes. He could leave and she might think it was a dream.

As his eyes became accustomed to the gloom, the faint glow of the streetlight made her silky bedcover gleam.

He knew how it felt; he'd lain on it when she wasn't there, took in her aroma from the pillows, stale perfume and warm sleep. He'd looked through her drawers, run his hands through her underwear, relished the silkiness.

His mouth was open as he stepped into the room, his breath coming too quickly. Stay in control. She was under her covers, lying on her side, facing him, the sound of her sleep so gentle. If he closed his eyes for a moment, he could smell her.

He knelt by the bed. Her face was inches away. Her lips, soft and full, her hair over her cheek, her fingers slender over the duvet. He reached out but stopped. Not yet. He'd always promised himself. Not that.

He closed his eyes again. The voices were back, the chants like a rolling rhythm, the wind blowing through the bedroom, the voices now like drumbeats, tempo increasing, his heartbeat racing.

He took long slow breaths to calm himself and let the voices fall silent. The drumbeat stopped. All he had left were the race of his heartbeat and the rise and fall of his chest.

He opened his eyes and gasped. Her eyes were open too.

Her arm moved quickly. He tried to move backwards, panicking, but he was kneeling down, so his toes jammed into the floor.

He saw the lamp just before it connected. Small but made of brass and with a narrow edge. She brought it down hard.

The last thing he remembered was the loud clunk when it struck his forehead and the blinding flash of pain. Then there was nothing.

One

Present Day

Dan Grant stood in front of the mirror. He was in his court dress: long black gown, stiff collar with bands, just two strips of white cloth drooping from it, stark white against the deep black of his waistcoat. But it wasn't his clothes he was checking. It was his nerve. He was looking for a flush to his cheeks, a giveaway look in his eyes, but everything looked as it should. Strong chin, resolute stare.

'Is it always like this?'

Dan turned around. It was Jayne, looking around the room.

'What do you mean?'

'Busy, noisy. Full of arseholes.'

They were in the robing room of the local Crown Court, where the barristers and solicitor-advocates readied themselves for the courtroom. It was cramped, with wall space taken up by lockers, the room lit by the large lattice windows that gave views over the wrong end of the city centre. Betting shops, an amusement arcade, a small paved precinct that led to the bus station which acted like a wind tunnel in the worst days of winter, litter blown into one corner. Everyone spoke in loud voices, the air heavy with stale cigarette and cigar odours but almost overpowered by too much perfume.

He raised an eyebrow and gave her the faint trace of a smile. 'Yes, mostly.'

The day was just starting, the room so different to the hush of the corridor outside, where footsteps echoed and people spoke quietly. The room was filled with the chatter of a new week, with talk of evenings out and cricket, whether anyone had tried the new restaurant out towards the hills, punctuated by the smack of leather bags landing on the tables as people pulled out their robes and papers.

'Mondays are always like this,' Dan said.

'Why?'

'It's when most trials are scheduled to start. Everyone is buzzing around, trying to plea-bargain the cases they were preparing last night. Tomorrow, it will be different. Trials will have been sorted, late guilty pleas entered, that kind of thing, slots in the court diary freed up, so it's back to juggling whatever cases are left.'

'And by Friday?'

'Sentencing, mostly. All those heartfelt pleas they don't mean.'

'*They*? You're part of them.'

'You think so? I thought you knew me better than that.'

'Yeah, sorry,' Jayne said. 'Don't ever be like them. The way they talk, the way they act.'

'It's all affectation, a performance. Take him, for example,' and Dan gestured towards a man sitting nearby, with smooth skin and slicked hair, peering over glasses he'd allowed to slip down his nose. 'He's not much past thirty but talks in a deep bumble, like he's some kind of retired colonel, and I can bet you he didn't talk like that when he was propping up the student bar a few years ago. It changes you, this job. Or rather, they let it change them.'

'Why hasn't it changed you?'

'Because we have different heroes. These lot,' and he gestured with a flick of his hand. 'They all want to be the whisky bore, the old country gent in front of the stone fire.'

'And you?'

'Just trying not to lose myself.' He looked down at her. 'And as for you, well, you look very nice.'

'Nice?' She grimaced as she ran her hand down her clothes: a dark trouser suit, plain white blouse. 'I don't think I do *nice*. It doesn't feel right.'

'This is how it's got to be. I need you in and out of court all week, keeping me updated. The judge has got to see you today, know that you're my caseworker. It's the only way you'll be able to sit behind me. I don't know how this thing is going to go.'

'Is it just you?'

'No, of course not.' He pointed to a woman sitting at a table in the corner, a dirty-looking horsehair wig on the table next to her, the grey turned to light brown. Her own hair was dyed deep brown and pulled back into a clasp, her cheekbones sharp, her nose pointed. 'She's my QC. Hannah Taberner.'

'Does she know what we've been up to?'

'No, and she doesn't need to know.'

'What happens when she finds out?'

'It won't matter. And she might not find out anyway, unless Robert Carter changes his story. He's the client.'

'Do you think he will?'

'I've no idea. All I know is that it's safer for us if he doesn't.'

'And if he does?'

'I don't do this job for the easy stuff.'

'I'm scared, Dan.'

He sighed. 'You're allowed to be.'

'What about you?'

'Apprehensive, but trials are like that, the fear of the unknown. Whatever we think will happen, it will probably turn out differently. Something unexpected will happen.' He picked up his court bag. 'Come on, let's get to the courtroom.'

'Shouldn't you wait for her, the QC?'

'Leave her with her thoughts. She's the main attraction, not me. Let her concentrate and focus, and we'll do what we have to do. There'll be time for you to get to know her later.'

'Is she any good?'

'Damn good. The jury will love her, and you will too, but right now, she's got a murder trial about to start and won't want some jumped-up solicitor-advocate like me distracting her.'

Dan threaded his way through the room, exchanging greetings with those who'd come up the same way he had, scrapping it out in the local Magistrates Court before ending up in the gown at the Crown Court, many solicitors choosing to do the work that had once been the preserve of barristers. The nods and greetings from the barristers were more brittle, their once exclusive club becoming eroded, most niceties stemming from the need to keep the work coming. Dan had no sympathy for them. The good ones were very good, but many had taken too much cash for not doing enough. They were never the ones in the police station at midnight, or taking the early morning calls from drunken clients.

The door closed behind them and shut out the chatter of the robing room, replacing it with the peace of the court corridor, tiled in black and white that echoed the clicks from leather soles.

There was talk of a new, modern building, but Dan liked the history of the place. It had dealt with murderers and the rest since

Victorian times, with people sent to the gallows from the rooms on either side of the corridor. Modern buildings were more suited to the work, with better acoustics and heating that didn't clank in winter, but they couldn't match the shadows of the past.

DI Murdoch was ahead, with a small group of people, talking in a tight cluster. He recognised them as the family of Mary Kendricks, the young woman murdered in a shared house a few months before. Dan was there to represent the man accused of her murder. The family stopped talking and glared at him as he got closer to the courtroom door. Dan looked away. There would be no point in saying anything.

The door to the courtroom was heavy to keep out any noises from outside. Once inside, he let out a long breath. This was it, the start of it.

The courtroom was empty, but soon it would become the focus of the drama, someone's tragedy played out as a public spectacle. The aim was to find the truth, but Dan wasn't there for the truth. His role was to conceal it, to distort it and present a different version of it. The truth, the whole truth, and nothing but the truth came second most often.

'I don't like courtrooms,' Jayne said, from behind him.

'You're the proof that justice can be done.'

'That doesn't make it a good memory.'

'It does to me.'

Jayne was a former client who'd once been accused of murder. After her acquittal, Dan suggested that she acted as his caseworker and investigator. Jayne had agreed, provided that she wasn't employed by him. She wanted the freedom she'd almost lost and, in the two years since then, she'd come in and out of his life whenever a case demanded it.

Dan looked around as he put his bag on the floor. The courtroom was vast, with high ceilings and walls lined with dusty paintings of judges, the windows covered in long green drapes. The lawyers' seats were wooden rows, the dock just behind, raised high and protected by security glass, the defendant sat like a specimen in a lab, the public gallery behind.

'Are you ready for this?' Dan said.

'I think so. We'll make it work, whatever the cost.'

Dan took a deep breath at that. It was how much the case would cost him that worried him the most.

Two

Fourteen Days Earlier

The town glinted in the early morning sun. A small spot on the northern map, somewhere between the large urban sprawls near the coast and the dark shadows of the Pennines.

The view was of old grey stone clustered in the town centre, nestled in the valley. Terraced streets ran up the opposing hill in tight grids behind the arches of a railway viaduct. Bright supermarket signs along the new ring road interrupted the mood, but they were a blip. The canal had built the town, like most in the area, as it cut through the valley and brought cotton from Liverpool, turned into cloth in the mills. Soot-stained chimney stacks rose high above the rooftops.

Those days were gone. The chimneys had been blocked off, home now to grass and bird's nests, but much better than the grey smoke that had once choked the town and obliterated the view of the high green hills that surrounded it. The textile mills were now either derelict and waiting redevelopment, or reinvented as new office premises.

Dan Grant smiled at the view. The town might be small, grubby, insular, violent, forgotten and derelict, but most of all, it was his. He'd played in the empty stone buildings, got lost amongst the rubble, learned to smoke on the banks of the canal, had his first kiss in the shadows of one of the low bridges, and lost his virginity in the alley behind a social club. All of his life lessons had been learnt and mistakes had been made in the collection of cobbles and stone blocks.

University had distracted him for a few years. He'd been tempted by big-city living and a glitzy apartment on the edge of the nightspots, but that had been ten years earlier and his home town had pulled him back, as he knew it would. He knew he'd got it right every time he walked to his office. The sun caught the dew on the hills and the breeze blew crisp and clean.

He paused outside his office doorway, craving a moment of peace before the day began. There was a steady hum of traffic, but it was mostly heading away from the town, queuing for the motorway. People were trudging down the hill to work in the shops and cafes in the town centre, but it could hardly be described as bustling.

For Dan, as a defence lawyer, his day would be another one at the town's rougher edges. Drugs, violence, theft, they were the mainstays. Sometimes a real injustice came along, a genuine case of a wrongly accused person, but most often his days were about processing the bad times.

Over the traffic noise came a steady click of shoes. Against the backdrop of railway arches, his boss walked towards him in a black fedora hat and dark three-piece suit, brightened by a mauve silk tie, matching handkerchief poking from his breast pocket. Pat Molloy played the part of a small-town eccentric very well. It was fake, developed over the years to make himself stand out, but at least Pat was trying. He was a splash of colour in a profession that was fast losing its gleam, lost in bureaucracy.

'Good day to you, Daniel,' Pat said, as he got close, his tone rich, enunciation exaggerated. 'You ready for the day ahead?'

'As always.' He stepped aside to let Pat walk in first, switching off the alarm as he went.

The office hadn't changed much in the ten years he'd been there. There was a square reception area with cheap carpet tiles and an old leather sofa against one wall, stuffing held in by black tape. A box of toys occupied one corner, for clients with children, and a reception desk in the other. The view of the street was through the name of the firm, Molloys, in gold-edged lettering on the glass.

Pat Molloy had set up the firm when the going for criminal lawyers was good. He'd made it a success by looking after some of the larger criminal families, where every success against the police, however minor, had spread his reputation and turned his name into the first people thought of when they found themselves in a police cell.

Pat had been a good teacher. Look after the local press, that was his advice. Tip them off about your cases and make sure the court reporter knows the addresses and facts, whether the client wanted the publicity or not. Most of all, include something controversial in any courtroom speech, because the court reports in the local press were free advertising, and there was no better advert than a headline.

The receptionist wouldn't be in for another half an hour. Margaret Ferguson had been with Pat since he started, an elderly woman with deep lines around her eyes, who fussed over Pat like she was his aunt. To Pat, she was Mrs Ferguson. To Dan, it was just Margaret.

Dan's office was on the floor above, overlooking the street. Pat preferred the room at the back, so that clients never knew whether he was in or not. Dan gave up his privacy for the view over the Town Hall and moorland hills. As he opened his blinds, the ritual for another week beginning, Pat appeared in the doorway behind him.

Dan turned round. 'How was your weekend?'

'Just splendid. Not one police station call out.'

'If we don't get the calls, we don't get the cases.'

'I know that, but sometimes, my dear Daniel, settling in with too much wine just about compensates. How was yours?'

'Routine. A couple of jobs in the Saturday morning court, but nothing major. An assault, just a Friday night scuffle, and a shed burglar.'

'Both out?'

'Yes. The fighter pleaded and the burglar was put on a tag.'

'I might have something more interesting for you,' Pat said, and his chuckle told Dan that he'd come across something good.

'What is it?'

'A referral from Dutton's. Conflict of interest. They want us to take it over.'

'Dutton's spotted a conflict of interest?' Dan was surprised. 'They never give up a client.'

'It was Shelley Greenwood's case. I had the Legal Aid transferred on Friday and was going to keep it myself, but I think it might be right for you. Do you want it?'

'What is it?'

Pat paused for effect, before he said, 'A murder.'

Dan's eyes widened. 'Shelley's given up a murder case? What's the catch?'

'They've done most of the work, because the trial is only two weeks away. I don't know how much more we can squeeze out of it.'

'Two weeks? What were you thinking? What happens if Duttons haven't done a good job and it all goes wrong? We'll get the bad publicity.'

'It's the Robert Carter case.'

Dan groaned. He knew of it, the murder of a pretty young teacher that had filled the national press. 'Pat? Have you gone mad?'

'But if they've done a good job, and Shelley is good, we'll be the ones on the court steps giving speeches to the cameras.'

Dan shook his head. 'Two weeks, Pat. And you agreed to take it? It's too much.'

'If you want to tell the bank manager, I'll pass on his number.' Pat lowered his voice. 'He won't be interested. Times are hard and I've just about had enough.'

'What do you mean, had enough?'

'Just that. I'm nearly sixty. I own this building and it's my retirement pot, but the overdraft is killing it. We've got to make money, and if this case keeps us trundling on for a bit longer, I'll take it.'

'Just back me up if it goes wrong.'

'Of course.' Pat stepped away from the door, some of his sparkle returning. 'They're sending over a copy of the file this morning.'

'I might want to use Jayne.'

'Are we still calling her that?'

'That's her name now.'

'You can't look after everyone, Daniel. Do your job, close the door and go home.'

'Just spreading a little happiness.'

'Be careful when her new identity unravels,' Pat said. 'If she's in the danger she thinks she is, some of that violence might head your way, especially when they find out your role in it all.'

Dan didn't respond.

He'd been at a police station on the other side of Manchester when he met her, there for a travelling burglar. Just as he was about to leave, a woman had appeared at the custody desk, scared, blood on her clothes, her cheeks tear-stained. When she was asked if she wanted legal representation, she looked at Dan and nodded. It didn't matter that he was from out of town. He was there, and that was all that mattered.

She was accused of murder. She'd been in a relationship, an abusive one. That had always surprised Dan, because Jayne was tough, one of the toughest people he knew, but somehow her boyfriend had weakened her enough that he felt free to abuse and demean her. The physical stuff had come eventually, but the phone messages disclosed by the prosecution read like a daily pattern of bullying. He belittled her, criticized her, taunted her by boasting of the women he'd slept with. It was a psychological drip-drip, until one day, she snapped. He'd been drinking and was insulting her, pushing against her, becoming nastier as she cowered. She'd been drying the knives, and in her hand was a carving knife. He taunted one last time, and before she knew it, the knife was in his leg, his femoral artery severed. She sat in the corner of the kitchen, screaming as he bled out.

The jury had formed a judgment on the deceased rather than Jayne and she'd walked free, the main problem for the prosecution being that the only witness was Jayne.

When her case ended, she wanted to run away. Her boyfriend's brothers and cousins were making threats to kill her. Dan drafted a change of name deed, so that Jade Winstanley became Jayne Brett, and she moved to Highford.

'If you want to use Jayne, fine, but all the work has been done,' Pat said. 'We're just holding the file to collect a fee.'

'Not if my name is on it.'

Pat didn't say anything as he turned to head down the corridor to his own room, but Dan knew he had no choice. Pat liked to play at being the boss but he couldn't function without Dan, and he knew it.

Dan looked towards the window once Pat was out of view. Pat had said it was just a case of holding the file and putting in the bill. He didn't believe that. The first thing he'd learnt as a young lawyer was that whenever your boss tells you that something isn't going to be a problem, it usually turns out to be the biggest problem of the month.

Three

Someone moved against her. Jayne Brett jumped. It was a warm leg, big and hairy. She moaned and buried her face in the pillow. Not again.

She opened her eyes. The sunlight caught the steady swirl of dust as it streamed in through the curtains that she hadn't closed properly. The hum of morning traffic filtered into her consciousness. She lifted her head but the day bit back with a sharp jab of pain and made her gasp. Her mouth felt dry, her skin sticky with sweat from stale booze.

She took deep breaths to make the pain in her head subside and to calm the nauseous roll of her stomach. What had happened the night before? The memories were just sketches, a collage of blurred images. She didn't need to lift the duvet to know that she was naked. What about the man next to her, whoever he was? She looked under the covers and groaned. He was naked too, lying on his side, his stomach slumping on to the sheet.

She needed to pee.

As she slid out of bed, the body in the bed stirred.

There was no need to cover herself, he'd already seen her naked, but still she scoured the bedroom floor for something to put on, anything to give out the message that the good times had ended. The T-shirt from the night before was crumpled in the corner, her bra on top, next to an empty wine bottle, something cheap they must have picked up on the way home.

She looked back to the bed as she slipped on her T-shirt. His dark hair was scruffy against the pillow as he smacked his lips; the morning was as cruel for him as it was for her. More brief flashes of the night before came back to her and she clasped her forehead. Laughing at the bar, a glass being placed in front of her, him moving closer, his face next to hers. Walking home, talking nonsense, kisses in the street, his hands in her clothes. After that, nothing. Not even his name. He was around twenty years older than her, his cheeks with that boozy redness against pallid grey skin. She checked for a ring on his wedding finger, but it was clean. At least she hadn't done that.

As she turned to go towards the bathroom, he said, 'Good morning,' although it came out with a croak. She looked back and he tried a smile, one eye still closed. He threw the duvet off himself and revealed his early morning pride like an achievement.

She didn't want to be cruel but he was never going to win a prize.

'You're going to have to deal with that yourself,' she said. 'I'm not good in the mornings.'

'Nor last night.'

'What, we didn't . . . ?'

'You fell asleep.'

She almost punched the air in relief. 'You have to catch me in the mood.'

'What about breakfast?'

'Not even toast.' She pointed at his crotch. 'Shoes on and home, cowboy. You can play with that at your own place.'

'I'm not in a rush.'

'I am.'

And with that she went to the bathroom and locked the door, leaning back against it, prepared to wait until she heard her front door slam. She'd been here before. Sometimes they sneaked out during the night. There were times when she'd done it, woken up in a part of the town she didn't recognise and ended up in a taxi, avoiding the disapproving glances in the rearview mirror.

They couldn't judge her. They didn't know her.

There was just silence on the other side of the door, so she sat on the toilet and put her head in her hands. Her world was spinning and she wondered how long her stomach contents would remain there.

She knew how it had happened. Alone in a pub, just wanting a drink, not looking for a hook up, but still the chancers talked to her. She would have been cool with them at first, not flirting, but then the booze would have taken hold and her mood changed. Just some guy fulfilling a need.

Her bed springs creaked. She flushed the toilet and then ran the shower to let him know that she was going to be a while.

As she wiped away the condensation from the bathroom mirror, she rubbed her face awake. Her eyes looked heavy, dark rings forming. She was twenty-five but felt older.

There was a knock at the door. 'Jo, your phone's ringing.'

It's Jayne, she thought, shaking her head, and shouted, 'Who is it?'

'The screen says *Dan*.'

She rushed to the door and threw it open. He was standing there, dressed, holding her phone out to her.

'Boyfriend?'

She held up her finger to ask him to wait, before taking the phone from him and answering, 'Dan, just give me a moment.' She held the phone to her chest. 'No, it's work, not a boyfriend.'

'Will I see you again?'

'I don't think so.'

A pause. 'Okay.'

He turned towards the door. She reached out and grabbed his arm. 'Look, I'm sorry, but you know how it is. Thanks for walking me home, and for, well, just letting me sleep.'

He looked down at her hand on his arm, before he patted it and said, 'No worries. Take care.'

And then he was gone.

She let out a long breath before putting the phone to her ear. 'Hi Dan.'

'What was all that about?'

'Just me being a bitch.'

'That's not news. Do you want some work? Two weeks at the most.'

'I always need work, you know that.'

'Good. I'll give you a call when I know more.' A pause, and then, 'Everything okay?'

'Quiet, you know how it is.'

'Okay, speak later,' and then he hung up.

Jayne sat down with relief when the phone went silent. She remembered now why she'd gone drinking, because her funds were getting low and she wasn't sure when the next pay cheque was going to arrive. She might as well enjoy the dregs of her account. Now, there was more cash on the way.

She slipped off her T-shirt and was ready for the shower to bring her back to life. Jayne Brett Investigations was back in business.

Four

There was a large crowd outside the local courthouse as Dan got closer. The sunshine brought them out, an early burst of summer for the court regulars as their cigarette smoke and laughter drifted into the air. Some were drinking cheap lager from cans, even though it wasn't yet ten in the morning. This wasn't the high drama of the Crown Court, where the serious cases happened, but the Magistrates Court, filled with the day-to-day humdrum.

The first-timers stayed indoors, staring straight ahead, not saying much, glancing towards the court ushers whenever someone was called into the courtroom, just wanting the ordeal over with.

The court was a typical northern civic building, a grand stone monument to a thriving industrial past, with a Roman portico held up by stone pillars over steps leading to double wooden doors. It was inside the building where it showed its age, cramped and drab. The waiting area was just four rows of plastic chairs bolted on to cracked floor tiles, the walls painted pale yellow with bulges in the plaster, a coffee machine the only way of getting a drink.

Dan pushed through the crowd. No one objected. Someone shouted his name, but Dan indicated with a point of his finger that he would see them inside.

The security men let him through without a frisk; one of the benefits he received from spending time talking to them, one of the few lawyers who did. Dan was thirty-four and had been a lawyer for only ten years, but had already learned where there was an advantage to be had. Sometimes people arrived at court without a lawyer and the security staff passed on Dan's details, a small gesture in return for his civility.

It wasn't just business though. Sometimes Dan just got tired of the conversation topics amongst the other defence lawyers. Golf club chat, moans about how they had to downgrade their Jaguar. Tales from the football, usually from an executive box. Times were tougher for defence lawyers, but those over fifty had already drained what they could from the system. It was the younger lawyers who struggled, who'd never known the good times and ended up in criminal law only because of the lack of alternatives. Criminal law used to be a path to a good career. Now, it was the refuge for losers and chancers.

Dan had chosen criminal law for a different reason: he enjoyed it. Even at university, when his contemporaries from the better schools were contemplating work in the City or firms with offices abroad, Dan had only ever imagined himself in a courtroom or a police station. He'd answered his calling, even if it was the one shunned by most young lawyers, who preferred to be paid more for doing work that wasn't nearly as interesting.

Dan was holding three files, his court appearances for the morning: a scrap metal thief, a drink driver, and the only one charged following a Saturday night fight, the drawback to winning the tussle. If two men fight, the winner goes to court.

It was easy to spot his clients. The scrap metal thief was in dirty jeans and work boots, the leather worn away from the steel toecaps, his hands scarred and burned, the after-effects of another night of burning away cable coatings to get to the metal in the core. The Saturday night fighter was young and smartly dressed, muscles in his shirt, and the drink driver was the only one in a suit, not yet certain how that extra drink will impact on his life.

It was Shelley Greenwood he was really looking out for though, keen to find out why she'd transferred a murder case.

Dan ducked into ushers' kiosk, staffed by retired police officers in black gowns, holding clipboards.

'Morning Daniel,' one said. It was Bob, his police days a long way behind him.

'You seen Shelley?'

'You not heard?'

He frowned. 'Clearly not. What is it?'

'She's in hospital. Rolled her car into a wall and ended up in someone's front garden. Happened last night.'

His stomach jolted. He'd been close to Shelley since university, being from the same town keeping them close. 'How is she?'

'In a bad way, so I'm told. There's something else, too.'

Whatever it is, everyone will know soon enough, Dan thought. Bob enjoyed the gossip around the courtroom. His usual conversation involved talk of the old days, suspects being held out of windows or blowjobs from prostitutes under the privacy of a police cape, the price for looking the other way. But gossip about a defence lawyer? That will keep him busy all day.

'Go on,' Dan said.

'They took a blood sample, but the rumour is that she stank of booze.' His glee was obvious in his voice.

Dan closed his eyes and let out a long sigh. He was used to hearing of lawyers on downward spirals, the long hours and poor company bringing them down. Criminal lawyers don't have a good record of either staying out of prison or avoiding being struck off. The clients want the little extras, like tip-offs for drug dealers whenever a user ends up in the cells, so that the lawyer can marshal the client, ensure that he doesn't swap information for more lenient treatment. The hardest part of being a criminal lawyer was keeping a distance.

Shelley was different to them. She was clever and hard-working and honest, and he couldn't stand to think of her as just another one taking a fall.

'Who's doing her work?' Dan asked. 'I was hoping to catch up with her this morning.'

Bob pointed along the corridor, towards Court One, the showpiece court, reserved for the overnight cases and sentencing hearings where prison was likely. 'Conrad Taylor, and he's not happy.'

Dan thanked him and threaded his way through the tangle of legs belonging to people who refused to move them.

The atmosphere was more hushed inside the courtroom. The ceiling was high, the dock at the back of the room, its brass rail scuffed and dull from the years of hands gripping it after people had emerged from the tiled stairwell that rose from the cell complex beneath.

There were three long rows of benches with uncomfortable wooden backs leading to the high desk where the Magistrates sat, the royal crest behind them, the lion and the unicorn. The court hadn't started, so this was the time when the lawyers crowded the prosecutor, gleaning from her whatever information they could, hoping to carve out some deal or agreement they could take back to their client as something victorious.

Conrad Taylor was sitting on the back of one of the benches, leaning over the prosecutor, his feet on the seat pads, files on his knees. The prosecutor was scrolling through her case on her laptop, trying to read what she could before answering Conrad's question. That was always the problem for the prosecutor: Dan had three cases that day, so knew each one well. The prosecutor had to know around twenty for that day, all the time trying to deal with interruptions from defence lawyers.

Dan approached them both. The prosecutor smiled briefly, before turning back to Conrad.

'No, I can't agree that,' she said, her irritation obvious. 'Your client punched him five times, and when he was on the floor. Fine, get him to plead guilty, but I'm not accepting a couple of slaps. The taxi driver was just doing his job, he didn't deserve to be attacked.'

'Come on,' Conrad said, his tone rich and deep, assured. 'You'll have ticked your box and the taxi driver won't thank you for dragging him to court. He'd rather be out there working.'

'And your client gets a slapped wrist.'

'Fine, have it your way. Not guilty, and let's see if he turns up for trial.'

Before the prosecutor could respond, Conrad stepped away and raised an eyebrow at Dan.

'It's you I'm looking for,' Dan said to him.

'If it's about Shelley, I've only just heard. That's why I'm here. This is her work.'

'It's not really about Shelley. I'll catch up with her myself. It's about Robert Carter.'

Conrad looked confused. 'What has that got to do with you?'

'Well, everything now.'

'What do you mean?'

'Pat doesn't want to run it himself. He's asked me to look after it.'

'Look after what? You're making no sense.'

'The Robert Carter case.'

'Why would you be running it?'

'You do know it's our case now?'

Conrad clenched his jaw and pointed to the door that led to the corridor. 'Outside.'

Dan followed Conrad out of the courtroom. Once there, Conrad walked to a quiet corner. He was smaller than Dan and leaner, his cheekbones sharp in his cheeks, his fingers skeletal as he gripped his files, but still he tried to intimidate, crowding Dan as he said, 'What the hell are you talking about, it's your case?'

'A conflict of interest, we were told. It's our case now.'

'Like hell it is. The trial is two weeks away.'

'I know that, which is why I'm surprised the Legal Aid was transferred.'

Conrad opened his mouth as if to say something, but stopped. He looked down for a moment before turning back to Dan. 'When?'

'Friday, according to Pat. You could ask Shelley about it, but she's not up to it, by the sounds of it.'

Conrad stared at the floor for a few seconds. 'I didn't know she'd done that, transferred it.'

'What's the conflict about?'

'If I tell you, you'll be conflicted too,' Conrad said, regaining his poise. 'Just babysit the case. The trial is two weeks away and there is no way the judge will adjourn it. Everything is done. All you have to do is to send someone along to sit with the QC and put in your bill.'

'I'm surprised the judge didn't object to this,' Dan said, trying to hold back his irritation at being told how to run his cases. 'You're giving up a murder client because you've got a conflict of interest, but really I'm just holding it so you can make out like you've given it up.'

'Most of what we do is pretence, you know that.' Conrad's voice was filled with condescension. 'And you don't get the file until we get your undertaking to settle our part of the fees. You might as well ask the court to transfer it back to us.'

'You've already sent it. It will be at my office this morning.'

Conrad stepped closer, taking deep breaths through his nose, as if he were about to issue a threat, but Dan stared him down.

Eventually, Conrad stepped away and stormed off towards the advocates' room. Dan decided not to follow him.

One thing he had decided, however, was that Conrad had just made him a lot more interested in his new murder case.

Five

The walls were closing him in. He paced, anxious, claustropho-bic, the light weak. Just a bed and somewhere for his clothes, a few personal items on a shelf. Pitiful.

His fingers teased at the scar she'd left when she hit him with the lamp. Four stitches. He shook his head at the memory. Yeah, some irony that she thought he was the violent one.

The night had changed everything. The memory made his fingers curl into a fist, his jaw clench, his moment of shame. Not because of what he was doing, but because he was caught. He thought he was better than that. He'd always taken his time, because there'd been others before her, but she'd almost brought everything to an end.

Cassie was her name.

It was raining when he saw her for the first time. She was rushing for a bus and there was an instant spark, like someone had clicked their fingers and snapped him awake. The rain stuck her clothes to her body, tall and lithe, but she was smiling, like colour in the gloom, her bag clutched to her chest. He'd known straight away: he needed to see her.

No, that made it too simple. It was more than that, because he could see her whenever he wanted. All he had to do was learn her habits. Everyone had a pattern, and they made it easier for him, gave him a way inside. But it wasn't the patterns he'd wanted. His need was much greater than that. He had to *know* her.

People lie to the world. They create a character, like what clothes they wear and how they behave. It's a display, nothing more.

What use was that? He could see that anytime, but the real her? That was different. He wanted to know how she was when no one else was around. Her dark side. Her shadow.

That thought spread a thin smile. Everyone has a shadow, some inner darkness to explore when alone. The more it's suppressed, the higher it bounces back. That's how it works. The jack-in-the-box. The spring. What was she keeping pressed down? So much light, so much fun. As high as that was, her darkness had to go as deep, had to be equal to the light.

Northern Soul had been Cassie's thing. That had surprised him. A secret world of dancers who pack out the social clubs and pub backrooms, spinning and twirling to the beat of obscure American soul. He'd watched her, hidden behind the bushes in her garden, the heavy bass and horns drifting through the slightly open window and along the lawn. She'd become so absorbed, singing to herself, her eyes often closed, her features in sheer rapture.

He'd followed her to an event once, in a local club. She rode a small blue Vespa most days, and the steady put-put of her engine, the clunk of her gear change, gave him warning when she was back, but she caught the bus to the dance. He travelled with her, the quiet man behind her on the bus, close enough to smell her shampoo and the light scent she'd sprayed on her neck.

Once inside, he sat in a dark corner to watch her. The music reverberated against walls covered in deep flock wallpaper, made wet by condensation from the sweat generated by the dancers, as they moved as a body, gyrating, body-flipping, spinning, clapping, the rhythm taking them to some other place far away.

She'd surprised him again though. He'd watched her dance in her home, and he thought he'd see more of that in the club. His eyes scoured the dance floor, hoping to see her shirt stuck to her back, her body visible as her perspiration made it see-through, but he saw something he loved even more. Her quietness.

She was standing at the edge of the dance floor, drinking through a straw, watching the dancers. Sometimes singing along, her eyes closed, feeling the songs, and other times just swaying to herself, lost in the rhythm. But she didn't let herself go in the same way as when she was alone. He was captivated. Why did she keep it all for when she was by herself?

He'd wanted to speak to her, but that would have spoiled everything. It would make her choose which person to show to him, and that's all he would ever see.

He'd carried on watching, waiting, wondering when he'd dare to do what he dreamed of.

All the nights since then had been spent thinking of how it had gone, his eyes clamped shut, his fingers gripping the sheet. The memories burned. The shock on her face, then the anger, the spluttered obscenity as she swung the lamp towards his head.

He should have realised she would turn like that. He'd seen some of her secrets. The angry emails she'd sent, which he saw when he'd looked through her computer, or the comments on a newspaper website that didn't seem anything like her. That was where her shadow came out, her spiteful, nasty side.

She was so beautiful, so fun, but her private thoughts were dark and hurtful. That was the balance, he knew, but did she really think he was going to hurt her? He'd wanted to know her, that's all. The real her. Was that so wrong?

What she hadn't known, when she hit him, was that there'd been other times with her. As he looked back, he knew one thing: it had all led to Mary. Now, when he closed his eyes, all he saw was Mary's blood, her beautiful face transformed into a mask, all of her light gone.

Six

Jayne left her apartment building and looked around, as was her habit. It seemed clear. All she had was the view of the town in the valley below, grey and grim, the tall chimneys reminding her what the town meant to her. It was derelict, obsolete. Her hiding place.

She lived on the top floor of a four-storey terraced building, one in a row of grand old stone houses that lined the road into the town centre. Some had retained their splendour, with stained glass panels on either side of painted wooden doors and polished tiles in the hallway. Others, like the building Jayne lived in, had fallen into disrepair from bedsit use, the windows dusty and with tattered old curtains. The hallway carpet was worn out and ripped in some places, from the footfall of five households crammed into one building.

Below her was a man who lived alone and had never worked, who spent his time smoking cannabis and shooting birds from his bedroom window with an air rifle. There was the young couple who'd painted their walls black and filled the house with the noise of a bass guitar that he practised late into the night. Next to them was the middle-aged couple who worked in a local hotel, who left for work in suits and returned drunk later in the day, where they screamed at each other until one of them fell asleep, and on the ground floor was a youth in his late teens who repaired an old Lambretta in the hallway, so she was frequently assaulted by the smell of oil and petrol whenever she ventured downstairs.

Above all of this was Jayne's apartment, squeezed into the eaves, rented from an elderly couple who'd bought the building as a way of providing an income in their retirement. They didn't care much for what it was worth after they died, with no children to leave it to, so the house was left to slowly fall into disrepair.

It was perfect for Jayne. Anonymous, where so many people came and went that no one noticed her. She hated feeling like she was on the run, but that's exactly what she was, hiding away, always expecting a visit from the family of her dead boyfriend. The jury had cleared her, but his family didn't see it that way. She'd been holding the knife, that's all that mattered. They'd find her one day, but until that happened, she stayed alert, hoping to see the threat before it was too late.

She looked down at her feet. They were cold, her pumps worn through on one of the soles so that she could feel her skin against the tarmac as she walked. The worn-out patch on the knee of her jeans was not fashion.

The breeze that blew through the valley cleared some of the fogginess in her head that lingered from the night before. She searched for some regret about the man who'd stayed overnight. There was none. There'd been too many regrets in her life. Tumbling into bed with some guy whose name she couldn't remember paled against most of them.

She set off for the town centre. She was hungry and the examination of her cupboards had reminded her that she needed money. She rummaged in her pockets. Just a few pound coins. Whatever work Dan wanted her to do, she needed to start straight away.

As she walked down the hill, her body felt too skinny, her clothes too loose. A car slowed next to her and she tensed. When she looked, it was a battered old Mazda, holes in the wheel-arch, with three young men in baseball caps and pale faces. The driver grinned as the passenger leaned forward and shouted, 'Hey, you want a lift?' and then laughed.

Jayne ignored them.

'Come on, I've seen you around and you always look like you need cheering up.'

Jayne turned to them. 'And you think you could do that?' She shook her head. 'I doubt it. Even all three of you together.' She flashed a smile, but it was filled with sarcasm. 'Have a good day, boys.'

The driver laughed as he set off, the passenger's middle finger extending out of his window.

Hiding away so often felt like a punishment. Perhaps it was no more than she deserved for what she'd done, but being recognised unsettled her. In Highford, too many people lived in a very small world and she was the newcomer to it. Perhaps the anonymity of a big city would have been better.

She thrust her hands into her pockets. She couldn't think like that. There was work ahead. That's why she'd remained in Highford, because she understood towns like it. There was work, and a new life to build. Focus on the future, not the past. Never go back there.

Seven

Dan checked his watch as he rushed up the hill from the court-house. He'd finished his cases and was keen to clear some paper-work at his office before the usual afternoon scramble.

Mornings had a familiar routine, with a couple of hours of sitting around in court, broken only when his cases were called. First-come, first-served applied to the defendants, not the law-yers, so he'd had to endure Conrad Taylor at his insincere best, although he hadn't seemed interested in hanging around, as if his spat with Dan had thrown him off somehow.

He'd tried calling Shelley but her phone was switched off. He'd visit her once he'd got rid of his afternoon clients.

As soon as Dan walked in, he saw there were three people waiting to see him. The waiting room hung heavy with the smell of their clothes, pungent with stale cigarettes and not enough washes. Margaret pointed towards someone in the corner of the room, his head against the wall, his mouth gaping open, soft snores drifting out.

'Your one-thirty has arrived early,' she told him. 'And your father called an hour ago.'

'Did he say why?'

'Something to do with his satellite channels not working.' She raised an eyebrow. 'And these two want to speak to you.' Margaret gestured towards two skinny young men in black jackets, their faces too pale, dark stubble in contrast.

Dan read her obvious disapproval.

They stood up and walked towards him.

Dan shook his head as soon as they got close.

'What do you mean, no?' one said.

'I gave you money last week,' Dan said. 'It was a one-off, a gesture of goodwill for all your past custom, but it's not going to become a regular thing.'

He opened his mouth as if offended. 'It was only a tenner, man. They've cut my money.'

'Yeah, and they keep cutting ours too.'

'We send you work. We come here and get other people to come here.'

'You send me scraps.'

'That's it then?'

'Look, I get your problem, but you can't keep coming here whenever you get short.'

'You get my problem?' The man shook his head. 'No, you don't. You just pretend like you do, but you're just a fancy lawyer, thinking that you're better than us.' He went to the door, his friend just behind him. 'Yeah, thanks man. I'll remember this,' and then he slammed the door, making the dozing man jolt in his chair before settling down again.

Margaret tutted. 'You can't keep giving money away.'

'It's part of the job, you know that, and sometimes I'm a sucker for a sad story.'

Margaret shook her head, but being a criminal lawyer wasn't just about the courtroom. It was a social service, sometimes a friend to turn to, the one person who won't look down on them when they're at their worst. Clients often asked for money, usually under the guise of a bus fare home from court or just something to get them through a couple of days, and sometimes Dan gave it, if they caught him in the right mood. His clients weren't often happy if he refused, but they stayed loyal, and the argument was never mentioned the next time Dan saw them, which was usually through the hatch in a cell door.

'What's that?' Dan pointed towards a large box on the reception desk.

'A courier dropped it off. Pat says that it's for you, so you'll have to carry it up the stairs.'

Dan lifted the lid, although he knew what it was: the Robert Carter file, copied and bundled into separate folders.

'It looks like it will keep you busy,' she said.

'No more than a fortnight.'

'Something interesting?'

'I'll tell you when I've read it.' Although he guessed that Margaret had already looked through the box. 'Give me a call when sleeping beauty rejoins the world.'

'Will do. Are we expecting any more?'

'I've got a two-thirty and a three-thirty, but they won't turn up. They never do.'

'Don't forget your father,' she shouted, as he went upstairs with the box.

He dropped it on to his desk. It landed with a thump and made his coffee-stained mug rattle. It must have alerted Pat to his return, because after a couple of minutes he appeared in the doorway.

'How was court?'

'Routine. Everyone wanted to plead guilty and the sunshine made the Magistrates lenient.'

'Not many go to prison these days.'

'You're sounding nostalgic.'

'Sometimes your clients need to expect prison, so you can be the hero for keeping them out. Now? We just process people.'

'That's right, people. My ego isn't important.'

'Not ego, old boy. Reputation, that's what it is, and it makes people come through that door.'

'I saw Conrad Taylor at court,' Dan put his hand on the box lid. 'Why didn't he know about this transfer?'

'Why should he? Robert Carter was Shelley's client, not his.'

'But Conrad's the senior partner. He didn't know the legal aid had been transferred.'

'Shelley can make her own decisions, and she saw a conflict of interest. Her professional integrity was on the line, and she knew he wouldn't see beyond the money.'

'It sounds like she's got more important things to worry about now. She rolled her car last night, with rumours of booze involved. She's in hospital.'

Pat closed his eyes for a moment and pinched his nose. 'How is she?'

'I don't know. I'm going up later.' Dan pointed to the box. 'I need to read this first.'

'Good man, I'll leave you to it.' Pat went towards the door but paused and looked back. 'Ignore Conrad Taylor. Do what you think is right.'

Dan smiled. 'I always do.'

Once Pat had left the room, Dan closed his eyes. He needed a moment's pause before he started to look at the file. Conrad Taylor might think that Dan's job was to babysit the case, but

Conrad didn't want to be the person hauled in front of the judge for missing something, or cited in the appeal courts. For as long as the case was his, he'd do what needed doing.

He needed the pause though, because as soon as he turned the first page, he'd be involved. Professionally, emotionally, morally. He cared about the verdicts, about justice, because for Dan it wasn't just an outcome. For some lawyers, the verdict meant the end of a case, nothing more to do than submit the bill. For Dan, the end of a case was a test of how he'd done, of whether his client's trust had been misplaced or not. It didn't matter that Robert Carter had chosen Shelley as his first lawyer. He was his client now, and Dan wasn't going to let him down.

He reached out and grabbed the first binder. He started to read.

The following hour was lost to Dan as he became engrossed in the case. He marked points of interest or things to explore with a red pen, but it was really about getting to grips with the facts.

There was a knock on his door. He wanted to ignore it, but the second knock was more insistent.

'Yeah?'

When the door opened, Jayne Brett walked in.

She looked dishevelled. Her hair was shoulder length but tangled and she had dark rings under her eyes. Her T-shirt hung loose over the waistband of her jeans, a green combat jacket over the top. Her white pumps looked ragged, a toe showing through.

She sat down on the chair at the side of the room. 'Is that the case?'

'No hello?'

'I've had a tough morning.'

'Work?'

'Life.'

'Who was he?'

She shrugged in apology. 'I never asked. Or if I did, I forgot.'

Dan laughed. 'I need your focus for this case. It's a murder case and the trial is in two weeks.'

'Won't all the work have been done?'

'I'm not interested in what other people have done. It's what I do that's important.'

Jayne lifted her feet on to the seat so that her arms were wrapped around her knees. Dan had spotted that look before, defensive whenever a murder case was being discussed, as if she was bracing herself against being reminded of her past.

'Go on then,' she said. 'Tell me about it.'

'You'll know it. Robert Carter.'

Jayne put her feet down, her eyes wide. 'The teacher case? Wow.'

The case had attracted a lot of media attention when the victim was first found; the pretty victims always do. She was Mary Kendricks, a young redheaded teacher who'd been found stabbed in the neck and body.

It wasn't just the murder that drew the press, although her good looks helped. It was the behaviour of the people who discovered her: one of her housemates, Lucy Ayres, and Lucy's boyfriend, Peter. As others were approaching the scene with flowers, ready to lay them at the end of a brick alley, Lucy and Peter watched from a distance, holding each other, kissing, almost as if they had no interest in what had happened in the house. For two days, the press reported on them, questioned what had really happened, focused on the two young people who were not displaying the public grief expected of them. That stopped when Robert Carter was arrested, and the media talk died right down once he was charged. They would have to wait for the verdict before they published anything else they'd found, the subjudice rules keeping everyone silent.

'Tell me about Mary,' Jayne said.

'She worked at a local primary school, not long from college. She couldn't afford her own place so she moved into the shared house. She'd lived in the house for a year or so when she was killed. Her friends make her sound pretty special.'

'They always do when they talk about the dead ones.'

'No, I think there's something in this. Fun, decent, studious.' He held up a photograph of Mary grinning for the camera, carefree and young, just starting to carve out her life. Her ginger hair caught the sun in the picture, and the light had brought out the freckles that spotted her nose.

Jayne reached out for the picture and studied it. 'She looks nice.' As she handed it back, she said, 'How did it happen? I remember some of the media stuff, but not the real detail.'

'It was at the end of a night out, Mary and her friends were at the Wharf. You know, the pub by the canal? All cask beers and stone floor.'

'A bit sedate for a night out with the girls.'

'Saturday night, they put bands on in the room upstairs. When Mary and her friends arrived, my new client was there, Robert Carter. Alone. He pestered Mary, something he'd done before. He made no secret of the fact that he liked her, but she didn't feel the same. Robert didn't seem a threat, but he imposed himself on Mary whenever he saw her. Mary was too polite to tell him to go away, but her friends said she resented him for spoiling her nights out.'

'Her housemates?'

'No. Two were away on a hen weekend and Lucy Ayres was with her boyfriend all night. They were in the throes of new love at the time so she didn't want to be away from him.'

Jayne made a gesture as if sticking her fingers down her throat.

'Yeah, and the next morning Lucy found her, stabbed,' he went on.

Jayne blinked at the word *stabbed*. 'How did Robert Carter end up there?'

'This is the part where his story makes no sense. Mary walked home with her friends, but she lived the furthest away, so she did the final half-mile on her own. According to Carter's interviews, he met up with her by chance and offered to walk her the rest of the way.'

'Some coincidence.'

'It doesn't look good, particularly as he lives on the other side of town.'

'So how did she go from walking home with him to being dead?'

'He said she invited him in for coffee, the old cliché, to say thanks. After half an hour or so, he went outside for a cigarette and Mary went upstairs to get ready for bed.'

'Didn't he take the hint?'

'Seems not. He was on the front step when he heard something in the house, as if there was someone else there, and then Mary screamed. The front door had closed and he waited outside, but when it had been silent for a while, he went around the back and went inside. Mary was injured, a neck-wound, blood everywhere. He tried to stop the bleeding but couldn't, and he panicked and ran out.'

'If there's any truth in that, it was a shitty thing to do, to leave her like that.'

'That'll be the hardest part, persuading a jury to like him after what he did. That's our case though, that he behaved like a coward and doesn't deserve our sympathy, but that doesn't make him a murderer.'

'How was she when Lucy found her?'

'You're sure you're okay to do this?'

'After Jimmy, you mean?' She shrugged. 'I need the money.'

Dan passed her a bundle of photographs. He didn't need to say anything as Jayne flicked through. He'd had to suppress his own sadness. It wasn't the blood or injuries that got to him, it was the waste of such a young life, vibrant and filled with so much hope, her dignity erased by the harshness of the flash bulb.

'When Lucy returned the following morning, the house seemed empty, but she sensed something wasn't right. She went into Mary's room, and there she was, just like in the pictures.'

Dan saw the photos again as Jayne looked through them a second time. Mary's body was on the bed but the duvet was over her head, just her bare feet sticking out. The pictures moved on to Mary with the duvet moved. She was naked, her jeans thrown to the corner of the room, her knickers and bra with them. Her white shirt was on the floor by the bed, soaked by the blood from a deep wound in her neck. There were some smaller puncture wounds in her side, with small trails where blood had trickled to the carpet.

'Didn't Lucy look under the duvet?' Jayne asked.

'She screamed and collapsed as her boyfriend called the police. But look at the blood. It's dried out and it looks obvious that Mary was dead. Who would want to look?'

'How did they catch him?'

'Carter's bloodied fingerprint on the wall by the door, inside the bedroom.'

'So where do I start?' Jayne took a deep breath as she handed the photographs back to Dan.

'Carter says that he wasn't in the room when it happened, so we need to show that someone else could have done it. There must be witnesses the police haven't found. A woman who lives on the street reckoned she heard a scream at around eleven-thirty. If we're looking for new suspects, we need to put them in the timeline, but a scream might have made people look out of their windows.'

'But the police will have done door-to-doors.'

'Yes, but people don't always like to talk to the police. That's where I want you involved. You can do it differently. And look into the other housemates, see what people say about them.'

'Won't the previous lawyer have done this already?'

'I don't care what Shelley did.'

'Can we do it in two weeks?'

'We're about to find out.'

'Anything else?'

'We'll see if any leads come back.'

She stood up. 'I'll meet you later to update you.'

'Where?'

'There's a new Italian that's just opened, Pizza Roma, on the High Street.'

'Okay, I'll see you in there at eight.'

Just before Jayne left, she paused. 'Why did Carter cover her up?'

'What do you mean?'

'Well, what's the case? That it was an intruder unknown to her, a stranger attack, a burglary gone wrong as Robert Carter smoked outside? Or was it a revenge attack for something, Mary targeted for reasons we don't know about? If it was either of those reasons, why was she still in bed, under the sheet? Carter said that he'd tried to help her but realised that there was no point and panicked. So why cover her up, if he was panicking? He'd just run, wouldn't he? No, it feels more like the killer was ashamed of it, couldn't stand looking at her.'

'Like passion wound up and let loose, and then the come down?'

'You said it,' she said, and left.

As he watched the door swing closed, Dan knew that he'd taken on a surefire loser.

He smiled. Those were the challenges he liked the best.

Eight

The house where Mary Kendricks was murdered seemed a good place to start. Jayne was sitting on a bench close by, aware of how she looked: scruffy, aimless, her hair unkempt, her eyes heavy. She had a notebook in her pocket, along with a pen and a camera. Those were her tools.

The plan was a simple one: hang around to see whether people will reveal the secrets they won't tell the police. She'd do the door-to-doors, like Dan wanted, but first she wanted to speak to the locals. They might help her find the right door to knock on.

The house Mary died in was in the middle of a terrace, with a small front garden behind a low wall. There was a bay window at the front and a low grey slate roof, typical of the long stone rows that lined the hills of the town, the homes built by the mill-owners to keep the workforce close by. Once devoid of indoor plumbing and made squalid by overcrowding, they were now tranquil starter homes, with double-glazing and hanging baskets taking the place of laundry stretched across the street.

Dan wanted to know more about Mary's scream so he could put it in the timeline. The street was quiet, with parallel rows of terraced housing on either side; there must have been people who heard something.

Mary's room had been at the back of the house so that was the place to start.

Jayne walked to the alley that separated the street from the one that ran behind. It was a long brick path with a small gutter in the middle, shaded by the high walls that bordered each yard and cluttered with wheelie bins and bags of rubbish, pizza boxes and torn cardboard stuffed in between. A cat with matted fur was chewing at a bag, dragging out chicken bones.

She walked slowly. Mary's house was the sixth one along. The brick wall that bordered the yard had been painted white and access was gained through a battered green wooden gate. Jayne looked around as she put her hand on the clasp, but there was no one watching her.

She'd expected the gate to be locked, but it opened as she pushed on it, the bottom of the wood scraping on some loose stones. It revealed a concrete yard with a white metal bench at one side. Moss covered the bricks and lichen made the floor slippery.

The house itself looked gloomy. A kitchen extension invaded the yard, an addition to the original design. Jayne peered in through the windows. The worktops were empty. Some of the cupboards were open. Nothing in them. The other occupants must have moved out. Jayne didn't blame them.

It was the view from the back of the house that interested her. Mary's bedroom had been on the first floor and she'd been killed in early November, so had her window been open? It would explain how her scream had been heard, but why did Mary have her window open late on a November night?

Her window must have been closed, which meant that the witness lived close by. The obvious answer was that she lived next door, and the scream was heard through the walls. The police don't put the addresses of witnesses in their statements, but what other answer could there be? If the window had been closed, the houses further along the street might have been too far away.

As she left Mary's yard, there was a noise. A gate closing, the sound of a latch coming down, the slide of a bolt. She looked up and down the alley. There was no one there. The sound had come from the yard opposite.

She went to the gate and listened. She thought she could hear someone breathing on the other side.

'Hello?' She tried to open the gate. It was bolted shut.

There was no reply.

'Anyone there?' She thumped on the gate.

Still nothing.

She frowned and set off back down the alley, glancing back to see if anyone opened the gate, but it stayed shut.

As she got to the front of the street and made her way to Mary's house, she noticed how the neighbour's house was different. Mary's house looked like just what it was, a house once occupied by a group of young people more interested in enjoying life than making a home. A CND sticker occupied a corner of one window, the only thing visible, privacy preserved by grey and sagging net curtains. The house next door, however, had flowers on the sill and the room she could see through the window looked ordered and neat.

Jayne knocked on the door and waited. She checked her notebook for the name of the witness.

The door was opened by a young woman with straggly blonde hair and a red sweatshirt stained in food. Behind her, there was a long hallway with a child's safety gate in the kitchen doorway.

'Helen Bolton?' Jayne said, as she passed over her business card.

'Yes, that's right,' she said, caution in her voice.

'Sorry to disturb you,' Jayne said, pleased that she'd guessed right. 'I work for the firm that represents Robert Carter.'

Helen looked at the card and then folded her arms, immediately defensive. 'I told the police I didn't want anything to do with it.'

'But you made a statement?'

'They wrote down what I told them and got me to sign it. They told me I wouldn't have to go to court, as I was just helping them out, but I got a letter telling me I've got to go in two weeks. I don't want to go.'

'Talk to me and you might not have to.'

Helen frowned. 'What do you mean?'

'You have to go to court because we want to ask you questions you haven't been asked by the police. If I speak to you now, we might have all we need.' Jayne hoped she wasn't going too far, because Dan hadn't made any decisions about anything, but she guessed that whatever Dan wanted to know, he needed to know it quickly.

Helen thought for a moment before stepping aside. Jayne took it as an invitation.

Her steps echoed as she went inside, the floor stripped down to the boards and stained white, the same in the living room, except the sounds were softened by a burgundy rug. The walls were covered in baby pictures, some natural, others formal studio shots.

'So, what do you want to know?' Helen said, as she sat on the sofa opposite. Her sleeves were rolled up her forearms, as if Jayne had interrupted her cleaning. She hadn't offered a drink so Jayne knew the visit would be short. A child was playing in another room.

Jayne thought quickly and cursed herself for not having any real plan.

'Tell me about the people next door.' It was the first thing that came into her head.

'I didn't really know them. We've lived here for fifteen years, and it seemed like the people changed all the time. What's the point in getting to know them?'

'Why do they change?'

'They're young, you know that. They move in with boyfriends or get their own place. Who'd rent long term with strangers?'

'So always women?' When Helen looked puzzled, Jayne added, 'You said they move in with boyfriends.'

'Well, yeah, I suppose. All girls together and all that.'

'You saw them around, then?'

'Yeah, sure, but I didn't really speak to them, and they didn't speak to me. That's how it was sometimes. There've been times when we've fallen out with whoever lived there, because we've got children, five of them, from twelve down to our youngest, and some of the neighbours get noisy, have parties that go on too late. Others are really friendly, will introduce themselves, make a point of talking. These? Like most, I suppose. They did their own thing, kept out of our way. Not friends, but not a problem. They'd say hello on the street but that's about it.'

'What about Mary, the woman who was killed?'

Helen softened at the mention of her name. 'I didn't know her that well, but her bedroom was next to ours. Our bedroom is at the back because there's a street light outside the front window and I can't sleep. We didn't hear much from her so

I reckoned she was decent enough. There'd been some years when the girl in that room has been, well, and Helen blushed. 'Let's just say enjoying living away from home.'

That made Jayne smile. 'And what about the night when Mary was killed?'

'I don't like to think of that, now that I know I heard someone die. That scream.' She shuddered. 'You can't fake something like that.'

'But is that all you heard, a scream? What did you hear before then?'

'Nothing much. I was watching television downstairs. There were bangs and things, some shouts.'

'How many voices?'

'I don't know. It's that scream I remember.'

'And you're certain about the time? Eleven thirty?'

'I looked at the clock straight away. I thought it might wake up the kids.'

'What about afterwards?'

Helen frowned as she thought back. 'Nothing. I listened out for a few minutes, in case there were more. I heard the back door go, but it went quiet after that.'

'The back door? Are you sure about that?'

'Absolutely. I heard the gate go.'

'Why didn't you call the police?'

'Like I just said, it went quiet. I've lived next door to that house for a long time and I've heard so many things that nothing surprises me. I just want them to make less noise and put the bins out on time. There was nothing else after that scream, so I left it. It was only the next day when I saw all the police outside that I thought it might be connected.'

'How long has the house been empty?'

'Ever since that night. They moved out and never came back.'

'Has anyone else ever mentioned to you that they heard anything? People must talk about it and you're right next door.'

'No, nothing, and I don't tell anyone about it.'

'Is there anything you missed out of your police statement?'

'What like?' The hostility was back.

'It's not a trick question. Just anything that you mentioned that they didn't think was relevant?'

After a few seconds thought, Helen shook her head. 'No, nothing.'

Jayne said her thanks and stood as if to go.

As Helen walked Jayne towards the door, she said, 'Will I still have to go to court?'

'I don't know,' Jayne said, truthfully. 'You've helped, though.'

Just as Jayne reached the street, Helen stopped her. 'Did he do it? Robert Carter? There must be good evidence against him if he's been charged, right?'

'He says he didn't. I can't do any better than that.'

Nine

Dan put the phone down. He'd arranged with the prison to see Robert Carter the following day. That was some progress. All he could hope for was that Jayne would come back with something new. His client needed to see something positive from the change of lawyer.

He pushed away the piece of paper he had in front of him, just a loose scrap that he was using to jot down his thoughts, but it was too frustrating. How could Jayne do in a day what Shelley hadn't managed in five months?

Something occurred to him.

He left his room and went to Pat's, who was turned in his chair, staring out of the window, his fingers steepled under his nose. Dan couldn't see what was so distracting, because the view was nothing more than a small car park and the rear of more offices. He knocked on the doorframe, interrupting Pat from his daydream.

'Daniel,' he said, his smile switching on as he turned round in his chair. He indicated with a flourish of his hand that Dan should talk.

'When did Shelley contact you about the transfer?'

Pat thought for a moment, his heavy brows shadowing his eyes as he frowned. 'Last Wednesday, I think. She called me and asked if I'd take it.'

'Shouldn't that be the client's choice?'

'Speed was of the essence, so she said. The trial is close. Once I said yes, she went the next day and got Carter to sign his life away to me. I got the case listed on Friday and it was transferred.'

'But why didn't you tell me? Getting a murder case just before the trial is a pretty big deal.'

'I was going to keep it, but,' and he shrugged. 'You've got the energy for it.'

'But Carter thinks he's getting Pat Molloy and he's got me instead.'

'He needs more than an old stager like me. The QC will take care of the trial. You'll be fine.'

'I'll be the junior on it.'

'What do you mean? A junior's already lined up, and you've never been a junior on a murder trial.'

'That's why I want to stay close. The QC will be the star turn, I know that, there for the tricky stuff, like the closing speech and the main witnesses, but at least I'll know what's happening in court because I'll be sitting right behind. And I might even be allowed to do some of the routine stuff, like the interviewing officers. I won't be there just to be a bag-carrier.'

Pat went as if to say something, but then waved his hand dismissively before turning back to his view of the car park.

Dan leaned against the doorframe. 'There's something I'm not being told. Like, why didn't Shelley come to me? We're old friends.'

'Just do what you do best,' Pat said, without looking back. 'Fight hard and it will all work out.'

Dan went back to his room. He had to call the prosecution. He'd flicked through the copied correspondence and saw the name of the lawyer. Zoe Slater. That was a relief. He liked Zoe.

Approachable, sensible, she'd done her time slogging out the days in the Magistrates Court and had graduated to preparing and serving the paperwork on the serious cases, making the day-to-decisions on murders and rapes and more, but never appearing in front of a jury.

He dialled and waited. He checked his watch, nearly four, and wondered if she'd be at her desk, but she answered just before her voicemail kicked in.

'Zoe, it's Dan Grant. I've inherited the Robert Carter case.'

'I hope you're not calling for an adjournment,' Zoe said, shot like a warning.

'Any chance of that?'

'None. The judge said as much when he agreed to the transfer. Anything else I can do for you?'

'I want to speak to the other tenants in the house.'

A pause. 'Why?'

'Because I need to find out about Mary.'

'But they're our witnesses. You can ask them what you want in the trial.'

'There's no property in a witness, you know that.'

Zoe sighed. 'There's nothing to know. Mary was a decent young woman. Worked hard, was popular, had a nice family.'

'But I need to satisfy myself. For that, we need to know more about Mary.'

'So that's your game, going out to tarnish her memory?'

'Give it a rest, Zoe. If there's nothing to find, there'll be no tarnishing.'

A pause, and then she asked, 'What's the conflict of interest? Has Carter changed his story? Did he admit it to Shelley?' Her voice softened. 'You can tell me, off the record, just between us.'

The newfound friendliness was fake. 'You sound worried that you've got the wrong man. You looking for reassurance?'

'Just curious. It's a good case. I wondered whether Carter had finally realised that.'

'I'll find out tomorrow when I see him.'

'And if he has?'

'I'll worry about that tomorrow.'

'Didn't Shelley ask around about Mary?'

'I don't know, and I can't ask her. She's in hospital. Rolled her car.'

There was a sharp of intake of breath. 'When?'

'Last night. I thought you might have heard about it. Defence lawyer crashes her car with rumours of drink being involved. I'd have thought the glee from the police would have spread the news quickly.'

'How is she?' Zoe said, ignoring the jibe.

'I don't know, but I'm going to see her later. I need to ask her about the case.'

'She crashed her car, is laid up in hospital, and you're going to ask her about your case? At least take some flowers.'

'Yeah, thanks for the tip.'

'When do you want to see these witnesses?'

'Tomorrow. After I've spoken to Carter.'

'I'll speak to DI Murdoch. It'll have to be at the station. I'm not giving out their addresses.'

Dan bristled but didn't say anything. The prosecution had no right to insist on conditions, because he could speak to whoever he wanted, but he didn't want to be accused of derailing a case so close to the trial date. He just didn't want to ask any questions under the scrutiny of the detectives.

'It will have to be tomorrow though, or else I'll speak to them in their homes. I'm sure I can find out the addresses.'

'You can't do that.'

'You know I can.'

A pause, and then, 'All right, tomorrow, I'll sort it.' Irritation showed in her voice. 'Anything else?'

'No, that's it for now, but I'll be in touch.'

'Yes, I'd guessed that,' she said, and then hung up.

Dan tapped the handset against his lip. He'd just fired the first salvo. Now for the battle.

Ten

There was a pub further along the road from where Mary lived, the sort that filled up with lonely lives looking for fulfillment in a glass. The sign outside creaked as it swung in the breeze.

Jayne had enough for a bottle of something. It would be a good source for rumours about Mary's murder, because there's no one more prepared to talk than the kind of bore who props up a bar.

The pub was dark. Even though the smoking ban had come in years before, the light that came in through the stained-glass windows was just a dirty swirl. A group of old men played cards in a corner, and three men in their early twenties played pool. Food was provided by a small pile of sandwiches under a clear plastic lid, with pork scratchings and peanuts sold from card displays that slowly revealed a semi-naked woman.

Everyone looked up as she went to the bar. The old men went back to their card game. The three men playing pool whispered something to each other and the one leaning over the table, taking a shot, laughed.

Jayne ignored them. For now.

She asked for a Becks, and when the barman brought back the drink, she said, 'Is it always this quiet?'

The barman looked around, scratching an old handmade tattoo on his forearm, a faded blue anchor etched into his skin. 'This is a busy day.'

She took a drink and felt her mood lift, as if the lager had swept away the last cobweb.

'Isn't the neighbourhood changing though?' she said. 'All buy-to-lets and young professionals not rich enough to buy a place elsewhere.'

'We're too authentic for them,' the barman said, the word *authentic* coming out with a sneer, the gaps where he'd once had teeth giving his voice a hiss. He shouted over to the men playing pool. 'Hey, when was the last time you saw one of the new locals in here?'

'Never,' one said. He considered Jayne for a few seconds. 'Fancy a game?'

Jayne raised her bottle to the barman and wandered over. She reached into her pocket and pulled out whatever change she had. 'I'm not sure I've got enough left.'

'Don't worry, it's on us,' he said, before putting some coins into the slot and pushing it home. There was a crash, followed by the slow rumble of the balls. He slapped the triangle on to the baize and said, 'I've never seen you round here before.' His voice had that Jamaican patois that the deadbeat white boys imitate.

'No, you haven't.' She didn't volunteer any more.

He set the balls up and said, 'I'm Callum,' before wiping blue chalk on to his cue. When he took the first shot, the air cracked with the noise.

Jayne put her jacket on a nearby chair and considered her shot, prepared to let the conversation take its own route. As she bent over the table, gazing down the cue, she was aware that Callum was behind her, checking out her backside as his friends at the other end of the table grinned and stared down her T-shirt. Fine, give them a look. She reckoned it'd been some time for those two.

She struck the cue ball hard, crashing a red ball against the cushion and making the two men flinch, splashing beer from their glasses on to their knuckles.

Callum laughed behind her. 'You asked for that, boys,' and then to Jayne, 'so what are you doing round here?'

'Why are you interested?'

'Because you came in and started asking questions straight away.' His gaze had turned hard.

'I'm not the police.' she said, taking a drink.

'Why do you think I'd be bothered if you were?'

'Because you're concerned about who I am and why I'm here. It doesn't take much to work out the rest.'

'But if you're the police trying to find out information, you're always going to say that.'

He had a point.

'I'm working for Dan Grant from Molloys.'

Callum tilted his head. 'You don't look like someone who works for a solicitor.'

'How well would I have fitted in here wearing a suit?'

'Good answer.' He grinned. 'So why are you here?'

'Do you remember the young teacher who was murdered just around the corner?'

'Found dead in her room?' Callum nodded as he thought back. 'I remember the police everywhere. Bad one, so I heard.'

'Dan represents the guy accused of murdering her.'

'I hope he's getting a rough time inside.'

'If he's the right person.'

Callum raised an eyebrow and then pointed to his two companions, who seemed content for him to lead the conversation. 'We've all been to court and we all knew we'd done it. We just lied about it. We lied to our briefs, to the police, to the court, and sometimes we got away with it. And guess what, we've got away with a load more stuff than we got done for. You're not talking to some div at a dinner party, all the hand-wringers, believing in the freedoms and all that shit. This is real life.'

He bent over the table and took a shot, standing when he'd sent the ball thudding into a corner pocket. 'So like I say, I hope he's getting some of what he dished out to her.'

'Play a game with me,' she said. When he looked to his friends and winked, she added, 'Not that kind of game.'

'Shame.'

'Pretend I'm not someone you want to fuck, just someone helping an innocent man. I need to find out if anyone else saw anything or knows anything about the people in that house. Who do I speak to?'

'That's easy, his Aunt Julie,' Callum said, and pointed at one of the men watching. 'She's like the mother of the street. Nothing goes on that she doesn't know about.'

Jayne drained her bottle. 'Thanks, boys. Time to go.'

'I'll text her now, tell her you're on your way round,' and Callum gave her the address.

Jayne headed towards the door.

As she went, Callum shouted, 'Are you sure you don't want to play any games? We could have some fun.'

'Maybe another time,' she said, and squinted as she headed back out into the bright sunshine.

Eleven

Dan's work was interrupted by a phone call from the custody office. One of his clients had been locked up. Like always, he stopped what he was doing and set off for the walk down the hill to the police station, a black leather folio under his arm.

He jabbed the intercom button and stared up at the CCTV camera over the door. When the door buzzed, he pushed and went in, and the echoes and clangs of the custody suite replaced the noises of the street, the fresh Pennine breeze replaced by the cell-stench of old feet and bleach.

The custody sergeant raised his mug when Dan walked in, offering a drink. Most defence lawyers get on with the police, and the conflict that took place in front of the prisoners was usually a charade.

Dan declined the offer. 'Where is she?'

The sergeant pointed towards a large glass room, where a young woman was pacing, one hand on her hip, the other on her forehead.

'She's been like that since she got here,' he said.

'What's she done?'

'Boyfriend threw her breakfast on to the street when she didn't make him one, so she attacked him.' The sergeant suppressed a chuckle. 'With a frozen waffle.'

'A what?'

'You heard. She threw a frozen waffle at him.'

'And he complained?'

'Yep. Hit him on the side of the head.' He shrugged. 'So, here we are.'

'You've got the exhibit, I take it?'

'It's in the freezer, in an exhibit bag.'

'He could have made his own breakfast rather than throwing hers out. Easiest way not to have a frozen waffle launched at you.'

'I'm guessing that's what you'll say once she's been interviewed and said nothing, and someone upstairs will say that it's not worth taking to court, and we'll all move on.'

Dan looked over to his client in the glass-walled holding cell, who'd stopped pacing and was staring at Dan and tapping her wrist, as if angry with him for keeping her waiting.

'Have you searched her for weapons?' Dan asked. 'She looks a little wound up.'

'What, foodstuffs?'

'Yeah, something like that.'

'She's clean, but if we keep her too long, we'll need to feed her, and the thought of it's making me nervous already.'

Dan grinned and set off towards the holding cell. Just as he got there, about to push open the door, there was a shout of, 'Dan Grant.'

He turned around. It was DI Tracy Murdoch. With skin stained by tobacco and yellowing eyes, the smell of cigarettes followed her everywhere.

'What can I do for you?'

'You've taken on the Carter case.'

'That's right. Found out this morning. I was just reading it.'

'You've had it less than a day and you're making trouble already.'

'Sorry, I don't get you.'

'Wanting to see the witnesses.'

'I've got two weeks to get my head round the case, so I'm taking shortcuts.'

'That's how it works, is it? Carter admits he's a murderer to his old solicitor, so they have to get rid of him. You take over and pretend he didn't say it, and the witnesses have to give up a day of work to relive their friend's murder with you. That's about right, isn't it?'

'They don't have to give up any work. I'll drive to their houses and speak to them when they finish, if they prefer, except it might not be easy to arrange for you to be there, so it'll be just me and them.'

When Murdoch's eyes widened, her nostrils flared, Dan added, 'I'll speak to them before the trial and you know you can't stop me, so cut out the horrified act.'

Murdoch turned and went to slam the door, except the slow hinge stopped her, so it brushed at the floor gently as she stormed off, marching down the corridor, shouting expletives that were lost as the lock engaged.

'I tried to be polite,' Dan said to the smirking custody sergeant.

'She's waiting,' he said, and pointed to his client, now staring at Dan through the glass.

'The fun never ends,' Dan said, and set off towards her.

Twelve

As Jayne walked along the street where Mary had lived, there was a woman standing in a doorway, her arms crossed, a cigarette in her fingers, smoke curling upwards and obscuring her face.

Jayne checked the house number of the street matriarch that Callum had given her. 'Are you Julie?'

The women took a pull on the cigarette. 'I got the text.' Her voice had a deep gravel from too many years of smoking. Suspicion filled her eyes as she looked Jayne up and down. 'Who are you?'

'I'm working on the Robert Carter case.' Jayne pointed along the street to where Mary had lived.

'That could mean anything. A writer. A copper.'

'No, I'm working for the firm that represents him. Molloys.'

'You're working for Pat Molloy?' Julie chuckled. 'You don't look like a solicitor.'

'I'm not. I'm a private investigator.'

'I didn't know they made them so young. How's he paying you?'

'Cash, I hope.'

'He's always been flexible about payments, has Pat Molloy.'

'How do you mean?'

'I didn't always look like this,' she said, and patted her stomach. She was dressed in a black skirt and a shirt that hugged large sagging breasts, her stomach not much smaller. Her hair was dyed too black and cut into a bob that framed her cheeks, making her face look even rounder. 'Yeah, Pat was good to me, back in the day,' and a twinkle in her eye made Jayne raise an eyebrow.

'You and Pat?'

'We were both young and I couldn't get Legal Aid. He'd help me out in court. I'd send him home to his wife with a spring in his step.'

'But he's a lawyer. They don't do things like that.'

'What, spend time with people like me?'

'No, I didn't mean that. I meant take payment like that, if that's what you meant.'

'Don't worry, love, I thought the same, but lawyers are the worst. You'd be surprised how many take drugs and enjoy the wrong kind of things. You can't stay buttoned up all your life. And what's a blowjob when I've just avoided a short jail spell?'

'I'll be taking cash,' Jayne said, and decided that she liked Julie. 'And I'm working for Dan Grant, not Pat Molloy.'

Her brow creased in concentration. 'The young one? A bit intense, from what I can tell.'

'He just likes to win.'

Julie sat down on the stone step and patted the space next to her. 'Pull up a seat.'

Jayne sat down next to her. Julie offered her a cigarette. Jayne declined.

Julie's skirt had ridden up to reveal the bright white slabs of her legs. Jayne liked that she didn't care.

'So you're here about the man who killed that poor girl over there,' and she jabbed a tar-stained finger towards Mary's house.

'He said he didn't kill her.'

'Yeah, and I've never shoplifted either,' Julie said, and coughed as she cackled. 'What do you want to know?'

'Just tell me about the people who lived there.'

'Quiet, that's what I remember. Boring, even.'

'Boring?'

'This area used to be a good one. We all knew each other, a community, families sticking together. Then the house prices shot up, the landlords bought up everything, and the people raised around here couldn't afford to stay when they left home.' She sighed. 'I blame the television people. You know, that Sarah woman, all the shows about buying up houses to do up and rent out. Suddenly, everyone wants a property empire.'

'Why don't you sell up? Cash in.'

'Because I was brought up here. It's my home. Now, it's all short-term renters. Some of them are okay, enjoy a good time, have parties and things.'

'The woman next door to where Mary lived didn't like the parties.'

'She would say that, snooty bitch.' Julie flicked the cigarette to the floor and ground it into dusty flakes. 'She spends too much time looking down her nose at us, thinking she's too good for the street. She loved it whenever the Bentley stopped by. She went straight outside, saying hello, sucking up to him, putting on the voice.' She wagged her finger. 'Never be ashamed of who you are.'

'Bentley?'

'A red one. Belonged to one of the parents, that was my guess. Summed this lot up. From good homes, just slumming it for a few years so they can brag about how they *kept it real*.'

'Did you ever speak to Mary, the woman who was killed?'

'Just hello and stuff. No real chats but she always smiled and said hi, unlike most who live round here now.'

'Did the police speak to you about the night Mary was killed?'

'They came round but I didn't speak to them. I never do.'

'Even though it was about a murder?'

'I don't help the police, that's it.'

'Why not?'

'Because they've never helped me.'

'What about Dan Grant? Will you help him?'

'Not if it gets that boy off.' She frowned. 'I don't help out the police but if he did what they say he did, I want him to stay locked up.'

'But do you know something worth hearing?'

Julie shook her head. 'I know someone said there was a scream, I didn't hear it, but her room was at the back, so they said, so I wouldn't hear or see anything if I'm in my house. I'm guessing that whoever did it ran along the back alley.'

Jayne remembered Carter's story, that he was at the front, having a cigarette, when he heard Mary scream. 'What about at the front of the house? Did you see anyone hanging around outside?'

'Why would I pay any attention? A lot of people went in and out of that house.'

'If you hear of anything, will you let me know?' and Jayne passed over one of her business cards.

'Yeah, sure.'

Jayne checked her watch. She had to go home before she met up with Dan. So far, all she'd learned was that the tenants in the house were quiet and one of them had rich parents.

With two weeks to go the trial, she doubted whether Robert Carter's change of lawyer was going to make any difference.

Thirteen

Dan checked his watch, out of breath as he rushed to his car. He wanted to visit Shelley at the hospital but he remembered the message from his father. He had time to call in, provided he could keep it brief.

The interview with his client had been short. He'd advised her to say nothing and Dan had complained during the interview that the case was too trivial to go to court. The duty inspector had agreed and Dan had one grateful client and a promise that she'd call him again next time.

Next time? There was always a next time for criminal lawyers.

The journey to the rest home was brief, where his father had lived since a stroke felled him two years earlier. His mind was still sharp, but the stroke had robbed him of his ability to look after himself, his left arm and leg useless. Instead, he bellowed his views on life from a room in a care home filled by men and women much older than him.

Dan drove too quickly, his mind on Shelley, and almost hit a car reversing out of a parking space. He waved an apology before he jogged across the tarmac and then slowed to a walk as he hit the warm air of the interior.

Dan hated the rest home. The air was too warm, too cloying, filled with the lingering aroma of boiled vegetables. Staff bustled by in aprons and smocks as residents sat hunched over on chairs along the corridor, their final days dragging by.

Dan's father had been an easy man to admire, big and strong and noisy, but a hard man to love. He'd been too busy looking for his next fight to bother with his children, his adult life spent in the trade union movement. Dan's kitchen was always filled with activists plotting the next campaign, evenings lost to smoky conversations and political dialogue.

Despite that, Dan looked for that man whenever he visited, but only ever saw shadows, withered by his stroke.

Dan tapped on his father's door and walked in.

His father lived in what would pass as an apartment in parts of London, but was really just a bedroom, bathroom and living room, with a kitchen at one end. The air had a faint smell of piss, and Dan hated pushing open the living room door in case he caught his father using a funnel. Fortunately he wasn't. He was sitting in his wheelchair in front of the television, watching cricket.

Dan sighed, exasperated. 'I thought your television wasn't working.'

'I've sorted it now. Rang them and gave them hell. Had to do this stupid thing with the box, turn it on and off again or something.'

'Why didn't you tell me?'

'What, so you didn't have to bother coming round?'

Dan lifted the bag he'd brought in, following a stop-off at a nearby shop. Four large bottles of cider. 'Will these make you feel better?'

His father pointed to the sink. 'Stash them under there.'

'They haven't rumbled your hiding place yet?' The staff didn't like him drinking. Dan guessed the reason. His father was belligerent when he was sober. Adding booze to it was like inviting the next fight.

'As long as it stays in here, they'll tolerate it.'

It was booze that had brought on the stroke. His body had tried to tell him years earlier to slow down, when drinking too much ale gave him gout and he'd roll around the bed in agony. Rather than slow down, he found a drink that aggravated it less. Cider.

The good times ended when a neighbour found him face down on the floor one Sunday morning, the stroke bringing him down a few hours earlier. Dan knew the booze was killing him, but alcohol remained one of his last pleasures; Dan felt he owed him that much.

There was a small glass on the side, which he reached for as Dan sat down, the bottles safely hidden.

'Are you stopping?'

'I've got to go to the hospital. A friend has had an accident.'

'Someone I know?'

'A lawyer friend. You've never met her, I don't think. Shelley.'

'Just a friend?'

'She's married.'

'Would that stop you?'

'Yes, it would. I'm going. I'll come back at the weekend and take you out.'

His father turned away and looked out of the window, towards a view of a garden fence. 'Don't bother. I don't want anyone to see me like this.' He turned up the volume on the television, the cricket commentators shouting now.

Dan took that as his cue to leave.

Just as he was about to close the door, his father raised his glass and winked. There it was, their relationship. Nothing was said, but they both knew the truth: they were the same. Stubborn bastards always looking for an argument.

The hospital wasn't far away, a sprawl of prefabricated buildings on the edge of the town, always threatened with closure but somehow it struggled on.

He checked his watch against the visiting times on the board. He had thirty minutes left.

Shelley was sitting on the bed when he walked in. She was dressed, a coat over her shoulders, her left leg bound tightly in thick bandages, her forearms resting on crutches. Her head was down. In front of her was Conrad, talking to her. Her husband, Mark, was leaning against the wall a few feet away.

Mark looked up as he approached, Shelley too. There was a long cut running down her cheek, held together by stitches, and a bruise on her jaw.

Conrad turned and glowered when he saw him.

'We were just talking, if you'll give us a minute,' Conrad said. He didn't fake a smile. His anger came out as a tremor in his voice.

'No, it's all right,' Shelley said, her voice weary. 'I get your point. I just want to go home.'

Conrad looked at them both, his jaw set, before walking quickly along the ward, the clip of his heels loud.

Once he'd gone, Dan said, 'Point?'

'Just work stuff.'

'When you're here? Does the man have a heart?'

'I don't want to talk about it.'

'Okay, no problem. How are you?'

'Tired.' She looked at Mark. 'Can we go?'

Mark dangled his car keys. 'Right away.'

Shelley grimaced as she eased herself into the wheelchair by her bed, her crutches on her lap and pointing forwards like jousting lances.

As Mark pushed, Shelley pausing only to say thank you to the nurses, Dan asked, 'What happened?'

'I crashed my car, that's all.'

'Someone else involved? Everyone all right?'

'Just ask the question, Dan. Drink?'

'Those are the rumours around the court.'

'And what do you think?'

'You're too strait-laced for that,' and he smiled. 'Unless you've changed since uni, you wouldn't know a wild night out if it hit you on the nose.'

'Someone had to look after you.' She sighed. 'The police took a blood sample, but that was routine, I know that. I hadn't been drinking. I lost concentration, that's all, was driving too fast. The police were bound to think it was booze.'

'But you're not going to admit that, right, the driving too fast?'

She smiled, but it was tired. 'I'll give myself the right advice, don't worry.'

They reached the warm breeze of the hospital entrance and Mark pointed to the furthest corner of the car park. 'I'm parked over there. Wait here with Dan, I'll bring the car round.'

As he went, Dan said, his voice more serious, 'What did Conrad really want?'

'What do you mean?'

'Come on, Shelley. I know Conrad well enough to know that he wasn't being touchy-feely.'

Shelley stayed silent as Mark got to their car and started to drive towards them. As he pulled in, she said, 'Just leave it, Dan.'

He was surprised. 'I won't, and you don't want me to. Is it because you've transferred Carter's case? Is that what it's about, the loss of a case close to the trial?'

'I'm not talking about it.'

'If you're in trouble, come to me. If it's something you can't tell Mark, I'll listen.'

Mark stopped and got out, to help Shelley in. Just before she strained to stand on her crutches, with Mark ready to take the wheelchair back inside, she gripped Dan's hand. 'Please, for my sake, leave it. Do Carter's case, submit the bill, and let me get on with my life.'

Shelley didn't look back as she clambered into her car.

As they drove away, Mark waved out of the window but there was nothing from Shelley.

If she'd been trying to prevent him from investigating further, she'd done the exact opposite.

Fourteen

Jayne had typed up her notes for the day, her recollections of her scout around Mary's neighbourhood dressed up as a formal report by adding a title page and the date. It didn't amount to much, certainly nothing that could be used in court, but it was all she had. Now, it was about the evening ahead, and she paused in front of the mirror as she decided what to wear.

She took off her T-shirt and threw it on to the bed. She frowned at her reflection. Her shoulders were too slim, she'd lost too much weight, and her skin was pale. She wasn't eating enough. She thought of Dan and reached for a dress that was hanging over the door, something she'd bought on a whim, flimsy and strappy, but hadn't had the chance to wear.

For a moment, she wondered how it would be with Dan, fantasies that slipped into her mind sometimes. It would be different, she was sure of that. More thoughtful, more tender, more for her, because it would mean something; his hands on her, soft kisses on her neck, his fingers pushing aside the straps, the dress falling to her feet.

Memories tumbled in too quickly, the glow gone. A knife plunged into skin, blood warm on her hand and then sticky on her face as her hand went to her mouth. Jimmy's blood. The metallic taste. Loud screams. Her screams. A knife fell to the floor.

She threw the dress into the corner of the room and found a shirt instead, plain white cotton she could wear over her jeans, under her usual army-style jacket. As she looked in the mirror, she realised she looked the same as she had at the start of the day. Just a little less bleary around the eyes.

It would have to do.

*

Dan was drinking wine and staring out of the window as he waited for Jayne. He was still in his work clothes, except his shirt collar was open and his tie was pulled down. The day had been long and the wine was starting to loosen him.

Dan had an urge to sink into the wine, but he knew he had to take it steady; he had something else planned for later and needed his car. Two waiters in black shirts were standing at the back of the room, looking bored.

The restaurant was at the end of the High Street, where the chainstores petered out to charity shops and take-aways, between a closed sandwich shop and a pub with a tiny front door, a relic of Victorian times. On a Monday night, the pub was quiet, just marking time until it became part of the week-end pub crawl.

Jayne almost crashed through the door, out of breath as she threaded her way through the tables.

'I was thinking that you'd found out something good and were still on the case,' he said, raising his glass.

'Do you never stop working? I thought we were dining out.'

'You sound hungry.'

'I forgot to eat today. Extra large pepperoni please.'

'Yes, that's hungry.'

'They'll box up what I don't eat and I'll have it for break-fast.'

'Why didn't you say?' He reached into his jacket pocket for his wallet. He pulled out fifty pounds and handed it over. 'An advance on payment. You've probably earned it already.'

'Thanks,' Jayne said, pocketing it. 'But I still want that pizza.'

A waiter brought over a wine glass for Jayne and took her order. Dan reached over for the wine and filled her glass. 'Business now, so that we can enjoy the rest of the evening. What have you found out?'

'Not much.' She took a drink, pausing to look at her glass. 'This is good stuff. The wine I get tastes a bit sharper than this.'

He wanted to push the whole bottle to her side of the table and get another one for her to take home, but said instead, 'Tell me about your day.'

She took another sip. 'I spoke to the woman next door who heard the scream.'

That surprised him. He raised his eyebrows. 'That'll get us noticed.'

'It just sort of happened. Did I do something wrong?'

He felt bad about the look of disappointment on her face, as if she'd been hoping that he'd praise her good work rather than react the way he had. 'No, that's fine. There's a proper way to do things, I know, and I play dirty only when the fair way doesn't work, but yes, time is short.'

'When I was your client, I wouldn't have cared how you did it.'

'I know, but if I'd played dirty in the case before yours, perhaps I'd have found your case harder, because no one would have trusted me.' A pause, and then, 'What did she say?'

Jayne leaned forward. 'You see, sometimes the wrong way is the best way. She said Mary was quiet, at least compared to the previous tenants, and the same for the rest of them. She heard the scream and that was it. Same with the street-mum further down.'

'Street-mum?'

'Just someone who fancies herself as the boss. She didn't hear the scream but said the tenants thought they were too good for the area. A red Bentley turned up one day. That's about it. Mary got a good report though. Sorry if you're hoping for some dirt on her, but Mary went unnoticed. Just a nice young woman.' Another swig of wine. 'What about you?'

'Nothing yet, apart from one thing, but I don't know what it is'

'Sounds mysterious.'

'I drove to the hospital to see Shelley. Something wasn't right. Conrad Taylor was there, and whatever they were talking about, it was serious, and she wouldn't tell me about it.'

'Why should she?'

'We go back years, right back to college. We started out at the same time and we've always shared confidences.' When Jayne smiled over her glass, he added, 'And that's all, confidences. But she clammed up on me.'

'It might not have anything to do with this case.'

'If he was checking on her health, she didn't look happy about it. She transferred the case to me without Conrad knowing, and he's angry about it, but Shelley won't say why.'

'How can you be so insensitive?' Jayne said, shaking her head.

'What do you mean?'

'Come on, Dan, not everyone is like you, wedded to the job. Shelley's rolled her car and ended up in hospital, and you think she should be interested in a case she's given away? Perhaps there's more to the accident than that. Was she drunk?'

'She says not.'

'And your clients always tell the truth? If she's rolled her car after getting drunk, you're a reminder of what she might have thrown away.'

'She'll need a good lawyer.' Dan said, and raised his glass.

'You're all heart.'

'She doesn't get a free ride just because she's a lawyer. The law applies to all of us.'

'Ah lawyers, those paragons of virtue.'

'What do you mean?'

Jayne swirled the wine in her glass. 'The queen of the street? She was one of Pat Molloy's old clients. Sounds like he did court work for blowjobs.'

Dan raised his eyebrows and then laughed. 'I've heard a lot of things about Pat, so nothing surprises me. Let's just say it was a different world back then.'

'More fun?'

'Less straight. Criminal law attracted talented people back then, and sometimes with talent you get misbehaviour.'

'What like?'

'Pat was once caught in a brothel. There was another night when he went to a client's nightclub and got so trashed that he ended up shouting like an old drunk in the town centre. He spent the night in the cells. Was turfed out in the morning, hungover, and he'd soiled himself.'

Jayne pulled a face.

'Yeah, and you can imagine how the police loved that, local defence lawyer in a cell. I know you think I'm too serious, not fun enough, but I've got a job to do. You should know that more than anyone.'

He cursed himself when a look of pain flashed across her face. There it was again, the memory, their past. He wanted to reach across and say how sorry he was, but that wouldn't be right. She'd been a client. That changed things.

'Yes, I know, and you know I'll always love you for that.' She flushed. 'Not love like that, of course.'

He saw something else in her eyes, for a moment, but it was gone before he could work out what it was.

'I'm glad your case went like it did,' he told her. 'And every time Pat took himself too seriously in court, got pompous, every lawyer and copper in the courtroom remembered when he'd walked home from the station in a paper suit, past all the punters, his clothes in a plastic bag because he'd shit himself. The police wouldn't let him call for a taxi or use his phone until he got outside.'

'Okay, I forgive you for being boring,' she said, laughing. 'So what now?'

'We eat, we drink, and then tomorrow I meet Robert Carter.'

'And me?'

Dan thought about that and then said, 'Try to find out about Shelley, why she sent Carter my way.'

'Why should that matter?'

'Because that firm never gives up a client, and Shelley gave up a murder client without telling her boss. Just see what you can find out.'

'And how will I do that?'

'You're the investigator.'

'Do you think it might be dangerous?'

'What makes you say that?'

'Just a feeling. Murder cases being transferred secretly. Pat Molloy not wanting to do it.'

'Perhaps he thinks I'll do a better job.'

Jayne frowned. 'No, it's more than that. You're just too close to see it.'

'You sound like you want out.'

Jayne drained her glass and reached for the bottle to pour another. 'I can't afford to be out.'

Dan thought about what she said and wondered whether she was right. He knew one thing: there was something different about this case. All he could do was hope that any danger stayed away from them.

It wasn't the risks that bothered him. It was the knowledge that he wouldn't shy away from them when they arrived.

Fifteen

It was the nighttime he hated most. Everything went quiet and he was alone with his thoughts. What happened to Mary had changed everything.

His mind drifted back to Cassie, it often did, pleasure mixed with pain. He'd seen more of her than she'd ever known.

He'd gone into her house as normal. She'd gone out to her soul club and he'd let himself in through the back door. He'd checked her emails and then her calendar, just to check whether she had any plans to stay out all night, but there was nothing written down. She'd be coming home. He squeezed under her bed and waited.

The opening of her front door had been loud in the silence. His breath caught. He listened out to make sure she was alone. No second voice. No giggle as she brought someone home. He couldn't bear that. Not that night.

She was alone.

He was patient as she went through her nightly routines. A drink of something from the fridge. Locking the doors. He'd smiled at the irony of that, her locking him in. He'd seen the patterns while watching from the garden, so he knew them all, but still it sent a ripple of excitement through his body, like a cold shiver followed by something he fought harder to control: a surge of desire. Being in her room was a whole new experience, because waiting for her made him keener to hear everything: the tune she sang to herself, the loud patter of her bare feet on the floor, the whispered endearment to her cat.

He had to control his desire. He couldn't take risks, but as she came upstairs, her steps slow, he was breathing hard.

The door opened silently, a slow sweep. Her legs came into view. Her shoes had been taken off downstairs, so he could see her bare feet. Soft, warm.

He closed his eyes. He had to stay in control, she couldn't know he was there.

Once he opened his eyes again, he moved his body slowly, almost slithered, so that his movement was silent but he was closer to her, her feet a short reach away.

She clicked on the lamp and sat on the bed as she took off her jeans, the metal lattice above him creaking. Her legs were shown to him in a slow reveal, just inches in front of him, his black cloth mask making him part of the dark space. Her calves looked so smooth, her muscles defined. Her T-shirt and bra went to the floor. He was desperate to peer out and glance upwards, but all he could do was watch her as she walked around the bed, her feet making soft noises in the carpet.

She clicked off the lamp and the springs clanged as she climbed into bed.

He allowed himself a small gasp of pleasure, although he stayed as still as he could. Her weight on the mattress had brought it closer to his face and he tried to control his breathing, his mouth open. Perspiration stuck the hood to his face as he tried to listen out, knowing her breaths, the rhythms of her deep sleep. He was waiting for those before he slid out, so he could kneel next to her and watch her, his outline just a shadow.

A few minutes passed and then there was a noise from the bed. A deep inhale through her nose and the softest gasp.

He jammed his eyes closed. Not that. Too much.

The bed started to move in regular motions, barely noticeable but for the gentle creaks. He lifted his head so that it was almost touching the mattress. His fingers gripped the metal lattice, as if he was pulling her closer, her weight trapping his hand, needing to feel her rhythm against his fingers.

He grimaced. He couldn't hold on.

He started to shuffle out from under the bed, his movements silent, desperate to see her.

He stopped himself. That was a weakness. He had to stay in control. Just lie back, enjoy the moment with her. What was she thinking of? Who? He slid his hand into his trousers so he could match her rhythm, just inches from her, the sound of his hand against the fabric lost against the steady movement of the bed.

Her climax came quick and quiet, no one to impress. He came with her, his mouth wide open in the hood, the material stretched across his mouth like a black scream. Her breaths came fast as she lay back and enjoyed the comedown.

All he could do was wait. His own need had slipped away, sated for the moment, the slow burn of shame creeping through him. Her sleep would come soon. A few minutes passed and her breathing became more regular. The sleep of the contented.

He waited for thirty minutes and then slid out from under the bed. He was silent as he got to his feet and stood over her. He couldn't see her properly, it was too dark and the eyeholes in the hood had moved as he'd shuffled across the floor. He lifted the hood slowly and almost gasped out loud when he saw her. So beautiful, so serene. So his.

He backed out of the room, keeping his hood up so he could see any obstacles, like clothes in the middle of the floor that could trip him and wake her.

Once he was out of the bedroom, he couldn't stop his grin. That had been their moment together.

He should have ended it there. If he hadn't gone back, Cassie wouldn't have hit him and his life would still be in one piece. And he would never have known Mary.

Sixteen

Jayne wasn't aware of Dan's driving. He'd kept the wine flowing and she hadn't noticed that she was the only one drinking it, and then the food and the gentle roll of the car had sent her to sleep. She jolted awake when Dan tapped her hand.

It took a few seconds for her to realise where she was, outside her own building. She wiped her eyes as Dan said, 'You okay here?'

'Yeah, fine.' She heard the slur in her voice. A pizza box was on her lap. She raised the wine bottle, the rest of the second bottle she hadn't finished during the meal. 'If you're after coffee, I'm going for this instead.'

'You need to get some sleep.'

Jayne reached for the door handle, but paused. She looked round at Dan, her mind screaming at her to keep on moving, not to say anything, but the booze made her go hunting for his gaze, looking to find something there.

It came to nothing. Dan was staring straight ahead, chewing his lip.

She unlocked the door and stepped out. It was clumsy, as she tried to keep hold of the pizza box and the wine. 'Goodnight, Dan,' she said, once she was on the pavement.

'Yes, you too.'

She slammed the car door and weaved her way towards her building, as she tried to work out the easiest way to get her keys from her pocket. She turned to give Dan one final wave with the bottle before she went inside, but he was driving away, his mind already elsewhere.

'Goodnight then,' she said to herself, as she stepped inside and leaned back against the front door.

She'd almost done it. In her drunken state, she'd almost leaned over and kissed him, just to feel his lips on hers for a moment, even if he'd pulled away. But she'd stopped herself, one small drop of self-control keeping her from making a fool of herself. Again. Her life had become a series of one-night stands, meaningless encounters for a few short hours, nothing more.

But every time she thought of wanting more, one thing came back to her: she'd killed the last person she'd loved.

She unscrewed the cap on the wine bottle and took a long swig. It was warm. She pushed herself away from the door. If she was going to lose herself in self-pity, she needed to do it in private.

There was music coming from the floor above. It was a Monday, for Christ's sake. The faltering thuds of a bass guitar as he tried out a new song. At least he couldn't complain if she stumbled around for a while longer.

She trudged up the stairs, taking care on the carpet as it slithered around on each step. The smell of cannabis got stronger as she got higher. As she went past the flat where music was playing, she banged on the door with her fist. The bass stopped for a moment, but started up again as she went up the next flight.

On the next floor, someone was watching her, the apartment door slightly open, the glint of an eye visible.

'Drunk again,' Jayne said, and raised the bottle. She swayed as she walked and took another drink straight from the bottle. Classy, yeah.

The door slammed shut.

Her apartment was up one step, with a small staircase inside to take her into the eaves. The lights on the stairs were on a time-switch; one push and they stayed on with just enough time to make it to the next one, except that Jayne had weaved her way up too slowly, so that the light clicked off as she got close to her door.

She reached out as she walked, knowing her front door was close, her keys in one hand, fumbling for the lock.

She put her hand on her door handle and jumped, startled. There was something there. A rustle of paper. She reached out more slowly this time, her nerves on edge. The paper again, and then her hand moved upwards, to the thin stalks of flowers, jammed in behind the handle.

Jayne's good mood left her as she turned the lock. She grabbed the flowers and closed the door quickly.

Someone had got into the building. Her breaths were fast, her panic rising. She turned on the light and read the card. *Thanks for last night. Let's do it again.*

No, not a good idea.

She marched into the kitchen and threw them into the bin. Yes, some big romantic gesture, but what was he hoping for when she opened the door? That she would fall into his arms and they'd go straight back into bed?

Tears prickled her eyes but she blinked them away. She wouldn't let those memories take over her life, but it had been that way at the start with Jimmy. Flowers, sweet nothings, texts all the time. Until she'd moved in. Then it had all changed. It became about control. The texts were about knowing where she was, who she was with, then abusing her when he didn't like the answers. She wasn't going that way again.

It was the blood she remembered. All that blood.

She put the wine in the fridge. The memory had wrecked her mood, and pouring booze on it wouldn't help. Was it her fault for letting him come home with her, because now he knew where she lived? One night didn't give him entry into her life.

She flicked off the light and went into her bedroom, flopping on to the mattress. She thought about getting undressed, but why bother? She was angry. She'd wanted to finish the bottle and think of better things. Now, all she could think about was Jimmy.

It was going to be a long night.

*

Dan checked his rearview mirror and watched Jayne as she weaved across the pavement, the wine bottle tucked into her elbow and the pizza box tilted. She needed to have a clear head tomorrow, and that wine bottle looked like it was going to be drunk fairly quickly.

He took a deep breath. Not for the first time, he'd wanted more than they had. She made him laugh and was attractive and so many times during the meal he'd had to stop himself from reaching across for her hand. Even as she was getting out of the car, he'd almost leaned across to kiss her, but he couldn't think like that. She was a former client and he couldn't cross that line. And what if she'd rebuffed him? It would ruin their friendship, their working relationship, and he valued both of those things. She wasn't in a prison cell. That should be enough for him.

He focused on the Carter case instead, and he knew where he was headed: to where Mary died.

It was a short drive, just around the deserted precinct, an empty strip of shops crammed into a sixties revamp that had cleared away much of the grandeur of the town centre. The streets were quiet as he crawled along the residential area, long terraced strips, the pavements jammed with cars.

He stepped out of his car and buttoned his jacket. The night was cold. There was a hill at the top of the road. During the day, it was a vivid splash of green in contrast to the drab grey of the houses. During the night, however, it turned into a dark and brooding silhouette.

He looked at his watch. Just before midnight, around the same time as Mary's neighbour heard a scream. That's why he was there, for the sensation of how it was at night, to listen to Mary's neighbourhood. You can't get everything you need from a file.

He turned as he walked. There were the blue flickers of television in many of the windows. A dog barked, and the sound of shrill laughter drifted from somewhere.

Mary's house seemed so ordinary. He'd expected it to seem ominous somehow, as if what had happened in there had somehow changed it, but it was just like all the rest.

An alley ran behind it, and it was the rear of the house that interested him more. His shoes made loud clicks as he walked.

He stopped and closed his eyes, tried to hear the sounds of the night as they might have been when Mary was murdered. The slight hum of cars from one of the main roads out of town.

The creak of gate hinges in the breeze. Something moved in a cardboard box. A cat or something. A gate banged against its post, not closed properly. There was someone talking in a yard, with smoke drifting upwards from a late night cigarette, just mumbles breaking the quietness. That was his first answer. They were noises barely made, just small sounds that would be lost in the daytime, but at night they drifted through the alleys and streets.

He opened his eyes, filled with the certainty that if Mary's scream had been loud, people should have heard.

But what could they have seen, if they'd looked?

The streetlight at the end of the alley painted the brickwork orange. The gateways that broke up the line of walls were dark chasms, small alcoves that provided a hiding space. The walls were high, six feet all the way along, so that any light that came from the rear windows was swallowed by the yards. Beyond the streetlight, the alley headed into darkness as it gave way to the countryside.

If Robert Carter was telling the truth, someone must have come through the alley and into the house from the back yard. When Carter came running around the corner, why hadn't anyone seen him, their attention drawn by the scream just minutes before?

The prosecution's case was mainly a forensic one, with Carter's fingerprint in blood by the door, topped off by an explanation no one believed. Carter's first mistake had been to talk. He'd come up with the first thing that came into his head, needing to explain away his forensic traces, and now he was stuck with it.

Dan sighed. He was veering into that grey area that clouded a lawyer's morality, where justice becomes confused by the desire to win a case, to see a client go home knowing that his lawyer has done his job well. Sometimes, the truth didn't seem to matter, which meant that Mary didn't seem to matter.

He walked slowly along the alley and stopped outside the gate to Mary's house. The house number was on the wooden gate in white plastic numbers. There was green twine pinned to the gatepost that had once held flowers. The house was starting to look neglected, with all the tenants living elsewhere. It would fill up again soon, Dan guessed, once the trial had finished and everyone moved on, but for now the empty house was a reminder of what had happened in there.

Dan turned to look at the houses that overlooked Mary's. The windows were all in darkness. He turned away but stopped. He'd seen something. It barely registered, but it had been there. Movement in a window, the sensation that someone had moved quickly, as if to avoid being seen.

The skin on the back of his neck tingled. Someone was watching.

Seventeen

Present Day

The jurors had been sworn in but the chairs were as empty as the judge's, who had decided on a break, the chance for people to have one last cigarette, coffee or toilet visit before the opening speeches. For the judge, it was the final opportunity to check with the lawyers that everything was ready, that there were no surprises to come. Dan reminded himself that the judge was the Recorder, the title of the most senior judge on the circuit, always used for the murder trials, so it would be *My Lord* and not the usual *Your Honour*.

Dan had recognised the awestruck stares of the jurors when they'd come in at the start of the day. It was something he felt himself whenever he was in the wood-panelled surroundings of the main courtroom, surrounded by pictures of long-dead judges, reminders of all that had gone before him. He was about to create his own small piece of history in courtroom number one, used for the high-profile cases.

A murder trial is what all jurors dream of from the day they get the letter; or, at least, for those who can't think of a good enough excuse to avoid jury service altogether. Something to talk about with friends, the insights only they can share. For a couple of weeks of inconvenience, they get a lifetime of dinner party gossip.

It's fool's gold. Robert Carter's case will change them. For the moment, they had a murderer and their private excitement.

Soon, they'd have a victim, with her family in the public gallery, bereft, lost, along with crime scene photographs that will come back to them in their nightmares.

Jayne leaned forward. 'What do you think of the jury?'

She was sitting directly behind him, deep in the well of the court, the dock behind her, where Carter was chewing his nails as he waited for his trial to start. Carter's QC, Hannah Taberner, was in the row in front of Dan, her papers open on a lectern that she'd brought into the courtroom.

Dan knew it was a trick, part of the mind games to come. The prosecution hadn't engaged a QC; government cutbacks, and the threat of more, meant that money had to be saved where it could. Instead, one of their more senior in-house advocates had been given the job, except that he wasn't a QC. It meant that he couldn't use a lectern or sit on the front row, and instead was seated along the same row of desks as Dan.

The prosecutor had sought permission to sit alongside the QC, but had been given the short answer: no. The message was clear to the jury, that the prosecution didn't care enough about Mary Kendricks to instruct a Queens Counsel.

Dan turned round and spoke in a low voice, so that Carter couldn't make out what he was saying. 'Not good.'

'Why's that?'

'Did you see how they swore the oath?'

'They swore on the Bible, like they were asked.'

'Exactly. The best jurors refuse the bible part and merely affirm, make a promise to come to the true verdict.'

'What, atheists? What makes them so special?'

'No, not that, because some devout people refuse to swear on a holy book. Don't swear an oath, let your yeah be yeah, that's what the bible says. If they affirm, believers or not, it shows conviction, that they will stand by what they believe is right. I look for those jurors every time, target them during the trial and watch for those moments when they scowl or wince or nod in agreement. If I can turn them into allies, I have friends in the jury room, and friends who will lead the dialogue. I need just three to hang a jury.'

'And for this trial?'

'You saw. They each mumbled their way through it and held the bible like they'd never seen one before. All followers, no leaders. That makes everything uncertain.'

There was a sudden thump as the Prosecution counsel sat down. Simon Parkin, his head a smooth dome whenever he wasn't wearing his court wig, his nose always pointing upwards, like a dog sniffing the breeze. He'd been a barrister in chambers for twenty years but had settled for the steady hours and pension rights of the prosecution a few years earlier. He smirked across at Dan. 'You're all dressed up just so you can carry her bags,' and looked towards Hannah, who sat poised in front of Dan.

Dan tried to control his frustration. It was his one weakness in the Crown Court, the sneers of other counsel. Dan's accent was untamed northern bluntness. He'd gone through the phase of trying to soften it, but had decided in the end that his attempt to fake it would sound worse than what he had. It gave away his origins though, a rough edge made smooth, and any hint that opposing counsel saw it as something to sneer at brought a response too quickly.

Hannah turned round and she was struggling with her pen. 'Can't get the damn lid off, screwed on too tightly.' She thrust it at Simon. 'Get it off for me, will you.'

Simon stood so that he could reach it. He gave it a twist and handed it back.

Hannah winked at Dan as she went back to reading her papers.

'You certainly know how to tug a forelock,' Dan said, smiling. He knew Simon's type. Head-butler type, always ready to suck up to the judge.

'Is Carter sticking with his nonsense then?' Simon said, ignoring the jibe and not caring whether Carter heard him.

Dan leaned over and spoke in a whisper. 'He is, so you better make sure you win.'

Simon's smile flickered before he chuckled to himself. 'It's not about winning, you know that.'

Dan recognised the slight glint of unease in his eye, because for a prosecutor, it was very much about winning, and there were some prosecutors who feared a solid case, because they can only get weaker as the tight threads unravel.

Dan's attention turned to the public gallery. It was at the back of the courtroom, where they struggled to hear the proceedings as the lawyers' voices got lost in the high ceiling. The room had been designed to be imposing, nothing more. Despite that, there were five reporters: one from a national newspaper, another from a television channel, along with two local ones and an internet hack looking to sell cheap copy. They were only allowed to report what was said in court, with no speculation or comment, although he knew from experience that the prosecution's opening speech was often reported as if it were fact. If the case slipped down the columns, that's all people would remember.

Mary's parents had been placed in one corner of the gallery, the furthest away from Carter, and their gaze was fixed forward.

The seats would fill as the case progressed, once Mary's friends had given their evidence and were able to watch from the sidelines.

There was a loud knock and Dan got to his feet. It was the judge's entrance, choreographed, archaic.

Dan closed his eyes for a moment. Now was the time. He could do as Carter wanted him to, but he wasn't ready to. He just had to persuade Carter to see the case differently, to do it his way, despite the danger it presented.

Eighteen

Thirteen Days Earlier

Dan woke with a start and then groaned as he felt a sharp jab in his back.

He'd slept on the sofa, too tired to go to bed, except that the sofa wasn't long enough. He'd ended up curled into an awkward position, papers from the Carter case all over the floor, separated into different sections.

He hauled himself upright and stretched out the aches in his back. He rubbed his eyes, hoping to massage some life back into them before he opened the curtains. The view reminded him why he was glad he'd turned away from city living.

His apartment was on the top floor of an old wharf building, where the barges had once docked, bringing the cotton from Liverpool before being winched in and loaded on to the wagons waiting in the cobbled courtyard on the other side. Oak beams ran across the ceiling and an old black iron wheel hung in one corner, a remnant of its history. Some concessions had been made to modern living, like the small window replaced by a door that opened on to a steel balcony, but mainly it was the twenty-first century somehow squeezed into an old industrial space.

He went to the balcony to let the sunshine kick-start his day. As he stepped outside, the early morning chill made him shiver. The canal curved in the distance, getting lost between long-deserted factories awaiting regeneration, the town always hinting at rebirth. The sun made the dew glisten on the hills and an early morning mist turned the town into light grey outlines, just the tall chimneys reaching through.

The wharf building had a large wooden canopy over the water, painted light blue. Barges lined the towpath, attracted by the pub next door. Smoke drifted from a small black chimney on one, and on another a woman was reading, a blanket round her shoulders. She raised her hand when she saw Dan. He waved back.

He turned and went back inside. As good as the morning felt, the town's darker side was drawing him in.

Dan thought back to the night before and his sensation of sudden movement when he was in the alley behind Mary's house. It was a curtain coming to rest, the faintest outline of someone watching.

He went back to the papers on the floor.

He'd put to one side the routine statements from the officers who'd handled exhibits or interviewed Carter. There was nothing to be gained from those. They'd be read out to the jury, or summarised into formal admissions, so that the jurors' attentions remained focused on the important things. The case was about what happened and who did what, not which officer handed over which scraps of paper.

The statements containing the real evidence were in a separate pile and he'd read all of those. His opinion from the day before hadn't changed, and it didn't look good for Robert Carter.

The case was simple. A bloodied fingerprint was on the wall by the door. They'd swabbed her body and found his DNA on her neck. He'd explained that away by talking about a brief hug she'd given him for walking her home, but none of that fitted with the evidence from the people who knew Mary: the other tenants, her friends. Carter had been someone who'd hung around and been a nuisance, and Mary had been too polite to tell him to leave her alone.

It was the third pile of papers that interested him the most: the list of items that the prosecution had decided they weren't using.

In any investigation, the police create records and documents that aren't needed for court. The unused material. That's where the acquittals are often found, in the documents that don't help the prosecution. Like statements from the witnesses who give accounts that help the defence, the results of the door-to-door enquiries, or the logs of calls made by witnesses who say something different when they are in front of a police officer with an eager pen.

The prosecution must disclose whatever undermines the case, but spending cutbacks have made it harder for the police to compile the schedules, so the list is sometimes put together without the disclosure officer reading everything properly. Carter's defence was based upon someone else being responsible. It was Dan's job to find another suspect, to spot something Shelley hadn't, and the best place to look was the schedule of unused material, to find that snippet of information that wasn't properly pursued.

He went back to the schedule. It ran to a hundred and fifty pages, each with the prosecutor's endorsement. Some items had been disclosed, like witnesses' convictions, but mostly it was a list of documents the police had but the defence team wasn't allowed to see.

It was reading them that had sent Dan to sleep the night before. He was more focused now.

Another hour passed before he found what he was looking for, fuelled by coffee, tucked away on page hundred and two. He jabbed at the sheet of paper with his finger.

He checked his watch. Nearly eight. He wanted Jayne to help. She needed to see everything in the case to get a feel for it, but it might still be too early for her. There were other things he'd noticed too that needed to be talked through, just to get his own thoughts in order.

He rang her. She answered on the fourth ring, her voice just a groan.

'You alive?' he said.

'I think so.'

'Can you come to my apartment? I want your opinion on something.'

The phone was filled with her sleepy breaths, and then, 'Okay, I'm up. Give me an hour.'

'I'll get the coffee on and make it half an hour.'

'Throw in a bacon sandwich and I'll be there.'

'It's a deal,' he said, and hung up.

*

Jayne stared at the handset as she yawned. No goodbye or thanks. Just 'it's a deal'. Dan's intensity was kicking in, becoming consumed by the case and normal human interactions were more limited. She'd relied on it once. Now, she wished he could learn to switch it off, because it meant early morning starts her body wasn't ready for.

She staggered her way to the bathroom, wincing at the occasional jab of pain to her head, grimacing at the smell of cold pizza coming from the kitchen. In the shower, she pressed her palms against the tiles as the water stung her skin like hot needles. By the time she emerged, her skin pink, she was ready for the day.

She threw on the clothes from the night before, collected her car keys, and left her apartment with wet hair.

Dan was cooking bacon when he buzzed her into his apartment, the air foggy with smoke. She flapped at the air. 'You trying to burn the place down?'

'I like it crispy.' He put some of the bacon into a soft bread roll so that it was peeking out of the side. 'Here. It'll bring you back to life.'

'Thank you.' She collapsed back on to the sofa, her hair still damp. 'It beats reheated pizza.' She took a large bite and said, her voice muffled, 'So what have you got that needs me this early?'

'This case. I'm making sure that you're up and about. Time is tight on this one. We need to decide what we're doing today.'

'You mean me, not us. You're speaking to witnesses and going to the prison.'

Dan paused as he made his own sandwich, the pan cooling with a loud hiss as he put it into the sink.

'I want you with me,' he said.

'Me? How come?'

'I want you to meet Robert Carter and the witnesses, just for another perspective.'

'A woman's perspective?'

'Why not? And when you're in court with me, you might remember something the witnesses said that I miss.'

'And Carter?'

'I just want your impressions. If you're working hard to help clear him, you should meet him.'

'It makes sense. And after that?'

Dan reached for a piece of paper. 'I was looking through the file and I found something strange.'

'Go on.'

He handed it over. 'This.'

Jayne quickly scanned the page. Nothing stood out. 'What is it?'

'From the unused material schedule. It's a summary of some of the house-to-house enquiries. There, the top item on that page. *No relevant evidence.*'

'I'm sorry, I'm not getting you.'

'Don't you see? *No relevant evidence* isn't the same as *no information*. It means that something was said, but a police officer decided it wasn't relevant. It's an opinion, not a fact. That's not how it should be. I want that to be my opinion, not someone else's. Don't forget, my job is different to the police. They were trying to catch who did it. Me? I'm trying to say who else might have done it, sow some seeds of doubt.'

Jayne put down her sandwich. 'I'm not hungry anymore.'

'What's wrong?'

'It's you, your outlook, it's all wrong. It's like you don't care whether Robert Carter killed her or not, that it's some kind of game. What if he did it and you set him free?'

Dan let out a long breath. 'I thought you were better than that?'

'Why?' Jayne folded her arms. 'Say it, Dan, because I know what you're thinking.'

'You don't.'

'Oh, I do. I'm supposed to like what you do because I was accused of killing Jimmy and my clever lawyer got me off? Is this how it's always going to be, that you see me as the scared young woman in a police station? I didn't know I was just another challenge, one more fight you had to win.'

'But you were glad I was there for you?'

'That's not the point.'

'It's exactly the point. I was there for you when you needed someone to fight for you. You're a strong and intelligent woman. A university graduate. What was it? A psychology degree?'

'Yeah, so I should have been better at spotting who he really was.'

'He weakened you, that's all. As soon as you were in love with him, he abused you rather than love you back. You were too scared to leave him, but dreaded every moment you stayed with him. What happened just, well, happened, and I fought for you, and now you're free.'

'No, you're missing the point, Dan. I didn't murder Jimmy.' She slammed her hand into the arm of the sofa. 'I lashed out. There was no other way to get him off me. I didn't mean to kill him. I wanted you to believe that, don't you get it, because I needed someone to believe me?'

'Why did that matter?'

'Because people thought I was a murderer and I wasn't.' She pressed her open palm against her chest, tears in her eyes. 'I needed someone to believe in me, and I thought you did.'

'No, you needed someone to fight your corner. Just believing in you wouldn't persuade a jury.'

She glared at Dan. 'So go on, did you believe me?'

'I choose not to have an opinion.'

Jayne got to her feet and went to the balcony door. She stared out for a few seconds before saying, 'How can you not have one?'

'Because it's one of the first things you learn as a lawyer. Don't you get that? I've chosen a career that helps rapists, and child molesters and fraudsters and all the despicable people you can think of.'

'And murderers.'

'Yes, and murderers, and if I started forming opinions, I'd crack. I would begin to judge them.'

'So it's a cop-out? You don't think about what they've done; you just try to get them off?'

'People need a voice. That's my job. The jury judges them, not me. It doesn't matter what I think. If they're guilty, they'll be found guilty, and I'm happy with that.'

'But being found not guilty doesn't mean they're innocent.'

'No, it doesn't. And now you're going to turn into the boring dinner guest by asking me how I sleep at night, when I help guilty people get away with it. I'll save you the trouble. I sleep at night because I'd rather we had the system we do. It's better than accepting what the police think.'

'And now you sound like some kind of civil rights type.'

That made Dan laugh and shake his head.

'What's funny?'

'I've spent most of my career with my father telling me the opposite.'

'Why?'

'Because he grew up in a different time. He was a trade unionist, old-style, where getting what you want involved confrontation, not compromise, where every battle was part of the struggle.'

'And he ended up with a lawyer for a son?'

'Yeah, and you can guess how that went down, like I've sold out somehow, turned my back on *my people*. He can't get it that the battles he fought have been lost. I fight in a different way, that's all.'

'How very noble.'

'Oh, come on. What's wrong? You still need to know that I believe you?'

'Yes. Is there anything wrong with that?'

'Okay, here it is. What I know is that Jimmy treated you like shit for months, longer even, and only you and he were there when he died. I know you and you're a good person. If you snapped because he had one more punch to land, then I understand that. People make mistakes.'

'So you don't believe me?'

'I didn't say that.'

'Dan, I was holding the knife before it went into his leg. I watched him as he bled out on the kitchen floor. I think about it all the time. If I hadn't grabbed that knife, or if I'd known how to stop the bleeding, or if I'd just hit him somewhere else on his leg . . . all those little things would have made it different. He would be alive, and his family wouldn't think I was a murderer. I'm always waiting for the knock on the door that tells me that his brothers are outside, or for the sudden blow to the back of my head. So yes, I want you to believe me, because then I'll feel a little less alone.'

Dan held up his hands. 'Okay, I get that.'

'Do you believe me?'

'You're the nearest I've got to believing a client accused of something so serious. I can see why there had to be a court case, because a man was dead and the only other person there was holding the knife that went into his leg, but your version made some sense.'

'That's the best I'm going to get?'

He shrugged.

'Bloody lawyers. Why must everything come with a get-out clause?'

'Years of training.'

Jayne laughed, despite herself.

'Think of it this way,' Dan said. 'You're going to help with this case, aren't you?'

'I need the money.'

'No moral issues for you?'

'Yes. My need to eat and pay my rent.'

'There you go. We all have our reasons for what we do. I won't lie to you, there have been times when I haven't felt proud of myself. Like when I've had to pass sobbing witnesses on a court corridor because I'd been able to make the facts seem different to how they saw them. That's the price I pay for the job I do.'

'Okay, I'm sorry.'

'So are you ready for Robert Carter?'

'I suppose so.'

'Someone on the street behind Mary's said something that a police officer decided wasn't relevant. I want to know what that person said, whoever he or she was. I need you to do a door-to-door, speak to everyone. I want to know what they say and whether they said it to the police.'

'Won't Shelley have covered this? You spotted it in one night. She had the case for five months.'

'I don't care what Shelley did or didn't do. It's what I do that's important.'

'When I was there yesterday, I thought someone was watching me.'

'From the house at the back, with the blue gate?'

'Yes. I didn't see anyone, but I thought I saw a gate close. And I could hear breathing on the other side.'

'For me, it was a curtain moving.'

'You went there?'

'Yes, once I'd dropped you off. I wanted to know what it felt like at night.'

'How did it seem?'

'Quiet, but that's not the important part.'

'What do you mean?'

'If people are interested in what we're doing, why isn't anyone saying anything?'

Nineteen

The mornings were the worst times. The day was just one big stretch ahead, not knowing whether any threats would come his way.

He'd gone to sleep thinking of Cassie. He'd awoken thinking of Cassie. He knew the reason: it all led to Mary.

He should have stayed away from Cassie once he'd experienced her, but he'd needed more. He always needed more.

She worked in an office not far from where she lived, a modern complex close to a concrete flyover. He could see into it from the second level of a nearby car park. He spent whole afternoons there, leaning against a pillar, hidden by the shadow of the level above, watching her work. He knew her routines. A coffee at eleven, always alone, shunning the kitchen skivers. Her lunch was always later than everyone else, when she'd do the same walk, just a bowl in her hand. Soup was his guess.

She went shopping twice a week, and he went with her, watching what she bought, what she *liked*. How she cooked for herself but bought a ready meal and a bottle of wine for a Friday night. Pinot Grigio. If she bought a DVD, she bought action films. She read thrillers.

He'd almost given himself away once, when he'd positioned his body so that he was blocking the wine she bought, so that she'd had to say, 'excuse me,' and brush against him.

Sparks. That's what he felt as her arm brushed his, as if he crackled with small explosions, his fingers slick around the bottle he was holding.

He should have flashed her a smile and stepped aside, and she might have exchanged a few words with him, given him her public face, distant and polite. He could have thought back to how she really was. His secret. No, *their* secret.

Instead, he mumbled something and stepped away.

That had been the beginning of the end with her. To be so close was torture. He had to go back and be in the house with her.

He should have planned it more, been in control, but he'd lost sense of the rules. Had he gone into her house without waiting long enough for her to be in a deep sleep? Or moved through the house too quickly? Had he made too much noise, were his footsteps too heavy?

As she'd swung that lamp, it was as if his love flew off into the night, ending in the darkness as it hit him.

He hadn't been unconscious for long. When he came round, she was pounding him with her fists, her fingers ripping at the hood he was wearing, her bare feet stamping down on him.

He'd cried out, tried to say that he loved her, but he couldn't make himself heard over her screams.

Those words she'd used. Ugly words. They cut him more than her fists. A side to her he hadn't seen. He should have guessed though. There's a piece of ugliness inside everyone.

She caught him with a good shot and he succumbed to darkness once more.

The police were called, of course, but a clever lawyer made sure he never saw a courtroom. He hadn't tried to attack her or steal anything, and the police couldn't prove how often he'd been in there or whether he'd seen her naked. The lawyer said he'd fallen between the raindrops, that the law couldn't get to someone who just liked to look around. He wasn't a burglar. He wasn't a voyeur.

He'd known that, of course, he'd done his research, but he couldn't go to her house anymore. He couldn't follow her any more.

And he didn't want to.

Until she'd attacked him, she'd been his secret. He'd wanted her shadow, but when he was faced with it, angry and violent and spiteful, it was ugly.

His life became empty for a while, until the day it all changed. *She* changed it. Mary. So sweet. Her poise. Her quietness.

He was in love. He knew it this time, stronger than before. His head felt clouded, unable to think clearly.

He loved the Mary everyone else saw, but he'd wanted more. He always wanted more. He'd wanted the real Mary. The secret Mary. He'd wanted her shadow.

Twenty

Dan and Jayne walked into the police station together. She'd driven home to put on something more formal before waiting outside with a notebook concealed inside a small black briefcase, something she'd bought in case her work ever required an appearance in court.

The police station was next to the courthouse, a building from the thirties made to look older. It blended in with the grand civic buildings nearby, Gothic expressions of merchant pride, with high white clocks on ornate stone towers. The station hung on to some of the original features, like the old blue lamp over the door and the tiny opaque blocks of glass that passed for cell windows, positioned just above pavement level, but the steps had been replaced by a concrete wheelchair ramp and the doors were automatic, leading into a tiled public area lined with crime prevention posters.

The counter assistant was her usual brusque self, insisting on seeing some identification, even though she'd met Dan countless times before.

'What's her problem?' Jayne said, as they sat down on a row of white plastic chairs, bolted to the floor.

'This place is about control. I let her win each time, because taking her on would just lead to a longer wait next time. Murdoch will do the same and keep us waiting.'

As they sat there, Jayne saw someone who looked familiar. A man was loitering by a building opposite, a scarf partially over his face, his hands thrust deep into his pockets, pacing, looking up and down the street. He'd been there when they came in, but it was only as time passed that she became suspicious.

She was about to say something when Murdoch appeared. 'Dan, are you coming through?'

Murdoch was holding the door open, her eyebrows raised, smart in a grey trouser suit brightened by a purple lanyard, her identification swinging from it.

'This is Jayne Brett, my assistant in this case,' he said as they went through the open door, pausing to let Murdoch lead the way.

Murdoch glanced over before she stopped in front of him.

'What game are you playing, Dan?'

'No games.'

'You sent someone to speak to a witness without asking us first.'

'The neighbour who heard the scream?'

'That was me, sorry,' Jayne said. 'I was looking round the neighbourhood and knocked on the door. It wasn't planned.'

Murdoch glowered at her. 'Make sure you don't do it again.'

'I'll do anything that gets to the truth in this case.'

'Include harassing witnesses.' Murdoch stepped closer.

'Asking questions isn't harassing.'

Dan put his hand in front of Murdoch. 'Haven't you considered that it might make it easier for the witnesses at court, because we don't have to probe them in the box? If we know the answer, we might not need to ask the question.'

'I thought the rule was that if you don't know the answer, you don't ask.'

He had to give her that one. 'So are you going to get out of my face, or are you going to stand out here and argue with me, just to make yourself feel better?'

Murdoch stared hard into his eyes, and then at Jayne.

'Spare me the *how can you sleep at night* speech,' he said. 'I've had it once already this morning.'

Murdoch turned and set off along the corridor. Dan and Jayne exchanged a roll of their eyes and set off after her.

Her pace was quick and angry, passing open office doors, all revealing desks cluttered with files and walls filled with posters and photographs and maps. Uniformed officers passed them, heading for the exit. Along one corridor, the lights of the canteen shone brightly, a small queue visible through the door. It was a snapshot of a station at work. Chaotic, noisy, untidy, but somehow efficient, all the teams fitting together to protect the town.

Murdoch paused outside a door. 'The witnesses are all in there. They know that they don't have to speak to you, so if they ask you to stop, you stop, okay?'

'I'll want to speak to them individually, of course.'

'You didn't say that.'

'Isn't it obvious? Unless you want to be accused of encouraging collusion?'

Murdoch thumped the door open.

There were three young women in there. They looked up as Dan and Jayne walked in, eyes filled with wariness. The air was filled with the sweet tang of perfume.

Dan introduced himself and then Jayne, to put them at ease. He didn't want them to be nervous. He wanted their unguarded comments, not a stiff front presented to stop them from saying anything they might later regret.

'Who wants to go first?' he asked.

The women exchanged glances until one of them stood up. 'Me first, if that's okay.'

The self-appointed leader of the group. Always the best place to start.

'Use the room next door,' Murdoch said. 'I'll be sitting in with you.'

Dan shrugged. He wasn't there to cause problems.

The woman was tall and elegant, her light brown hair pulled back into a leather clasp, wearing leggings and a long fawn jumper.

They were all shown into a small room with an armchair in one corner and a table and four chairs in the other. It looked like one set aside to take down witness statements.

The woman sat down and crossed her legs. 'I'm Lucy Ayres.'

Jayne recognised the name straight away. It was the woman who'd found Mary and had been the subject of the press stories before Carter was charged.

'I was sorry to read about you finding Mary,' Dan said, his voice low. 'It must have been awful.'

Lucy swallowed. 'It was.' She hadn't been expecting sympathy. 'What can you tell me about her?'

Jayne opened her notebook to take down what was said. She hadn't been assigned the role of Dan's secretary, but it made her presence there look more normal.

Lucy straightened. 'She was just a lovely girl, a dear friend.' Lucy was well-spoken, not a trace of the north in there. 'I'd only been living there for a few weeks, but Mary made me feel welcome straight away, inviting me out for drinks and helping me to settle in.'

'How did you end up living at the house?'

'My job. I'm training to be a lawyer, although you probably know that, because it's on my witness statement. I needed somewhere to stay, and a woman from my office knew there was a vacancy because someone had just left. We were a bunch of young women beginning our careers, and I couldn't stand the thought of moving back home after university. It was fun somehow, as if we were still at college.'

'How was it in the house?'

'Before Mary was killed?' Lucy shook her head in sadness, although there was something rehearsed about it. 'We all just clicked. That's the best way I can describe it.'

'And Mary?'

'Like I said, a lovely girl.' Lucy uncrossed her legs and then crossed them again.

Dan leaned forward. 'I know it's not nice to speak ill of people who've died, but sometimes getting to the truth is needed. Mary must have had some faults?'

Lucy tilted her head, her eyes filled with regret, looking between both Dan and Jayne. 'If she had, I hadn't spotted them.'

'But you hadn't known her for long.'

'No, not long at all, but we'd become friends.' She looked down and it seemed as if she was about to start crying, but when she looked up again, her eyes were clear. 'Mary isn't the only victim in this.'

'What do you mean?'

'I've never seen a dead body before, and to see something like that, well, I can't sleep, can't eat. It replays in my head all the time.'

'Did you look under the cover that was hiding Mary?'

'No. We went in, and I was going to, but we just knew. I left the room as Peter called the police.'

The name made Jayne look up from her note-taking. Of course, Peter. She remembered him from the press reports, the boyfriend holding her when they were close to the crime scene. He was the person pacing outside. He was waiting for Lucy to come out.

'Were you at Peter's all night?'

Lucy nodded. 'I feel so guilty, because I'd stayed away. It meant that Mary was alone with him, with Robert. If I'd known what was going on, well . . .'

'Tell me about Robert.'

'What do you mean?'

'Just what I said. What kind of person is he? How well do you know him?'

'Not well at all. He was just someone who used to hit on Mary.'

'But was he a pest? Did she complain about how he behaved?'

'She'd try to avoid him but she was always nice to him. Mary was like that. Polite, friendly, didn't want to upset anyone.'

'I wasn't asking about Mary. I was asking about Robert. Was there ever a situation where he seemed dangerous, like he followed her home, or turned up at the house?'

Lucy paused, surprised at the sudden barb in Dan's questioning. She glanced across at Murdoch before she shook her head slowly. 'No, I can't think of anything.'

'What about the people on the street behind?'

'Sorry, I'm not with you.'

'Was there anyone on the street behind who made you or Mary uncomfortable, who seemed intrusive? Watching you or hanging around?'

Murdoch leaned forward. 'What has this got to do with anything?'

'I'm just asking.'

'But I can't see the relevance.'

'We're not in court yet,' Dan said. 'If there's nothing useful, we'll know not to pursue it.'

'It's okay,' Lucy said, and then, 'no, there was no one from the street behind who was a problem. They were nice neighbours. People were friendly.'

Dan smiled. 'Thank you for your time.'

'Am I done now?'

'Yes, you've been helpful.'

Lucy got to her feet and held out her hand to shake. Dan was surprised. He stood and shook.

'Nice to meet you, thank you,' she said, and he detected a slight flicker of her eyelids as he met her gaze. She didn't look towards Jayne.

'Yes, thank you,' he said.

She dropped his hand and turned to go, and presented her back to him as if he was meant to look at her behind as she went.

'It's probably best if you don't go back in there,' Dan said, pointing to the door that opened into the room where the other witnesses were waiting. When Murdoch took a deep nasal breath, he added, 'It's for Lucy's benefit, because I can't accuse her of saying anything to the other witnesses if she hasn't had the chance.'

'But they could spend all night tonight colluding, if they wanted.'

'That would be after I've got their answers.'

Murdoch clenched her jaw, and then nodded at Lucy that she should leave the station.

As Lucy headed for the exit, Dan said to Murdoch, 'I'll want to see item three hundred and five from the unused schedule, top of page one hundred and two, the door-to-door enquires from the street behind.'

'That's up to the prosecutor, not me.'

'But you could show me, to stop me wasting her time. You know what some prosecutors are like, that it's all about the rules. You? Aren't you about getting to the truth?'

'I'm about following the rules as well. You'd be the first to criticise me in court if I didn't. Another witness?' Murdoch went into the witness room before returning with another one of the women from the house.

Dan smiled, to put her at ease. It was time for the same again. Give nothing away. Just get the detail and compare it afterwards. He had the feeling he had something useful already. He just didn't know what it was.

Twenty-one

The police station visit behind them, Jayne looked up at the building where Robert Carter was spending his time before his trial.

It was an old Victorian prison, a dark shadow on the edge of the city centre at the other end of the motorway to Highford, with stone cell-blocks rising above high red brick walls, razor-topped. The windows were small and shielded by bars; any view of the outside world restricted, always just out of reach.

The area around the prison was seedy, the worst end of the city, where prostitutes prowled and few people walked after dark.

Dan was walking ahead as Jayne thought back to their meeting with the witnesses. All three women had said the same thing: Mary was sweet, and Robert Carter was a pest, but nothing had hinted at what was to come. Unless Robert Carter had anything unusual to say, there wasn't much to be gained from looking for a side to Mary that no one else knew about. No drug debts or a dark, secret life. If there were deeper secrets, it would take longer than they had to find them.

The last of the women had been less forthcoming. Beth Wilkins. She'd seemed nervous, reluctant, more than just not wanting to be there. She hadn't said anything different to the others, but it had been the way she'd said it, as if it was a script, a mantra to repeat. She hadn't met Dan's gaze. It might have been nerves about the case, or even anger that Jayne and Dan were trying to ensure that

Mary's killer stayed free, but whatever the reason, Dan had put a big tick next to her name. If Beth had behaved that way because she didn't want them intruding, she'd created the opposite effect.

They jumped the relatives queue at the front gate, because legal visits took priority. Jayne remembered the haunted looks of her own parents when she was awaiting trial: a mix of shame and fear, any pleasure in seeing her tainted by security clearances and the painful goodbyes and suspicious glares from those in passing cars and buses. It was the children who saddened her the most, brought up to see this as normal.

Their route to the visiting room involved a walk across an open courtyard, past a sniffer dog straining on a leash, in company with two other lawyers, then photographs taken and stuck to their clothes, so that no one was ever tempted to swap places with the prisoner.

They were left on their own in the room as a guard went to collect Robert Carter. Prisons were all about echoes. Large doors closing. Boots on concrete floors. Keys in corridors. Jayne listened to them as they waited, knowing that soon one set of noises will be for them.

'Did you see Peter outside the police station?' Jayne said.

'Peter?'

'Lucy's boyfriend. Remember all that smoochy stuff by the crime scene? He was hanging around outside.'

'Perhaps he just gave her a lift.'

'Yeah, maybe.'

They were interrupted by the rattle of a key as Carter was brought in, wearing loose jeans and a grey sweatshirt, topped off with a red bib.

He sat down with a slump and put both arms on the table. He scowled and put his head to one side.

'I'm Dan Grant. I'm your new lawyer. And this is Jayne Brett. She's your investigator.'

Carter sniffed and tilted his head the other way. He looked at them both. 'Yeah, Shelley said I was getting someone new.'

'We've got two weeks to get your case together.'

'It's already together.'

'Did she tell you why there had to be a swap?'

'Conflict of interest or something. Like she was the one who mattered.'

'I'm here now. That's just the way it is. So talk to us.'

He looked at Jayne when he said, 'What about? I didn't do it.'

She crossed her legs and folded her arms.

'That isn't enough,' Dan said. 'You can't go into the witness box and just say that.'

'Who says I have to say anything?'

'Look out of that window,' and Dan pointed towards the courtyard surrounded by the gloomy cell-blocks, which contrasted sharply against the vivid blue of the sky. 'If you don't talk, that's your life, perhaps for the rest of it. That cell block, those walls, those bars. I can't make you give evidence, but you'll be convicted unless you persuade the jury you're innocent. Your fingerprint is in that room and your DNA is on Mary's body. Her friends describe you as a pest, someone who wanted Mary but couldn't have her. What conclusions do you think the jurors will reach?'

When Carter shrugged, Dan said, 'That you're guilty. That you followed her home and forced your way in, because that was the only way you could have her. You tried to rape her, and when she screamed, you killed her.'

'No!' Carter slammed his hand on the desk. 'I'm not having that.'

'So tell me what happened.'

He waited for a while before he pointed towards the file. 'It's all in there. I told Shelley how it was and I'm sticking with that story.'

'The truth is never a story, nor do you have to stick with it.' Dan sat back. 'Give me more detail. Where did you see Mary that night?'

'At the Wharf pub. There was a band on.'

'Had you arranged to meet Mary?'

He paused. 'No, she was just there.'

'And did you approach her, or did she approach you?'

'What do you mean?'

'If you're sticking to the story, as you put it, you ended up at Mary's house, so one of you had to start off the conversation.'

Carter tapped his fingers on the table. 'It wasn't like that. I saw her when she was walking home.'

'Was she alone?'

'Yes. Her friends lived on the way, and she must have just left them, because I saw her walking the last part. I offered to walk her the rest of the way.'

'What were you doing in that part of town?'

'I don't know what you mean.'

Dan jabbed his finger on the desk. 'First rule when you give evidence: don't be vague and evasive. If the jurors think you're holding back in some way, they won't believe anything you say. So tell me again: what were you doing in that part of town?'

'Just walking around,' he said, and shrugged like a ten-year-old. 'It was a nice night so I went for a walk to clear my head before I went home.'

'Because your wife didn't like you drunk?'

'Exactly.'

'But Mary's house was completely the wrong end of town. That was some walk.'

'There's no point in walking it off if I just go straight home.'

'Okay, so you saw Mary. You walked her home. What happened when you got to her house?'

'She said thank you and invited me in, asked me if I wanted a drink.'

'And you said yes, rather than go home to your wife.'

'I behaved like a shit. So what?' He folded his arms and sat back like a petulant child. 'That doesn't make me a murderer.'

'Did you try anything with her?'

'I don't understand.'

'It's a simple question. You liked her, so everyone says, and she's invited you in for coffee. You must have thought you were about to get lucky?'

'Mary wasn't like that.'

'And you?'

He pursed his lips before he said, 'I liked her. Who wouldn't? She was a nice person, and pretty too.'

'But she wasn't interested in you?'

'The subject didn't come up.'

'So how did the cigarette thing happen?'

'She didn't want me smoking in the house. Mary went to get ready for bed, so I smoked outside.'

'But why didn't you go home? You were just friends, so you said, and she's dropping a big hint, saying that she was getting ready for bed.'

'We were talking and getting on, and we hadn't finished our coffee.'

'That's weak,' Dan said. 'You wanted more. Isn't that obvious?'

'You're making it sound bad.'

'And you think the prosecution won't?'

Jayne leaned forward. 'How did she end up naked?'

'How do you mean?'

'She was found naked, and she was going upstairs to get changed.'

'I don't know. Perhaps whoever killed her disturbed her just as she was getting ready.'

'And she was in bed,' Jayne continued.

'She was under the covers. She might have been protecting herself, if she was caught as she was getting changed.' He sat back and glared. 'I don't know. All I know is that I didn't kill her. I was at the front, smoking, and I heard a shout, some furniture crashing, and then,' and Carter stopped as his chin trembled. He wiped his eyes and took a deep breath before continuing, 'And then I heard her scream.'

'What did you do?' Dan asked.

'I didn't know what to do, whether to go inside or not, because I didn't want to get dragged into anything.'

'By *anything*, I presume you mean it being found out that you'd gone back to another woman's house rather than go home? What about poor Mary?'

'Yeah, it makes me look cruel, and I'm sorry about that, but I can't change it. There was this scream, but it was cut short, like someone had hit her. There were more bangs, and then it went quiet.'

'What happened next?' Dan said.

'I left it a few minutes. I expected Mary to come downstairs, to tell me what had gone on, but she didn't. I heard a bang inside, like a door closing, and the front door slammed shut. You know how they do sometimes when another door is opened and it creates a draught. I presume it was the back door, because I ran round there and the door was open. When I got to Mary's room, she's covered in blood and, man, I'm nearly sick right there and then. But I can see a big wound at her neck, on her chest, and the blood was just, like, gushing out. It smelled awful, and she was so white.'

'Alive?'

Carter looked down and took some breaths. When he looked up again, he said, 'No. I tried plugging the wound with her T-shirt, but it was a waste of time. Her face had that empty look, like it was the same girl but whatever it was that had made her special was gone.'

'What did you do then?'

'I panicked and ran.' He blinked away some tears. 'I know it sounds bad but what else could I do? I couldn't save her. I hadn't seen who'd killed her. I had to protect myself, don't you see? No one knew I was there and I could see how it would have looked.'

'But the police caught up with you.'

'My fingerprint. It was on the system because I got into trouble a while back.'

'The stalking case.'

'That was blown out of all proportion,' he said, his anger flaring quickly. 'She was a pretty girl and I liked her.'

'By following her around?' When he didn't answer, Dan asked, 'Did your wife know about her?'

'It was just a stupid infatuation, so she forgave me. And I didn't mean to scare the girl. I liked her, that's all.'

Dan rubbed his forehead. 'Is there anything you think I should know that you haven't just told me?'

'What like?'

'Did you see anyone else hanging around when you walked her home, or do you know whether anyone else liked her? This is the rub, Robert: if you didn't kill her –'

'I didn't.'

'So who did? That's the problem I'm having. All I get is what a nice woman she was and how she had no dark side or dodgy friends. And whatever the papers say, attacks like that don't happen often, and for it to be a random attack while you were having a smoke outside – a man who liked her but couldn't get her to like him in the same way, when he has a record for stalking someone – well, it's like adding all the improbables together, which just makes it even more improbable.'

'That's how it happened, all right.'

'What happened to the cigarette?'

'I smoked it.'

'The tab, the filter? The police are pretty thorough with these things, and I didn't see any mention of a cigarette end.'

'I must have mashed it with my foot. It was windy. It could have blown away.'

'I'll get the weather report, to check. We need something to back up what you say.'

'I've told you the truth. I've nothing else to say.'

'Did you cover Mary up again, after you'd tried to save her?'

'I must have done, because I've seen the pictures and know how she was found, but I wasn't thinking straight. I was scared.'

Dan considered Carter for a moment and saw that he wasn't going to add anything else. 'Fine, that's your version. Here's some advice though: make yourself look sympathetic, less defensive. People make mistakes, do stupid things. You've got to make twelve people think that your only mistake was leaving Mary, that you're a victim just like she is. If you go in there with attitude, they won't like you, and that's your first battle lost. No tantrums, no temper. Got it?'

'I understand.'

'Have you got a suit to wear?'

'No. My mum bought me one, but I've lost weight in here. It didn't fit the last time I was in court. And it was old-fashioned.'

Dan couldn't stop his smile.

'What's so funny?'

'I've just seen it in court so many times, defendants wearing suits badly, as if they've just bought them for court.'

'Why else would someone like me need a suit?'

'Fair comment. What about your wife? Will she have a suit that might fit, an old one of yours?'

Carter jumped up, knocking the chair back. He jabbed his finger at Dan. 'You keep away from her.'

'Why? What's wrong?'

'I'm not talking to you anymore.' He banged on the door. 'Boss, boss!'

'Robert, what is it?'

He banged again, louder this time.

Dan sat back, bewildered, as the door opened and Carter shot out, as if desperate to get back to his cell. The guard shrugged. 'Wait there so I can show you out,' and then followed Carter.

Dan turned to Jayne. 'What the hell was all that about?'

'He doesn't want *you* anywhere near his wife.' Jayne frowned. 'Do you have to do what he says?'

'Not really. I'm the lawyer, not him, but I don't want to lose his trust so close to the trial.'

'There is one way to do it, if you want to know about his wife.'

'How's that?'

'Carter didn't specifically say that *I* couldn't speak to her, did he?'

Dan grinned. 'I knew you were perfect for this case.'

Twenty-two

Jayne parked her car, collected from the cobbled car park by Dan's apartment building, and went back into the alley behind the house where Mary died. She wanted to have another look, because Dan had felt the same she had, that he was being watched. If people were showing an interest in what they were doing, they needed to know who, and why.

She turned as she went, to see whether there was anyone at either end of the alley, waiting to trap her, but there was no one there. She wasn't trying to be quiet, and had gone home first to change into heavier boots, so that her footsteps were loud enough to attract attention.

She stopped when she reached the yard where she thought she'd seen a gate close. The wood was old and rotten, jagged at the top, blue paint flaking from it. She tried the handle. It was locked. She stepped back to look up at the rear window. It was in darkness, but still there was something sinister about it, as if there was something, or someone, just in the shadows.

Jayne noted which house it was and headed round to the front of the street. It was time to start knocking on doors.

There were just over thirty houses on the side closest to Mary's. They were all identical except for the doors. Just a long row of grey stone broken by white sills and doorways. Cars were parked at the side of the road in an unbroken line and two young mothers with prams chatted further along the street.

Jayne took a deep breath as she reached into her coat for her pad and pen. Cold-calling wasn't something she enjoyed. She preferred the spying, the following. This was too direct.

She knocked on the first door.

A man answered, rough-shaven and in a faded yellow jumper with a coffee stain on the front. The sweet aroma of cannabis drifted out of the door.

He leaned against the door frame and looked her up and down before saying, 'Yeah?' One hand was down the front of his tracksuit bottoms and, although it looked like it was there for want of a better place to put it, Jayne spotted something in his expression she didn't like.

She passed over her business card. 'I'm speaking to the people on the street about the murder that happened in the house behind.'

'The young teacher?'

'Yes. It happened late at night so there's a possibility that someone heard something.'

'The police came round the next day. So what's it to do with you?'

'I'm just trying to find out if anyone heard anything, that's all.'

'That doesn't answer my question. What's it got to do with you?'

Jayne grimaced, as she knew how it was going to go once she gave her answer.

'I'm working for Robert Carter, the man who's accused of her murder.'

The man gave a small laugh. 'Good luck.' He slammed the door, leaving Jayne staring at it, just an inch from her nose.

The responses from the other houses were not much different. A mixture of closed doors, heard nothing, knew nothing. It was only when she got to the house she was really interested in, from where she thought she had been watched, that things changed.

Her knock was a friendly rat-a-tat-a-tat. After a few seconds, stubby fingers moved the slats of a Venetian blind. Jayne smiled and gave a little wave, hoping to disarm.

The chain stayed on as the door opened, and a woman's chubby face peered through, wary eyes hiding behind small round glasses with wire frames under tight grey curls.

'Hello?'

Jayne passed a card through. 'I'm here about the murder in the house on the next street.'

'Why are you speaking to me?'

'You live right behind the house, overlooking the room where it happened. I only want to ask a few questions.'

'Yeah, but why you?'

'I'm working for the firm representing the man charged with her murder.'

There was a pause before she closed the door in order to take off the chain. The woman looked Jayne up and down and then gestured towards a room at the back of the house. 'Just go in there, love.'

Jayne thanked her and went inside.

Like most terraced houses, there were two rooms on the ground floor, with a kitchen extending into the yard. The room at the back was where most people congregated, closest to the kitchen, the front room being the traditional parlour, used for entertaining or by parents when the children had gone to bed. They were habits from a long-lost era, but they clung on, as habits do.

Jayne waited for the woman to make her way into the room. Her progress was slow and she was breathing heavily as she made it in and slumped into a high-backed chair in the corner. Old and overweight, she filled a patterned dress, her legs covered in thick brown tights and forced apart by a stomach that had expanded into rolls and sagged into her lap. A wooden cane was propped against the chair arm. A television flickered, but the woman pointed the remote at it and turned it off.

There were framed theatre flyers around the room, and a couple of press cuttings, the newspaper yellowed by the light that shone in. There were some posed shots of a young man, collars up, either turned towards the camera or staring into the distance.

'What was your name again?' she said, not looking at the business card clutched between her fingers.

'Jayne Brett.'

'And it's about the girl in the house?'

Jayne suppressed her sigh. 'Yes.'

'It's not me you want. It's Mickey.'

'Your husband?'

Her eyes narrowed. 'My son,' she said, and pointed to the photographs. 'He's an actor. Very successful,' before she bellowed, 'Mickey!'

As she waited, the woman said, 'At least you're nicer than the last one.'

'How do you mean?'

'The solicitor. She shouted at Mickey. I don't know why.'

'There's been a change.'

'Good.'

Jayne was about to ask more when there were the sounds of movement above her, followed by footsteps on the stairs.

The man from the photographs appeared in the doorway. In his thirties, he was small and wiry with an easy smile, his hair dark and short, stubble showing on his chin.

'Yes?' he said.

'This is Jayne,' the woman said, and held out the business card. As he took it from her, she said, 'It's about the woman who died over there,' and pointed towards the window. 'I don't know anything about that, but you said you might.'

'Do you?' Jayne said to him.

'Come through here,' he said, and to his mother, 'I'd rather talk in private.'

He led Jayne into the front room. The television turned back on in the other room, the volume loud. He closed the door. 'I'm sorry about Mum. We don't get many visitors.'

Jayne glanced at his hand. A wedding ring.

He must have spotted her looking, because he raised his hand. 'Separated, which is why I'm here.' He grimaced. 'I didn't have much choice. My wife kept the house and I had to go somewhere.'

'I'm sorry. I wasn't prying.'

'It's fine. I tell everyone. I don't want anyone to think I'm the sort of man who never left home. Came back to Highford about ten months ago and I'm still here, waiting for the divorce to be sorted.'

'She said you're an actor.'

'Moved to London to tread the boards.'

'Have you been on television? Will I have seen you in something? Or do you have a stage name?'

'My stage name is my proper name, Michael Ellis, but at home it's plain old Mickey. I've had bit parts mainly. A couple of lines in a soap and a few adverts, but I got by on stage work. I loved that the most. Getting into a character's head, working out the motivations.'

'Not much work round here, I bet.'

'No, nothing at all. That's why I went to London. I used to love playing in the old Empire as a kid, just amateur stuff, but even that's closed down.' He blushed. 'But you're not interested in my acting career. What do you want to know?'

'Is there anything you can tell me about the woman who died?'

Mickey licked his lips and swallowed. He looked as if he was about to say something, then stopped, before walking towards the window and turning his back to Jayne.

'Mickey?'

He sighed heavily. 'Mum's wrong, I don't know anything about it.'

'Why did you bring me in here just to tell me that?'

'Because she thought I liked Mary, and that I know more about her than I let on.'

'And do you?'

'No, nothing.'

'How well did you know her?'

'I saw her around.'

'Is that it?'

'Yes, nothing more. She said hello if we passed in the alley, and we even talked once, but just like how you would with a neighbour.'

'Is that your bedroom at the back of the house?'

He nodded.

'Did you see me in the alleyway yesterday?'

There was a long pause before eventually he said, 'Yes. I was at my computer.'

'Your bedroom faces Mary's. Could you ever see into her bedroom?'

He frowned. 'You're making me sound creepy, like some kind of voyeur.'

'It's a natural question. We need to find out more about her and you've got a room that looks towards hers, where she died. I'm bound to ask.'

'All right, I get that. Sometimes I saw her, yes,' and he blushed.

'You used to watch her?'

'No, nothing like that.' Frustration crept into his voice.

'What was it like?'

'I spend a lot of time on my computer. I play games, and talk to people on the Internet. I get lonely, I suppose, and I have to do something with my time. What's the alternative? Sit down here, with my mother. I tried writing a book, just for something to do. Mary's bedroom was at the back, and if she left her light on I could see her, but it was nothing funny. I wasn't spying on her.'

'Did you see her on the night she died?'

'I don't know anything about it.'

'That isn't the same as no.'

'I'm going to have to ask you to leave.'

'Is there something you want to tell me?'

'Go, please.'

'Why won't you talk to me?'

'I said go!'

'Mickey?' his mother shouted from the other room.

Jayne raised her hands. 'I'm sorry, all right. I'm just trying to find out what I can.'

'You're going to have to leave.'

His mother banged on the wall with her walking stick.

'I'm going.' Jayne tapped her business card, which Mickey had clamped between his fingers. 'You've got my number, in case you remember something.'

Mickey didn't answer as Jayne went towards the door. Once she was back on the street, she glanced back towards the living room window. The Venetian blinds closed.

At least there was something to report, she thought, and made a note of the number in her book. Now for the rest of the street.

Twenty-three

Shelley Greenwood lived in a small cottage on a main road, on the edge of a small stone village nestled in a hill, not far from Highford.

Dan didn't know the area well, most of his time spent with Shelley had been down at the court or during after-work drinking sessions, but he knew he had the right house when he saw the crushed Mini, the roof squashed in on one side and the window smashed. Dumped there by the tow-truck and awaiting the insurance assessor, was his guess.

He knocked on the door at the side of the cottage, part of a glass porch, but had to wait a while for the door to open as he listened to the regular thump-click of someone walking on a crutch, almost drowned out by the frantic barking of a small dog.

When Shelley answered, she said, 'I knew you wouldn't leave it alone,' and turned and hobbled into the living room.

Dan followed, Shelley's small terrier almost tripping him as he jumped up at her legs. They were in a square room with uneven whitewashed walls and a large stone fireplace, with beams across the ceilings.

'How are you?' Dan said, sitting down on a large fawn sofa. 'I don't mean your injuries,' and he pointed at Shelley's leg, 'but, you know, you.'

Shelley threw the crutch to the floor as she slumped into a chair close to the fire, opposite a television. She silenced the talk show, the lie detector results pending. 'What, how am I after nearly killing myself? Oh, just great.'

'Have you heard anything from the police yet?'

'Guess what, I'm not really in the mood for this. Just tell me what you want.'

'Shelley, we've been friends for a long time. Maybe I'm just concerned.'

'You could have sent a card and flowers. It's about the Carter file, so get on with it.'

'Okay. I'm curious about why you gave up the file.'

Shelley shook her head. 'That bloody case.' She put her head back and looked up at the ceiling. 'I tried to do the right thing, that's all.'

'What do you mean?'

There was a long pause before she said, 'I can't tell you.'

'You make it sound like there's more to this than it seems.'

Her laugh was sharp and bitter. 'Oh, there's lots more, believe me, but you're not going to get it out of me.'

'Why not?'

'Look at my face.' She sat forward and pointed at her scar, her eyes wet and angry. 'And my car. Everything ruined.'

'But what does that have to do with the Carter case, because you make it sound like it's connected?'

'You're not going to give up on this, are you?'

'You must have wanted me to have it for a reason.'

'I tried to do something right, and it all goes wrong. I should have done what most lawyers do, just bank the cheque and move on.'

'And you regret it because you crashed your car?'

'There's more to it than that. You can't know. You don't need to know.'

'Tell me one thing at least.'

'Go on.'

'Where had you been, before the crash?'

'Wild Manor.'

'The hotel?'

'Yes.'

'Who were you with?'

Shelley paused at that, wiping her eyes and blowing her nose before saying, 'I'm not telling you.'

'Why not?'

'Because I don't have to. Isn't that enough? All I know is that I don't want anything to do with that case anymore. I shouldn't have transferred it, but it's too late now.'

'So what should I do?'

'Just don't dig too deeply. For my sake.'

'Do you think I will pay any attention to that?'

Shelley thought about it for a few moments. 'No, probably not.'

*

Jayne's journey to the Wild Manor Hotel didn't take long, acting on a text from Dan. *Check out who Shelley was with Sunday night. Wild Manor Hotel.* She looked at herself in the mirror. She'd found Shelley's picture on the Duttons website and she was similar enough in looks to pass for her, if the other person had only met Shelley briefly. Dark hair, similar figure. She didn't know whether Shelley was a regular there, but it was worth a try.

What Jayne didn't want to do was drive into the hotel car park, because one look at her car would give away her lie. Not many lawyers drive an old blue Punto, with one window that didn't quite close properly and her passenger door crinkled from an accident she'd had the year before. She wasn't too bothered about her own appearance, because if they knew about the accident they would assume she'd had a rough couple of days and put any difference in looks down to that. But her car was certainly no courtesy car.

She was trying to write up her visit to Mickey's street, her laptop on her knee, but the memory of Mickey was troubling her. He knew something, she was sure of it. He lived just on the other side of the alleyway and had taken an interest when she and Dan had been snooping around. The entry on the unused material list said that there was *no relevant evidence*, but was that witness Mickey, and, if so, what had he told the police?

Jayne knew what Dan would do if he thought there was something suspicious about Mickey: deflect some attention towards him, just to throw some doubt around. Did she want to be a part of that? Making him a pariah on his street?

It was a cliché too, the lonely man on his computer, with few friends apart from his dependent and ageing mother, watching Mary, the pretty young teacher.

Jayne stopped typing and looked out of the window as she realised something else: she was looking at it from the wrong angle. This was the law, where truth often came second. Dan would think like a defence lawyer, interested only in persuading twelve jurors that they couldn't rule out Mickey as the killer. The truth of that possibility didn't matter.

That thought soured her mood. Her job wasn't to help prove Robert Carter was innocent, but merely to deflect attention on to someone else so that Robert Carter could walk free. The criminal justice system didn't always provide justice.

She took a last slurp of a thick-shake and tossed the cup into the passenger footwell. She was struck by another cold reality: she wasn't doing it for justice. She was doing it for the money, because she couldn't afford to say no. Was that the price of her morality? It wasn't very high if it was.

Jayne stepped out of the car and on to a rutted and muddy grass verge. The view was into a valley, the glint of the canal at the bottom, the valley sides threaded by drystone walls and the gleam of a river in the distance.

She trudged towards the hotel until the soft squish of her footsteps was replaced by the crunch of gravel from the driveway, which swept towards stone pillars at the entrance. No neon sign, just Victorian lamps lining the driveway and spotlights in the flowerbeds, with long conservatories running along the back that made it popular for weddings through the summer.

As she went inside, her cheeks warmed from the heat of the fire blazing in the hearth close to the reception desk, even though it was a nice day outside. Comfortable chairs crowded the fire, the sort of place an elderly gent might sleep off a few lunchtime brandies.

The young woman behind the reception desk gave a cheery smile. 'Can I help you?'

Jayne returned the smile, aiming for her most disarming. 'Hi Kelly,' she said, spotting her name on a small tag on her lapel. 'I just need to ask you something,' and she rolled her eyes in mock-embarrassment. 'I came here on Sunday evening for a meal and, well, on the way home I crashed my car and the police are saying I was drunk. Of course, I wasn't, and I need to find the person I dined with to prove it.'

Kelly looked confused. 'Why don't you know who you dined with?'

'Because it was a first meeting with a client and I can't remember his name, but I can hardly go to my boss and tell him that.' She leaned closer to whisper, 'You'll get me out of a real hole.'

Kelly looked unsure as she logged on to the diary on the computer, the screen facing towards her. When she stopped typing, Jayne knew she was on the right page.

'I'm not sure I can,' Kelly said, glancing back towards a doorway that led into an office, filing cabinets visible.

'Please, just print off the diary and I'll be able to check it against the computers at work.'

'No, I can't, I'm sorry.'

Jayne leaned forwards over the counter to try to see the screen. 'I'll know it if I see it though.'

'No, please, you can't do that,' Kelly said, agitated now.

'It's okay, I might have his name in my phone.' Jayne pulled her phone from her pocket. She turned on her camera but made as if she was scrolling through something, her thumb flicking just a few millimetres from the screen.

'I can't help you, not without speaking to my manager,' Kelly said, glancing again towards the doorway behind her.

'It's okay, you're helping me.' Jayne swiveled the screen towards herself, taking a picture at the same time.

'Hey!' Kelly pulled the screen back towards her.

'I'm sorry. I'm in a real bind, that's all.'

A woman appeared from the office behind. She was older and more authoritative, frowning at Jayne's appearance. 'Everything all right, Kelly?'

'Yes, I'm fine,' Kelly said, her eyes fixed on the screen. She tapped some keys and Jayne guessed that the diary was no longer showing.

'It's all right, thank you,' Jayne said. 'You've been very helpful.'

Jayne turned and walked out of the hotel lobby. She took her phone out of her pocket and navigated to the picture gallery. There it was: the diary for the bookings from Sunday night.

Now they might be able to work out the identity of Shelley's dining companion. More importantly, they might be able to find out why Shelley was so keen to keep it a secret.

There was just one more stop for the day: Robert Carter's wife.

Twenty-four

As Dan walked into his office, Margaret handed over a slip of paper with a phone number on it.

'Can you ring Zoe Slater at the CPS. That's her direct line.' She raised an eyebrow. 'She sounds like a little madam.'

'Enthusiastic, that's all.'

He could guess what it was about: the door-to-door log he'd spoken to DI Murdoch about. He was supposed to go through the prosecutor, but that could mean a delay. He'd tried a shortcut but it could be at the expense of some goodwill.

He put his bag on the chair in his office and dialled Zoe's number. When she answered, Dan had to hold the phone away from his ear. She was shouting and it was shrill.

'You shouldn't go straight to the police for that kind of stuff,' she said.

'Why not?'

'Because there are rules.'

'Show me the rule that says I can't ask the police.'

'You know that isn't how we do things.'

Dan grimaced at her volume. 'So what does it say?'

'What does what say?'

'The document concerning the door-to-door enquiries, from the unused schedule. I presume you've read it.'

'It isn't disclosable. It doesn't undermine our case, so I don't have to show you.'

'But you must have seen it to make that decision.'

Zoe didn't answer straight away.

'You haven't seen it.' He smiled to himself. He knew the answer.

'We don't have to see every document,' she said, her tone more defensive. 'We can rely on the police description.'

'Didn't the words *no relevant evidence* concern you?'

'I don't know what you mean.'

'That's an opinion, not a fact. Didn't you want to test it yourself? Like you said, you make those decisions, not the police.'

Zoe didn't answer, although Dan could hear papers being turned as she looked for the right page.

'Look, I get it, you're overworked' he said, as he waited for her to find the entry. 'Half your lawyers have left and the ones still there have to somehow pick up the slack. So you just looked at what the police said could be disclosed and signed off the rest.'

'That isn't how it is,' she said, but her voice was quieter, her anger gone.

'If you won't hand it over, I'll get the case listed tomorrow so a judge can decide. You know what will happen, you'll have to admit you've never looked at the document. The judge won't be happy and he'll remember your name. Even if you have seen it, the judge will order disclosure anyway. It's what they do. Judges have never cared about the disclosure rules. If we want it, we usually get it.'

'We've already had that hearing.'

Dan was surprised. 'When?'

'At the plea hearing. Shelley tried to get it and was told no, because she got a judge who applied the rules, rather than some old boys network.'

'I didn't know that.'

'You do now.' Her voice softened when she said, 'I get it, Dan, you're under pressure because this case has landed on your desk, but I'm not bending the rules just because it's you.'

Dan shook his head when he replaced the receiver. That was one small battle lost.

Prosecutors were not much different to him, just criminal lawyers who'd chosen one side, often for nothing more than the better hours and not having to go to a police station at midnight.

He went towards the kitchen to make himself a drink, knowing that he had work to do on his other files. He passed Pat's office on the way. There were raised voices in there.

Dan went in without knocking, worried in case it was a client being aggressive. Instead, Conrad Taylor was there, standing and pointing at Pat in anger. He whirled round when he realised Dan was there.

'Here he is, superstar,' Conrad said, almost spitting out the words.

'What are you talking about?'

'We want that case back. Robert Carter. He's our client.'

'Not anymore.'

'It's just one little case. Why do you want it so much?'

'I could ask you the same.'

Conrad walked over to Dan and jabbed a finger into his chest. 'Because it makes my firm look bad, that we couldn't hang on to a murder case.'

'Is that all it is?' Dan pushed his hand away and stepped closer, making Conrad back away.

Conrad thrust his chest forward. 'What do you mean?'

'You're getting pretty agitated about *one little case*,' and Dan made speech marks with his fingers. 'You'll get paid for everything you've done, so it can't be about the money. What else is it? Because it's amazing what you find out if you dig deeply enough.'

'What the hell are you talking about?'

'I'm not telling you. It's my case now, so everything is confidential. You know the rules.'

'Don't be an idiot, Dan.'

Dan held his ground and stared at Conrad, who looked away after a few seconds and started to pace.

'Let's get a few things straight,' Dan said, a harder edge to his voice. 'Don't get in my face again, because I don't take backward steps. You jab me in the chest again and I'll throw you down the stairs. And don't come to my office and shout the odds. The case isn't yours anymore. I decide what to do on my files, not you. Got it?'

Conrad glared at Dan, and then back at Pat. 'Who do you think you are?'

'I'm the person in charge of the case.'

Conrad clenched his fists and stormed out of the office, slamming the door as he went.

His footsteps echoed through the building as he rushed down the stairs. Pat said, 'What the hell have you been uncovering that's got him so wound up?'

Dan stared at the closed door. 'I don't know, nothing so far. But Conrad has made sure that I want to find out a whole lot more.'

*

Sara Carter's house was a semi-detached on an estate that Jayne knew well from serving domestic violence injunctions, the neighbourhood blighted by unemployment and booze and drugs. A group of teenagers loitered nearby, their hands in their jogging pants, hair cropped skin-close at the side and then plastered to their scalps on top.

The gate creaked as she stooped to open it. Someone had painted in some of the bricks with white paint. A plastic pedal-car was abandoned on an overgrown lawn, alongside a path made of crooked paving slabs with grass sprouting between.

Jayne knocked on the door. Someone shouted inside, a woman's voice, and then her outline grew in the frosted glass in the door panel. When it was opened, she was holding a cigarette in one hand and using her leg to hold back a young girl, perhaps only three years old, from running out of the front door.

'I'm Jayne Brett. I work for Robert's solicitor.'

She looked confused. She took a long pull on her cigarette and said, 'I've never seen you before, and you don't look like you work for a law firm.'

'There's a new firm involved now, and I'm their investigator. Can I talk to you?'

There was a pause before she said, 'Yeah, sure,' and stepped aside.

The hallway was tiled in a way that spoke of a lack of carpet rather than a design feature, but the living room was different. The smoke hung heavily, but otherwise it was clean and nicely furnished, with a large comfortable sofa and candles dotted around the room, even though the clean wicks told Jayne that they were for decoration rather than a cosy night in with a bottle of wine. Photographs of the young girl adorned each wall but there were none of Robert Carter.

She offered Jayne a drink, but she declined.

'It's Sara, isn't it?'

She nodded.

'I hope you don't mind me asking you about Robert. It must be hard, I know.'

Sara looked to the ceiling as her chin trembled before she wiped at a tear with her finger and let out a long breath. 'You don't know the half of it. I know people talk about me when I walk down the street. I see their looks, as if it's somehow my fault.'

'Your fault? I don't understand.'

The young girl was leaning against Sara's leg and sucking on her thumb, staring at Jayne.

Sara kissed her on the top of her head. 'Tammy, go play in your bedroom and let me talk to this lady.' The little girl ran away up the stairs.

'Tell me, why could it be your fault?'

'Because he was dopey on that woman, on Mary, like he was dopey on that other girl a while back, so you can just guess what they think of me, that I wasn't good enough for him. I couldn't keep my man happy and all that, so he went off looking for it elsewhere, and if he hadn't, Mary would still be alive.'

'People don't really think like that.'

She laughed. 'You're kidding?' She took a last drag of her cigarette and stubbed it out in a glass ashtray that looked like it had been stolen from a pub. 'Maybe in your world. It's different round here. People have to fight hard for a good life and they get hung up on old-fashioned values.'

'I saw Robert this morning. He said he didn't do it.'

'Yeah, he said that to me too.'

'Did you believe him?'

'I want to believe him.'

'That isn't the same.'

'It's as far as I'm going to go, because that little girl upstairs is his flesh and blood, and I don't want her growing up thinking her daddy could do something like that.'

'But could he? You know him best.'

Sara took a deep breath. 'I don't know, because I thought I knew him, but really, what did I know? He's a lazy, lying, cheating scumbag, and I hadn't spotted it. But murder?' She shook her head. 'If I didn't know him as well as I thought, who knows?'

Jayne leaned forward. 'Did Robert's other solicitor ever ask you to give evidence for him?'

She swallowed. 'What could I say? I wasn't there when she was killed.'

'You can testify as to his character, to say whether he's ever been violent . . .' A pause, and then, 'Was he?'

'No, never that.'

'Can I ask what he was like sexually? Was he aggressive or forceful?'

Sara took a deep breath, as if deciding whether to answer.

'Don't be embarrassed,' Jayne said.

'No, never. But if he ever asked, I let him have me, even if I didn't want it. That's what a wife is for, isn't it?'

No, it wasn't, Jayne thought, but that argument was for a different day. 'There's one more thing I want to ask you,' she said. 'When you were mentioned, Robert ended the interview, became angry. It was as if we'd flicked a switch.'

'He was like that with me.'

'When?'

'A couple of weeks after he'd been locked up. I'd taken Tammy to see him, because she was missing her daddy, and I didn't know what was going on. I just had to know, to look him in the eye and work out if he'd done it, because it felt like my life had been destroyed too. He was all upset, telling me that I shouldn't have brought Tammy and how he wished he was home, but he became angry when I told him about those men who came to see me.'

'Which men?'

'Two guys. Big, they were. You could see their muscles even in their suits, and one had a shaved head covered in scars, like he'd once been bottled. I knew they were trouble. If someone knocks on your door in a suit around here, it's either a detective or a gangster, and they weren't the police.'

'What did they say?'

'They wanted to know what Robbie was saying. I told them I didn't know, that I hadn't seen him since he was arrested, but they scared me. No smiles, nothing nice. They told me that I had to tell them if Robbie said anything to me about the case, and that I had to tell Robbie that they were thinking of him, that they'd been to see me.'

'Did they say who they were?'

'No, and I didn't ask. Just big guys.'

'How were you going to tell them if you didn't know who they were?'

'They said they'd be watching.'

'That sounds scary.'

'It was.'

'And when you told Robert, he freaked out?'

'Yes. Told me not to come back, not to talk to anyone.'

'If you find out who these men are, will you let me know?'

Sara shook her head. 'They were nasty people, and I've got Tammy to think about.'

Jayne reached across and gripped her hand, gave it a reassuring shake. 'I understand. If you change your mind, speak to Dan Grant at Molloys. He'll look after you.'

'And what are you going to do?'

'I'm going to keep on asking around. It's what I do.'

'You need to be careful. You seem nice and Robbie isn't worth it.'

Jayne let go of her hand. 'I'll be fine.'

'I'm sure you think that, but,' and Sara let out a long breath. 'Like I said, they were nasty guys.'

Twenty-five

Dan was back in his own room when he heard footsteps on the stairs, and for a moment he wondered whether it was Conrad back for a second bite, but they were lighter, faster. Dan waited for whoever it was to appear, and he smiled when Jayne bounded into the office.

'You look like someone bringing important news,' he said.

Jayne flopped into the chair in the corner, dangling a leg over the arm, her foot swinging lazily.

'Not been a wasted day,' she said, and pulled her phone out of her pocket. 'I found out who Shelley was dining with.' She grinned. 'Conrad Taylor.'

He was confused. 'Conrad?'

'I went to the hotel and got a picture of the booking list from Sunday night,' and she waved her phone. 'There was a C *Taylor* listed at nine o'clock, and a table for three.'

He leant back in his chair. 'He's been here this afternoon, throwing his weight around. Do you know him?'

'Yeah, but not well. I've tried to talk to him at court, to muscle into his firm for investigative work, but not got anywhere. He has his own favourites.'

'Yeah, I'm sure he does.'

'What do you mean?'

'Oh, nothing.'

'Come on, you can't throw me a teaser and then pull it back.'

'Let's just say he keeps a tight rein on his cases and his firm.'

Jayne sat up. 'You make it sound like he's not on the level.'

'I'm not sure he is. For Conrad, it's all about the winning, not being a good lawyer.'

'How do you mean?'

'It's just the little things. The small stunts. Let's say a violent husband was my client and his wife came here and said she wanted to withdraw the complaint, and wanted bail conditions removing so he could go home. What do you think has happened?'

'She might be genuine.'

'Or more likely he's gone to round to her house and told her what to say and who to say it to. The old days of a case being dropped as soon as the victim demands it have gone. The police want to make sure she's not being bullied into dropping it. That's why I'd tell her to go to the police and let them look into it, because they can check everything out. What do you think Conrad would do?'

'Go on.'

'He'd march her across to the court and try to get the bail conditions removed. I watched him do it once, and when the prosecutor tried to speak to her in private, he wouldn't let her, insisted on being there.'

'He can't do that, can he?'

'The police look at lawyers from time to time, but they're difficult to take on, so they get away with it as long as they stick to the small stuff.'

'But if I were in trouble, would I be bothered about playing by the rules? Is that how you salvage your conscience, by playing nice? You're a defence lawyer too. You get paid to help people weasel out of things.'

'Not if it turns me into a crook along the way.'

'But you'd know how to protect yourself.'

'No, I see the line. Some lawyers can't see it.'

'And you can?'

'I try to.'

'What did he want with you?'

'He wants Robert Carter's case back.'

'And you told him to get lost?'

'Something like that.'

'Is he having an affair with Shelley?'

Dan was surprised. 'What makes you say that?'

'Shelley was dining with Conrad.'

'If it's an affair, it's a funny way to keep it secret, having a table for three.' Dan tapped his pen on the desk. 'If Shelley was dining with Conrad, and it had something to do with Carter's case, why didn't Conrad know that the case had been transferred?'

'Perhaps she didn't want to tell Conrad.'

'But he would have found out the next day.'

'If Conrad wants the case back, Shelley would have known he wouldn't be happy. Why ruin a good meal?'

'There must be more to it than that,' Dan insisted. 'Have you found anything else out?'

'A cliché.'

'I don't understand.'

'Remember the house at the back, where you thought some-one was watching, and I thought the same. Well, there was. A man in his thirties, Mickey Ellis. He's split from his wife so he's living there with his mother.'

'And you think he's a viable suspect?'

'He's got a view straight into Mary's bedroom and he acted weird. He took me into a different room so he could tell me something, and then went on to say that he didn't see anything.' Jayne sighed. 'I didn't like telling you but his mother told me that Carter's previous lawyer had shouted at him, so it was going to come out, because Shelley must have spoken to him.'

'Why would she shout at him?'

'He didn't say.'

'And why didn't you want to tell me about him?'

'Because he might be innocent, just some quiet guy. Do you remember that landlord in Bristol, when the woman was killed in her flat? Joanna something?'

'Joanna Yates. Yes, I remember. The landlord was Chris Jeffries.'

'The landlord was innocent, but until they caught her real killer, everyone thought he was the guilty one. You're going to do the same. You want to create another suspect to build some doubt. I know how it works. But what if he's got nothing to do with Mary's murder?'

'Then he's got nothing to worry about.'

'No, he's got a lot to worry about. It's not about what the police do to him, because they think they've got their man already. It will be about how you'll destroy him, because you'll blame him for what happened to Mary so that Robert Carter can walk free. How do you think his neighbours will react? They'll drive him from of his home. Perhaps even worse. He seemed an okay guy. Quite attractive really. He's just a hit rough patch, and we're going to make it worse.'

'What, you think I should ignore him because you like him?'

'I think you should only throw blame his way if you can prove that he did it.'

Dan shook his head slowly. 'That's not how the system works, you know that. It's dirty work sometimes. I have to look after Robert Carter, no one else.' When Jayne frowned, he added, 'You don't have to help me.'

'That's not fair. You know I need the money.' A pause and then, 'I went to see Carter's wife, Sara.'

'And what did she say?'

'She hates Carter for what he's done, but that's no surprise. She told me that two thugs went to see her.'

'Thugs?'

'Two big men in suits. Told her to let them know what Carter was saying, but when she told Carter about them, he went off on one, told her not to come see him again.'

'Who were they?'

'She didn't know. They told her that they'd be watching and would know what she was up to.'

'That's pretty strange, for a murder like this, some stalker fixating on a young woman.'

'Perhaps it's not like that at all then, and we've got two weeks to find out.'

'Keep digging,' Dan said.

'Are you sure? Carter doesn't want us to, and it's starting to sound dangerous.'

'That's exactly why,' he said. 'Try to find out who else Shelley was dining with on Sunday night. You might discover something that means we can forget all about the man on the street behind.'

'Okay. And you?'

'Unless you can come up with something, I'm starting to run out of ideas. Which isn't good news for Robert Carter.'

'If he did it, if he killed Mary, that won't bother me.'

'But if he didn't?'

Jayne got to her feet. 'Okay, I get it, keep on digging,' and she left the office, her footsteps not quite as enthusiastic on the way out.

*

His fingers were clenched into tight fists, his knuckles jammed against his forehead. He was trying to blot out the noise but he couldn't.

The scratches were back. Niggles in his mind that he couldn't ignore. He didn't want to them to come back, but they had, and he felt powerless. Like an alcoholic who stumbles into a party, or a crack addict who hits the hard times again.

He had to fight it. The sweep of the lamp through the air. Mary covered in blood. He couldn't go back.

He clamped his hands over his ears. They had to stop. Small knocks, like someone tapping the back of his head.

It was more than sound though. It was something surging through his body, a need driving him, so that he had to follow the urge to make it go away.

He moved his hands away and took a deep breath, his shoulders slumped. Is this what his life was to be?

He wasn't even sure what it was about her. She was no Cassie or Mary, who were bright and happy, but quiet with it. He'd wanted to see their darker sides, because they were hidden so deep that it felt like he was getting a secret. With her, she hadn't seemed cheery or light. No, it had been very different. It was as if there was some darkness inside her that was trying to get out, something barely concealed. It was the way her eyes narrowed when he looked at her, as if she knew he could see into her and it was her way of protecting herself, just closing down her gleam for a moment.

What was her secret?

He swallowed. He needed to know. More than anything right then, he had to find out.

Jayne Brett. What was she hiding?

Twenty-six

Jayne was back at the hotel again, peering through her windscreen, her car parked further along the country lane. She was looking out for employees who might help her find out the identity of the third person at the meal with Shelley and Conrad Taylor.

It was the end of a warm day and the sun was dipping behind a hill, casting red streaks across the sky, midges swirling over the warmth of her engine, ticking quietly as it cooled. Her window was open and the gentle sounds of summer drifted in. The last song of the birds in nearby hedgerows, the rumble of distant tyres, the gentle swish of branches in a soft breeze. It was one of those times when she enjoyed her work, where she could almost forget about what had gone on before in her life and allow herself a smile.

She wound up her window and folded her arms across her chest, the warm evening sounds blocked out, replaced by the creak of her car seat.

She had to wait another thirty minutes before she saw the right person.

Jayne had gambled on there being a shift change, the lunch-time staff giving way to the evening workers, and she'd got it right. There'd been a steady stream of people leaving, with many of the younger staff being collected by parents or partners. People were drifting in to replace them, in cars that said that they couldn't afford to eat there, parked around the back, out of sight.

She had an idea of the sort of person she was looking for. The hotel was plush, and she knew one thing about hotels like it: they attracted people who thought they were better than everyone else. Jayne hated that, and she knew some of the waiting staff would too, because they'd be made to feel less than worthy.

There was no point in looking for the young and eager, who saw their job as the first step on a hotel career. Or the students earning extra money to top up their student loans, decent kids with no gripe against their employers. No, Jayne reckoned she needed the person who'd ended up working there because there wasn't much else, where every day at work was a reminder of how their life hadn't turned out as they'd hoped. Instead, they had to suck up to the people who spent more on wine than they earned during an evening. She wanted the disenchanted who hated their jobs, hated their bosses.

Then she saw him.

He was walking towards the hotel along the lane, his black shirt hanging loose over his trousers. He was smoking and dawdling, putting off the moment he went inside.

Jayne got out of her car and walked towards him. She smiled as she got closer, making him straighten up and throw his cigarette into the grass verge.

'Hi, I'm wondering if you could help me,' she said.

His eyes narrowed, suspicious at first, so Jayne widened her smile, gazed into his eyes as if she was desperate for his response.

'Yeah, sure.'

'I came to eat here the other night, with someone called Conrad Taylor. Sunday night. Nine o'clock booking. There was someone else there and I don't know who it was. I was promised a job and can't get in touch.'

'Why don't you just ask this Conrad?'

'Because he's a sleazeball, like most of them are, thinking I can be bought for a few drinks. You know what these sports car types are like.'

He snorted a laugh at that. 'We get nothing but them here.'

'Self-centred arseholes?'

'Yep, plenty of those.'

'I tried to get the details from reception but they just about sneered at me, like I wasn't good enough for their place.'

'They're like that with everyone, so don't take it personally.' He shuffled nervously as he added, 'I'd have told you.'

'So can you help me?'

'How?'

'I don't know how the business works, but there must be some way of finding out who it was. Any CCTV, or who paid the bill?'

'I can't get the footage but I can ask around.'

'Oh, would you?'

'Yeah, sure,' he said, and his eyes turned more interested as he tucked in his shirt. 'But what's in it for me?'

'My everlasting gratitude, if it gets me the job.' Her smile was flirty, her voice teasing.

That got his attention.

'How do I get in touch with you?' he asked.

Jayne reached into her pocket and scribbled her number on to a scrap of paper. 'Just text me.'

He read it and then put it into his shirt pocket. 'I could get sacked for this.'

'Would that bother you?'

'No, I hate the place.'

'Thank you,' she said, and skipped back to her car.

Once inside, she watched him as he walked into the hotel with more purpose than before. She hoped he didn't get into trouble, but like Dan said, it's a dirty job sometimes.

*

Dan was parked further down the street from Mickey's house. He'd already walked up and down, just to get a feel. A terraced house, just like all the rest, although the blinds looked dusty and there were cobwebs in one corner of the window.

He'd thought about knocking on the door, but he couldn't think of an opening. Jayne had already been to the address so what could he add? It would make Mickey think he was about to become the focus of the case and he didn't want that.

But Dan needed to see him, just so he could picture him. Dan didn't have to blame Mickey for the murder, all he had to do was raise a line of inquiry the police didn't pursue, but he'd have to make Mickey a credible suspect. The oddball loner, creepy guy staring from his bedroom window. A perfect cliché for the jury.

Jayne was right though; the people in the neighbourhood would fix on him as an easy target. It would be more than just innuendo that never makes it beyond the court door. It would be the wink, the nudge, the lapse into silence as he passed people on the street. Perhaps anonymous letters through his door. Dan needed to see him, to turn him into a human being, not some note on one of Jayne's reports.

He had to do his job though. What would the military call it? Collateral damage. The phrase makes it innocuous, a tragic casualty. He had no idea how the military people dealt with their consciences, but Dan knew he had to confront his own.

He was trying to work out a reason to knock on the door when it opened. A man stepped out and rushed along the street, his head down, hands thrust into the pockets of a brown leather jacket.

Dan stepped out of his car to follow him. The man's pace was fast, so Dan had to trot to catch up when he rounded the first corner.

He went into a shop. Dan followed, just as a way of getting close to him.

He was by the counter as Dan went in, sharing a joke with the shopkeeper and buying a packet of chewing gum. His accent was soft northern, his manner easy. The shopkeeper called him by name.

Dan went to the fridge and selected some milk, to avoid suspicion. He always needed milk.

Once the door had closed, Dan paid for the milk and left. He had what he wanted. He'd seen Mickey the man, just a normal person, polite and pleasant. If he wanted to cast any suspicion his way, Dan had got a sense of the person who'd be getting the backlash.

His mood was sour as he got back into his car.

He didn't go straight home. Instead, he detoured to his father's rest home.

His father was watching some old television movie from the seventies when he went in, with Peter Falk on a cruise ship. His half-full glass was clasped in his good hand.

'Two days in a row,' his father said, without looking up. 'And why do I get the honour?'

'To see how you are. Isn't that a good enough reason?'

His father pulled a face and turned towards him. 'I know you. You've never visited me two days running, so there has to be a reason. That's the thing with people like you.'

'People like me?'

'Lawyers. Everything you do has a motive.'

'Let's not go through this again.'

His father took a long swig and drained his glass, then clicked his fingers and pointed at a sideboard filled with old country and western records and horror books.

'A refill?'

'What else?'

Dan went to the cupboard and brought out the cider bottle, filling his father's glass. As he put it back in the cupboard, his father said, 'We fought hard against people like you. The courts, the lawyers. I don't understand why you went that way.'

'How much have you drunk today?'

'Not enough. And I'm right, you know it. We fought to make the world a better place, because sometimes you've got to bring everything crashing down in order to rebuild. But they used the courts to defeat us. And what do we have now? No mines, no mills, no industry. What future do young people have now? Call centres? Those at the top make money by moving money. What happened to making things? You can't run a country by shuffling money around.'

'The world's changed, Dad.'

'For the better? Bullshit. And yet my son goes to work in the system?'

'I help those beaten by the system.'

'No, you make them part of the system, by making excuses for them.'

'You're drunk.'

'No, I'm angry.'

'The revolution is over, can't you see. You lost.'

'No, *we* lost. We all lost.'

'You're missing a bar to lean against so you can rail against the world. I'll take you to one, if you want. Get you out of this room.'

His father shook his head. 'I've told you before, no one is seeing me like this. I want them to remember me as I was, not like this,' and he gestured with his hand towards his withered left arm, spilling cider down his front.

'I can take you out. Think about it. You can take me on a battlefield tour.'

'I don't understand.'

'Show me where you worked, where you fought the good fight, tell me what it meant.'

'You lawyers have a good way with words, and like you said, we lost.'

'Do you regret the fights though?'

'No, not one.'

'But good people were caught up in it. Not everyone shared your vision. Some people were happy to have a job and pay their bills and didn't want to risk everything by striking. What about those people, the ones who were hurt along the way?'

His father's eyes narrowed. 'Sometimes you've got to decide what the right thing is, what you think justice is. You don't change anything by pleasing everyone. Principles are important. Stand by what you believe in.'

'Even us lawyers?'

'Especially you lawyers. Don't be someone who can be bought.' A pause, and then, 'Have you got what you wanted?'

'It's good to see you, Dad. I was passing, that's all. I must come again.'

'To have an argument?' his father said, although there was mischief in his smile. 'I've spent my life arguing about one thing or the other. That's what I hate most about the world today. No one argues anymore, no one fights. We just get offended at things, so no one dares say anything.'

'I'll come and see you again this week,' Dan said, and in his father's smile, he got an inkling of what had driven him throughout his own career. Whatever his father thought about him, Dan knew that he got many things from his father. Dan just didn't know how many of them were good.

Twenty-seven

Jayne had turned into the short path that led to her front door when someone stepped in front of her, as if he'd been waiting on the other side of the wall.

She stepped back, shocked, ready to run, when she saw it was the man from the other night, the one who'd left the flowers.

'What are you hanging around for?' she said, the words snapping out. 'You're creeping me out.'

He held up his hands in apology. 'I don't mean to. Did you get the flowers?'

'Yes, I did.' She was about to tell him not to do it anymore, but when she looked into his eyes, she saw kindness, not danger. He was dressed in work clothes, a green polo shirt with a logo and matching trousers, along with cement-splattered boots. 'Thank you. They were nice, but remember what I said, that I'm not into having a boyfriend right now. I still mean that.'

'I know, and I get that. The flowers were to say thank you, that's all, nothing more.' He laughed. 'I know nothing happened, but I don't often get to wake up with a woman as pretty as you.'

That softened her anger. 'You're not going to get a repeat if you hang around where I live every day.'

'Yes, I know how it looks, but it's not what you think.'

'And what am I thinking? That you're someone who can't take no for an answer?'

He flushed with embarrassment. 'I can see how you might think that, but the flowers were just a gesture, nothing more.'

'So why are you here?'

'Just to say hello, I suppose. I was hoping you might want to do it again, go for a drink or something.'

'How long have you been waiting here to find that out?'

'An hour or so. I was about to leave, but here you are, but I can see that it's a no. I'm sorry.'

'It's okay. Look, you're a nice guy, but I'm just not ready for anything. You alright with that?'

He held his hands up. 'Oh yes, absolutely.'

He turned to go and Jayne went to the front door. Just as she got there, he turned and shouted, 'Something else too. There's someone hanging around.'

Jayne's hand was on the door handle but she paused, her skin chilled by goosebumps. 'Who?'

'Just some guy looking up at the building. He seemed nervy, as if he didn't want to be seen, but he was looking high up.'

'Towards my flat, you mean?'

'I can't say for sure.'

'What did he look like?'

'Average height, smartly dressed, short dark hair. That's all I can remember, sorry. I just wanted to warn you.'

'Why did you think I needed to know?' Jayne said, turning round, anger creeping into her face. 'There are a lot of flats and bedsits around here.'

'Just a gut feeling, nothing more.'

Jayne closed her eyes and reached out for the door to steady herself. Could it be Jimmy's family, out looking for revenge?

'You all right?'

Jayne opened her eyes. 'Yes, fine. Just tired.'

'I just thought you ought to know.'

'Thank you,' she said, before going into the building and slamming the door behind her. Her mouth was dry. Her hand trembled as she wiped her brow.

Get a hold of yourself. She'd always known the day would come. All she could do was deal with it.

She rushed up the stairs, enjoying the brief comfort of familiar sounds. Music from the ground floor. The steady thump of a bass guitar from the floor above. She had her keys in her hand as she approached her own door, and once inside, the door closing quickly, she leant back against it. She let out a long breath of relief.

She cursed herself for feeling that way and put her keys on the table by the door. She went along the short hallway, towards the kitchen at the end, where she enjoyed her meals overlooking the town. The daylight had gone, the roads picked out by the orange glow of streetlights, clustered in the town centre but thinned out to ribbons as they snaked over the hills. Looking northwards, the sky was dark, no light pollution to spoil it. It was different in the other direction, where the glow from Manchester bled over the hills, visible from her bedroom, but it was the darkness she craved. It made her more invisible somehow.

There was a bottle of wine in the fridge, left to cool before she went back to the hotel. She poured a glass and swirled the wine for a moment, but winced when she took her first sip. It was cheap.

The second sip wasn't quite as bad, as she got used to the taste. She turned to the window again, to the hills caught in faint silhouette. Somewhere over there was her past. She could never return there. Too many memories.

There was a noise.

She held her breath, her glass still, her body tensed.

It wasn't much of a noise. Footsteps possibly, just the sound of someone walking outside her door, but Jayne was attuned to every sound out there. She'd chosen her apartment because of its location. It was at the top of a nondescript building. That made it a trap, but at least if there was someone outside she'd know. It gave her the chance to protect herself, to slam the door and turn the key, to call someone. She always checked the peephole before she opened it. She would only be caught out if someone waited for her by crouching down or was pressed against the wall.

She put the glass down and listened. Her nerves tingled. The hairs on her arms stood proud.

There it was again. A soft shuffle, the faintest creak.

What should she do? Call the police? But say what? That there might be someone in the communal area of her apartment building? That wouldn't get her far.

She looked out of the window, trying to see something different. A car she hadn't seen before, or a group of people? Nothing. Just everything as it always was.

There were two choices: barricade herself in or investigate.

She drained her glass. She wasn't going to hide away. That choice led to a life of never going out. No, she would confront whatever it was.

Her footsteps were light as she made her way back down the hallway. There was definitely movement outside. Soft footsteps, the creak of floorboards, the faintest of breaths, someone moving in small circles.

Jayne's breath caught in her chest, her stomach in turmoil, sweat flashing across her palms. She thought about getting a knife but too many bad memories flooded back.

The door loomed large. She pressed her hand against the wood as she reached it, as if she'd be able to detect the person through vibrations.

She clicked off the hall light and moved herself closer to the peephole, her breaths coming faster, more nervous, tremors inside like tickles in her heart, building, rising.

The view outside filled her mind as she peered through, her fears seen through a fisheye lens. Her breath came back at her with heat, misting up the glass.

There was no one there. Perhaps all she'd heard was one of the other tenants moving around, or a visitor leaving.

Her apartment felt like it was trapping her, not shielding her. She had to get out.

She grabbed her keys and flung open the door, ready to rush down the stairs and get into her car, drive the country lanes just to feel the breeze cool her brow.

There was someone in front of her, in shadow, his back to the light on the landing.

She screamed but a hand lashed out, covered her mouth and pushed her backwards.

And then she was falling, stumbling over a table leg, unbalanced by the person rushing at her, the light in the hallway blurred as she fell to the floor, her breath crushed out of her as he landed on top.

When she tried to scream again, she couldn't. His hand was too tight across her mouth. She reached for something from the table, the lamp, anything to hit him with, but there was nothing there.

The time had come that she'd always dreaded.

She closed her eyes and wondered if she'd ever open them again.

Twenty-eight

Present Day

Simon Parkin sat down, his opening speech finished and his first witness announced. He sat back and seemed pleased with himself. It was about looking calm and confident, his poise reassuring the jury that everything he'd said was true.

The steady tap of his middle finger against his thumb gave away his nerves.

The speech had been all drama, verbal punches to the gut as he described the story that would unfold, with Mary's life reduced to being a victim and Robert Carter as the deranged stalker. The judge had already delivered the warnings about the sombre nature of the case, and how the jurors mustn't discuss it outside of the courtroom. Some would take it seriously, but there were always bound to be a couple who wouldn't be able to cope with staying silent, who'd whisper trial secrets over a wine glass or in private messages on social media.

Dan glanced back to the public gallery as he spoke, to gauge the reactions of those listening. Mary's parents held hands and stared resolutely ahead. The trial would be an ordeal for them and Dan wished he could make it less so, but this was the process, however painful it became.

Dan noticed other people there too. Lucy's parents, but their attention shifted to Dan as he looked and Lucy's father met him with a long stare. There was another woman further along, her focus on Carter, her jaw set. She looked familiar.

Lucy Ayres was the first witness to be called. It would be a good opening for the prosecution. Bring in the woman who found Mary's body, let her recount the horror, the blood, how sweet Mary was, how awful it was for her.

Dan turned round to Jayne as the court usher disappeared into the witness room with his clipboard. 'Who's the woman at the end, staring at Carter?'

Jayne looked towards the public gallery. 'That's Sara, Carter's wife.'

'I thought she was having nothing to do with the trial?'

'He's the father of her child. Perhaps that counts for something. Her daughter will ask about him when she's older.'

'I've seen her before.'

Before he could say more, the court usher re-emerged, Lucy behind him.

Lucy stared ahead as she walked towards the witness box, but all eyes were on her. She didn't glance at the dock, where Carter sat impassively, almost as if he wasn't paying any attention. She smiled at the judge as she entered the box. She was the sole focus of attention in the courtroom, the witness box raised high, the lawyers lower down in the well of the courtroom. It was her stage.

Dan turned to the jury. A couple of them were gazing sympathetically at Lucy. Simon Parkin had set out her part in the story in the prosecution's opening speech. It had been a bad thirty minutes for Carter, the person portrayed as the loner who pestered Mary, made her uncomfortable, who seemed to turn up wherever they went, and Dan guessed that it wasn't about to get any better. The case would be simple: he was the man who lost control when Mary spurned his advances. It would be hard not to be persuaded by it.

Lucy's voice was strong as she gave her oath. Simon tried to put her at ease by asking her to keep her voice up and to direct her answers to the jury, not him. The message was simple: they were the important ones, not the lawyers. Ten out of ten for ego stroking.

Simon started simply. 'Tell the court about Mary.'

Lucy looked upwards and blinked away what were supposed to be tears but, when she looked down again, her eyes and cheeks were dry.

'Mary was a dear friend.' Her hand went to her chest when she said it, just in case there was any doubt as to her sincerity. 'I'd known her for just a few months, when I moved into the house, but we hit it off straight away.'

'How would you describe Mary?'

'A wonderful, warm, generous person, as nice a person as you'd meet.' She looked towards the public gallery as she said it, a nod of comfort to Mary's parents.

'Tell the court how you got to know her.'

'I moved in to the house, I needed somewhere to stay, and we just hit it off. We went out together, had some real fun. She was funny and lively and everything you'd want a friend to be.' She took a deep breath, as if to compose herself. 'It was scary moving into that house, because I didn't know anyone else there, but Mary made me feel welcome, as if we'd been friends for years.'

Dan looked down. This was very bad for Carter. He might be able to repair some of the damage, but for as long as he was playing dumb, it was all going against him.

After a few more minutes on their close friendship, Simon asked, 'Do you know the defendant, Mr Carter?'

She looked to the dock. Her eyes narrowed before she turned back to the jury. 'Yes, I know him.' Her voice had gone flat.

'When did you first meet him?'

'I was out with Mary and the other two girls from the house, just having a drink, when he came over to talk to her.'

'Can you remember when this was?'

She made a show of trying to recall the date, even though Dan knew it was in her witness statement, the one she'd read before she came into court.

'The first Thursday in September. We were in the Wharf pub, that was where we went, usually, and he walked over.'

'Did he talk to you?'

'Just to say hello. It was all about Mary, not the rest of us.'

'Did Mary respond?'

'Only as Mary would. Politely, friendly.'

'How long did they talk for?'

'The first time? Thirty minutes, but we made our excuses to go as he had her sort of pinned into a corner, almost as if he were trying to separate her from us by putting his back to us.'

'And there were other times?'

She nodded. 'Plenty. It seemed like it was every time we went out. We'd go into a pub and he'd turn up.'

'On his own?'

'Every time.'

'Did Mary ever confide in you how she felt about this?'

'It was as if she hated the attention, because if we said anything about him, she'd pull a face, or go quiet and change the subject.'

Dan looked back at Carter again, who was now clenching his jaw hard. At least he was staying quiet. Dan was expecting an outburst, but so far he'd listened to his advice.

As he looked at Carter, Dan's eyes drifted towards the public gallery and to Carter's wife. She was glaring at Carter, but there was something in her expression that surprised Dan. He'd expected hatred or loathing, but instead it was something closer to confusion.

She noticed Dan watching her and looked away, her brow furrowed.

There was something there.

Twenty-nine

Thirteen Days Earlier

Jayne punched out, struggled and tried to bite the hand clamped over her mouth.

A male voice said in her ear, 'I'm sorry, I'm sorry, stay still.' His breath was warm on her face. She could smell mints and the soft aroma of cologne.

Her hand reached out, flapped at the carpet, looking for something to use as a weapon.

There was something small. A pen. That would do.

She gripped it in her hand, about to swing. Something stopped her. The knife. Jimmy dying. A murder trial.

The man pressed down on her. Heavy, threatening. His jacket had slipped off his shoulder in the struggle, and a button had popped from his shirt.

She grabbed the pen and plunged it his chest.

The man cried out as the pen sank in, her clenched fist meeting his body, dampness spreading out against his shirt. Sweat? Blood? It didn't matter, because he scrambled off her and reached for the pen, yelling in pain.

Jayne kicked out, caught him between the legs, his breath punched out of him. He curled up and rolled away. He seethed through gritted teeth, before letting out a long moan of pain.

She kicked out again, sensing his weakness, in anger this time, catching his upper leg.

She lay there for a moment, looking up, panting hard, before crawling along the hallway towards the kitchen. She was seeing things from a distance, the sounds faint, just the rush of blood through her veins in her head.

Once she got to her feet, she reached for the knife drawer.

Some part of her told her to stop, but still she reached for a carving knife, wanting to attack him for attacking her, her self-control not working. The handle was steel, cold in her palm, the blade long and sharp.

She bumped against the walls as she went back along the hallway, in shock, the view ahead almost monochrome, as if seen through a strobe light, flashes of images. A man rolling in pain. Her door swinging open. Blood. A pen thrown to one side.

She stood over him, breathing hard, wanting him to feel the terror she had, sweat running down her face, her chest.

Then she stopped. The light from the kitchen shone on his face and she recognised him, the scene getting some of the colour back.

'Mickey?'

He looked up and pain was etched across his face. 'I'm sorry, I'm sorry, I didn't mean to scare you.'

Jayne slumped to the floor and rested against the wall, throwing the knife underneath the table, where it joined old pizza flyers and lost coins.

'What the fuck are you doing here?' Her chest rose and fell as she tried to get her breath back. 'No, I'll say it differently. How did you know where I lived?'

He grimaced as his hand went to his chest. 'I researched you. It was easy.'

'How come?'

'Because your email address is on your business card, so I searched for it, which led me to your social media accounts. You've taken photos and shared them, just moans about having no money and staying in, but it read like you were drunk when you posted them. They showed your flat and the view. It made it easy for me to find the building and then match it against the view. On the internet, I can travel down your street and check it out. So I've been waiting around.'

'You could have just emailed me.'

'I wanted to speak to you because I needed to say what I've got to say in person.'

'Why didn't you say something when I was outside? I told you to contact me if you had any news, not this,' and she pointed at the discarded pen, blood on its tip staining the hall-way carpet.

'Because you were talking to that guy. I was just over the road, in a doorway, and when you went inside you looked scared, checking around, so I became uncertain and stayed outside.'

'And pushing your way into my flat, taking me by surprise, scaring me, would just be fine, would it?' She opened her eyes, incredulous, and shook her head. 'Look at my hand,' and she held out her right hand, palm downwards.

He turned away and looked at the floor.

'Look!' She kicked out at him.

When he raised his head, her fingers were trembling. 'You scared me, you got it wrong.'

'I was going to knock.'

'Why didn't you?'

'Because *I* was scared.'

'Of me?'

'Of everything. But then you opened the door like you were going to attack me, and you screamed. I panicked, thought I had to make you quiet.'

A face appeared in the open doorway. It was one of her neighbours, the bass player from downstairs.

'Everything okay?' His hair was dishevelled, the droop of his eyes telling her that he was too stoned to help even if she needed it.

Jayne looked at Mickey, grimacing, his hand on the injury from the pen, and gave a breathless nod. 'Yes, fine. My friend surprised me, that's all.'

The man looked down at Mickey, then back to Jayne, before he shrugged an okay and went back to his own life.

When the door clicked shut, Jayne pointed to the living room. 'We need to talk.'

Mickey grunted in pain as he got to his feet before limping to the living room. He took off his leather jacket and there was blood spreading across his shirt. Jayne watched him go and then let out a long breath when he went into the room. She heard the creak of the sofa springs.

Jayne thought about taking the knife with her but decided against it.

She hauled herself to her feet and followed Mickey. He was sitting in the corner of the room, at one end of the sofa, both hands in view.

'Talk to me.' Her words came out in short angry bursts. 'Why are you here?'

'That woman, the teacher, Mary. The night she died.' He closed his eyes and groaned. 'I'm not supposed to say anything.'

His tongue flicked to his lip. 'But it's not right, and I don't know what to do.'

'What isn't right?'

'That I don't tell the truth. Mary was nice. She'd wave at me whenever she left by the back gate, if she saw me in the window, or if she passed me on the street.'

'Were you looking out of the window on the night she died?'

Mickey paused.

'Come on, Mickey. You've come here because you want to talk to me. So talk. Did you like her?'

He shook his head. 'Not like you're thinking. She was pretty and seemed friendly and fun, but I'd just come out of a messy split and wasn't ready for that again. And she was ten years younger than me. I'm not exactly a catch right now, living back at home.'

'But you used to watch her in her bedroom.'

Mickey looked down.

'It's all right. Don't be embarrassed. Just do the right thing.'

'Not on purpose,' he said. 'My computer is in the back room, upstairs, and it faced her room. Sometimes she didn't close her curtains. I didn't go up there to watch her, or even look out for her, but I saw her sometimes.'

'But you didn't close your curtains, to stop yourself seeing?'

'What can I say? She was an attractive young woman. I might not be married anymore, but I'm still a man.'

Jayne moved closer to him and knelt down. 'Did you see something on the night she died?'

Mickey took a deep breath.

'Talk to me, Mickey. If not for me, because of how you just scared me, say it for Mary.'

He stared into Jayne's eyes. 'I heard her scream.'

Jayne's eyes widened. 'Were you on your computer?'

He nodded.

'Did you look over?'

'Straight away. I mean, who wouldn't? And that scream.' He ran his hand over his head, brushing his hair. 'It was pure fear, something you can't fake.'

'Could you see into her room?'

'No, nothing. The curtains were closed, but the light was on.'

'What did you do?'

'I turned off my light so no one could see me watching.'

'But you carried on watching?'

'Yes. I wanted to know what the hell was going on, but it had gone quiet and there was nothing to see. So I waited.'

'What did you see?'

'It was a couple of minutes later when I saw them.'

'Who?'

'Two of them, running out.'

'Two?' Jayne felt the tingle of something important. 'Are you sure?'

'I'm sure.'

'Did you recognise anyone?'

Mickey didn't respond straight away. Instead, he looked at his hands, rubbing one palm with his finger.

'Mickey, talk to me. Who was there?'

When he looked at her, Jayne saw the confusion in his eyes. And something else too. Fear.

'That's what I couldn't understand,' he said, and he began to tell his story.

Thirty

Dan was in bed when his door buzzer sounded. He raised his head from the warmth of his pillow and opened a bleary eye to look at the clock. Eleven-thirty.

He wasn't going to answer, it might just be kids messing around, but then it sounded again. Two buzzes this time.

He wrapped the pillow around his head and wished he could ignore it, but he knew he wouldn't get back to sleep if he didn't check what it was about. He stumbled out of bed and went into the hallway, rubbing his eyes. He jabbed the button and said, 'Yeah?' His voice was slurred through drowsiness.

'It's me,' a voice said, crackles coming through the intercom.

Dan rubbed his eyes. It was Jayne. He would have to stay up now.

He pressed the button until he heard the door downstairs click. He stretched and opened his apartment door, so that Jayne could walk straight in, before going back into his bedroom. He found a pair of grey sweatpants and a T-shirt, his TV clothes, for when he settled down with a bottle of wine, maybe two, and went on a *Netflix* marathon.

He'd started a bottle of wine before he went to bed. They might as well finish it. The bottle clinked as he opened the fridge and reached for two glasses. He was pouring the wine as Jayne came in. From the loose focus of her eyes, Dan knew he was merely topping her up. He held a glass out anyway.

'This is late,' he said.

Jayne took the glass and curled up on the sofa, her knees tucked underneath herself. 'I've had an interesting night.'

'And you thought you should share it.' He took a sip and grimaced. It didn't taste as good after an hours sleep. 'Has something happened?'

She took a drink, pausing only to raise her eyebrows and nod appreciatively. 'Better than the stuff I get,' she said, almost as if to herself, and then, 'I'm not doing this anymore.'

'Doing what?'

'Living in fear. Always looking over my shoulder, worrying about the next knock on the door, or who might be waiting for me.'

'Jimmy's family?'

'Yes, them, and others.'

'Have Jimmy's family ever done anything to you?'

'They threatened me when I was at court. You know that, and you knew it would happen. You said I had to be brutal about him.'

'No, I said you had to be honest, because you were fighting for your life.'

'But have I won it back yet? All the time I was telling my story, they were glaring at me, hating me.'

'He was part of their family, and they were grieving. I told you to expect that.'

'But they told me that they would get me someday.'

'People say things when they're angry or upset.'

She drained her glass, gulping it down, before holding it out. 'Well, not anymore. This is the new me.'

He topped her up and said, 'I'm glad to hear it, but what's brought it on?'

'I've been barricaded in. Everything I do is about seeing the threat coming. And I can't stop it, can't help myself. But I've had enough of it. I'm not hiding anymore.'

'That's what I've been trying to tell you all this time.'

'Sit next to me,' she said. When he didn't move, she added, 'I won't attack you.'

Dan moved to sit next to her. She looked up at him, her eyes glassy, large and green and doleful.

He looked away. He'd seen something in her eyes that he shouldn't.

She placed her head against his arm and spoke more softly. 'I should have listened to you.'

'We don't have to do this, just because you're drunk.'

'I'm not drunk.'

'You're more drunk than I am.'

She poked him in the arm and giggled. 'You need to live a little.'

When Dan turned towards her, she tried to stare into his eyes. Her gaze was soft, her pupils enlarged.

Dan stood up and went to the window. He couldn't let it go that way.

'What's brought this on?' he asked.

She put her head back. 'Mickey Ellis came to my apartment.'

'Mickey? How does he know where you live?'

'He said he worked it out from social media. A couple of pictures I'd posted.'

'What did he want?'

'I thought at first that he'd come to scare me. And he did, creeping around, pushing me into my apartment. But he had something to tell me about the case, and he's scared too, so it made me think about my life, about how I live it. I was telling him that he's got to do the right thing, how he can't let fear rule him, but look at me. Everything I do is about being scared. Knowing the escape routes, not being in small spaces where I can be trapped.'

'What did he say?'

'When Mary screamed, Mickey was in his room. He turned off his light to see what was going on.'

'Did he see anything?'

'Yeah, he did, and get this.' She took a long sip of the wine. 'Two people came out of that house a minute later.'

Dan was confused. 'Two?'

'That's what he said. Through the back yard and then up the alley. They must have just got around the corner when Carter rushed round.'

'Is he sure?'

'Seemed it. You see, he's not bad like me. Doesn't drink. He's a good boy for his mother. So everything is clear. He told me everything.' She put her glass down. 'Come sit down again.'

'No. I mean, not yet. I need to make a note of this, while you remember it.'

She stretched out and put her head back. 'Work, work, work.'

'Wait there. Let me get some paper.'

He rushed to the bathroom and splashed his face with water. He needed to wake himself up. Jayne might not remember as much in the morning so he needed to get it down. He used the toilet and went back into the living room.

He stopped and looked around. He couldn't believe it. She was gone.

He slumped into the chair and groaned. He'd got it wrong. All he'd wanted to hear about was the case. Jayne had wanted more. Now? She was in a huff with him and had taken off, knowing that she had information that he wanted.

He finished his wine and took the glass to the sink. He was about to turn off the lamp in the living room when he looked along the hallway. There was something on the floor. A boot outside his bedroom door. Next to it, a sock. A small white sock.

He walked slowly along the hallway, not sure what he'd find. The clothes weren't a sexy trail, but discarded as Jayne had taken them off. The light from the hallway was enough to provide a glimpse into his room.

Jayne was in his bed, the rest of her clothes on the floor in a crumpled heap. She was naked, the sheets pulled back, her breasts small and pink, her stomach taut, her body lithe and pale against the dark triangle of her hair, her head turned towards the doorway.

Dan leaned against the doorframe. If she'd intended to make her intentions clear to him, it had been spoiled when she'd fallen asleep. Her right hand hung loose over the edge of the bed and her breath was soft and regular.

He went to her and took her hand in his, light and warm, and moved it so that it was on her body. He covered her with the bedclothes and moved some strands of hair from her forehead. He watched her sleep for a few seconds before giving her a gentle kiss on her forehead and going back to the living room. He grabbed an old sleeping bag from a cupboard, knowing that he had a long night on the sofa ahead.

Her body was on his mind though as he turned off the light, but the reason for her visit came back to him. Mickey had disclosed something important to Jayne, but Dan had no idea whether she would remember it in the morning.

Thirty-one

Jayne winced as she tried to open her eyes, pain slicing through her forehead. Hungover again. She took a few deep breaths to calm the fast roll of her stomach, her face buried into her pillows.

Something was different. The pillow felt softer, the room brighter than normal. She turned her head and squinted, sun streaming through white vertical blinds. She wasn't at home.

Then it came back to her. She was in Dan's bed. She'd gone round the night before, after Mickey's visit. She put her face back into the pillow and let out a long moan. What had she done?

She had to clench her jaw at the acid rise of bile. She thought she was going to throw up, so she took more deep breaths, warm through the pillow. Her moan turned into a groan as images flashed into her head. Sitting next to Dan. Then her stumble towards the bedroom and the idea that she would tease him into bed by lying naked, just because it seemed like a good idea at the time. Yeah, subtle. Well done.

Perhaps she was wrong, maybe it was part-dream. She glanced down and lifted the sheet. No, she wasn't wrong. She was naked.

She turned over and covered her face with her hands. How could she face him now?

There was a tapping on the door before it was pushed open. Dan was in his work clothes: a blue striped shirt with plain blue tie and dark trousers. He looked fresh, his hair still wet from the shower.

She covered her face with the sheet. 'Go away.'

He laughed and put something down on the cupboard next to her. 'You need to get up. You never finished your story.'

She uncovered her face. There was a mug of tea next to the bed. 'I made a fool of myself.'

'Let's just say that it was an interesting end to a case conference.'

'Stop it, you're not helping.'

'I know, but sleeping on the sofa didn't help me much either.'

'You could have climbed in. I was in no fit state to jump on you.'

Dan backed out of the room and gave her one of those damn enigmatic smiles of his. She thumped the pillow in frustration. What did he mean? That he might have been the one doing the jumping? Or that he wasn't interested anyhow?

Then she remembered the story. The real reason why she'd gone round. Mickey.

Her stomach heaved as she stumbled out of bed. Her phone was on the floor, having fallen out of her jeans. It was flashing a blue light. A message. She didn't recognise the number but, when she read it, she knew who it was from. She whistled to herself. It had just got more interesting.

She pulled on her T-shirt, long enough to reach her legs, and shuffled into the living room. She ran her hand through her hair in an effort to straighten it, her mug of tea in the other.

Dan was looking out of his window when she went in. She felt a stab of guilt when she saw the sleeping bag on the sofa.

She stood next to him and cupped her mug in her hands. Her mouth was dry and she could taste the wine on her breath.

'Nice view,' she said, gasping as she took a drink. The surface of the canal glinted, so that it was almost looked like starbursts, with only the faint outline of a barge visible. 'Hurts my eyes though.'

'Finish your story.'

'Are you always this businesslike?'

'One of us has to be.'

'So we're an *us*?'

He raised an eyebrow before taking a drink, although Jayne thought she saw the faintest of smiles.

'You were telling me what Mickey saw. Two people came running out of the yard and up the alley. Is that right?'

'Oh yes, that. Where did I get up to?'

'To that point. Who were they? Did he see them? Did he know them?'

'He knew them all right. At least, he knew one of them.'

She took a drink. She enjoyed dragging it out.

'Jayne?'

'Lucy Ayres.'

'Lucy? The housemate? The person who found her, along with her boyfriend?'

'The one and the same.'

'But they didn't return until the morning. That's when they found her.'

'According to Mickey, they were there not long after the scream, running away.'

Dan stepped away from the window and put his mug down. He pulled on his lip. 'Lucy lied.'

'Or perhaps Mickey lied? You were all set to blame him before.'

'But does it matter? How does it help Carter?'

'It puts someone else at the scene, and might make someone else responsible. That's what you wanted. I thought you'd be happy.'

'You're forgetting one thing,' Dan said.

'Which is what?'

'The other person might be Carter, but he hasn't mentioned Lucy. What am I going to do? Get Mickey to call my client a liar?'

'I know something else too.'

'Tell me.'

'You remember the hotel where Shelley dined with Conrad? I flirted with a waiter to get him to find out about the third diner, and guess what: I got a text during the night.'

'Stop dragging it out.'

'The bill was paid by someone called Dominic Ayres.'

'A relative of Lucy's?'

'I'm guessing so.'

Dan turned to stare out of the window again, except Jayne didn't think he was really looking. His focus was more distant, as if he couldn't really see anything.

'We need to know more about him and Lucy,' he said eventually. 'If Dominic Ayres was with Shelley and Conrad, it was to do with the case. We need to know why, because whatever is going on, Shelley is staying quiet. '

Jayne put her mug down and walked towards the doorway. 'You see, sometimes the best stories are worth waiting for.'

'Where are you going?'

'I'm going to use your shower.' She smiled. 'You've seen me naked now, so I don't have to be embarrassed about asking you to help with the hard to reach places.'

'I've seen you naked before, remember.'

'When?'

'When you were waiting for your trial. I saw the real you, the vulnerable you, the scared you. The you that was in here,' and he patted his chest.

'I prefer it this way,' she said, before lifting the T-shirt over her head and throwing it at Dan. 'Just in case you change your mind.'

Dan laughed and threw a tea-towel at her.

As she left the room, she knew Dan's eyes were on her.

Thirty-two

It was mid-morning as Dan waited by the canal on a bench that gave a good view over the town. The scene ahead was spoiled by a supermarket, and some of the older buildings in the town centre had been cleared away to make a car park, but the town was slowly modernising itself. Some of the crumbling old mills were being developed into office spaces, and those that were cleared away created green, open spaces.

The canal was quiet. The towpath didn't attract walkers this far up and there weren't many boats; the canal had a long stretch without any locks to make queues, so the ones that were there just flowed past.

It was the solitude Dan needed. He'd had an hour to think things through and create some sort of order out of what he'd learned. Lucy Ayres running out of the yard. Dominic Ayres dining with Shelley, linked to Lucy. Sara Carter threatened. He tried to work out what it all meant, but his mind kept going back to Jayne from the night before. That would be a complication he didn't need, but the memory of the desire in her eyes, of what he felt within himself, was distracting him.

He needed the privacy for his meeting too. Not for himself, but for DI Murdoch, because this was a conversation he wanted to keep secret, and he guessed that she'd want the same.

He was drinking coffee from a foam cup as he waited, the steam warming his face whenever he lifted it, fighting back the crisp breeze blowing from the high hills. The day was bright but was struggling to get warm. His foot teased loose stones, kicking them into the water, enjoying the small splash.

There was a noise behind him, footsteps on concrete, small pants of exertion. When he looked round, it was Tracy Murdoch.

She glanced around as she got closer, as if she was scared of being seen. The police station wasn't far away, in a stone block just the other side of the supermarket.

She sat down next to him and put her hands in her trouser pockets. They both looked as if they'd got lost, sitting by the side of the canal in suits, like nervous lovers.

'So what is it that's so important?' she said.

'I'm coming to you because I trust you,' Dan said.

Tracy stared at Dan for a few seconds before she said, 'Beware of lawyers bearing compliments. Everything they say is meant as a trap.'

'No, I mean it. I've known you as a detective since I first started here, and do you know why I trust you? Because you fight hard but you fight fair. There are some coppers who'll play it straight, and some who'll do anything to win. You've never tried any silly tricks with me, like keeping stuff from me before we go into interview. Even yesterday, with those witnesses. You didn't like going along with it, but you did, because you knew it was the right thing to do, and that's why I'm here. Or rather, why I wanted you here.'

She flicked at some strands of hair that were blowing into her face. 'What do you want, Dan?'

'Your help.'

'What, in getting Robert Carter off? Is this why you've brought me here, to recruit me as some free-of-charge investigator?'

'No. In discovering the truth. That's what it's all about, isn't it, finding the truth?'

'The truth is that Robert Carter killed Mary. I'm sure of it. I've done my bit. We all have.'

'But what if I could persuade you of another truth?'

'In your world, there isn't another truth. Just confusion mocked up as doubt.'

'What turned you so cynical?'

'Dealing with lawyers.'

'I asked for that, I suppose,' Dan said. 'But what if I could show you an actual truth? Not doubt. No tricks. Just truth, but a different one to the truth you think you have?'

'You're talking in riddles and I've no time for this.'

Dan put his cup down. 'I came into some information this morning. I don't know what it means yet, but I'm going to look into it. I might need your help.'

'I'm really not sure about this.'

'But your job is to investigate, not take sides.'

'I know my job. How do I know this isn't part of a game, that you're making out like you're playing fair but really you're just wanting to use me?'

'You don't. But you know me. Don't confuse doing a good job with not being straight. If I'm a lawyer you don't trust, fine, that's my fault.'

Tracy turned away at that and fell silent.

They both stared out at the water for a few moments before she said, 'Most of us think you're okay.'

'Just okay?'

Tracy laughed. 'All right, more than that. We were talking about this just the other day, how the old guard has gone. We were wondering who we would use if we got into trouble. Go back ten or fifteen years and there were some good lawyers around. Crafty, shifty, but we would have all used them like a shot. Now? All the good ones have retired and none of the young ones fill you with confidence.'

'There's no money in it anymore.'

'But you chose it.'

'Because it's what I always wanted to do.'

'You chose right then, because your name was the one that came up. Most agreed that they'd use you.'

'So trust me on this then, that I'll be honest with you. I just don't think I can be open yet.'

Tracy nodded to herself. 'Okay, I'll play along. What do you want?'

'I might have to ask you to look into something for me, but if you do, I want you to forget I asked if it doesn't go anywhere. I don't want the Judge having a go at me because it looks like I'm trying a scattergun defence. This isn't on Carter's instructions and it's not fair if it rebounds on him. I've only met him once and he stormed out.'

'So why are you doing it if he hasn't asked you to?'

'Because my job is to do what's best for him, even if he doesn't realise it.'

'You're just fishing around.' She got to her feet. 'Don't take me for a mug.'

'No, I'm not, trust me. I can't disclose what I've found out, not yet, but I will, if it comes to something.'

'And if it does?'

'I'll see where it goes.'

'Dan, do you realise what you're asking?'

'Of course I do. I'm asking you to help me prepare my client's defence, if what I think turns out to be true. But, and this is the thing, I trust you to chase the truth. That's all I'm asking. The outcome of the case doesn't matter if it's the right one.'

'You're a defence lawyer. We have different views of that.'

'I'm talking about actual truth, not the way things are spun in a courtroom.'

Tracy stared at Dan, doubt in her eyes, until she said, 'If you can persuade me it might be true, I'll look into it.'

'And if I've got it wrong?'

'Then it stays between you and me. But you've got to give me a clue.'

Dan thought about that for a few moments before he said, 'Lucy Ayres. Got any doubts about her?'

'None. Decent young woman. Trainee lawyer. From a rich family.'

'Dominic Ayres?'

'Her father.' Tracy frowned. 'Are you going after her?'

'I don't know. Possibly. I just wanted to know whether there were any doubts about her.'

'None. You're wasting your time.'

'Okay, forget I said it, but if I find something out though, you'll check it out?'

'Only if it's worth doing.' She checked her watch, just to let him know she had to be somewhere other than with him.

'There is one other thing,' he said.

She sighed. 'Go on.'

'I need to speak to one of the housemates again. Alone.'

'Hey, come on.'

'I'll speak to her anyway, because I'll be able to find her, but I'd rather you knew.'

'Which one?'

'The one I spoke to after I finished with Lucy. Small, with glasses.'

'Beth Wilkins?'

'That's her.'

'I'm not giving you her number.'

'So give her mine. Tell her it's only her I'm talking to. No one else.'

'Why should that matter?'

'I just think it will.'

Tracy agreed and then went quickly down the steps that took her into the supermarket car park.

Dan watched her go before he turned back to the canal. He listened to the gentle lap of the water against the canal bank, better than the noise of traffic from the town below. The beep of a reversing lorry, the distant rattle of a train.

He had no idea whether he was wasting his time, or even whether Robert Carter would approve, but for the first time he felt like the case was getting somewhere. He had to move quickly though, because the trial was only twelve days away now.

When his thoughts went to the threats made to Sara Carter, and the way Shelley was rattled about something, he wondered something else: whether he was putting himself in danger.

Thirty-three

Jayne was in Dan's apartment, using his desktop PC to research Dominic Ayres. She needed to go home and get some fresh clothes, but she was enjoying the greater luxury of Dan's flat, with the view along the canal. She looked for Lucy first though. Whatever Dan wanted to know about Dominic Ayres, everything started with Lucy.

Lucy's profile from her law firm came up at the top of the search.

Jayne recalled her casual clothes from the police station. The media images showed her in a scarf and coat, her hair blown in the wind. Her professional profile was much more as Jayne expected, a picture of self-confidence. She was the newest member of the team and, standing in front of a bookcase filled with law books, she oozed arrogance and conceit and self-assuredness. Everything expected of a lawyer in one photograph.

Jayne went to the social media sites next, but the privacy settings were too high to let her browse properly. She could look at the profile pictures, but no more.

It was the search results further down that she found most interesting: the reports from the newspaper websites from around the time of Mary's murder.

Although much of the reporting was on what had happened to Mary, many had focused on Lucy and Peter's behaviour as they loitered near the scene. There was a picture of Lucy with

Peter, her arms around him, but it wasn't a picture of two grieving people looking for support. It was a photograph of a young
couple in love, smiling and kissing as if they were enjoying a
sunny afternoon in the park. Just behind them, the crime scene
tape was visible across the alley.

As she looked, Jayne knew she was right about seeing Peter
outside the police station the day before.

The comments below the articles slammed them, calling
them inappropriate. Jayne had thought the same at the time, but
if nothing else the images had kept the story in the media.

One of the later reports showed Lucy with her father, Dominic.
She smiled to herself. She'd found him, described as a successful
local businessman, standing with Lucy's mother in front of a large
house in the countryside, both sporting stern faces, going public
with his defence of his daughter, explaining how people react
differently to shocking situations. All the press had seen was their
daughter trying to put up a brave front.

As she kept searching, letting the coffee bring her round,
she found more news stories, except this time they were about
Dominic's business empire. Or, rather, his property empire.

The stories were mostly complimentary, portraying him as
someone who'd rescued part of the town.

According to the press reports, in the nineties huge swathes
of the town were derelict, with whole streets of terraced housing standing empty, people leaving the area for opportunities
elsewhere and the young house buyers preferring the shiny new
estates built on the sites of cleared away industry. They were
offered for sale at bargain prices and Dominic Ayres bought up
two streets.

He was the local hero, lauded for his enterprise, for saving part of the town that was going to be demolished. That's how he'd pitched it to the press, how he hated to see the heritage of the town lost to the bulldozers and was determined to regenerate the area.

He made the houses habitable and offered them out for rent, and soon the streets were full again, no longer the long lines of steel plates over windows and ripped out piping.

Time hadn't been kind to the regeneration and Jayne knew the part of the town they were talking about. It was bleak and barren, with isolated strips of housing facing each other over open patches of rubble and land where some streets had been knocked down. She'd served court papers around there and it had been scary, groups of kids circling her as she tried to find the right house. The doors were plywood sheets and some of the windows were broken.

As she kept on looking, she found a source for more information: a local residents action group was featured in the local paper, complaining about the condition of the properties. The picture showed three women in front of a pebble-dashed terraced house with graffiti daubed next to the window, along with a name. Alison Reed.

She had somewhere to start.

Then Jayne remembered the areas of law practised by Lucy, spelled out on the firm's website. Civil litigation and landlord and tenant disputes, acting for the landlords.

Jayne wasn't sure how relevant it would turn out to be, but it was important to know your adversaries.

Thirty-four

Dan rang the doorbell and stepped back.

DI Murdoch had texted him the number of the witness, Beth Wilkins, and he'd squeezed in a phone call between his court cases; his daily grind didn't let up just because Carter had come along. Beth had been reluctant at first but eventually agreed to speak to him, provided that it was at her parents' house.

It was on a new estate aimed at the high end of the market. Large detached houses sat back from a road that curved gently. There were no trees to darken the street or block the view of the four-by-fours and sports cars on the drive, the houses double-fronted, many with white pillars and leaded windows and driveways wide enough to hold three cars.

It was missing some life though. There were no pedestrians; no young couples with prams or people walking dogs, or any of the things that make a community. It was too far out from everywhere, slotted on to what was once a field at the end of a road that didn't go anywhere. The only noise was the gentle fizz from the overhead pylons that cut through the estate and stretched into the distance.

He turned round as the door opened. Beth Wilkins. Small and mousy, plain-looking, with short hair and glasses. She was dressed in a plain black jumper and leggings, as if she spent her life trying not to be noticed.

She seemed nervous but brighter than the day before, when Dan had spoken with her at the police station. There, she'd been sullen and withdrawn. That was the reason Dan wanted to speak to her. He didn't want to hear from anyone keen to tell a story. He wanted the stories that people weren't keen on telling.

'Thank you for seeing me,' he said.

'Come through.' She set off down the hallway, to a brightly-lit kitchen at the back.

Dan almost had to squint as he went in. The sun streamed through large windows and glinted off bright white cupboards and steel utensils hanging from a rack. Beth carried on through to a conservatory that gave him a view over a long garden, with lush lawns broken by flowerbeds, a birdbath in the middle.

She sat down but didn't offer Dan a drink. Instead, she sat forward, her hands on her knees, expectant, almost.

'What can I do for you?' she asked. 'The trial is just over a week away, so this feels a little weird. I didn't know it worked like this.'

'It doesn't normally, but I've only just got the case so I need to move quickly.' He pulled out a voice recorder. 'Are you all right with me recording this?' When she looked surprised, he added, 'It's to protect both of us, so no one can twist what was said here.'

'Good, yes, I'm glad, because that's what I'm worried about, that I'll get to court and everything I say will get twisted. Lucy's a trainee lawyer and, boy, the things she's told me . . .'

'Don't worry about court. It's just answering questions, so all you have to do is be honest. It's the answers that are important, not the questions.'

'I wasn't expecting counselling from the defence.'

'I just want to follow on from when we last spoke.'

'I didn't say much.'

'No, you didn't, which is why I wanted to speak to you again.' He clicked on the voice recorder and set it down on the table. 'You were good friends with Mary, so your statement said.'

Beth stared at the red light on the recorder for a few moments before she said, 'We were friends all through school and then university. Not best friends, but part of the same group. I got a room at the house and, when another room came free, I told Mary about it. She moved in.'

'What about Lucy?'

Beth scowled. 'Friend of a friend. We used to share with another trainee lawyer, but she moved in with her boyfriend. We needed someone quickly because we're all on low wages, and the girl who left suggested Lucy.'

'What did you know about her?'

'She was just starting her training contract but didn't want to go back to her parents. Like all of us, she'd gone away to university, so going home was like going backwards.'

'What did you think of Lucy, when she first moved in?'

Beth frowned. 'Everything was fine at first. Lucy is one of those people who's just a little too much, do you know what I mean? Like, everything has to be about her, and it was easy to get swept along at first. She'd drag us out for nights out, or organise a big girlie night in, music and wine, but sometimes we just wanted a quiet night. The thing is, we were old friends, so we knew each others' rhythms. For Lucy, all that mattered was Lucy.'

'What about Mary? Lucy described her as a good friend.'

Beth's jaw clenched again. 'Anything but. Yes, it was fine at first, but Lucy is demanding, needs attention, and Mary just wasn't into that.'

'What do you mean?'

'Lots of examples. If we had a night in, even if it was just sitting around and watching TV, Lucy would do things to make herself the centre of attention, like talking about her father's money, bragging almost, or trying to start conversations about sex. We were all girls together, so we'd talk about stuff like that, but for her it was as if it was about all the numbers, like how many she could get. If we went for a drink, she wasn't happy unless some guy was drooling over her.'

'I thought she had a boyfriend.'

'If you mean Peter, she'd only been seeing him for a couple of weeks before Mary died, not that it would have stopped her. Even sex was an attention-grabber.'

'What do you mean?'

'Volume,' Beth said. She leaned forward and spoke in hushed tones, even though they were alone in the house. 'We were all single women, so we had guys sleeping over sometimes, but who wants their friends to hear you with a man? Lucy? She didn't care. It was almost as if she wanted us to hear her, so we'd know that no one has better sex than her. That's what she was like; everything was about impressing people. So after Mary died, her statement had to be all about how Mary was her best friend and no one felt grief like her. Mary's murder became all about Lucy, and how awful it was for her to find her.'

'And that wasn't true?'

Beth shook her head. 'She was starting to grate on Mary. You see, Mary was no prude, but she didn't like the way Lucy flaunted herself. She was too open about things, as if she didn't care who could see her. Lucy was lazy too, never helped out with the housework. I just wanted an easy life but Mary, well, it got to her in the end. They argued a lot. Lucy used to call Mary an uptight bitch, or a frigid little princess. That was her favourite one. Really spat it out when she said it.'

Beth paused and frowned. 'Why the interest in Lucy? Is this what this is all about, that you're going to deflect attention on to Lucy?'

'Just curious.'

'It sounds more than that. I'm not telling you this just so you can spin some lies to get Robert Carter off. I didn't like Lucy, still don't, but the police must have some good evidence against him, or else he wouldn't have been charged.'

'I'm just trying to find out more about what happened. Like I said, I've only just got the case, so it's all new to me. Tell me how Lucy responded to Mary being murdered.'

Beth paused, as if she was deciding whether to answer. Eventually, she said, 'Over the top, just like her, as if she had to grieve the most. I've lost a lifelong friend and Lucy's behaving like she and Mary were practically in love, especially when the cameras were there, because then it was really all about the display, cuddling Peter, as if Lucy would fall apart without him. That was the worst part of it. It was as if Mary's real friends were pushed into second place. In the end, however, I realised that it wasn't a competition.'

'Why didn't you put any of this into your statement?'

'Why did it matter? I told the police about Mary, and Robert Carter, not Lucy. And I didn't know then how she was going to behave.'

'What do you mean?'

'Acting like she's the real victim. For finding her, for losing her. There's only one victim in this, and that's Mary, but not in Lucy's world.'

Dan clicked off his voice recorder. 'Thank you.'

'Why? I haven't done anything.'

'You've just given me a clearer picture.'

Once he got outside and back into his car, Dan stared forward, deep in thought. There was something going on with Lucy, and if Mickey was right, she'd lied to the police.

The only question was why no one was prepared to talk about it.

Thirty-five

After all the research, it was time to seek out Lucy, which took Jayne to Manchester.

South of Highford, Manchester was like a whole different country. Highford was an enclosed little world nestled in the hills, sheltered from everywhere, the sort of place you stumbled across if you were lost, rather than seeking it out. Manchester was the industrial north in its pomp and swagger and snarl. Its history was visible in the businesses built into the old redbrick railway arches, and its future in the glass blocks and new open spaces.

Lucy worked in a law office on Deansgate, on the third floor of a grimy and outdated concrete building, with views along spluttering lines of traffic and next to the neo-Gothic splendour of the John Ryland Library, its Cumbrian sandstone dark against the shiny new architecture that surrounded it.

Jayne had found a bench further along Deansgate that gave her a view of the front entrance of Lucy's building. She was sure Lucy would leave the office for her lunch. The area around it was busy and vibrant, aimed at people like Lucy, the young professional, with designer shops and pubs and bars of wood and chrome. Jayne didn't fit in, with her chainstore jeans, ratty pumps, her baseball cap and sunglasses. They made her look conspicuous, but she and Lucy had met at the police station so Jayne needed to look different.

It was nearly an hour before Lucy appeared, making Jayne edgier with every passing minute. Jayne almost missed her as she bustled out of the front door, her head down, her fingers flitting over the screen of her phone, but once seen, she was hard to miss. She was elegant, in a tight skirt and heels, her legs toned, her stride confident. Jayne watched her go past and then slotted herself into a cluster of people by a traffic crossing.

Men glanced at Lucy. She had that mix of elegance and haughtiness that men seem to like. Some exchanged raised eyebrows with their companions after she'd gone past. Others saw her and then looked down quickly. Lucy didn't notice. Or perhaps she did and just expected it.

Lucy was heading for Crown Square, the area in front of the Crown Court that had been transformed from an open concrete square to an area buzzing with bars and shops.

Jayne threaded her way through the crowd as she tried to keep up, scared of losing her in the busy streets. At first, Jayne thought Lucy was heading for one of the high-end bars, but she kept on going past all the doorways and headed straight for a man loitering near the grass bank in front of the Court. He looked up as Lucy got close. As she threw her arms around him and kissed him, he didn't reciprocate. Instead, he pushed her away by putting his hands on her hips and said something to her, his body language animated.

Jayne recognised him from outside the police station, and from her internet searches earlier that day. It was Peter Wilde, Lucy's boyfriend. Tatty leather jacket, a hooded top underneath, torn jeans and stubble that added to his rough charm, his hair unkempt and to his collar, dark and greasy-looking. If he had a job, he looked like he was taking time off.

Things seemed tense between them. Peter looked around, anxious, and whispered something to Lucy. He indicated with a tilt of his head that Lucy should follow him and set off walking.

They headed away from the square and turned into one of the side streets, towards a coffee shop that traded on not being one of the chains but did its best to replicate one. It was dark inside, the walls exposed brickwork, with an old bike fastened to the wall.

Jayne tried to get a good view through the open doorway as Peter went to the counter and Lucy found a table in the darkest corner. She waited outside until Peter took over two coffees and a sandwich. She pondered whether she should go in, but she wanted to know how they were with each other. Quiet and relaxed, or nervous and edgy? Once they were both settled in, Jayne went inside and ordered the smallest coffee they had before grabbing a seat by the window.

She pretended to text and held the screen in their direction, took a few pictures to show Dan later. She put her phone away and faked gazing out of the window. Lucy and Peter were deep in conversation, huddled over, with Lucy pushing her sandwich away as he spoke.

Jayne made a show of checking her watch every few minutes, as if she were waiting for someone, but kept her gaze towards the front, relying on the reflection in the window to see what was going on. Lucy was sitting back but looking away. Peter's hands were gesturing dramatically, as if making a point, but Lucy didn't seem interested.

Jayne turned to get a better look, but as soon as she did, Lucy stared at her, before leaning in to Peter and whispering something.

She'd been spotted. She cursed herself. That wasn't in the plan.

There was movement in her peripheral vision. They were leaving.

Annoyed with herself, she turned and watched them as they left the café. Lucy just stared straight ahead, walking quickly. Peter paused by the door and looked straight at Jayne, his glare direct and angry.

As they both split up outside, Jayne thought about which one of them to follow. She'd been spotted, but that didn't mean there wasn't still value in pursuing them, because Lucy and Peter will behave differently, knowing that she was watching. That could still reveal something.

It was an easy choice to make. Lucy had walked out, cool and focused, whereas Peter had given himself away. Follow the one showing emotion, she thought, because he'll react the most.

She left the café. It was time to be visible and to see what that produced.

Thirty-six

Dan waited outside Shelley's cottage as he stared at the wrecked car on the gravel patch by the side door. He'd called her a few minutes before and she hadn't sounded pleased at the idea of another visit from him.

It took a few minutes for her to get to the door. When she opened it, there were rings under her eyes and she looked exhausted. The stitched scar stood prouder than when he'd seen it the day before, the skin around it inflamed.

She didn't say anything. Just turned around and hobbled back into the cottage, leaving the door open as the only hint that Dan should follow her. When she went into the living room, she slumped into a chair by the unlit fire.

Dan sat opposite, leaning forward, trying to assess her mood.

'You don't have to keep checking on me,' she said.

'Don't be like this.'

'Like what?'

'Pushing me away. I know you're unhappy, because you're hurt and scarred and your car is trashed, but you need your friends.'

'I've got Mark.'

'You need more than Mark.'

'Why?'

'Because I get you.' He held up his hand as her eyes narrowed. 'I know Mark knows you better than I do, but he doesn't know the lawyer side of you, perhaps doesn't understand that side of you.'

'Lawyers are nothing special.'

'No, but how many other jobs involve keeping dangerous people on the streets and are still regarded as a noble profession? How often has Mark driven to some remote police station at two in the morning because someone has been caught burgling a lonely pensioner's house? How often has Mark been asked how he can sleep at night? I know the answer: never. And this is something we've chosen to do.'

Shelley put her head back and blinked quickly, tears flicking on to her eyelashes. 'We've been friends a long time, good friends,' and then a teary smile. 'I wanted more, once.'

Dan returned the smile. 'I know.'

'Hey, Mr Ego, how did you know?'

'Just from how you behaved, at times. A look you gave me.'

'And why didn't you act on it? Was I that ugly?'

'Just the opposite, you were gorgeous,' he said, his voice soft. When she raised an eyebrow, he laughed and added, 'Still are. It would have spoilt things though, because we were such good friends, and then Mark came along and he's right for you.'

'Yes, he is.'

'But we're defence lawyers. We're supposed to stick together.'

'Be honest with me about one thing, Dan: would you be here right now if you didn't have the Carter case?'

Dan didn't answer. She was right, and they both knew it.

'The lawyers of this town will do nothing for me,' she said. 'I'm just more competition out of the way, one more lawyer no longer fighting for partnership.' She slammed her crutch on the chair arm, making dust fly up. 'I fought hard for that. Damn hard. I wanted to make a difference.' She wiped her eyes. 'That sounds so stupid now.'

'Why are you out of the way?'

'Because of that damn case. Robert Carter.'

'I don't understand. Have you still got a job?'

'I'm not sure I want one anymore.'

'Fight for it, Shelley.'

'I've always fought for it, don't you get it? It was different for me. I wasn't naturally academic. I had to work hard, revise through the night, fight back my panic. At the same time, I had to watch all those who could drift and drink through the year and then turn up for the exams. Bully for them, except it was the same in my job. Mark's always called me a stress head, because I brought work home with me and worried about getting things wrong, whilst others just breezed through. I envy people like them. Like you.'

'What do you mean, people like me?'

'Those who just have it in them. The fight, the eye for the detail, you've got it all in there,' and she tapped the side of her head. 'That's why I wanted the case to go to you.'

'You're good at what you do too. We all have different skills. Some can just bullshit their way through a mitigation speech, but they never get the good cases. Others – you're like this – are about the graft, the commitment. So what if you have to work a little harder, become a little more obsessive? That's your skill, that's what you bring. Stick with it.'

'Thank you,' she said, some of her anger gone.

'But why should the Robert Carter case cost you your job?'

Shelley didn't answer.

'What are you scared of, Shelley?'

She clenched her jaw. 'Who says I'm scared?'

'I do. I can see it in you. Who is it? Conrad? Are you scared of him? Change your job and he won't matter.'

'Conrad is a fool.'

'What about Dominic Ayres, Lucy's father?'

Shelley's mouth dropped open. 'Don't go there. You don't know who you're messing with.'

'And yet you still did the right thing in passing the file to me.'

'No, seriously Dan, back off from there.'

'That's not what you want me to do, though. That's why you gave me the file, because you had the choice of doing as you were told and hiding behind Carter's instructions, but instead you gave it to me because you knew I'd look.' When she didn't answer, he asked, 'Who do I need to be careful of?'

'Everyone.' Shelley leaned forward. 'What is Robert Carter saying to you? Is he sticking with his story?'

'It seems that way.'

'So there's nothing you can do. Play it his way, if that's how he wants it.'

'And if it's not how I want it?'

'Come on, Dan, you know that isn't how it works.'

'But what if I can persuade him to do it my way?'

'Which is?'

'That he wasn't alone with Mary. Lucy was there too. That changes everything.'

Shelley sat back and tapped the floor with her crutch. 'You think that?'

'That's what I've been told.'

She nodded to herself. 'Who have you spoken to?'

'A witness who saw her there.' Dan hadn't seen any mention of Mickey in the file, so he didn't want to give up his name.

'And Henry?'

Dan almost faltered, his mind going quickly through what he'd read, whether the name meant anything. Nothing came up, but that didn't mean it wasn't in the file somewhere. One of the first tricks to learn as a lawyer was not to react when you get an unexpected answer. 'Yes,' he said, lying, to see where it took the conversation.

'Are you going to use him?'

'I haven't decided yet.'

'Well, good luck with that. Just make sure you get him to court in the morning. He'll have had a few cans by then anyway, but at least he'll still make some sense.'

'If you're not going to work with Conrad anymore, why don't you work with me on this case?'

'No. I don't want to see that file again. I'm sorry for what happened to Mary, but there's nothing I can do to bring her back, and this way her family will get closure, because someone will go to prison for the rest of their life. I'm not risking anything to alter that. Will you?'

'I'll do the right thing, whatever that is.'

Shelley sighed. 'Yeah, that's what worries me.'

Thirty-seven

Jayne followed Peter as he rushed away from the cafe, weaving through the crowds, not giving way to anyone. He looked back a couple of times but Jayne was trying to blend into groups of people as she walked, always trying to be behind someone taller than her. The occasional sidestep and a glance ahead kept him in view.

He was tall, which made him easier to follow, his hair visible above the crowd. Jayne put her hands into her pockets and tried to make herself smaller by hunching her shoulders, although she guessed she was probably making herself look more suspicious. Peter walked past some of the pubs, but thankfully didn't go inside.

He turned down a side street and Jayne trotted to keep up, so that she could see if he went into a nearby building. As she peered around the corner, he disappeared into an alleyway that ran between two main streets.

Jayne cursed before she jogged across the road, worried about losing him.

As she turned in, she couldn't see Peter ahead. He must have run through, knowing that he was being followed, or else ducked into the Irish bar further up, waiting for her to go past.

The light dimmed as she walked along. The sun shone at the other end and cars streamed past, along with shoppers from a nearby department store, but the alley was deserted. She'd lost the security of the crowd.

She thought about ducking back, accepting that he'd got away, but she didn't want to tell Dan that.

She walked slowly. The streets around had turned into a hum of distant traffic. A drain outlet dripped water into a puddle. The clangs and shouts of a kitchen at work echoed between the buildings.

As she passed a doorway, someone moved towards her. A hand gripped her collar and dragged her into the shadows. She gasped as she was slammed into a steel door, her head banging on the metal. Her sunglasses fell to the floor. The smell of stale piss filled her nostrils and the shape of a man blocked the view ahead as a hand went round her throat, pinning her against the door.

'What are you doing?' the man said, his teeth bared, stale coffee on his breath.

Jayne pushed back, kicking out, her foot landing feebly against his leg. She was pushed against the door again, his hand tighter. She tried to shout out but the hand around her throat choked off her voice.

He put his mouth to her ear and hissed, 'If you promise not to scream or run, I'll let go.' He shook her. 'But you've got to talk.'

Jayne struggled some more, but he was strong. She nodded and then sucked in huge breaths as his grip relaxed, bent over as she caught her breath.

As he stepped back, the light from the pub caught his face. It was Peter.

'I know who you are,' he said, bending towards her so he could speak quietly, his voice filled with anger. 'You're working for Robert Carter, but why are you following us?'

'I'm an investigator.' She was panting hard, her hand rubbing her throat. 'It's what I do.'

'But what are we to do with anything? This is witness intimidation.'

She stood straight. 'Why did you lie about being with Lucy?'

'I didn't.'

'She was there. She was seen leaving the house just after Mary screamed. We can prove it. What you said in your statement can't be true.'

He moved towards Jayne again but she was expecting him this time. She pushed his arm away and stepped to one side, the alleyway behind her, with space to run. 'If you grab me again, I'll scream. Watch that pub empty and see what happens when they see a woman being attacked in an alleyway.'

Peter stepped back and put his hands out. 'Okay, okay, calm down. I just want you to leave us alone.'

'And you think this will achieve it?'

'Lucy didn't do it. She was at my place, with me, all night. Let me warn you though: if you try to spread blame our way, or accuse me of anything, I'll come after you.'

'It looks like we've got an impasse here.'

'What do you mean?'

'I'm going to carry on investigating this case, and I'll go where the investigation takes me. You don't scare me.'

Peter glared at Jayne for a few seconds. 'You don't know who you're taking on.'

'Maybe. But that won't stop me.' She smiled when she said, 'Are you going to leave now, or do I start screaming?'

Peter stared at her for a few moments longer, before turning and running along the alleyway. Jayne stayed where she was until he disappeared into the shoppers and then leant back against the door. She held out her hand. It was trembling.

The case was getting dangerous. As sweat trickled down her forehead, she found herself laughing. For the first time since she'd moved to Highford, after months of serving court papers, she felt alive.

Thirty-eight

Dan rushed into his office. Margaret looked up, surprised, a sandwich in her hand.

'What is it?' she shouted, her mouth full of food.

He was breathing hard from exertion. 'Since we've taken over the Carter file, has anyone called Henry tried to ring me, or been to the office?'

'No, nothing like that.' The words came out muffled. 'Why, are you expecting a call?'

'I don't know, but if an old drunk comes looking for me, don't send him away.'

'Dan, there are always old drunks looking for you. It's your client base.'

'This one is called Henry.'

She waved her sandwich to tell him that she understood.

Dan went up to his room and lifted the box that contained the files on to his desk. He took out those that were filled with the witness statements and other schedules, the meat of the case, and put them to one side. He hadn't paid much attention to the correspondence file, a jumbled collection of letters and notes attached to a clip.

He'd skimmed them before, looking for any evidence of a change of instructions, because Shelley was obliged to write to Carter after every visit or phone call. Some of the letters were just requirements of the job, the lengthy letters setting out how the firm works and how the costs are paid, running to around five pages, none of them ever read. Now, he was looking for something specific.

His hands flicked through the pages, his eyes scanning quickly, looking for any reference to a Henry.

He found it in the middle. On a scrap of paper, wedged between two thick letters.

Henry Oates called in about Robert Carter. Drunk, as usual. Told him to come back but he said it was urgent. Had information.

He pulled out his phone and called Shelley. When she answered, he lied. 'Would you believe it, but I missed Henry when I was at yours. Where does he hang out?'

'By the flower beds at the end of the precinct.'

He thanked her and hung up.

As he rushed through the reception area again, Margaret shouted, 'Where are you going now?' When he turned, she added, 'In case someone asks. One of your existing clients, for instance.'

'Just for a walk in the sun.'

'Don't obsess, Dan.'

He gave her a wave as he went.

Just as he got to his car, he noticed someone on the opposite side of the street, looking up at the office. A young woman with a pushchair. As Dan watched, she turned towards him and looked as if she was about to shout something. He paused for a moment and wondered what she wanted, but decided to keep going. He had to find Henry Oates.

The town centre was at the bottom of a small hill, a pedestrianised strip that was once the hub of a thriving town. The town planners had pulled down the old buildings in the sixties and replaced them with featureless brick and glass, now worn out and faded. The road had been paved over and dotted with trees and raised flowerbeds, so that the street never looked full anymore, despite the efforts of the coffee chains at creating a Parisian effect by putting chairs and bistro tables outside.

Dan missed how the town used to be sometimes, when it seemed to work as one, with everyone taking the same fortnight off work and the working week was about hard graft in the mills, followed by long weekends of football and booze. Things had changed. The smoke had gone from the air and people worked in jobs that were less likely to kill them, but the town seemed to have less purpose, nothing to bond people together other than shared geography. A walk along the precinct involved passing too many people who seemed to have nothing to do apart from smoke and exchange vacant stares.

There was a group of drunks ahead. They were easy to spot: their clothes were dirty and dishevelled, their faces flushed, with one man standing and talking animatedly, making a point that would make no sense to anyone else. The others in the group nodded sagely.

'Henry?' Dan said, as he got close, making them all turn round.

The man standing narrowed his eyes as he tried to focus. He looked at someone facing him on a bench. 'Henry, he wants you.'

The man turned to Dan before standing, wobbling slightly. Dan recognised him as a court regular, one of those who view it as an interruption, nothing more. He was holding a green bottle half-filled with something that Dan couldn't imagine ever wanting to taste. He passed it to the woman next to him, who raised it in salute.

'Yeah, that's me.' He was squinting as he spoke, leaning to one side, his body not attuned to the day.

'I need a word. Shelley Greenwood sent me.'

There was a moment of confusion before he turned to the others and said, 'My brief,' and shuffled away from the group.

Dan sat on a bench further along, scattering pigeons. Henry sat next to him. He smelled of smoke and sweat. His fingertips were stained brown, with the cuffs on his jumper ragged, loose threads hanging down.

Dan reached into a bag, he'd stopped at a shop, and pulled out a four-pack of strong beer. Henry's eyes brightened when he saw the gold cans. He reached for them but Dan pulled them away. 'Not yet. You've got to talk to me first.'

Henry's tongue darted to his lip as he glanced back to his friends. Dan knew that Henry's life was just about getting through another day, hour-by-hour, drink-by-drink.

'Don't do this to me,' Henry said.

'Do you want the beer or not?'

'Okay, I'll talk,' and he snatched the can from Dan. The snap of the drink being opened was followed by thirsty gulps. His lips glistened as he took the can away from his mouth.

'Tell me what you know,' Dan said.

Henry belched. Dan winced. The stench was old booze and decay.

'About what?'

'You know about what. The woman who died.'

'I don't know anything about that.'

'You do.'

Henry shook his head and took another long gulp, worried that Dan was going to snatch it away from him.

'You didn't ask me which woman,' Dan said, and leaned closer. 'You know who I'm talking about. You spoke to Shelley and told her something. I want to know what it was.'

Henry looked up to the sky and tapped a fast rhythm with his foot. 'That was in confidence, man.'

'So is this. I've taken over from Shelley.'

Henry pointed at Dan. 'I know you. I've seen you around the courts.' His finger wagged although he swayed. 'I used you once, after a lock-up. You're all right.'

'So talk to me.'

'I saw him.'

'Who?'

'The guy the police locked up. I saw him with a woman.'

'When?'

'The night she died. I remember because I saw it on the news the next day. I'd been hanging out all day and was sitting on a bench near the swings. They walked through.'

'They?'

'Both of them. The woman who died and the bloke who killed her.'

'Why did you remember it?'

'Because they talked to me.' He scratched his head. 'No, more than talked. He was joking with me, like, taking the piss, but her? She told him off. Can't blame him though. Look at me. So I was lying down and he called me sleeping beauty and went to take my bottle away, but she said no, give it back. I remember the woman he was with. Very nice. Pretty. He was panting like a dog.'

'How did they seem together?'

Henry grinned, not much more than a row of brown stumps. 'Like they couldn't wait to get home. She told him off, and he said he was sorry, but they were cuddling and kissing, like they'd just had a great night.'

Dan tried to hide his surprise. This was something new. Not Carter as a pest, or even Carter as a friendly chaperone, but Carter and Mary as more than that.

'Are you sure about this?'

'Damn right. When I saw them on the news, I said how could it be that it went so bad because they were all, well, you know, loved up and that.'

Dan tried to think it through, how it fitted, his instinct telling him that it was something important but his mind not yet able to work it out.

'Is that it? Do you want more, or are you done?' Henry looked at the cans of beer as he said it.

Dan pushed them towards him but kept a right grip. 'Is there more?'

'I've told you what I told the plod.'

'The police? Why do you say that?'

'Because I told some copper about it, except he looked down at me like I was nothing. That's why I told Shelley. I was doing the right thing.'

'Who did you tell in the police?'

Henry shrugged. 'I don't know his name, but he was walking through town and I recognised him as plod. We'd been talking about it,' and he waved his drink towards the other drinkers. 'They said I should speak to him, so I did, but he wasn't interested.'

'Okay, thank you,' Dan said, and let go of the cans.

Henry wouldn't be much use as a witness, he would come across as unreliable, but what was important was that he'd told the police and it had been ignored. That gave him an argument to present to the jury that they weren't getting the full picture.

Sometimes, a defence was about nothing more than blurring the clear lines. Henry Oates might have given him something he could use.

Thirty-nine

Murdoch was finishing her lunch, some noodle concoction in a plastic pot washed down with coffee, when the phone rang.

She thought about not answering, her hand going to the packet of cigarettes by her cup, her eyes going to the window, but she knew she couldn't avoid it.

'Hello, DI Murdoch.'

'Tracy, it's Dan Grant.'

She suppressed a groan. 'What now?'

'Henry Oates.'

She paused and wondered why the name sounded familiar, but nothing came back to her. 'What are you talking about?'

'Why did you keep him secret?'

'Dan, you're talking in riddles, and I need a cigarette more than I need this conversation.'

'He's one of the town centre drinkers. He saw Mary when she was walking home but I haven't seen any mention of it anywhere. Not in any statement. Not on the unused schedule.'

Town centre drinker. That's why his name was familiar. Murdoch had done her town centre stint, chasing shoplifters and moving on the boozers. Her mind flashed back through all the statements they'd taken, all the snippets of information, the phone calls that turned out to be not much at all. 'He won't be on the police file if he hasn't spoken to us. I can't disclose what I don't have.'

'He tells it differently. He said he spoke to the police and no one was interested.'

Murdoch rubbed her brow with her fingers. 'Does it matter? If he's just some town centre drunk, we're not going to use him, and neither are you.'

'That's not the point, and you know it. There's a witness who saw something and he contacted you. Now, one of two things are correct: either someone didn't make a note of it, which will just sound inept in front of the jury . . .'

'Hang on, Dan.'

'Or else you've hidden the information,' Dan continued, oblivious. 'Which makes you look even worse.'

Murdoch took a deep breath. 'I'll call you back,' she said, and slammed the phone down.

She stood up, the chair rocking backwards, her hands on her hips, her jacket splayed. 'Everyone, this way.' The typing and shuffling of papers stopped as everyone looked towards her. 'The Robert Carter case. Does the name Henry Oates ring any bells?'

There were some furrowed brows, until someone said, 'One of the losers who hangs around the shops?'

'That's him.'

'Locked him up a few times, just minor stuff. Pissing in doorways, stealing, that kind of thing.'

'Has anyone spoken to him about the Mary Kendricks murder?' There was silence as Murdoch looked around the room. 'Come on, anyone? If I find out that someone here isn't speaking up, there'll be consequences.'

A detective at the front of the room coughed. 'He spoke to me,' he said, his voice quiet and hoarse.

Murdoch turned to him. DC Edwards. Old-school, a coppers' copper who still missed cracking heads in the weekend van, with a nose that spoke of too many rugby games, his neck in a roll over a shirt collar that was too tight.

'When?'

'A couple of months ago now, I can't remember properly.' The redness that had crept into his face spread over his scalp, shaved and buffed to a shine.

'But you made a note of it, right?'

A pause, and then, 'Well, no.'

Murdoch closed her eyes for a moment and took a deep breath through her nose. When she opened them again, she said, 'Don't explain it to me. Explain it to Dan Grant.'

No one spoke as she stormed out of the office. She really needed a cigarette.

Forty

Dan was in a small square, overlooked by shops that populated the less wealthy end of town, as the chainstores faded away towards the covered market. Cobblers, drycleaners, shops selling used video games. He dodged prams and people strolling in their lunch hour. He saw lawyers he knew, some detectives, but he turned away. He had to think. He tapped his phone against his lip.

He had a problem with Henry's story. If he'd told the police the same thing he'd told him, they would have been interested. Murdoch didn't sound like she'd heard anything, and she was right, Henry wouldn't be a great witness. But you can't choose a witness. And what if Henry was right? If the police hadn't been interested, why not? His story put Carter with the victim. Although Carter had always admitted being with Mary, there should still be some record of what Henry had said.

And why hadn't Shelley been more interested? Henry helped rebut the police account that Carter was some kind of unwelcome stalker. Yes, Shelley knew about it, but it was more of an aside than anything else. Despite how bad a witness Henry would be, Dan had found him easily. Was there something else? Had Henry missed something out?

Most lawyers concentrate on the inconsistencies, wedge open any cracks in the prosecution case and give the jury something to focus on. Dan had a different instinct: explore the gaps, look for the things that aren't said. Inconsistencies are good, but the real gems are the things that the police choose not to highlight, because jurors won't convict if they think they're not getting the full story. When taking a witness statement, the police don't always write everything down, because they can focus too much on building a case. Investigations are geared towards proving what the police think they know as the truth. Dan tried to work out what the evidence didn't say, rather than what it did.

He called Jayne, to see if she'd found out anything.

'How are you getting on?' he said, as she answered.

'I was caught and warned off.'

'Who by?'

'Peter, the boyfriend. The bastard had me gripped round the neck.'

'A violent type?'

'He told me I didn't know who I was messing with.'

'Who did he mean?'

'He didn't say.'

'Are you wanting to back off?'

'I don't back off. I just want to know what to do next.'

'Where are you?'

'Just got back to Highford. Where do you want me to go?'

'Look more into Dominic Ayres, see what you can find out.'

'Will do. And you?'

'I've just got a lead, some old drunk who saw Carter and Mary together. We'll talk later,' and he clicked off the phone.

He had to go back to Shelley.

The journey didn't take him long, just a short drive to her village. When he pulled on to her street, she was leaving her house, trying to control her dog, desperate for exercise, as she used her crutch.

Dan rushed towards her, slamming the car door. 'I've just spoken to Henry.'

'Back again,' she said, weariness in her voice. 'For once in your life, Dan, think about something other than the case.'

'What do you mean?'

'Just forget about Robert Carter, like I've said. I shouldn't have transferred it.' She tapped her crutch on the floor. 'My body feels beaten up and I've probably lost my job. Right now, I don't want to talk about it.'

Dan held up his hand. 'Sorry. I get focused on things, I suppose. You know how I am.'

'Yeah, which is the only reason I'm forgiving you.'

'Which way are you heading?'

'To the park. I need to get out, and this fella,' and she waved the lead over the dog's nose, making him turn in wild circles, 'doesn't care if I'm injured or not. He needs to run. Walk with me.'

'Yes, I'd like that.'

'Progress will be slow.'

'I wasn't expecting a sprint.'

They set off together, Shelley leaning heavily on her crutches.

'Why didn't you tell me you were with Lucy's father at the Wild Manor?'

Shelley didn't answer at first. Instead, she kept her gaze to the floor and exhaled in discomfort. Eventually, she said, 'You're good. That's why I wanted you to take the case. Now, I'm not so sure.'

'Why did you keep it quiet?'

'Because I thought it was better that way. You've got the case. You defend it how you want to, but I've got to look after myself, no one else.'

'So what about Lucy's father?'

'I don't want to talk about him.'

'But why?'

'Because I blame him for this,' and she lifted one of her crutches. 'I don't want to push him any further.'

'Why is it his fault?'

'Because I should have been paying attention, it's a twisting road and it was dark, but my mind was on other things.'

'What did he say to you, Shelley?'

She didn't answer.

'Should I be wary?'

She nodded. 'Very.'

They were closer to the park now, approaching the railway bridge, the open space beyond it, a grassy field framed by barren hills, was heather-topped. Shelley's dog was straining on the lead.

'Why is Lucy's father dangerous?'

'Because he doesn't lose.'

'But I don't understand. Why should he lose anything?'

'I've said too much.'

'No, you haven't said enough. Why isn't there any mention of Mickey in the file, the guy from the street behind? I know you spoke to him, because his mother said you'd lost your temper with him, heard you shouting, but why isn't there a record of it in the file?'

Shelley stopped to lean against the railway bridge. It was a stone wall, only waist height, the bridge flat, a long-defunct road given way to grass. Shelley released her dog from the lead and watched as he ran into the park.

Dan was about to say something else when there was the sound of an approaching train. It was part of a long curve, where the tracks came down from the Pennine hills and started the long journey through the cotton towns, viaducts carrying the rails high above the terraced streets as they cut across the valleys.

The engine was loud as the sound echoed between factory walls, the noise of the wheels making conversation difficult.

Dan waited for the train to pass, glancing down at the driver as it passed under the bridge. Once it had rumbled into the distance, she said, 'I was told to lose it.'

Dan opened his mouth as if to say something, then paused. 'Who by?' he said, eventually.

'Conrad.'

'Why?'

'Because he's the boss.'

'What is he scared of?'

'Losing work, it seems.'

'There's got to be more to it than that.'

'Conrad and Dominic go back a long way. They're friends from childhood, apparently. I didn't know that.'

'Is Mickey telling the truth?'

'Why do you say that?'

'This could just be about Lucy's reputation. You saw how the press went after her when Mary was killed, but if Mickey is telling the truth, she's a real suspect. Perhaps Dominic didn't want you to trash Lucy just to help someone like Robert Carter.'

'I'll let you work out the rest for yourself.'

'What, there's more?'

She shook her head. 'I've said too much already.'

'Don't hold back on me, Shelley.'

'No, go.'

'Why were you shouting at Mickey?'

Shelley looked down and said nothing.

He considered whether to stay and try to extract more information from her, but the clench of her jaw told him that he would be wasting his time.

He checked his watch. He had a client, and he was late. 'We'll speak again about this.'

'No. I've said enough. I just want to get better and go back to work if they'll let me, and for us two to go back to being friends.'

'I can promise the last part.' He kissed her on the cheek, the one without the scar, and set off jogging back to his car. Once inside, the engine running, he paused to watch Shelley for a few seconds, just a small figure in the distance. But he could make out how lonely she looked, staring over the railway bridge, her arms resting on her crutches.

There were more truths to be found. That gave his day more purpose.

He set off quickly, one of the neighbours turning to watch him go.

Forty-one

Jayne skirted the town centre as she headed for the area regenerated by Dominic Ayes, before she turned into a small maze of speed humps and brick walls covered in spray paint.

Her edginess had lifted as she drove back from Manchester and the city became nothing but a grey blur in her rearview mirror. As she passed moorland hills and the bright gleam of a reservoir, it had felt like she was coming home. Her sanctuary. Highford had appeared in the valley as she went over the brow of a hill, caught by the sun, a world made small by the way the hills surrounded it.

The romance was lost as she rounded an open circle of wasteland next to an electricity substation and came upon three parallel rows of houses, with the first street one-sided, the opposite half too derelict for renovation. The land in front was sparse grassland littered by drinks cans and two open patches of brown grit where bonfires had been lit, with five caravans lined up along a fence on the other side.

There was a shop visible on a street further along, but it was hard to tell whether it was still in business, with the windows hidden by brown metal mesh and the paintwork old and shabby.

A group of men were sitting on the kerb, passing a cigarette along.

Jayne wound her window down. 'I'm looking for Alison Reed.'

'Are you the press again?' one said.

'Yes, sure,' Jayne said, figuring that it might get her further than the truth.

'She likes her face in the paper, that one,' he said, and pointed further along. 'The house at the end.'

Jayne thanked him and drove to the end of the street, a wooden fence bringing an end to the roadway. As she parked outside, Jayne noticed graffiti on the wall. Just a tag, the sort of meaningless scrawl favoured by those whose sole ambition was to write the scrawl in as many places as possible.

She stepped out of her car. The men at the end of the road were watching.

The door was opened straight after knocking, by a short woman with dark-hair wearing a large jumper, out of keeping with the season.

'Alison Reed?'

'Yes?' She folded her arms.

'I'm working for a law firm and I want to ask you a few questions about Dominic Ayres.'

Her eyebrows raised. 'You his friend or foe?'

'Foe, probably. Or at least, I will be soon.'

Alison stepped aside. 'Come on in then.'

The house felt cold when they went inside. The carpet looked threadbare and the cheap sofa had arms that had worn shiny. The fireplace was blocked off by a steel plate.

Alison must have seen her looking. 'My landlord won't service the fire, even though I've got a carbon monoxide detector that tells me it's dangerous.'

'Is your landlord Dominic Ayres?'

'Who else?'

'And the newspaper reports said that you've campaigned against him.'

'I had no choice. I've got damp in all the bedrooms upstairs and he won't do anything about it. A lot of the other tenants are the same, but they're already in hock to him.'

'What do you mean, hock?'

'Hock. Debt. His rents are high, more than anyone gets on benefits. Let's be honest, who'd choose to live round here? I was homeless before I got this place, and was glad of it, but Dominic Ayres is a bastard. If tenants fall behind on their rent, because Christmas gets in the way or they go away for a spell, prison or something, or just because they have money problems, does he evict them? Hell, no. There's a clause in the tenancy that over-due rent will be subject to an interest charge of ten per cent a month, drafted as an administrative fee.' She waved her hand towards the world beyond the window. 'All these people are in debt to Ayres.'

'But how can they ever pay?'

'How do you think? Threats, intimidation, and if that doesn't work, sudden repairs that drag on and on. Take my damp. I threatened legal action but it made it worse. He sent someone round to make roof repairs, saying that he thought the problem was there. All that happened was that they took some tiles off, over my bedroom, and covered it in blue plastic, all through winter. It was so cold I had to sleep down here, and I've got two children. What sort of life do you think they have?'

'Why don't you move?'

Her laugh was bitter. 'How easy is it to get somewhere new now? They all want deposits and bonds we don't have, to live in houses we can't afford, and want references from previous landlords. Anyway, the ones left here have got some power back.'

'What, the residents' action group?'

'No, that fizzled out, and those guys who came down were scary. Big guys in suits. Polite, but that made them just scarier. No one cares about us. We're just the forgotten people in a forgotten town.' She frowned. 'You know, I thought my life would be about more than this.'

'But how does this help Dominic Ayres?' Jayne said. 'He gets hassle and people who can't pay their rent.'

'That's where our power is, because even though these houses have paid for themselves a thousand times over, it's on good land. Bulldoze these and he'll get a small fortune. Manchester has got too expensive, so young couples are looking this way now. I know that, because my cousin works in an estate agency. This town is the next big boom town, so they say, and we're stopping him from cashing in. He wants us out, but I'm not budging.' She smiled. 'We've got the power back, although there's not as many of us as before.'

'I don't understand.'

'Tenants. Can't you smell it in the air?' When Jayne looked confused, Alison said, 'Weed. The houses are full of it.'

Jayne thought back to her own building and the sweet tang that often drifted upstairs. 'Everyone smokes weed now.'

'No, not smoking it. Growing it. If a house becomes empty, it gets rented out by a local letting agency, which is just a front really, because the house is always rented out to some young sap who doesn't really live there. That's not what the papers say, of course, because it's all official, benefits paid there, housing benefit and everything. Someone comes in and kits out the rooms with the lights and foil linings and extractions systems, bypasses the electricity meters, and plants the weed. It's a twelve-week turnaround. Grow it, crop it, grow it again.'

'Who are these tenants?'

'People in debt, most likely. To dealers, to Ayres, who knows? Ayres is protected though, because it's through a letting agency, distant from him. Too many houses on this street are just cannabis factories now, the rent paid for by the council, and as soon as the rest of us leave, he'll sell the land.'

'How come the police don't raid them?'

'You tell me.'

'Who deals with his legal work?'

'Some firm in town. I can't remember their name.' She paused. 'Hang on,' and Alison went to a small computer desk in the corner of the room. When she opened one of the drawers, documents sprang up like a jack-in-a-box, in no order at all. She rummaged through until she found what she wanted. 'Here you are,' and she passed a letter to Jayne. She recognised the letterhead, Duttons. Conrad Taylor was listed as one of the partners.

'I thought it might be his daughter doing his work,' Jayne said. 'She's training to be a lawyer, but not with Duttons.'

'Lucy?' Alison rolled her eyes. 'Did we used to hear about her.'

'What do you mean?'

'When you first meet Dominic, he's a charmer, and that's how he sucks you into all this. You think he's a friend, someone who'll look after you, so he'll chat, but it always turns to her, pretty precious Lucy. Yeah, there I am, at the bottom of the pile, and he thinks that I want to know about his daughter's pony lessons or her private school, with my kids worrying about their next meal or who'll be hanging about near the school when they walk home. I'll tell you one thing though: she's his weak spot.'

'What do you mean?'

'He dotes on her. I can see it in his eyes when he talks about her. His pride and joy. He'd do anything for her.'

'Anything?'

Alison drew out her words when she said, 'Absolutely anything.'

*

Shelley stared down at the tracks.

How the hell had it got to this? Flashback a week, and she had a career. She thought back to Dan, jogging over to his car. She used to have that urgency. What did she have now?

She closed her eyes and let the breeze caress her cheeks. She had two choices: fight for it, or accept it was over and seek fulfillment elsewhere. She had friends, a loving husband. No more missed evenings because of time spent at the police station. Did her career matter that much? Wasn't it just about paying the bills?

No, it was more than that. Her career defined her.

She opened her eyes and looked towards the park. Harry, her dog, was darting around with no real purpose. She almost laughed. It was a metaphor for her career. She should head over that way before another dog arrived on the scene, but she didn't have the energy.

It was quiet around the park. Just the occasional car from the road near her own home and the odd person taking a short cut to the pub across the park. A man strolled in her direction. She turned away. She wasn't in the mood for the cheery hello.

She stared down at the tracks. She knew the train times from living so close to the line. There'd be another one along soon.

There was a bark. She looked into the park. Harry was looking at her, rigid, alert.

She turned back to the tracks. If he wanted to play a game, he'd need to wait for a better day. She glanced backwards. The man was getting closer, his hands in his pockets, his head down. Something about him made her nervous. He looked familiar, but she couldn't place him.

There was a rumble in the distance, distracting her. The next train.

She curled the dog's lead into a ball and put it in her pocket.

There was a sudden noise behind her. Quick footsteps, crunches on loose stones.

She turned, surprised.

The man rushed her.

His hand went over her mouth with a slap, cutting off her scream. She tried to hit out but she was too unstable. Her crutch fell to the ground.

He was reaching for her legs with his other arm, bending down. Harry barked, angry yaps. She pushed back but he was too strong. He got his shoulders under her stomach as she bent over him. She flailed at him, but they were just ineffectual thumps on his back.

His hand relaxed, allowing her a scream, but it sounded distant, mixed in with the slow metallic rumble from the tracks, the rustle of her clothes as he got his shoulders under her midriff, grunting as he pushed upwards. Her back scraped against the edge of the bridge as she leaned backwards.

His hand reached upwards and gripped her round her throat, stopping her shouts, pushing her backwards all the time. She tried to punch him, but her blows were weak, striking his head and having no effect as his shoulder pushed upwards, lifting her feet from the ground.

Shelley gripped his jacket, her fingers trying to hold on, but it wasn't enough.

One last heave and she was hanging over the bridge, her hair hanging down, swaying, her arms hanging uselessly, only prevented from falling by his grip around her legs.

She was screaming again but it was drowned out by the noise of the approaching train on the other side of the bridge, the horn sounding as it rounded the long sweeping bend.

He let go of her legs. Her feet kicked once against the bridge and then she was falling, hair wild, the air rushing by, her arms wheeling, the sound of Harry growling.

Her head hit the rails with a crack and everything blurred. There was a sharp jab of pain in her shoulder and her leg, her body over both rails. The track vibrated but the sounds were distant. She tried to move but couldn't. The sound of the horn became louder, brought her round. Everything was sideways.

As her view became clearer, all she could see were metal wheels, the screeches deafening.

Her mind willed her body to move, but she was caught. There was no way out.

The last thing she saw was the contorted face of the train driver. She closed her eyes. Make it quick, was her only thought as the train wheels struck her.

Then there was nothing.

Forty-two

Present Day

Simon Parkin paused as he turned over a page of his notes.

He'd taken Lucy through the friendship, leading up to the night in question.

He coughed before he said, 'I'm going to take you now to the night Mary died.' Lucy straightened herself. 'Did you see her during the evening?'

Lucy shook her head. 'I saw her before she went out, that's all.'

'How was she?'

'The same as ever. Happy, looking forward to her evening.'

'Did she mention whether she had any plans to meet anyone?'

'Just two of her friends. The other two girls in the house were away and I was staying at Peter's, my boyfriend's flat.'

'Did you stay there all night?'

'Yes. It was the weekend, so we decided to get some wine and, well, have some fun.'

She blushed when she said it.

'When did you go home?'

'In the morning, just before eleven. I went with Peter because I was going to change my clothes and then we were going shopping.'

'Did you sense anything untoward when you got to the house?'

'Yes, because it was strange. We came in the back way and the door was open. I don't mean unlocked, but as if it hadn't been closed properly, not quite on the latch, so that all we had to do was push it. We went inside and it didn't seem like anyone was in, so I was pretty annoyed that it had been left insecure.'

'What did you do once you were inside?'

'Shouted for Mary. She didn't answer.' She stared at Carter. 'Now I know why.'

Hannah leaned across to Simon and whispered, 'Control your witness.'

Lucy must have seen Hannah, because she said, 'I'm sorry, but, well, it's difficult, as you can imagine.'

'Did you go into Mary's room?'

'I knocked on her door but there was no answer. I was angry with her, but then I saw blood on the door, like a big smear. I was worried then, and then . . .' She paused as her chin trembled. Her palm went to her chest again. There were tears this time, running slowly down her cheeks. 'Then, it swung open, and we saw her.'

Simon paused.

Dan looked across at the jurors and they were transfixed. He could have done headstands and he didn't think they'd notice. All their attention was fixed on Lucy.

'Did you go into the room?' Simon's voice had grown softer, drawing the courtoom closer.

'I stepped inside but couldn't go any further. I screamed, I couldn't move. It was, well, just horrible. We could see blood on the floor and on her arm, where it was hanging out from under the duvet. Peter closed the door and called the police.'

'Did you go into the room at any other point before the police arrived?'

'No, never. Like I said, I went inside, stopped, and went out.'

Simon gave a small bow to express his gratitude for her evidence. 'I've no more questions at this stage.'

Lucy nodded her relief and turned towards Hannah, who had risen to begin her examination, but the judge intervened.

'It's been a long day,' he said, and pointed towards the clock. It was four o'clock. 'This seems like a good place to stop for the night.'

Hannah bowed. 'As it pleases, My Lord.'

The judge turned to Lucy. 'I'm sorry, Miss Ayres, because it does mean you'll have to come back tomorrow, but it's important that people hear what you have to say and are not too tired to pay attention.'

'It's fine,' Lucy said. 'I'm doing it for Mary.'

As Lucy stepped out of the witness box, Dan watched her go, until he saw her father staring at him again.

Dan turned away.

It had been a good day for the prosecution. They'd had the opening speech and then the first witness, who described the horror of the scene and what a beautiful person Mary had been. More than that, the notion of Carter as an obsessive stalker had become fixed in their heads.

Yes, a very fitting end to the first day.

Dan stood as the judge exited, followed by the jury, who filed out of a side door, going home with the knowledge that Mary Kendricks was an intelligent young woman, with a long career ahead of her and was loved by many. And they had seen that Robert Carter had sat through Lucy's account expressionless, almost as if he wasn't a participant.

Dan looked back towards the dock. Carter was staring straight ahead, his jaw set, as handcuffs were clicked on to his wrists and he was led down the tiled steps into the cell complex below.

As Hannah gathered her papers, Dan said, 'Will the jury buy all her simpering about her special friendship with Mary?'

'The other housemate, Beth Wilkins, will undermine it,' she said. 'She'll allow us to speculate that Lucy didn't know much about what Mary really thought of Carter, but there's still a problem, because Beth doesn't like Carter either. We might lose all that we gain when the prosecution re-examine her. And, of course, there'll always be the biggest problem of all.'

'Which is?'

'If not him, who?'

Dan looked back at Dominic Ayres. He was leaving the court-room, his hand on Lucy's back as they went through the door. Mary's parents were still in their seats, with her mother wiping tears from her eyes.

Dan looked away. It would have been a tough day for both of them, even if it had been Lucy who played at being the victim.

'Remember one thing,' Hannah said. 'For the jurors, cases like this are all about playing at being detectives, their private little murder mystery, with the signposts to the killer all laid out for them like a road map. That is where the problem is, because in all the murder stories, the real villain turns out to be some-one you least expect, but at least there is another villain. All we can do is untangle a few threads and ask them to release the only suspect. It doesn't matter what the judge tells them about *beyond reasonable doubt*, because they'll only let him walk away from this if they think he's innocent. A young woman died. The burden of proof comes a poor second to that.'

Dan sat back. Hannah was telling him what he already knew, but he'd been hoping for more optimism.

As Hannah shuffled along the bench, Dan followed, until the calm velvet of the courtroom was replaced by the harsh tiles of the court corridor.

Dominic Ayres was ahead of them as they made their way to the robing room. Hannah strode confidently past them, but she didn't have the same recent history with him as Dan had.

Mary's parents were talking to Lucy, who was smiling her sincerity at them, but they turned their backs on Dan as he went past. Dominic glared at Dan as he got closer.

Dan looked away. The game wasn't over just yet.

Forty-three

Twelve Days Earlier

Dan was back at the local Magistrates Court, fresh from his visit to Shelley. Why had she kept Mickey secret? She'd been told to lose him, she said, but why? Had she expected him to find Mickey anyway? Is that why she'd transferred the case without Conrad's knowledge, knowing that Dan would discover the same thing that she had.

He'd phoned his client to tell him that he was going to be late and it turned out that he wasn't going to attend anyway. The slur to his voice told Dan that the next appointment ought to be in the morning. Missed appointments were part of the job.

He was at the court to meet Murdoch. He was loitering by the door, leaning against the stone pillar and looking out over the open square in front of the library opposite.

He smelled Murdoch before he saw her, the scent of stale tobacco drifting towards him. The police station was connected to the court, so that the overnight prisoners could be brought blinking into the brightness of the courtroom from the dark tiled corridor underneath.

'Henry Oates,' Dan said, as he turned. 'Do you want me to repeat the question, or have you managed to locate the information?'

'Don't be an arsehole. Follow me.'

They walked back into the courthouse, along a dim corridor that ran by one of the small courts at the rear of the building, reserved mainly for traffic cases and those trials where the defendant wasn't expected to go to prison. She stabbed a few numbers into the keypad and went into the police station, holding the door for Dan.

This was an area of the station Dan rarely saw. His visits were confined mainly to the cell complex, where everything was sterile; plain cream walls, broken only by posters advising prisoners of their rights and that lawyers had to surrender their phones. This part of the station was bustling, with pieces of paper fluttering on walls, showing maps of the town or pictures of crime nominals, those people who accounted for most of the low-level crime. The police wanted them put away so that they could smarten up their crime figures. Dan recognised some of the faces and wanted them at large, to keep his own work ticking over. It was a dirty job sometimes.

Murdoch turned into a room behind a frosted glass door. In there was a male officer sitting at a desk, the chair leaning back, his lips pursed. Dan recognised him. Andrew Edwards. He'd fallen out with him a few times when dealing with prisoners. Edwards was the confrontational type, one of those who'd advance too closely if he didn't like the advice a client was getting, thinking that he'd get his way if he breathed stale coffee over him. What he'd never worked out was that tactics like that, bullying, aggressive, made Dan even more determined to fight against it.

Murdoch gestured for Dan to sit down. He shook his head. He was fine to stand. He folded his arms.

'Tell him,' she said.

Edwards sat forward, his chair clumping to the floor. 'I spoke to Henry Oates.' His mouth was set in a scowl, his eyes narrowed. 'He had nothing to say, the ramblings of a drunk, so I didn't note it down. That's all there is. No secrets, no conspiracy.'

'What did he say?'

'Like I said, nothing. He reckoned he'd seen Carter on the night, with Mary, but he couldn't even get the night right. Said it was the Friday, and he remembered it because he'd been into town and there was some kind of event on, the local radio station holding a roadshow, but that was the day before, the Thursday.'

'But there should still have been a note of it,' Dan said. 'He's a witness who's given you information.'

'If it's the wrong night, he's no witness at all. How do you know about him? Did he come stumbling into your office?'

'When you ignored him, he spoke to Shelley, because however much of a hopeless drunk he is, he'd seen a murder victim just before she was killed, along with the accused. He thought it was important.'

'What did Shelley do about it?'

'Not much. But I'm not Shelley. What did he say about how Carter and Mary were?'

'Just walking together.'

'Are you sure about that?'

His eyes narrowed even further. 'Yes, I'm sure. What are you getting at?'

'Henry remembers them more vividly. And I'll tell you something else too, that it causes problems for your case whichever night it was.'

'What do you mean?'

'Henry said Carter and Mary were more than just friends. They were kissing, being romantic as they made their way to her house.'

Edwards paused before he said, 'So what?'

'Think about it,' Dan said, his tone implying that he knew DC Edwards didn't spend much time thinking at all. 'It doesn't matter whether it was the night of the murder or not, it shows that Carter wasn't the oddball pestering her.'

Edwards folded his arms. 'But if it isn't the night of the murder?'

'Then it's even worse for your case, because then Carter and Mary are a regular thing.'

'Or perhaps he was just showing off, making out that Mary was his girlfriend, and she was too polite to tell him to get lost?'

'Maybe, but you can see how it's relevant.'

Edwards shrugged.

'Anything else?' Murdoch said to Dan.

'No. We can deal with the rest of it in court.'

'What do you mean?' Edwards said, his eyes darkening.

'Work it out,' Dan said, as he walked out of the room, heading back to the corridor.

Murdoch caught up with him, out of breath from the short dash. 'Happy now?'

'No.'

'What do you mean? Yes, he's been sloppy, dismissing Oates like that, but it doesn't mean anything.'

'Is he a good copper?'

Murdoch thought about that. 'A bit old school, if you know what I mean.'

Dan did. Brusque, no nonsense, the focus on the case, getting 'justice', not on promotion.

'That makes it worse. I can't work out why he didn't make a note of it, because it doesn't matter how much Henry is an old soak, he said something worth hearing that might have led to more enquiries. If he saw them acting like lovers on the way home, you might have checked for more CCTV near there or done some more knocking on doors. No, it sounds more like Edwards wanted to ignore it, and that makes me uncomfortable.'

'Shelley ignored him too, by the sounds of it.' They'd reached the door into the court. 'How is she?'

'I've just been to see her. She's fine. She'll come back fighting.'

'Good.' She held open the door. 'You're reading too much into this thing with Henry.'

'We'll find out soon enough.' He knew that Murdoch was watching him as he set off, the door not closed.

Andrew Edwards. Something wasn't right, and Dan needed to know more.

Forty-four

Murdoch was back in the squad room, fresh from her meeting with Dan and was making a round of drinks for the team, when there was a shout from the other side of the room.

'We've got another dead one,' a detective said, holding up his phone.

Murdoch looked up. 'What is it?'

They didn't need any more homicides. There was a Major Incident Team on the other side of the county, and there were enough egos there who'd fancy a speech in front of a camera.

The detective held up his hand as he listened. 'We'll be there,' he said, and put the phone down. 'Someone's been run down by a train.'

'Forget it. Leave it to the transport police. We've too much on.'

'They're saying it doesn't look like a suicide. Who takes their dog for a walk when they go to kill themselves?'

'Don't read too much into that.'

'You don't know who it is.' He paused for dramatic effect. 'Shelley Greenwood.'

Murdoch put the spoon down. 'Carter's former lawyer? Are they sure?'

'They found her purse at the side of the tracks, and a neighbour knew the dog. It was barking at the bridge, running round in circles, distressed.'

'Get your jacket, you're coming with me.' She pointed to a detective at the other side of the room. 'Get CSI there, and a team of uniforms to knock on doors.'

She rushed out of the room, ignoring the need for a coffee. The coincidences were mounting.

The journey didn't take long, the town not yet hitting what passed for rush hour. The detective who'd taken the call, Tom Snape, was in the passenger seat, and he wasn't saying much. He hadn't been on the squad for long and it seemed like he'd chosen silence over the risk of saying something he'd regret. Murdoch couldn't decide which she preferred. She'd opened the window and was trying to smoke a cigarette before they arrived. Tom didn't say anything, but his frown told her that he wasn't impressed.

She didn't care. She wasn't allowed to smoke outside the station, bad for the police image, and smoking had been banned from the yard after complaints from people using the offices above. She wasn't going to be told what to do in her own car.

She pulled alongside the yellow crime scene tape that had been stretched across the entrance to the bridge. Before she got out, she stubbed out what was left and slipped it into the box to finish later. If one of her own cigarettes contaminated a crime scene, she'd never live it down.

'Too close,' she said, looking along the street towards the cottages that lined the road. The path leading to the bridge was on a bend in the road, crossing the railway lines to a park on the other side.

'What do you mean?' Tom said, trying to discreetly sniff his sleeve for the smell of cigarettes.

'They've only blocked off the bridge to stop gawpers. It's a potential crime scene, not a bloody privacy guard.'

Murdoch climbed out of her car and approached a uniformed officer keeping guard by the tape. 'How many people have you had here before we came up?'

'Seemed like half the street, ma'am.'

'Who put the tape up?'

'The transport lot. It'd been up for half an hour before I was stationed here.'

Just great, she thought. The chance of getting anything useful forensically from the bridge was reduced to nil, because it could have been carried there from any part of the street.

She went into her boot and pulled out two white paper forensic suits from a box, kept there for those late night calls. She passed one to Tom. 'Suited and booted, young man. The scene might be wrecked already, but no one is going to blame us.'

Once they were dressed in the paper coveralls, they both went under the tape. Murdoch said, 'You okay with bodies? This isn't going to be good if she went under a train.'

'I worked on traffic for three years. This will be easy.'

'Easy?'

'With car crashes, you get complete bodies, just banged up a bit. Or people screaming. That's worse. This,' and he pointed towards the bridge. 'She'll be body parts, nothing more. A butcher's window.'

Murdoch took a deep breath. 'You must be a joy at parties.'

As they walked on to the bridge, there was a further line of tape, to keep people away from the centre, presumably the point where she'd gone over the edge. Murdoch stopped to look over. The train was stopped a hundred yards further along. Behind it, rags were strewn along the track, either stuck to the sleepers or lying in the grey gravel along the track edges, flapping in the slight breeze in the midst of people wearing garish green bibs.

'Come on,' she said, and headed for the grass bank that ran down to the tracks, accessible by jumping over the wall and into a patch of long grass on the other side. 'It looks like we're the only ones wearing this garb.'

Her paper suit caught and snagged on the grass and thistles as she made her way down, her arms out, steadying herself against the risk of slipping. Tom had asked to go first, some kind of manly gesture, to sweep away the high weeds for her, but she'd told him no, she didn't need help. The paper covers over her flat soles made her wish she'd accepted his offer, just because he'd be a soft landing if she stumbled forward.

A man with a clipboard and green coat walked over, taking long strides so as not to step on the sleeper edges, the long grey hairs he'd combed over his scalp rising up in the wind. As he got closer, Murdoch held out her identification. He seemed to take longer than he needed to, checking out who she was before he held out his hand to shake.

'What have you got?' Murdoch said, ignoring his gesture.

'We thought she was a jumper at first. This is the worst place for it, because the bridge is just a path, so no one is going to drive past and stop them. And people loiter because of the park. It's hard to know who's a risk and who's just enjoying the view.'

Murdoch looked towards the static train and understood the problem. The bridge was one of the few over the tracks, because the railway lines ran high over the valley and cut across on a long viaduct. Most of the town was below the tracks rather than above them.

'How's the driver?' she asked.

'Distraught. It's his second fatal but this one shocked him. The last he had was someone stepping out, and he saw it coming a long way off but just couldn't stop in time. This one seemed to drop right in front of his cab.'

'Did he see anyone on the bridge?'

'No, nothing. She came from the other side of the bridge, if you know what I mean. He could see the edge of the bridge nearest to him, but not the side from where she jumped.'

'But now you're not sure she jumped?'

'It doesn't seem right. When we went up there, to close it off, her dog was going crazy, like running round in circles and then going to the edge of the wall and trying to see over, barking like mad.'

Murdoch knew Tom was right, that people don't take their dogs with them to commit suicide.

'At least we can time the death accurately, because of the train,' he said.

'Provided she was alive when she went over the bridge,' Murdoch said. 'It's one hell of a way to disguise an injury.'

She looked back along the track. Now she was closer, the scattered pieces of cloth were much more than that. They were wrapped around what she knew were body parts. They glistened in the sun, the light catching the occasional brightness of bone, exposed by the crushing impact of the train wheels, or the wetness of the blood soaking through the clothes. Patches of bare skin gleamed.

Murdoch closed her eyes and pinched her nose. She knew Shelley Greenwood. She was one of the good ones, a lawyer who played it straight. She fought for her clients but never fed them a story, and afterwards, when the adrenalin of the interview had subsided, the arguments finished, she was good company, had no beef with the police. Knowing it was her, scattered along the line, brought it too close.

'We know she wasn't alone,' the man said.

That caught Murdoch's attention. She opened her eyes. 'What do you mean?'

'When the news came through, the driver of the train before said he saw two people on the bridge. He was heading away from town, so she was on the side nearest to the train. He noticed them because he always looks at the bridge, just in case.'

'Why don't you put up suicide fences?'

'Because it's easy to get on to the tracks further along. If they're going to kill themselves, they'll do it down there. Somehow bridges reduce it, because it takes more bottle to jump from a height, more nerve than just lying on the track and closing your eyes.'

'Can he remember what the other person looked like?'

'It was a man, that's all.'

There was a shout. It was the uniform manning the tape. 'Ma'am? Can you come here?'

'You wait here,' she said to Tom Snape, who was clenching his jaw as he took in the grotesque scene in front of him. Perhaps it was different to working the traffic cases.

Murdoch scrambled back up the grass bank, her shoes slipping more than on the way down, so that she fell forward on to her hands twice. She wiped her hands and took deep breaths when she got to the top. Her breaths were hoarse. She tapped her pocket, felt the reassurance of her cigarette packet and lighter.

The uniform was with a woman sitting on a low wall, wiping her eyes. Her hair was grey and straight, thinned out by age, and the redness brought on by tears was the only colour to her cheeks.

The uniform gestured towards Murdoch and said to the woman, 'Just tell her what you told me.'

The woman sniffed back whatever tears she had left. 'I saw her, Shelley, walking with her dog. She was using a crutch. She's my neighbour.' A deep breath. 'She was with a man.'

'Did you know him?'

'No, I've never seen him before. I was watching television and I saw them go past, and I noticed them, well, because of what happened, with her car and everything. I like Shelley.'

'What was he like?'

'Tall, a bit dapper, in a suit and tie, but around the same age as her. Early thirties.'

'How did they seem?'

'Just normal, you know. Talking. Funny thing, though.'

'What?'

'When he came back along the road, without Shelley, he was running.' She held up her hand. 'Not like a mad dash, but a fast jog. I thought it was strange. He got into his car and drove away.'

Murdoch said thank you and told her that someone would be along later to take a statement.

A man in a suit. Running. She remembered the meeting from earlier and how Dan had said he'd been to see her. The man had to be Dan, and the timing of Shelley's death suggested a connection to the Carter case.

Now, Dan would have to answer her questions.

Forty-five

The scratches were back. They'd been playing in his head all day, like they were on a loop, a needle stuck in a groove, but they were different songs. First Cassie, and now Jayne, her guardedness making him want to know more, all wrapped up by the sound of Mary's scream.

He lay back on his bed and put his forearm over his eyes. It seemed easier that way, because he shouldn't dream of what he couldn't have. The hours spent watching Cassie, staring at her office, or in the bushes at the end of her garden, and all for nothing, because he'd been found out in the end. He had some of her secrets but she'd never be the same again. She'd hold something of herself back, always wondering if someone was watching. He'd spoiled her.

But how could he think that he could control his thoughts, because it was something inside of him, that need to know? Who'd understand, even if fate did intervene to punish him? The swing of Cassie's lamp. The terror in Mary's final moments. What lay in store for Jayne?

But what did he know of her? Not much.

He closed his eyes for a moment and stretched out his fingers to release the tension. Tremors of excitement quivered in his stomach and drew his chest tight. It was always like this when he first started his dreaming. His want, his desire, all unfulfilled, and that's how it had to be.

What would Jayne's bedroom be like? That was always a clue. Cassie's had been tidy, with her clothes folded neatly and all the drawers aligned. He'd liked that at first, because it meant the shadows were even more concealed, and the deeper they were, they higher they bounce back. He felt the scar on his head. He'd found that out, sure enough.

Mary's had been untidy, which he'd preferred, because it meant that she wasn't buttoned up. He'd learned from Cassie that sometimes what he found out was too much for him. Mary's drawers were open haphazardly. Dirty clothes had been thrown into a corner of the room, knickers and bras. He'd wanted to pocket a pair, but things had gone wrong.

What about Jayne? Young and beautiful but she'd held something back, her eyes filled with caution. What were her secrets once the lights went out?

He swallowed and opened his eyes. He needed to focus on the ceiling, bland and ordinary, apart from the small crack that ran from one side to the other. He couldn't obsess, not again.

But every time he told himself that, the urges got stronger.

*

Dan was in his office, catching up with correspondence, when his phone rang. It was Jayne.

'Hi Jayne. How you getting on?'

'Not bad. I found something out about Dominic Ayres: his property empire is mainly tenants who get bullied into leaving or end up in debt to him, or else the houses are just small cannabis factories.'

'He's got a drugs empire?'

'No, he's got a property empire that other people use to grow drugs in. He keeps a distance. And guess who does his legal work? Duttons, that's who.'

'Shelley's old firm?'

'The one and the same.'

'That's interesting.'

'And there's more. You remember I told you how Sara Carter had been visited by heavies in suits? It was the same for Dominic's tenants. I'm thinking that whoever visited Sara had been sent by Dominic.'

Dan realised that Jayne was right. Dominic's name was coming up too often.

'What next, boss?'

'Take some time off, you've earned it. I'll catch up with you later.'

When he hung up, his phone rang again. It was Margaret on reception, who must have been waiting for his line to clear.

'There's someone called Lucy Ayres here,' she said. 'She wants a word with you.'

He almost laughed at the coincidence. Dan thought back to Jayne's account of being attacked by Peter. And now Lucy was at his office? 'Show her into the interview room, please.'

The firm had a room next to the reception area that they used for interviews. It ensured that clients didn't get to walk through the office and come across handbags and jackets and know the whereabouts of the best computer equipment. Representing thieves was all about keeping them from temptation.

Dan picked up his dictation machine as he went downstairs, switching it on and placing it on top of a notebook. He concealed the small red light with his hand clasped on the edge of the notebook.

Lucy stood up when he walked in. She strode towards him and held out her hand, confident, smiling. She was dressed more formally than when he saw her at the police station, in a business suit, her blouse open, her hair tied back neatly.

He shook it and smiled back. He knew what her gesture meant, that this was lawyer-to-lawyer. He was happy to play along if it made her less defensive.

'This is a surprise,' he said. 'I thought you'd be at work.'

She let go of his hand and sat down again. She crossed one leg over the other, making her skirt ride up her leg. 'I took the afternoon off because I wanted to talk to you away from the police. Some things are bothering me.'

Dan sat down, placing the dictation machine on the desk, the red light on top facing him. 'Fire away.'

She put her palm to her chest and blinked rapidly, taking a long breath before she spoke. Her eyes remained dry. 'I can't understand why you're coming after me.'

'Who said I was?'

'I saw her at lunchtime, your assistant, the one who came with you to the police station. She was following me.'

'Your boyfriend saw her too. He assaulted her, so I'm told.'

'He was scared, couldn't understand why she was there.'

'You're a witness in a murder case. We look at the witnesses, just to see what we can find out. Sometimes it helps our client.'

'And sometimes it doesn't?'

'That's right.'

'And which has it been?'

'Come on, you know I can't disclose anything.'

'But you're harassing witnesses. The police won't like that.'

He shrugged away the threat.

Lucy pulled her chair closer and spoke more softly, looking into Dan's eyes all the time. 'I want you to know how hard it's been for me. You saw how the press portrayed me just after Mary was killed. Can you imagine how that must have been, seeing yourself on the front pages, reading the insinuations? Does it matter that I didn't conform to what everyone thought I should have been like? How would you have preferred me to be? Wailing at the police line with flowers in my hand? No, this happened to me, not anyone else, and I dealt with it in my own way, by shutting myself off from it.'

'Why are you telling me this?'

'You wanted to speak to me before. Why not now?'

'I wanted to speak to all the tenants.'

'How many of the others have you followed since?'

'I'm not disclosing my client's case or discussing how I conduct it.'

She sat back and tossed her hair. 'I'm not here to cause problems. I'm here to help you, if anything.'

'How so?'

'If Robert Carter is innocent and you want to find another suspect, you're wasting your time with me. It won't help your client.'

'But then again, you would say that.' Before she could answer, Dan said, 'You've come a long way to tell me this. You could have emailed me or called me.'

'I was coming this way anyway. And the personal touch is sometimes better. I hope you don't mind.'

'Not at all,' he said, his tone as insincere as hers.

'Do you believe me then, that you're wasting your time by looking at me?'

'It doesn't matter what I believe. It's what will help Robert Carter, nothing more.'

'That's no answer.'

'It wasn't meant to be.'

But you've no evidence to implicate me, so you can't just accuse me in court. That's right, isn't it, that you've nothing, that you're just fishing around?'

'We've got this.'

'What do you mean?'

Dan leaned forward, so that his face was close to hers. He lowered his voice too, but it had a harder edge, with none of the seduction Lucy was attempting. 'You've come here to try to change how I defend my client. Now, you're trying to find out what I know, to find out what Shelley told me. I don't like that.'

'No, I'm not doing any of those things. I just want to live my life and not be the victim in this case.'

'Mary Kendricks is the victim.'

'I know that,' she said, and anger crept into her voice. She sat back. 'I found her, remember?'

'How could we ever forget?'

'Don't you think I've got a right to know what you're going to say about me? And don't tell me you're not going to say anything, because I was followed today, which tells me differently.'

'You're a lawyer,' Dan said. 'I'll give you a lawyer's answer, which is no, you don't have the right.'

'Robert Carter is an evil man.'

'Is he?'

'A creep, a weirdo, and I hope he gets what he deserves. You should think about that.'

'I think about it all the time, and I do my job just the same.'

Lucy stood up and grabbed the door handle. Just as she was about to open the door, she turned back to Dan. 'I came here to help you.'

'No, you didn't. I'll see you in court.'

She slammed the door as she went. Paper fluttered on the desk.

Dan clicked off the dictation machine and sat back. There was something significant in what had just happened. He just wasn't sure what.

Forty-six

It had been a long day, Dan thought, as he stared out of his apartment window. The Carter file was exhausting him and he wondered whether he'd taken on too much.

Jayne was on her way over. He'd asked her for updates. She was bringing over a report of what she'd found out that day and promised to bring food with her. Indian.

He'd fought against the idea of opening a bottle of wine, worried that it was becoming too much of a habit. He remembered those times in his childhood when his father would return from some meeting about industrial unrest somewhere, the revolutionary spirit fuelled by booze, and his aggression. Not physical violence, but Dan and his mother knew how to stay quiet as he ranted at the television, because any challenge to his opinion ended up with a thrown glass or a kicked door.

He gave in, the need for some relaxation taking over any self-restraint, knowing that Jayne would want some of the good stuff to go with her food. He was holding a wine glass as he looked out over the town, his favourite view, with Jayne's empty glass waiting for her. Streetlights lit up the town grid, the town centre like bulbs thrown into a box, jumbled together, so different from the regular stripes that ran up the hillsides. Given a different history, it would have been picturesque, with steep climbs and a winding valley, stone buildings and old slate roofs wherever he looked, but it had never really shaken off the industrial past. Too much of Highford stood derelict. Dan's apartment building was part of the town relaunch, rebuilding along the canal, but the good news hadn't spread. The old mill buildings stood mainly empty and burnt out.

His doorbell rang.

He checked his watch. Seven o'clock. It was too early for Jayne. He clicked on the intercom to check the security camera. It was Murdoch, with two other detectives.

He thought about not answering, unsettled by the group visit, wanting a break before he went back to Carter's file and any updates from Jayne, but his curiosity was piqued. Had they found something out to help Carter?

He jabbed at the door release button and watched as they pushed their way in.

The footsteps got louder on the stairs. Dan opened his apartment door and waited, until Murdoch arrived on the landing, wheezing, the two males detectives behind her panting. 'Doesn't this place have a lift?' she said.

'Yes, you missed it.'

Murdoch gestured towards the two men with her. 'DC Snape, and you remember DC Edwards from earlier.'

Dan held the door open for them as they walked into his apartment. 'Unforgettable.' He gestured towards the sofa as he sat down in a chair. Murdoch and Tom Snape sat but Edwards went to the table where Robert Carter's file was spread out.

'Keep away from that,' Dan said.

Edwards looked up and smirked. Something wasn't right.

Dan turned to Murdoch. 'What's going on?'

'Shelley Greenwood. When did you last see her?'

Dan was puzzled. He was about to shoot out the answer but he was troubled by the question. It was no innocent inquiry, and Dan's instincts told him to be careful, because if the police ask an unexpected question, it's best to stay quiet until the reason becomes clear.

'Why are you asking?'

'To see what answer you give.'

'You're going to have to do better than that.'

Edwards tutted. 'Mistake,' he said, almost to himself.

Murdoch shot him a glance but he was too busy flicking through the correspondence clip to notice.

'Leave that alone,' Dan said, his voice rising, angry now, and then to Murdoch, 'what kind of cheap stunt is this?'

'Shelley Greenwood is dead,' Murdoch said, her tone blunt.

'What?' Dan's mind was working fast, trying to process the information.

'This afternoon. Went in front of a train from the bridge at the end of her street.'

'That's not possible,' Dan said, confused, his mind whirring fast as his shock blurred with his memory of how she'd been: reflective, sad, quiet, but suicidal? No, he hadn't thought that.

'When did you last see her?'

'Just before I spoke to you. I told you that.'

'What time?'

'I don't know exactly. Two thirty, possibly. What time was I with you? Three o'clock?'

'What was she saying?'

'Not much.'

Edwards was still leafing through the correspondence file. 'I said leave that alone!'

'We might need to look at that,' Murdoch said.

'No way, that's privileged.'

'You know it isn't. I looked at the rules on that before I left. We can get a warrant to look at whatever you've got that you think is privileged, if it's in connection with a crime or where it might prevent serious bodily harm.'

'Well done, Inspector. So go get one.'

'Why don't we just discuss it first? Haven't you learnt that it's often better to cooperate with us rather than work against us?'

Dan closed his eyes for a moment. Images of Shelley flashed through his mind. The young fresher at university, one of his first friends, laughing at the excitement of being away from home. Then they were both young trainee lawyers in Highford, nervous, building their careers. They'd drunk together, laughed together, bitched about work together. It felt like some trick, Murdoch using fake bad news to find out what he knew.

Dan opened his eyes. 'Cooperation with you is for when there is nowhere else to turn, and if what you're saying is true, how could you use it for your own agenda? She was a damn good friend of mine.'

'There's no agenda.'

'So why are you here? Carter's former lawyer jumps in front of a train and you're so callous that you'll immediately use that to get to him? I thought you were better than that.'

Murdoch pursed her lips. 'I didn't say she jumped.'

That hit Dan like a punch. 'You're saying she was killed?'

Edwards started a slow clap.

'Enough,' Murdoch said, irritated, and then to Dan, 'you were the last person seen with her.'

'How do you know it was me?'

'You admit being with her.'

'There might have been someone else, after me.'

'Do you really want to go that way?'

Dan sat back and ran his hands over his hair. He let out a long breath. 'I'm not going any way.'

'Will you come to the station with us, to answer questions?'

'No.'

Murdoch looked surprised. 'No? Why not?'

'If Shelley was killed, it was something to do with Carter's case. I don't know why, but it just seems that way. I know I haven't done anything, and you know I haven't. I was with you just after I spoke to Shelley and you saw how I was. You want me to tell you all about Carter's case, which I'm not going to do, because the last person who tried to do something about it is now dead. I owe it to Shelley to keep my mouth shut.'

'Why were you running?' Murdoch said.

'When?'

'When you left Shelley. A witness saw you running back to your car. A train driver saw you on the bridge with her. Not long after, she ended up on the track. Why did you run?'

'Bullshit.'

'Were you running?'

'I'll tell you what,' Dan said, getting angry. 'If you want to play games, how about proving it was me on the bridge? How do you know we didn't talk in the house? How can you prove it was me running? Have they named me?'

Murdoch stayed silent.

'What about my registration plate?'

Again, Murdoch didn't respond.

'If you're playing games, I'll play the proof game. Prove it was me and I'll think about talking.'

He glowered at Murdoch, who sighed and shook her head. 'You leave me with no choice.'

'Which is what?'

'Dan Grant, I'm arresting you for the murder of Shelley Greenwood.'

'You're kidding.'

'You do not have to say anything –'

'You leave that file alone.'

'But it may harm your defence if you fail to mention when questioned –'

'I know the bloody caution.'

'Something which you later rely on in court. Anything you do say may be given in evidence.' She went to her jacket pocket and pulled out cuffs. 'I won't be needing these, will I?'

'No,' he said, and got to his feet. 'Let's have your fun then.'

Dan checked that Edwards had left the file where it was before they all left his apartment.

It was going to be a long night.

Forty-seven

Jayne was hungry as she arrived at Dan's apartment building. Two curries were in a plastic bag, with rice and naan, and the aroma was making her salivate. At least she didn't have to wait for Dan to buzz her inside; being his occasional overnight guest had got her a spare key.

The apartment seemed strangely silent when she went inside. There was a half-empty wine glass on the table near the window, with another glass next to it.

'Dan?'

No reply.

She put the bag on the side and went looking for two plates. She got the wine from the fridge and filled her own glass, sighing with pleasure as she took a long sip. As she spooned the food out on to the plates, she shouted again, 'Dan?'

No response. In the bathroom, she presumed, or getting changed. She was too hungry to wait. As soon as she got a fork, she sat down at the table and started to eat, the Carter file pushed to one side.

She closed her eyes in pleasure. Hot and spicy tender chicken, it was the best food she'd had all day.

Once a few forkfuls had taken the urgency from her appetite, she left the table and went for a look round the apartment. His food was getting cold.

She pushed open the bedroom door. Empty. As she glanced across to the bathroom, the door was ajar, meaning that he wasn't in there either.

Great. Must be a police station visit or something. He'll have his food when he gets back.

She went back to her own meal, and was halfway through it when her phone rang. When she pulled it from her pocket, the number was shown as private.

'Hello?'

'Is that Jayne Brett?'

'Yes.'

'This is the custody office at Highford police station.'

A voice in the background said, 'Let me speak to her.' She recognised it as Dan.

'Mr Grant wants you to know of his whereabouts, that's all.'

'How long will he be? And why can't he use his own phone?'

'He's under arrest. He may be here for a while.'

She put her fork down, surprised. 'Arrest? What for?'

'I can't tell you. He's entitled to have someone made aware of where he is, and he chose you.'

'Let me speak to him.'

A pause, and there was more conversation in the background, before the sergeant came back on and said, 'Hang on.'

There was the sound of the phone being handed over and then Dan said, 'It's nothing to worry about.'

'What the hell's going on?'

'Shelley's been killed.'

Jayne gasped. 'What? How?'

'I can't say too much, but they've dragged me in here for it.'

'But why you?'

'They're grasping at straws. It'll be fine.'

The sergeant spoke up in the background. 'Pass me the phone, Mr Grant.'

'I've left the Carter file out, and it needs tidying. Can you do that? Leave it very tidy. Put it all away.'

'Yeah, sure,' she said, confused.

The sergeant came back on. 'Thank you, Miss Brett,' he said, and hung up.

She pushed her plate away, no longer hungry.

Shelley Greenwood, dead? That can't be.

Jayne looked at the Carter file. Grasping at straws? Is that what it was about, the Carter case? And why did Dan want it putting away? What did he mean?

Then it dawned on her. He'd been arrested, and if there was a connection to Carter's case, someone might come back for the file. When he said put it away, he meant hide it.

She bundled all the papers together and put them back in the box, which was on the floor next to one of the chairs. She grabbed her jacket and key, picked up the box, then left the apartment.

From Dan's tone, she guessed that she should keep moving.

Forty-eight

Dan stared at the floor in the glass-walled reception cell.

It was opposite the custody desk, so that the sergeants could keep watch on those waiting to be processed. Even though he'd been booked in, he hadn't been transferred to a proper cell. He knew why: he was the sideshow, a defence lawyer arrested, and it seemed like every officer in the station needed to visit the custody area, normally a place of quiet, waiting for the next arrival from the vans and cars that pulled up outside.

His feet tapped out a fast rhythm, just to keep his focus. He'd been in this holding cell before, waiting with clients for the beginning of an interview. When he'd first started out as a lawyer, things weren't this refined. He'd been shown into cells to face the stench of plastic mattresses, dirty socks and unbleached steel toilets, nothing to protect him from an angry client but an emergency buzzer that he hoped someone would answer. It had taken an attack on a female solicitor, pinned against a wall, some pervert's hand up her skirt, her hand thumping the buzzer, for things to change.

He tried not to think of his own plight. He had Shelley on his mind. She was a good person. Why would anyone kill her?

The door opened. It was Murdoch, Edwards just behind her.

'You okay, Dan?' She sat next to him.

He raised an eyebrow. 'What do you think? You make it sound like it's nothing to do with you, but you're the one who arrested me for murder, and we both know it's bullshit.'

'You were the last person seen with a murder victim, running away from the scene. I can justify this.'

'Do you know what false imprisonment lawsuits cost now? I'll be getting five hundred pounds an hour for this charade. Keep going as long as you want, because that'll be ten times what I get when I come here with a client.'

'You still sure you don't want a lawyer? It's a serious offence. You should have someone with you. You're too close to be objective. What's the saying, that someone who represents himself has a fool for a client?'

'I'm not close to anything. I didn't have anything to do with Shelley's murder.' He held out his hands. 'And why would I want to get someone who isn't as good as me when I'm already here?'

Murdoch got to her feet. 'Come on, we're wasting time.'

Dan followed her out of the holding cell and along a dark corridor lined by grey steel doors. The sharp clips of Murdoch's footsteps echoed. Dressed in foam slippers given to him by the custody sergeant, Dan's footsteps were just shuffles.

At the other end was a door that led to a small collection of interview rooms. He'd been in them enough to know what they were like, windowless and bare, intended to make the interviewee uncomfortable, to want out, to say anything to get out. Would he feel different about them when he was the suspect?

Murdoch opened the door to let Dan go in. 'Do you need anything? A drink? Water? Nothing stronger, I'm afraid.'

'No, I'm fine.' He went inside, going straight to the nearest chair, so that he was in the centre of the room, facing into the corner.

'Not there,' Edwards said, and pointed to the chair furthest away. 'You sit over there.'

'No, I'm fine here.'

'But suspects sit in that corner.'

'Not this one. If you want this interview to stay civil, I stay here.'

Edwards was about to say something else but Murdoch interrupted him. 'Sit where you want, Dan,' and she raised her eyebrows at Edwards.

That was round one, Dan thought. The psychology of the interview room meant that he was supposed to be under pressure, to react differently, and he had to fight against it. The layout was meant to add to that. A seat in the corner. No windows. Nothing on the walls to distract him. No posters to stare at, to provide a focus that would help him avoid the questions. The interrogator was meant to be the only focus of attention.

Murdoch put her folder on the desk and started to go through the preliminaries, her tone friendly, checking Dan was comfortable, explaining how she just wanted to clear up a few things.

'I know what it's about,' Dan said, interrupting her. 'The interview, the reasons, the aims. Just press the button, caution me, and get on with the questions.'

Edwards sat upright, bristling.

'I know that this is the rapport stage,' Dan said, putting his hand out, stopping any outburst from him. 'You want me to be your friend, to trust you, so that when you press the button to begin recording, I'm already talking.'

'Perhaps I'm just being human,' Murdoch said.

'No, you're not, because there's a formula. It's how you're trained.'

'And how are you trained?' Edwards said. 'To be a jerk?'

'No, I'm trained to engage in theatre, to not worry about upsetting people when I do my job. And right now, a friend of mine has been killed and you're wasting time with me. So get on with it,' and he pointed towards the microphone taped to the wall.

Murdoch scowled.

'The rapport part of the session not gone so well?' Dan said.

Murdoch pressed the button to record and went through the usual preliminaries again, like telling him how he could get copies of the recording, and once she'd cautioned him again, reminding Dan that he didn't have to say anything, she said, 'Tell me about Shelley Greenwood.'

Dan sat back and folded his arms. He stayed silent.

Murdoch looked surprised and the atmosphere in the room became hostile. 'Nothing to say?'

'You've just told me that I don't have to say anything.'

'But it may harm your defence if you do not mention, when questioned, something you later rely on in court,' she said, exasperated now, her voice rising a notch.

'This isn't going to court,' Dan said, meeting her angry stare, turning his head to meet the same from Edwards. 'You know that, and I know that. This is just the part where you want me to open up, to tell a long rambling story, to give you all the background. Once I'm done, you'll trawl over that, try to trip me up. You know I haven't done anything, but you think I'll get scared and tell you anything to get out. I'm a hostage, nothing more.'

'What are you talking about?'

'You think I've got information that will help. Perhaps confidential information. By locking me up, you're hoping I'll get scared and tell you everything I know.'

Murdoch pursed her lips, anger flaring in her eyes. She jabbed the button that stopped the recording. 'Don't be so bloody self-important. Do you think this is really all about you? There's a dead woman on the railway tracks, with a family wondering what the hell happened, because all they know is that she'd had the worst week of her life. There's a train driver who saw her on the tracks and didn't have the time to stop, who saw that final look of terror in her eyes as his train went over her. So stop making it all about you.'

'She was my friend!' He slammed the desk with his hand.

Murdoch's lips stayed pursed and Edwards folded his arms and glowered.

'Why do lawyers always think they're better than us?' Edwards said.

'We don't, I just don't think I have to do as you say just because you want me to.' He looked towards Murdoch. 'I'll do you a deal.'

'What kind of deal?'

'I'll tell you anything you want to know about Shelley, provided that it doesn't impact on Robert Carter's case. I'll go further, even: if it will help him, I'll tell you. But you've got to stop seeing me as your enemy. I'm not working against you. I'm working for my client, nothing more.'

Murdoch stayed silent as she thought, a few seconds passing before she said, 'Shall we turn the machine back on?'

Dan shook his head. 'The first condition is that we stop this charade. Book me out of custody, then take me to a room where we can talk properly. You make me a coffee, we talk about our social lives, that kind of thing. And one more condition.'

'What?'

He looked at Edwards. 'He isn't there.'

Edwards dropped his arms, his jaw clenched, and he looked as if he was about to launch himself at Dan.

'Why?' Murdoch said.

'Because he doesn't like me. He oozes it, and as long as he's there, he makes me want to stay quiet, just to annoy him.'

Murdoch looked at Edwards, and then back to Dan. 'Okay.'

'You can't be serious,' Edwards said.

She glared at him. 'The operational decisions are mine.'

Dan stood up. 'Come on then. I want to spend some time at home tonight.' He glared at Edwards. 'I'd say *no offence*, but it wouldn't be true.'

As Dan turned towards the door, waiting for Murdoch to follow him, he knew he'd made himself an enemy, and an angry and vindictive one. What Edwards didn't know was that Dan had done that on purpose. All Dan had to do now was see what Edwards did next.

Forty-nine

Jayne was in her car, parked close to the police station, with a view of the entrance. She was browsing the internet on her phone for news of Shelley Greenwood, but there was nothing there. Dan had said *killed* though. Not suicide or an accident.

But why had Dan been arrested? Just because he was a recent visitor?

She checked her watch. She wasn't sure how long she'd stick around for, because from her own experience she knew that the interview phase could stumble on for a few days. In her case, however, she'd actually been the one who'd killed Jimmy. Whatever the reason for it, the knife had been in her hand as it plunged into the top of his thigh. The job of the police was to find out whether her descriptions of the relationship, of the abuse, were true, by speaking to neighbours and friends, and then after hours of interviews she had to re-enact it on video.

Those memories still made her shudder. Being made to act out what she'd done, the police analysing everything, even though the stabbing had taken a moment, just a flash of steel and then he staggered backwards. What if she remembered it wrong? For Dan, it would be different, surely? They'd realise he had nothing to do with what happened and let him go, and she'd be waiting for him.

Headlights came up behind her. She hunkered down into her seat so that she became invisible. The car was driving slowly, quietly. As it went past, she whistled. A red Bentley. You don't often see money like that in Highford.

Then she remembered. The woman who lived near to where Mary died said that a red Bentley used to visit the house, and Lucy's father was a rich man.

She wound down her window and listened out. A tyre scraped on a kerb and then there were the gentle clunks of two car doors.

Jayne stepped out of her car and tried to close her door quietly. The air was still, the town quiet.

She kept her footsteps light as she got to the end of the side street. The Bentley was parked next to the junction, its rear end visible from where she was standing.

She flattened herself against the wall and eased her head round. The lamppost on the other side of the street shone straight through it. There was no one in the car.

There was a pub further along. The Fleamarket. Once upon a time it was a lounge and tap room kind of place, but some time in the past the dividing walls were torn down and it was turned into a wood-lined open space, witticisms painted on the beams and guest beers chalked on to a blackboard. As she got closer, she could see two men in suits sitting at a table closest to the door. She recognised Dominic Ayres from the press photographs she'd looked at earlier, and he was with a bald man squeezed into a suit, scars on his scalp.

She remembered what Sara Carter had said about the men who'd visited her.

They weren't there for the fine ales, Jayne guessed, so she knew it was worth hanging around.

She crossed over the road and into the open square in front of the courthouse, which gave her a dark corner to watch from but with a view straight into the pub. Dominic and his muscle stared into their drinks, two half pints, not talking. If it said anything, it was that they were waiting for someone.

Jayne didn't have to wait long.

A man left the police station and walked straight across the road towards the pub, his hands in his trouser pockets, looking around as he went.

When he walked in, Dominic looked up and raised his glass.

The man went to the bar but, rather than joining Dominic once he'd got his drink, he went to a fruit machine on the other side of the bar, drawn like a moth to the flashing lights.

He put his drink on the top and started to feed money into it. Dominic and his muscle exchanged glances before Dominic gestured with a flick of his head towards the man on the fruit machine. The muscle left his seat and joined him at the machine.

The muscle spoke to the man, who never took his eyes from the spinning reels, his hand going to the money slot like it was automatic.

A few minutes passed and the muscle pointed at the man's glass and then at his watch. Dominic sat and watched. The man stepped away from the machine and drained his drink, before heading for the exit. The muscle followed, Dominic draining his glass, letting them get ahead of him.

Jayne cursed. They were leaving, but the Bentley was between where she was and her own car, so she'd be spotted if she ran for it now. Instead, all she could do was put up the collar on her jacket and walk casually past, hoping that no one looked.

The men were quiet as they got into the Bentley. The muscle was driving. Dominic and the other man got into the back.

The car started with a purr and pulled away almost without Jayne noticing. As soon as she got into the side street, she bolted for her car, her keys ready.

It started on the fourth turn of the key, and she had to rev it a few times to ensure it didn't cut out. By the time she got to the junction, the Bentley was gone.

She drove hard along the same road, hoping to see it further along, passing three more side roads before she saw it setting off through some traffic lights further ahead.

She was able to get through with the lights still on green and take up a position behind it, although she hung back so that they didn't notice her car.

They were heading out of town, towards the dark hills that blotted out the stars, broken only by the occasional dot of light from a farm or rural cottage.

There were more traffic lights ahead, showing green, but not for long. The Bentley sped up as they turned amber, and Jayne was too far behind to catch up before they went red.

She went to accelerate, just to get through them and hope that no one else set off on the green, but she saw the yellow and blue checked markings just in time. A police car waiting to set off.

She braked hard. Being stopped for going through a red light wouldn't help her. She banged her steering wheel in frustration as the Bentley carried on. The policeman in the car stared at her as he drove the lights. Jayne returned the stare and waved an apology. He kept on going. By the time she looked back, the Bentley had disappeared.

Jayne put her head against the headrest and groaned.

All she could do was turn round and head back, and revert to her previous plan of waiting for Dan.

Fifty

Dan accepted the drink from Murdoch. They were in a quiet room at the station, where the dirty cups and scattered papers showed that it was used by a team that had long finished its shift.

Murdoch opened the window. She shivered as the cool night air rushed in and reached into her pocket for a cigarette. She lit one and blew the smoke outwards. She held her hand outside, the smoke trails being blown back in. 'I'm sorry about Shelley. You were friends, I know that.'

'Thank you. I just can't believe it though.' He sat down and took a drink. 'She was feeling down, but she wasn't suicidal, so yes, I get it that you think someone killed her. She was worried about losing her job because she'd transferred the Carter case. Conrad Taylor didn't know anything about the transfer, but it was more than that.'

'What do you mean? She was depressed?'

'No, scared. Very scared. She knew something about the Carter case but wouldn't say what it was. She was getting some of her fight back though. She was just taking Harry, her dog, for a walk, to get out of the house, nothing more. Who takes their dog with them when they want to kill themselves?'

'Yeah, that's what we thought.' Murdoch took another drag, putting her head out of the window again to blow out the smoke. 'Was that you running back to your car?'

He took a drink. 'Yes, you know it was, and I'll make a statement if you need me to. I was rushing to get back.'

'Did you see anyone else hanging around?'

'No. It was near a park though, so perhaps whoever did it came from there. I wasn't paying attention anyway.'

'Remember how hard it is for witnesses the next time you have a go at them in court.'

He glared at her. 'This isn't the time to score points.'

She took another drag of her cigarette before she said, 'Yeah, I'm sorry.'

'So if you think she was murdered, and you accept it wasn't me, who else could it be?'

'You tell me, Dan. It seems like you're closer to the Carter case than I am. Or so you think.'

Dan thought about how much he should say. Robert Carter was sitting in a prison cell, and Dan didn't know if he was guilty or not, but he knew that there were people on the outside who'd been visited by Ayres's thugs.

'If I tell you, I'm trusting you.'

'Why shouldn't you trust me?'

'Because sometimes being a cop is just about getting a result, a box ticked, a positive outcome. The truth of it doesn't always seem to matter.'

'I'm not like that.'

'Yeah, I know, which is why I didn't want Edwards here.'

'He's all right. Like I said before, he's old-school.'

'No, he's more than that. He concealed something.'

'He made a judgment and got it wrong. You're seeing conspiracies at every turn, when really it's just people making mistakes.' She stubbed the cigarette out on the wall outside, sending sparks flying into the darkness below, and turned back into the room, closing the window behind her. 'That doesn't make him a bad copper. A lazy one? Yes, maybe, but if something happened to your loved ones, you'd want someone like Edwards turning up.'

'Someone who'll get the job done, leave no stone unturned?'

'Something like that.'

Dan took a drink and said, 'What do you know about Dominic Ayres?'

'Not much. I know he's from a wealthy family, but that's it.'

'Dominic Ayres is a nasty slum landlord and wannabe loan shark. If you want to improve your drugs busts, a lot of his rental properties are nothing more than cannabis farms.'

'We don't often get tip-offs from defence lawyers.'

'Just give them my card when you kick the door in. Someone has visited Carter's wife and told her to stay out of the case, but also to keep them informed about what he's saying. They sound like Dominic's thugs, from what we can work out. I don't know why they would do that, unless there's a connection with Lucy.'

'Any threats?'

'Does there need to be? It's about spreading a message with subtlety. And do you know who Shelley was with on the night she rolled her car? Dominic Ayres, and her boss, Conrad Taylor. The same Conrad who didn't know that she'd transferred the case to me.'

'Why did she do that?'

'She wouldn't say outright. A bout of conscience, I think, because she knew something about the case that Conrad wouldn't let her pursue.'

'And it was connected to Dominic?'

'I'm guessing so. Remember, his daughter's involved in the case. It might even involve her and Conrad wants to keep Dominic sweet, because Dominic could just transfer all his legal work to another firm.'

'What, you think Shelley found something out about Lucy?'

Dan thought about what Mickey had told Jayne, and then thought of Shelley, now murdered, and decided to keep some of it back.

He shrugged. 'Who knows? Perhaps it was nothing more than deflecting suspicion on to Lucy.'

'Perhaps Dominic was just protecting his daughter's reputation.'

'Yeah, perhaps.'

'You don't sound convinced. Is there something you should be telling me?'

'Not yet, but I want you to do something for me.'

'What?'

'Get me something for the trial. I want to go through you, not the CPS.'

'I can't do that.'

'Why not?'

'Because it isn't how it's done.'

'I thought you were the investigator?'

'I am.'

'So investigate. If there's nothing in it, it goes nowhere.'

'And if there is?'

'I reckon you'll want to know.'

Murdoch studied Dan, who met her stare until she said, 'Tell me then.'

'I want you to check on Lucy's alibi, and her boyfriend's, for the night of Mary's death. I want the cell-siting for their phones.'

'Why?'

'Because I want to know where they were.'

'At Peter's flat, having sex.'

'That's what they say.'

'You got any evidence that says otherwise?'

'Some.'

'And are you going to tell me?'

'Not yet.'

'Why?'

'Because Shelley died today. You think she was murdered, so it makes sense to hang on to some things for now, just to keep people safe.'

'The cell siting won't prove anything, you know that. The phone looks for the nearest mast, and if that's busy it searches for the next. Her phone might show up at a mast five miles away.'

'I know that, but it's a start. Let's see what it shows.'

Murdoch thought about that. 'I'll see what I can do.'

'One more thing.'

'What?'

'Don't tell anyone.'

Murdoch got to her feet again to throw open the window once more, her hand already opening the cigarette packet. 'Why should I help you?'

'Because you're more interested in the truth than you are in just getting a conviction.'

She put a cigarette in her mouth and turned back to Dan. 'If you cause me any problems with this, I'll spend the rest of my career trying to end yours. You got that?'

'I won't let you down. Trust me. Work with me.'

'Okay,' she said eventually, lighting her cigarette, blowing smoke into the cold air outside. 'Aren't you worried?'

'About what?'

'Shelley Greenwood was murdered today, and you think it's because of some secret she had. You think two thugs are scaring people. What makes you think you won't be next?'

'I might be next, but if I learned one thing from my father it's that you never back down from a fight, because then you lose the chance to win.'

Fifty-one

Dan turned his collar up as he trudged away from the station, heading for the nearest taxi rank. The route there was dark, all the offices in the buildings around closed until the morning, just large stone shadows.

As he walked, he became aware of an engine sound behind him, the exhaust loud, as if it was running with a hole in it.

He tried to ignore it, but the car was travelling slowly, right down to his walking pace. His fists tensed in his pockets, ready to fight if he had to, thinking about Shelley. A window rolled down and a voice he recognised said, 'Get in.'

It was Jayne.

He climbed in. 'I'm hungry.'

'I was expecting more of a thank you, or maybe even a hello.'

'Sorry. I haven't had the best of evenings. Hello. Thank you.'

'Wasn't it instructive though?'

'What do you mean?'

'You got a few hours in your clients' shoes. Not every lawyer gets that chance.'

He raised an eyebrow. 'You'd be surprised.'

'You're out. What happened?'

'A good friend was killed today, that's what, and I was the last person seen with her.'

'How was she killed?'

'Thrown from a railway bridge. They knew I hadn't done it, but arresting me made me a hostage for information.'

Jayne frowned. 'Can they do that?'

'Not officially, but they do. Take a murder where there are a few people around. Those people might not talk to the police, but they soon get talkative when they think they might get the blame.' He held his hands up. 'I'm not complaining, I was an obvious suspect, whether they believed me or not. They were hoping I'd tell them everything.'

'And did you?'

'No. Just what I wanted to. Did anyone come for the file?'

Jayne gestured with her head to the back seat. 'They'd have to find me first.'

Dan looked behind his seat. The Robert Carter file was there. He smiled but it was laboured. 'You're good.'

'A compliment? I don't get many of them.'

'Stop being so needy.'

'I've been doing your work for you tonight. I don't think a compliment is out of order.'

'What do you mean, my work?'

'I didn't know when you'd be released, so I came down here to wait for you. If they were going to come back for the file, there was no point in me staying in your apartment. I brought it with me instead.'

'I like your style.'

'As I was waiting, a red Bentley came past. Dominic Ayres. He sat in The Fleamarket with his hired hand, until they were joined by someone from the police station.'

'What did he look like?'

'Forties. Thickset. Bald, but like it was shaved.'

'It sounds like Edwards, but it doesn't fit.'

'What do you mean?'

'Murdoch thinks he's just a bad copper, lazy and arrogant, but not a corrupt one. Why would he be meeting with Dominic Ayres?'

'You're being too generous,' Jayne said. 'I've been on the end of police officers like him. They're different when the lawyer or inspector isn't there; they become nasty. When I was locked up, after you'd gone home, people just like Edwards came to the cell door and dropped the hatch, taunted me about what had happened. They treated it like a game.'

Dan turned towards her in his seat. 'What did they do while they were in the pub?'

'He's a gambler. He went straight to the bandit, a pint on the top. I could see him through the window, and it was as if he couldn't tear himself away.'

'Interesting. Gamblers have money troubles, and if he's a copper, he's a gambler with secrets to sell. What happened?'

'They all left together, went off in Dominic's Bentley.'

'Did you follow them?'

She grimaced. 'I did at the start, but I lost them. Sorry. I was hanging back, and they sped through a light that had gone red by the time I reached it. The last I saw they were heading out of town.'

'I've got an idea where they might have gone,' Dan said. 'Head out of town in the same direction.'

'I thought you were hungry.'

'I am, but it can wait.'

As Jayne drove, Dan peered ahead, trying to see shapes in the headlight beam, some indication that they were heading in the right direction.

They left Highford and drove along a country lane bordered by hawthorn hedges, the grey tarmac twisting upwards, the trees giving way to open moorland, the town below becoming a knot of orange streetlights.

'It's along here somewhere,' he said, almost to himself.

'What is?'

He strained into the darkness before he slapped the dashboard. 'There,' and pointed.

Jayne followed his gesture. 'I can't see anything.'

The hills ahead were just shadows, silhouettes against thin clouds backlit by a half-moon, the faint traces of stone walls snaking up them like snail trails. The occasional white clusters of sheep were the only bright spots, their fleeces catching the moonlight.

'Pull over,' Dan said.

Jayne found a space in front of a wooden gate and crunched to a halt, her front wheels finding the edge of a ditch. 'What is it?'

'Those yellow lights, just behind those trees over there. It's the home of Dominic Ayres. I found it on the Internet, in an article in one of the country set magazines, but it's been a long time since I've come down this road.'

'But what are we doing here?'

'Seeing who's here.'

'DC Edwards?'

'Exactly.'

Dan stepped out of the car. The glow of Manchester was far in the distance, but everywhere else was in darkness. His footsteps crunched loudly as he closed his door. Jayne joined him.

'We're sneaking around now?' she said.

'I thought you did this for a living,' he said, and set off walking.

There was a field between Jayne's car and the line of trees in front of the house. The grass was rutted, used by sheep, so that their way across was uneven, their shoes getting muddier as they went, and worse.

'There'll be security lights,' Dan said, his voice low. 'He's got money and a house in the countryside, so he'll know how to protect himself. Have you got your camera?'

She reached into her pocket and held it up. 'Never without it.'

'Get it on a night setting. We'll find somewhere to steady it and see what we can find.'

As they got closer, the house loomed larger. It was an old farmhouse, wide more than long, but modernised, with a large window at the front that went the full height of the building. It had blinds rather than curtains, so that it was more like an office block in the country than open hearths and high back chairs.

The field ended at a drystone wall, chest height, that lined a small grassy track that curved around the property, bordered by another wall, like an old public right of way from before the house was built. The open courtyard in front of the house was beyond it, where there was a wide fountain lit by dim blue lights, out of place in the setting.

'We'll need to get over the wall and around the back to see in,' Jayne said. 'They'll see us if we cross the courtyard.'

Dan looked over. She was right. The track between the two walls curved round to a part of the house that wasn't accessible from the field they were in.

'I should have dressed better for this,' Dan said, as he went first and scraped his chest on the stones before landing with a thump on the other side. Jayne clambered over more slowly, carefully, wedging her feet into the dry cracks until she was able to swing her leg over and drop down.

'Come on,' Dan said, and crouched down as he went along the path, Jayne behind, their shoes squeaking in the moisture.

The part of the path by the field had been open, giving a sweeping view of the countryside from the house, but became overgrown and thick with overhanging bushes and trees as they got to the side of the house. Once they'd followed the track to the back of the house, they knelt down behind the wall. His shoes glistened.

'We need to get a good view of the inside, to see if he's there,' he whispered.

He raised his head above the wall and looked towards the back of the house. Jayne reached into her pocket for her camera. It made a loud chime as it turned on, making her curse, before she fiddled with the settings. She reached up to place it on the wall before zooming in and panning over the house.

Dan moved back, so that he was looking at the house through the small screen on the back of the camera.

'Zoom into the window,' he said.

'Should we be doing this?'

'Why?'

'These people sound dangerous. Sara has been threatened. Carter's behaving as if he's scared. Shelley has been murdered.'

'I know all of that,' he said. 'I'm as nervous as you are, but I'm doing this for Shelley. We've got to make it right.'

Jayne made the lens whirr, and it went out of focus a few times, until it settled on a view of a few people sitting around a table. She pressed the shutter and took a picture.

The flash on the camera illuminated the back of the house.

'Shit, I'm sorry,' Jayne said, pulling the camera away. 'I had it on the wrong setting.'

'Has anyone moved?'

Jayne put the camera back and zoomed in. She moved it slowly, panning along the house. 'I can't see anyone.'

There was a noise. A door opened. Someone's voice. Footsteps on stone slabs, getting closer.

Jayne pulled her camera down and jammed it in to her pocket. They both sat down on the grass, their backs pressed into the wall, trying to blend into the darkness.

Dan tried to slow his breathing.

Footsteps got closer. There were quick breaths on the other side of the wall, then growls. A dog.

Jayne reached out for him, gripped his forearm.

Dan jabbed his finger towards the ground, they had to stay put, and then held out his hand, palm downwards. Stay calm.

A few minutes passed. There was the occasional shuffle of feet, a sniff, a cough. Dan closed his eyes. He thought back to Shelley and how she'd ended up on a railway track not long after he'd spoken to her.

The footsteps moved away and a door slammed.

Jayne went to shuffle along the ground but Dan stopped her, held on to her hand. He shook his head, barely visible in the darkness.

A few more moments passed, the night silent, before the footsteps returned and the door opened once more. It had been a test, to see if they'd come out of their hiding place.

When the door closed again, Dan gestured towards her pocket.

Jayne took out her camera and put it under her jacket to mitigate the light from the display as she turned it on. She messed with one of the dials to zoom in on the one picture she'd taken. She smiled, caught in the camera glow, and handed it over to Dan.

He looked and smiled with her. DC Edwards, playing cards with Dominic Ayres.

He handed the camera back and pointed towards where she'd left the car.

It was time to go.

Fifty-two

Jayne took off her shoes before she got into her building, covered in mud after her trudge through the fields with Dan. All she craved was the wine she had left in the fridge and a bath.

The building seemed quieter than normal. The thump-thump of the bass playing was missing.

She crept up the stairs, not sure what she might accidentally stand on in her socks. Just as she got close to her own apartment, the door of the constant cannabis smoker flew open.

Jayne stepped back. He swayed in the doorway, his eyes unfocussed. The landing was filled with the sweet smell of what he'd been smoking and growing.

'Someone was here again,' he said, his voice just a drawl.

Jayne's chest tightened. 'What do you mean?'

'Just that. Some guy in the building. I keep a look out on who comes through. I have to, you know,' and he gestured towards his apartment.

'Has he left?'

He shrugged. 'Maybe. Maybe not. I haven't heard him go downstairs, but, you know, I've been chilling so I miss stuff sometimes.'

'Okay, thanks.'

'You want any help?'

'No, I'm fine, thanks.'

He gave a long lazy nod and went back into his apartment.

Jayne closed her eyes and took a deep breath. Someone had been up to her apartment. She could turn round and go, find help, get someone to look around her apartment. But she wasn't like that. She had to know.

She climbed the final flight to her apartment door, swallowing hard, her nerves like fast flutters. There were too many possibilities. Jimmy's family. Whoever had visited Sara Carter. Whoever had murdered Shelley.

As she examined her door, she saw nothing different. No tool marks where someone had forced entry. No damage anywhere. She tried her key. It worked like normal.

Her door swung open. It was dark within. As she went inside and closed her door, she stopped.

Something was different. She couldn't describe it. Was it a smell? Or something more indiscernible, like it had fallen silent just as she walked in, or the slow settle of dust?

It all looked normal. The hallway stretched ahead. The kitchen at the end, her bedroom the first room on the left, the living room the next along. Orange light streamed in from the street-lights outside, catching the swirls on the kitchen window where she hadn't cleaned it properly. Nothing looked out of place.

There was something there though. She didn't believe in a sixth sense, but there were goosebumps on her arms that she couldn't control.

She clicked on the hallway light, ready for someone to come at her. She let out a long breath. There was no one there.

She edged along the hallway, trying to keep her footsteps silent, wary of a creaking floorboard. As she strained her ears, she picked out more sounds. Music drifted up from the flat below, the steady thumps usually comforting, but now they just emphasised the silence in her own apartment. A siren sounded somewhere outside.

She cursed herself for letting her imagination get the better of her, but she'd lived her life in Highford waiting for someone to come for her.

Her keys clattered as she put them on the table in the hallway.

There was a noise in one of the rooms. An object moving, like something knocked against the dresser. It had been barely audible but it was there. She wasn't imagining things.

But it was a noisy apartment building. The radiators clanged sometimes. Doors often slammed, music was always playing.

It wasn't that though.

Her living room came into view. It seemed just as she'd left it. Some cups on the floor. A dirty plate on the chair arm. She turned on the light. No one there.

Only her bedroom left.

It was dark, with no streetlights at the back and the curtains closed. The door was partly shut. She pushed at it. Something was different. The creak had gone. She liked that creak, because it gave her warning when she was asleep that someone was entering her room. It was no longer there. The door opened silently into the bedroom.

She thought about backing out, but that was letting her fear take over. That wasn't going to happen.

Her hand reached out and clicked on the light switch. Nothing. Still darkness.

Her stomach turned.

It was just the bulb. Be rational.

She stepped into the room and tried to use the light from the hallway to check whether anything was different. It all looked the same. Her bed in the middle. Her wardrobe across from it. Drawers on either side of the bed. A lamp.

Of course, the lamp.

She went towards the bed to walk round it and stopped. There was an aroma, something new. It was hard to pinpoint, except that it didn't smell like her room anymore.

The space was narrow between the end of the bed and the wardrobe, so she edged round slowly, feeling her way in the darkness, her legs against the bed.

There was another noise.

She stopped. She was at the corner of the bed, the darkest part of the room just behind her. She wasn't breathing, every muscle in her body tensed.

It was there again. Soft movement, the sound of someone getting comfortable. Light breaths just behind her. Hers? Or someone else's? Her skin went cold.

'Who's there?'

No reply. Static crackled along her back. She walked quickly to the lamp to click it on. Nothing. Clicked again. Still nothing.

Another sound, more movement. A breath, the sound of exertion.

Someone was in the apartment with her.

Jimmy's family. Maybe worse. She had to get out.

She scrambled over the bed, the springs bouncing. More sounds of movement, feet on the floor.

She ran for the door, slamming it shut as she stumbled into the hall. There was the sound of screaming, distant, unreal, then she realised it was her own. Something thumped against the bedroom door. She bolted along the hallway, grabbing her keys as she went, her hand fumbling with the lock as she opened it, her hands slick.

She could alert people, the others in the building, but she didn't want to wait. Get outside. Run. Those were her only thoughts.

She took the stairs two at a time, her breaths loud in her head. Her only thought was getting away. She sneaked a look back as she reached the first landing, but there was no one there.

She'd got it wrong, was seeing shadows. Something had fallen over as she'd gone over the bed. It was her imagination, that's all.

It didn't matter. She couldn't stay there. Get out, she told herself, driven by an inner alarm.

She knew where she was going.

Fifty-three

The night had been long for Dan. The news about Shelley and then the adrenaline of the arrest had drained him, but any thought of resting up had ended when Jayne had arrived at his apartment, tearful and scared. All he could do was give her a blanket and his sofa and make sure his apartment door was locked.

He'd stayed with Jayne, awake in a chair opposite her, fuelled by anger. As the first strains of sunlight appeared over the horizon, he'd known that he had to speak to Murdoch. The case was getting dangerous and it was no time to play games.

He was outside the police station, waiting for Murdoch. The town was quiet. The sun blinked off the large supermarket windows on the other side of the ring road. He'd left Jayne on the sofa, asleep under a blanket. Murdoch would be starting early; the senior detectives always did whenever there was a new murder, and Shelley's case was less than a day old. They started early and finished late, and the detectives who wanted to impress were compelled to match the hours. Murdoch would be too tired for the confrontation, but Dan was more concerned about the Carter case than about Murdoch's temper.

He'd been there for over thirty minutes before her car swung into the station car park and headed for the furthest corner, closest to the station's rear entrance. Dan ducked under the barrier and walked towards it. Murdoch was climbing out as he reached her.

'What's going on?' she said, startled at being approached. 'Got some news on Shelley?'

'No, I'm here about the Carter case.'

She slammed her car door. 'Give it a rest, Dan. You got up early for this? Do things the right way if there's something else. Write to the prosecution, get it listed in court if you want, but just stop bugging me about it.'

'This way is more effective.'

'But it isn't the only case I've got. No, more than that, because it's nearly over. The trial is in less than two weeks and I've got other things to do. Like trying to find who pushed Shelley Greenwood from a railway bridge, which I thought would interest even you.'

Dan bristled at that as she set off towards the entrance.

'DC Edwards,' he shouted after her.

She stopped and turned slowly. 'What about him?'

'He's bent.'

'What are you on about?'

'He's got money trouble, is my guess.'

Murdoch walked back to him and put her hands on her hips. 'This had better be good.'

'Whilst we were having our chat last night, do you know where he was?'

'You're about to tell me.'

'He was throwing his wages into a fruit machine in The Fleamarket.'

'He's allowed to relax after work.'

'Not if he was doing it with Dominic Ayres.'

'Dominic Ayres?'

'That's right. The father of Lucy Ayres, one of your key witnesses, and the bigshot no one will touch.'

'How do you know he was with Dominic Ayres?'

Dan unrolled the piece of paper he'd been holding and handed it over. It was the photo Jayne had been able to take the night before. Not particularly clear, the flash stopping the long night-time exposure she'd been hoping for and reflecting from the window, blocking a good view of the person closest to the glass, but there'd been enough light inside the house to show the one thing that caused Murdoch to raise her eyebrows: DC Edwards playing cards, a glass next to him.

'That's at Ayres's house. Taken last night, just after he was driven there by Dominic Ayres.' A pause, and then, 'Do you know what I think?'

'You're going to tell me anyway.'

'Dominic Ayres wanted someone on the inside, because he wants to make sure that his daughter isn't dragged into it. He knows Edwards, so he uses him. Or perhaps worse than that?'

'Worse?'

'He plays on weaknesses. That's what his thugs do, play on weaknesses. He bullies his tenants. I think he's bullied Carter, because two thugs visited Carter's wife, wanted to know what Carter was saying. I think those were Dominic's men, and they've put the frighteners on Carter so that he plays dumb, let him know that they know where his nearest and dearest are, that they could hurt them if they wanted. And guess what, it's working, because I don't think he's telling the truth. Instead, he's hanging on to his story, hoping that it will be believed, even though we both know it won't. Edwards has a gambling problem. He went straight on to the fruit machine, and then he was playing cards with Ayres, probably losing back all the money that had been given to him. Gamblers are easy targets. Ayres gave him a way out, and it meant keeping him in the loop.'

'Why are you telling me this?' Murdoch said, looking down at the picture.

'I'm going after Lucy Ayres, like I told you. I just thought you should know.'

'Bullshit. The defence only ever disclose something if it's to give them an advantage. You could have saved all this for the trial, make us out to be blinkered and corrupt, then propped up Carter's weak defence with a few conspiracy theories. Instead, you come to me, waving this around,' and Murdoch held up the photograph. 'You want to know what I think?'

'I can't wait.'

'You're panicking. Carter isn't telling you anything, so you know you can't go down this route at court. You're hoping to derail it now, that we get nervous and pull the plug, tell the CPS that we've got new evidence that we need to investigate and we're not sure of Carter's guilt. There's one problem with that: we are sure of Carter's guilt, and it's not our call, it's the CPS's. If we tried to pull it, they'd be suspicious, wondering whether we'd been doing deals behind their back. No, Carter's trial is soon, and at the moment you're looking desperate.'

'Perhaps I want to see justice done without Dominic Ayres interfering, because Robert Carter deserves a fair trial, whatever he did.' Dan pointed at the picture. 'And you need to make sure he gets one, unless you want some rogue detective letting Carter walk free. I told you last night that I want the phone records for

Lucy and her boyfriend. This,' and he pointed at the picture still in Murdoch's hands, 'should make you try a little bit harder. I want him off the investigation.'

'You can't tell me what to do.'

'You reckon? I've warned you about him. If you want to go to trial with that stain over your case, do it, but if you do, know that I'm going after Edwards. He will be a stench over the prosecution case.'

Dan turned to walk away.

He waited for a shout from Murdoch, maybe the sound of her trying to catch him up, but there was just the angry stomp of her feet and the slam of the station door.

He'd got what he wanted, Murdoch engaged.

Fifty-four

Dan listened out as he opened the door to his apartment. He checked his watch. Not yet eight. No sounds. The curtains were still drawn and Jayne was still asleep.

He was carrying coffees bought from a nearby garage. As he walked into the living room, Jayne's long hair was sprawled out over the cushion at the end of the sofa. The rest of her body was under the blanket he'd thrown over her, but it had ridden up and was showing off most of her legs, pale in the gloom.

He put the coffee on the table and opened the curtains. When the light streamed in, she groaned and pulled the blanket higher.

He sat on the sofa next to her and put his hand on her shoulder. 'Come on, sleepyhead, it's coffee time.'

'What time is that?' The words barely audible through the drawl.

'Almost eight.'

She lifted her head, just one eye open. 'Yeah, not my best look.' She yawned and swung her legs down, keeping the blanket over her shoulders, and got to her feet to shuffle to where her coffee was, on the table by the window.

'Where have you been?' she said, once she'd taken her first swig.

'To see DI Murdoch.'

'Did you tell her about someone being in my apartment?'

'No, I didn't. We'll go round later, both of us, and have a proper look.'

Jayne nodded, her hands cupped around her coffee, and returned to the sofa. 'Did you show her the photograph?'

'It didn't help her mood.'

'Is she going to do anything about it?'

'No, but she will. For all of her fire, she's honest and I trust her.'

She pulled the blanket around herself again and rested her head on Dan's shoulder. 'So, what now?'

'I need more information on Lucy. I'm waiting on Lucy's phone location, as well as Peter's. Find out what you can about him too.'

'You going all out for her?'

'I can't see any other option. If Dominic Ayres is behind all of this, the intimidation and threats, why is that? If Lucy's got nothing to do with it, he's behaving pretty strangely.'

'What's your theory?'

Dan went to the window and stared out at the view as he thought. Eventually, he turned round and said, 'I think Shelley got too close. She found Henry Oates, discovered that Carter and Mary had been seen cosying up to one another, so knew Lucy's story wasn't true, or at least, wasn't the complete picture. And she had Mickey too, pointing the finger at Lucy. How else can Dominic Ayres's behaviour be explained?'

Jayne pondered on that for a few seconds, before saying, 'But why would Lucy kill Mary? And more importantly, why would Robert Carter stay quiet?'

'Most of the good reasons are the simple ones. An argument gone wrong? We know that there was more to Carter and Mary than unrequited love on his part. We've a witness who puts them together as a couple, holding hands, looking affectionate. That's different to how Lucy painted it, which is very convenient, when you think about it.'

'Oh yeah, our great witness, a local drunk.'

'That doesn't make him wrong. Why would he lie? He's not getting any reward. And I'll tell you something else about all the drunks and tramps I've represented: their lives are a mess, but they're honest about their failures. Yes, they steal to get money to pay for booze, but when they're caught, they admit it. I wouldn't trust many with a tenner, but I'd trust them not to bullshit me.'

'I get that, but the jurors won't have your experience. They won't believe him and you'll look desperate, rolling out some drunk to spin them a line.'

'But it's all we have.'

Jayne took a drink of coffee as she thought about that. 'Okay, if it's true that Lucy was involved, what's the story?'

Dan sat opposite. 'Let's assume that Carter and Mary were together, that he wasn't some stalker. We can guess why no one else knew: because he was married, and Mary was a good person caught up in a situation she didn't like being in. But how can you control your heart? It would explain why Carter turned up whenever Mary was out on the town, and why Carter is sticking to his story. Because it's partly true.'

'Yeah, but it makes it worse in another way, because if Carter was having a thing with Mary, is the reason even simpler, the oldest reason in the world: a lover's rage? Was she planning on ending it? Or maybe the other way, that she was going to tell Carter's wife, give him an ultimatum? Did the after-sex talk go badly? If they were lovers, you've got passion, which makes more sense than some fixation got too strong for him. It'll stop him being a weirdo stalker, losing it because she won't sleep with him, but he'll still be seen as a killer.'

'But if that's true, why is Dominic Ayres behaving like this? If he's trying to deflect attention from his daughter, he's doing just the opposite.'

'Are we sure Dominic is behaving like anything? I mean, what has he really done? Someone has visited Carter's wife, then put some pressure on Shelley. That could just be about keeping the blame away from Lucy.'

'Shelley is dead. That's more than pressure.'

'It might not have anything to do with Lucy or Dominic.'

'Okay, let's forget for the moment about Carter and Mary. How might Lucy be involved? That must be the key.'

'Are we sure that Mary was the one he was fixated on?' Jayne said. 'That comes from Lucy, but if she's involved in the murder, it doesn't count for anything. Carter is staying pretty silent, apart from the finger in the ears impression; you know, all la-la-la, I can't hear how strong the evidence is and I'll just say I was outside. Yeah, like that's going to work. What if his fixation was Lucy? Let's face it, she's a striking woman, and she's got that coldness that some men seem to like. What if it's about blind loyalty? He loves Lucy so he is protecting her, is willing to go to prison for her.'

'You're forgetting one thing. Carter's DNA was on Mary. How did that happen?'

'I didn't say any of it made sense,' Jayne said, and went back to drinking her coffee.

'What about this?' Dan said. 'Carter is walking Mary home, because he's sweet on her and it's dark and he wanted to make sure she got home safely. They bump into Henry on the way, and Carter plays up to him, makes out like Mary's his girlfriend, because he wants her to be. Mary doesn't tell him not to because she's too polite, doesn't want to offend Carter, it's only some drunk anyway. They get back to her house and Lucy is there, being showy, annoying, perhaps stoned or drunk, fired up by something, and she taunts Mary for being uptight. It goes on and on, tempers flare, Mary lets loose with her feelings about Lucy. Things get out of hand, and Lucy holds Mary down and goads Carter into raping her, to give it to the "uptight bitch", because that is how Lucy thinks of her.'

'Would he do that?'

'What, would he rape her? The obsessive stalker, the married man chasing the woman who's too good for him? Yes, he would. And it wouldn't matter which woman he was fixated on. Did he rape Mary to please Lucy, or did he rape her because he couldn't control himself? But Mary screamed. Loud enough for the neighbours to hear. That's when they know it's gone too far, so Lucy panics and stabs her. She gets her boyfriend to give her an alibi. Perhaps he was even there, egging Carter on. In the morning, they go to the house to make the discovery, their stories in place.'

Jayne finished her coffee and sat back, huddled under the blanket. 'There's another problem.'

'Go on.'

'That makes Carter a rapist. I'd rather be a murderer than a rapist. I don't think he'll go with that as a story.'

'He doesn't have to go with any story. That isn't how it works. He tells me what happened, not the other way round.'

'That isn't how it's sounding.'

'I can still pitch some scenarios to him. Sometimes a person has to be shown that the truth is worth telling.'

'So, you'll try to get him to go with rape rather than murder?'

Dan stared into his coffee as he thought about that. Eventually, he said, 'Yes, you're right, he won't go for that. I'm going to see him this afternoon. Let's see if I can open him up.'

'And if he latches on to a more convincing lie and gets away with murder?'

'That isn't our problem. If he walks, we've done our job.'

'And Dominic Ayres? What will he do to Robert Carter if he blames Lucy?'

'That isn't part of our worry.'

'It should be, after what happened to Shelley.'

'That's just how it is.'

'If your client ends up dead?'

'A young woman died. Let's sort out that battle first.'

'And what about me?'

'What do you mean?'

'Someone has been in my flat.'

Dan held out his hand. Jayne took it. 'Stay here. The sofa isn't the comfiest thing, but it's only until the trial is over.'

'The sofa?'

He stared into her eyes as his mind turned over the answer. 'Yes, the sofa.' His tone was unconvincing.

'Understood. And thank you.'

'Good. Now let's get to work.'

Fifty-five

Dan sat poised at a desk as he waited for Robert Carter to be brought to him.

He'd been granted a small interview room. It wasn't usual to get an appointment so quickly, but with the trial so close the prison had made an exception.

He looked up as a key jangled in the lock and the door was opened by a large man with a chain attached to his belt loop. Carter trudged in behind him, wearing a grey sweatshirt under a red bib.

'How long have I got?' Dan asked.

'You're good for an hour,' the guard said, and pointed towards a button on the wall, next to the light switch. 'Just buzz if you want out before then.'

When they were left alone in the room, Dan pointed to the chair. 'Sit down.'

Carter did as he was told and crossed his arms. 'Why the attitude?'

'Because your trial is soon and we need to get your story straight.'

'It's not a story.'

'It's always a story when it's being told to the courtroom.'

Carter sat up and leaned forward. He scowled. 'What else do you want to know?'

'Tell me about Mary.'

Carter's jaw clenched. 'What about her?'

'How long had you been seeing her for?'

Dan let the silence grow as Carter stared at him. A few minutes passed before Dan said, 'Well?'

'I hadn't. She was just a friend.'

'You don't sound convincing.'

'I don't care what you think.'

'You should, because if you're not convincing me, you've no chance with a jury.'

'It's like I said. I saw her walking home and I made sure she got there safely. She wasn't like that.'

'Like what?'

'The sort of woman who would be involved with a married man,' he said, and then his anger seemed to dissolve. His eyes filled with tears. He wiped them away before saying, his voice cracking, 'Mary had a pure soul. She was a special person.'

'You loved her.'

'I didn't say that.'

'Do you think you can be this evasive when you give evidence? You've got to appear honest, someone who can't wait to tell his story, so the jury believes that you wouldn't hurt her.'

Carter looked down. A tear dropped on to the desk.

'Tell me about Mary,' Dan repeated. 'Where did you first see her? How was she with you? How would you describe your relationship?'

'I saw her in the Wharf pub, the first time,' he said. 'She was with a group of women, but she didn't look like she wanted to be with them.'

'How do you mean?'

'They were being too noisy, like they were drunk but didn't know how to handle it. She came to the bar, it was her round, and we got chatting as she waited to be served. It was natural, good. When she was leaving, I was having a smoke outside. She said goodbye, just being friendly, and when she came into the pub the next time she was the one who started the conversation.'

'Why do you think she did that?'

'Because that's how she was. Friendly.'

'Nothing more than friendly?'

Carter didn't answer.

'How often did you walk her home?'

Carter's lip twitched. 'Just that once.'

'Why that night?'

'I saw her, that's all.'

'Did you know where she lived?'

'She'd told me the area.'

'Were you waiting for her?'

'I was walking off the beer.'

'Did you kiss?'

Carter frowned. 'I don't know what you mean.'

'Don't be evasive. Things happen between adults, even if they don't plan it. You liked her, everyone can tell that, and Mary had been drinking. Did you kiss?'

Carter took a few deep breaths. 'Why do you want to make her look like the sort of person who'd sleep with a married man?'

'As opposed to the man who's actually the married one?' Dan said, his eyebrows raised. 'Don't you worry about the jury judging Mary, because they'll be too busy judging you.'

'But what about her memory?' Carter sniffed away his tears and wiped his sleeve across his eyes. 'Whatever I say will stay with people and she's not around to stand up for herself.'

'Okay, I'll fill in some of the gaps and you tell me how near I get.' Dan stood up so that he was leaning over Carter, so close that he could smell the roll-up cigarettes and the hours spent locked in his cell. 'You met up with Mary. She was drunk, but knew what she was doing. You kissed and you both ended up in bed. She had sex with you, but the afterglow wasn't as sweet as she hoped. You regretted it, because you're married. Or perhaps it was Mary who had the regret, because you'd probably dreamed of that moment, wished it was Mary every time that your wife slid into bed next to you.'

Carter shook his head but said nothing.

'Was it an argument? Did you feel rejected and lashed out in a moment of madness, not meaning to kill her? Or was it Mary? Did she talk about telling your wife and you panicked, grabbed the first thing to hand? A knife?'

'No!' Carter slammed his hand on the table.

'Don't lose your temper in the witness box.'

'Fuck off.' He some deep breaths to calm himself. 'I told you, I was outside having a cigarette. I heard her scream.'

'But the jury have got to believe you. I can tell you what they will think if you try to clam up. They'll think you went home with Mary and misread her signals.'

'No.'

'That you tried to force yourself on her, but she didn't want that, except that you'd decided that it was going to happen anyway, the night had come, so you kept on at her, holding her down, forcing yourself on her.'

'No, no, no.'

'You raped her, and when she screamed you stabbed her.'

'No!'

'Do you think the jury won't think that? Can't you see how easy a tale it is to tell?'

'I did not rape Mary. I did not kill Mary. I was outside –'

'Yeah, yeah, let me guess. You were outside, having a cigarette, when you heard her scream.'

As Carter put his head on the desk and his arms around his head, Dan stepped back, frustrated. He looked down and said, 'Lucy Ayres.'

'What about her?' Carter's voice was muffled.

'What did you make of her?'

'What has Lucy got to do with anything?'

'Just answer the question. That's all you have got to think about now. Don't answer a question with another one. It's the first refuge for a liar, to buy time.'

He lifted his head up. The sadness in his eyes was replaced by a hard glare. 'I'm not lying.'

'Just answer the question.'

Carter thought for a few moments, before he said, 'Stuck up. Full of herself, like she thought I should admire her, like every-one should.'

'Did you see her at the house that night?'

'I'm not doing this.'

'Why won't you answer?'

'I'm going back to my cell.'

'Why don't you want me to visit your wife?'

'Leave her out of it.'

'Jayne went to see her.'

He sat back, his eyes wide. 'I told you not to.'

'She's an investigator, so she did just that, investigated. Sara was scared.'

'You bastard.'

'Who went to see her? Have they got to you?'

He got to his feet and went to the buzzer, jabbing at it, before pacing in front of the door.

'This is your life,' Dan said. 'Were they sent by Lucy's father?'

Carter jabbed at the buzzer again and glared at Dan.

Somewhere in the distance a door was unlocked and footsteps got closer.

As the door was opened by the same guard as before, Carter said, 'I've told you what happened,' and rushed out of the room.

The guard raised an eyebrow.

Dan put his hands on his hips and looked towards the ceiling. Whatever truth there was to be uncovered, he'd have to do it without his client's help.

Or let Robert Carter talk his way into a murder conviction that would mean he spent the rest of his life behind bars.

Fifty-six

Jayne had followed Dan's instructions and gone to find out more about Lucy's boyfriend, Peter Wilde.

He lived in a flat above a betting shop, accessed by a small green door between the bookies and the barber next door. This was the flat where Lucy and Peter said they were on the night Mary was murdered, at the opposite end of the town to where Mary and Lucy shared a house.

Jayne was in a small café, close by. She hadn't expected Peter to be there, but there'd been some movement inside his flat. The café was probably once a thriving business, part of a small collection of businesses serving the surrounding streets, but it seemed to rely mainly on workers wanting bacon sandwiches, with just a few tables by the window.

She'd just started her second Styrofoam cup of instant coffee when Peter's front door opened. He was wearing a long black coat with a scarf around his neck, although it seemed more of an affectation than anything to do with the climate. He looked both ways before setting off, almost as if he expected someone to be watching him. Had she been seen?

Peter trotted across the road, a leather bag over his shoulder, and headed down a long terraced street that would bring him out close to a main road, which carried the traffic into the town centre.

Jayne left her coffee behind and set off after him.

He was around fifty yards ahead but she was able to keep him in view. She stayed on the opposite side of the road, using the shade from the line of houses to obscure herself. He was walking with purpose, so she had to occasionally break into a small jog to keep pace.

His change of direction took her by surprise.

He had seemed like he was heading to the end of the street but turned suddenly into one of the side streets, almost as if he hadn't planned to go down that way.

Was it a trap? Jayne contemplated running to catch up, but she remembered how he'd waited for her the day before and attacked her. She decided to stay on her side of the road and get a good view down the side street, so that she wouldn't run the risk of being confronted by him again.

She quickened her pace. If he'd spotted her, following him would be a waste of time. If he hadn't, all that mattered was that he was still visible.

When she was opposite the junction, she'd lost sight of him. There was just a short street that led to the main road, with open fields beyond, the traffic in a steady stream. She knew the road, it was long and straight, so he'd be easy to spot.

She walked towards it with caution, checking the alleyway, wondering if he was waiting for her there.

He wasn't. Just the usual scattering of wheelie bins and cardboard boxes.

The view widened out as she reached the main road, with the carriageways wider and a bus lane on one side.

She looked both ways, trying to spot him, but he wasn't there.

She put her hands on her hips, turning around. He was gone.

The morning wasn't going well.

She was about to turn round to go back to her own car when her attention was grabbed by the diesel rumble of a bus setting off from the other side of the road, bound for a town ten miles away. As she looked, someone was walking along the aisle to take a seat. Peter.

As he sat down, he glared at Jayne. She had been spotted.

She turned away, angry.

Peter was being very elusive, always conscious of someone following him. If he'd hoped to put her off, he'd done exactly the opposite.

If she couldn't follow him, she'd go back to what other people had said about him, and look for some clues in the press reports.

The library was the place to start.

*

Dan wondered where to go next as he left the prison and waited for his phone to come to life. He was frustrated that he'd got nowhere, which meant only one thing: he would just have to let the trial run.

But there was something he was missing. Nothing Carter had said would make Dominic Ayres behave in the way he had.

He walked quickly, wanting to get back to his office. As he got to his car, thankfully still intact, he noticed a light flashing on his phone. A voicemail.

He checked it as he climbed into his car. By the time he'd turned on the engine, his fingers were white with rage, clenched around the steering wheel.

It was from his father's rest home. His father had received visitors. Two of them. Both men. One smartly-dressed, wealthy looking. The other just a thug in a suit, bald-headed with scars.

Whatever had been said, they'd left his father agitated, angry even. He'd smashed a vase with his walking stick and demanded that Dan went there.

He didn't need asking twice.

The journey was quicker than usual, a dash along the motorway and then through the narrow streets of Highford. As he went through the door, one of the care home staff shouted out, 'Mr Grant?'

He stopped.

She was walking along the corridor towards him, her feet silent on the heavy carpet.

'Yes?' His impatience showed.

'I'm the one who called earlier,' she said, and folded her arms as she stood in front of him. 'We can't have him behaving like that. It frightens the other residents.'

'Behaving like what?'

'His temper. Some have complained about him before, the way he rants at the television news, and worse when he's had too much cider. He can't go on like this.'

'Let me speak to him,' Dan said, and set off towards his father's room.

'You've got to tell him to stop.'

Dan raised his hand in acknowledgement and then paused outside the door to his father's room. The corridor was too warm and the cloying smell of steamed vegetables was still heavy in the air following lunch. He had to calm down, because he needed to know what had happened without getting into an argument.

He knocked on the door and went inside. There was a television playing, the volume too loud. His father was hunched in a chair facing the television, a glass next to him, filled with cider.

A large plastic bottle sat next to him, squeezed in the middle by his one good hand.

'They called you then,' he said, as Dan sat opposite.

'Yes, they did, and they're not happy with you.'

He reached for his glass and took a drink, raising it in mock salute. 'Not for the first time. I'll survive. So will they.'

'Do you have to be so difficult all the time?'

'You know the answer to that,' he said, although there was the gleam of a half-smile.

Yes, he knew it all right, he thought. He'd had a lifetime of knowing how his father thrived on being difficult. 'What set you off?'

His father put the glass down and turned towards him. 'I had visitors.'

'So I heard. Did they say who they were?'

'I didn't need any introductions. Dominic Ayres and one of his apes. A nasty little sod.'

Dan was surprised. 'You know Dominic Ayres?'

'It's a small town. I make it my business to know these people.'

'I don't understand.'

His father sat back, and Dan got ready for a lecture.

'My politics wasn't just about strikes,' he said, and the way he stared into the distance told Dan that his father had transported himself back to when he had battles to fight. 'We tried to help people, to stick up for them, protect them against greedy bastards like Ayres.'

'I still don't understand.'

'Slum clearances. The council sold off whole derelict streets for virtually nothing, wanted developers to create something vibrant. That's where Ayres came in. Just like his father. Robert

Ayres. Leader of the council back in his day, and a complete bastard. Tried to get rid of half the workforce to put services out to tender, except that we got wind of it and protested. We had banners and pickets outside the town hall for a month before he backed down.' He put his glass down. 'We thought direct action had worked, at first.'

'Hadn't it?'

'No. He backed off because he'd been trying to give the services to companies run by people who'd given him gifts, like holidays and a car, and he was rumbled. Like them all, bloody rotten. The tenders were scrapped because he was bent, not because of us.'

'And Dominic is just like that?'

'Worse, because he's mean with it. I could see it in his eyes. Cold and arrogant. The old man was a bastard because he thought it was the only way to claw himself to the top. He was a fighter. Dominic? Spoilt, that's all. He wants it all because he thinks he deserves it.'

'I know about his properties, but why was he here?'

His father thumped the floor with his walking stick. 'Why do you think?'

'Because of me.'

'Damn right, because of you.'

'What did he say?'

'He wanted to know what you were up to. Talked about whether you were like me.'

'Stubborn?'

'I prefer *determined*.'

'What did you tell him?'

'I told him to leave, and to make it damn quick.' He banged his stick on the ground once more. 'I'm not scared of people like him.'

'He didn't pass on any message, or tell you anything?'

'That was the message. Don't you get it? It's the usual tactic of the bully. Let me tell you, son, real danger comes quietly, because you fill in the gaps in your head. It's how you frighten yourself that gives you the most fear.' He leaned forward on his stick. 'That's how they used to break us, back in the day.'

Dan sat back, knowing that he was going to get another war story, but he didn't mind this time. His work had caused his father to get a visit. He owed him some nostalgia, if nothing else.

'If we got a strike going, someone would get a visit,' he continued, his eyes misted by fond memories. 'Not one of the ringleaders. It would always be someone who just went along with the vote.' He scowled. 'Democratic vote, you understand. So someone with kids would get a visit, because they were the most desperate for the money, and they were told how the strike would close the factory, and then where else would they work? All polite, all friendly, and when they started to flinch, the extra pressure would come. They'd tell them about the money the bosses would lose, and how it would make people unhappy. They'd know the kids' names, where they went to school, making polite conversation. No direct threat, but there didn't have to be one, because once they left the fears started to play out, the ones that kept them awake at night.'

'That's industrial tactics. You can't compare that with this.'

'Why? What the hell are you caught up in?'

'It's a case, that's all. And it's not fair that they came to you.'

'Don't you worry about me. They know what I think of them.'

'It's not your fight.'

'It is now, because they came to me. And I don't back away from fights. You should try it.'

'Sometimes I think we're too much the same.'

'So go after them. Take the fight to them.'

'Is that what you did?'

His father smiled. 'Late night visits can happen at anyone's house. And sometimes they're not so polite.'

'I've heard enough.'

'You going to back down?'

Dan paused as thought of Dominic Ayres trying to intimidate his father. 'Not a chance.'

Fifty-seven

Dan knew where he was going.

He drove quickly, using the tight bends to keep his adrenalin flowing. Things were getting out of control. He had to put a stop to it.

The hedgerows flashed by, his hands gripped tightly around the steering wheel. Don't think about it. Keep going. If he thought about what lay ahead, he might back out. But Dominic Ayres had gone too far now.

The Ayres house loomed ahead. It stood out more in the daylight. The night before, it had seemed like a typical stone house nestled in the hills, but the sunlight made it look like a copy, with the mortar too neat, the stones too polished, the brick driveway too clean. Roses made an effort on either side to climb up the walls, but they were not established enough.

Dan drove quickly up the driveway. He jumped out of his car and banged on the door. It wasn't a knock with his knuckles but a thump with his fist.

He stepped away from the door and looked up at the house, checking for anyone peering out, any threat.

The door opened. Dan expected one of the bruisers, but a woman answered, in her late forties, her hair blonde but not natural, in an expensive-looking jumper and her shirt collar up. Dan recognised Lucy in her.

'Yes?' She said it as if it were a privilege to disturb her.

'I need to speak to Dominic.'

'And you are?'

That was all the answer he needed, because her answer spoke of whether she would allow him in, not whether Dominic was there.

Dan rushed forward and brushed past her. She shouted out and grabbed at him, her country gentility lost in the snarl of her teeth. Dan brushed her off. 'Which way?'

'You're a trespasser.'

'Get an injunction. Which way?'

'Who are you?'

'Where's Dominic?'

She pulled a phone from her pocket. 'I'm calling the police.' But her voice lacked conviction as her finger hovered over the screen.

'It's all right,' a voice said. Calm, composed.

Dan turned. Dominic Ayres was walking towards him, his hands in his pockets, looking nonplussed.

'We need to talk,' Dan said.

'In there.' Dominic pointed to a room off the hallway.

Dan went in first.

It was a large room with a low ceiling, a television built into its own slot over the fireplace and spotlights in the ceiling. The windows that picture-framed the hills behind were wooden, but clean and new.

Dominic closed the door and gestured for Dan to sit down.

'Forget the pleasantries,' Dan told him. 'You've gone too far.'

'I've gone too far?' Behind the politeness, there was menace.

'You visited my father.'

'Just saying hello to my father's old adversary.'

'You're involving family. That's too far.'

'But you're allowed to drag my daughter into your tawdry little case?'

'I know your source. DC Edwards. He's off the case now.'

'My source?'

'We can play games if you want. How about poker? He enjoyed that. What happened? Did you win back the money you paid him for information?'

Dominic paused as he took that in, before saying, 'For someone who does what you do, I don't quite get your moral compass.'

'For me, it's about doing my job, not about morality. You're the guy with the skewed morality.'

'You don't know anything about me.'

'What about trying to interfere in an investigation? Sending your goons to Robert Carter's wife? Intimidating my father? That tells me all I need to know.'

'You're dragging my daughter into this.'

'She dragged herself into it.'

'How so?'

'She was there.'

'Where?'

'When Mary was killed.'

Dominic walked over to where Dan was standing. He stopped right in front of him and invaded his space, looking up at him.

'Don't you dare.' Dominic snarled the words through gritted teeth.

'Is that what the visits are about? To Carter's wife? To my father? What happens next? Do I become another Shelley Greenwood?'

Dominic stepped away. He went to the window and looked out.

Dan's attention was drawn to his surroundings. There were pictures of Lucy on every wall. In her school uniform, and then her graduation shots, her hair in curls then, flowing out from underneath the mortarboard. Lucy on a horse. Lucy in the netball team. It was all Lucy.

'I won't have this,' Dominic said. 'Right at the start, the press latched on to Lucy. But why? Because she didn't behave like they expected? Well, that's just Lucy.'

'She was there.'

'Where?'

'When it happened.'

'And you've got a witness?'

Dan stayed silent. He wasn't prepared to reveal what he had, and what he didn't.

'I won't let Lucy become a scapegoat.'

'Why's that? Because of how it reflects on you? What about Mary?'

'No, because it will reflect on her forever. I won't have her life ruined for Mary's sake. No, not for Mary. For Robert Carter.'

'And I won't stop fighting the case my way.'

'It's not just your father though, is it? What about your assistant, Jayne? What about the danger you're putting her in?'

'Is that a threat?'

'You take it how you want.'

'Stop it!'

It was Lucy's mother, standing in the doorway, wiping tears from her eyes.

Dominic turned away from Dan.

'Just stop it, both of you,' she said. 'Posturing, facing up like that. Mary died. Lucy's character was attacked in the press just for being a little different, until they caught that man. You go, leave us alone,' and she pointed at Dan. 'You've made your point.'

'Do I make my point?' Dan said, staring at Dominic. 'Keep away from my father.'

Dominic shook his head. 'For as long as you're attacking my family, no one is off limits.'

'No one?'

'You, Dan Grant. And anyone who helps you.'

'Did you go to her place?'

'Her?'

'You know who I'm talking about. Jayne Brett, my assistant.'

Dominic folded his arms. 'Like I say, no one is off limits.'

'Just go,' Lucy's mother said again.

Dan looked at them both, saw the contempt in their eyes, and headed for the door.

Just as he got there, Dominic said, 'Take care, Mr Grant. For the sake of all the people you care about.'

Dan pushed past Lucy's mother and rushed to get outside. He needed air, light. He needed more than anything to be away from the poison they projected.

And he needed to think about Jayne.

*

The computers at the library were occupied by an unusual collection of people, mainly those who were not used to using computers at home. A retired man browsed a family tree website, a woman read an online newspaper, and two young men in their twenties were doing some research for college.

Jayne had the Internet at home, or she could use Dan's Wi-Fi at his place, but there were other resources available at the library that she didn't have at home. Like electoral rolls or older newspaper reports.

She started with the five days of press reporting Lucy and Peter had endured before Carter was arrested and charged.

In the absence of a pending court appearance, the press had relied on profiles of Mary and raised questions about her lifestyle, which made her parents walk out of a press conference. This had forced one newspaper into a long apology once it was realised that Mary had been everything the press wanted from a victim: pretty and wholesome.

The media attention shifted to Peter and Lucy. It was mainly photographs rather than explicit allegations, but the nature of their behaviour was highlighted, with words used like *inappropriate* or *disrespectful*, or even *just bizarre*.

They hadn't helped themselves. It seemed like all it took was a camera lens for Peter and Lucy to start performing.

It was in the comments section that the allegations flowed more readily, underneath the disclaimer that the newspaper sites did not endorse any of the user comments. For every comment posted that people react differently in different situations, there were ten times more attacking how they behaved.

Most of the newspaper coverage was about Lucy. Peter was almost a footnote, described as a student, nothing more.

Jayne was about to delve into the online forums when her phone buzzed in her pocket. The screen said it was Dan.

She ran out of the library so that she could answer.

'Hello?'

'It's over.'

'What do you mean, it's over?'

'Just that. Carter won't change his story and too many people have been hurt.'

Dan sounded flat.

'Are you okay? It's not like you to give up.'

'I'm not giving up. It's just that I've nothing to fight with if my client won't change his instructions.'

'But we can still look. We might find something better.'

'If Carter gives us a different tale, we'll run with it, but for now we're stuck with what we've got.'

'What about if I keep on looking?'

'No, we're done. I'm sorry, but thanks for helping, and if you can come to the trial, you can be the caseworker. Same rates. It'll help you out a bit.'

Jayne looked back into the library. Her computer screen was visible, showing a web page about Peter. 'If it's because you're worried about me, don't. I'll be fine. Or if it's because you want me out of your apartment, I can go back and ask my neighbours to look out for me.'

A pause and then, 'Yes, that might be a good idea. Just post my key in the letterbox. Send me your bill and I'll see you at the trial.'

And with that, he hung up.

Jayne slumped on to a nearby bench. So that was it. All over. As she thought about it, she realised what she'd miss most, and it wasn't just working with Dan. No, it was more than that. It was the chance to have a purpose, to mean something.

She'd miss that.

Fifty-eight

Present Day

Dan looked up at his office as he parked his car on the small piece of tarmac in the yard behind. It was all in darkness, apart from a light shining through the blinds in Pat Molloy's room. He should go home, he was tired, but being in court all day meant that he hadn't got round to the small jobs usually squeezed in between cases or client appointments. The bills to submit. Letters to clients, to make appointments they won't keep. Briefs to counsel. The routine trawl through his filing cabinet so that no file went untouched for more than three weeks.

It had been a long day, watching Lucy simper at the jury and enduring the threatening glares from Dominic Ayres.

He checked around as he made his way to the front door, cautious about anyone watching. The trial was attracting a lot of interest, and Shelley's murder reminded him that the threat existed wherever he went.

Dan headed for Pat's room, wanting some company before he started to open files. Pat was asleep, his head back against the chair, some papers spread in front of him.

Dan leaned against the doorjamb and tapped on the door. Pat jolted awake. His glasses tumbled from his nose and on to the desk in front of him.

'You're back,' Pat said, as he scrabbled for his glasses. An empty whisky glass told Dan what had caused the drowsiness. 'There was someone looking for you, a woman, said she had some information for you.'

'Did she say who she was?'

'No, but she seemed pretty anxious. I told her to call back.'

'What did she look like?'

'Young, stressed.'

'I don't have many clients who look at ease with the world.' Pat chuckled.

'Go home,' Dan told him. 'If you're going to drink alone, this isn't the place to do it.'

'Eileen is coming for me. She won't let me drive anymore. Worried that I'll crash.'

'If you're knocking that stuff back, she might be right.' Dan pointed to the glass.

'As I get older, I cherish my pleasures more. There isn't much excitement in my life, but things that make me happy? Plenty, and this fine single malt is one. That's what I look for in life, happiness. You should remember that.'

'What do you mean?'

'You don't smile enough, Daniel. You're too serious about everything.'

'Isn't that what you like about me, though? I remind you of your younger self. You didn't take on Dan Grant. You took on a version of Pat Molloy from thirty years ago.'

He swatted his hand towards Dan. 'It was a different world then.'

'What do you mean?'

'Where have all the characters gone? The wily old lawyers who tried every trick they knew, who could run a trial from notes written on the back of a cigarette packet. Retired, that's where. This job should be fun, because it's about peoples' lives. Their dramas. Even your old man knew that.'

'My father?'

'It's a small town, Dan, and I remember him back when he was in his pomp, back in the eighties, ready to fight for any cause he could. Perhaps it was that I was looking for, the reflections of your father, not me. He did it because he enjoyed it, and anyone who got into trouble because of it, he sent our way.'

'I didn't know that.'

'He asked me not to tell you, because he didn't want you to think he'd got you the job. He didn't, but he's a proud man from a different era, and wouldn't expect favours like that. It was a game, and there were some good players. Now, it's all money woes and tight procedures. There's been no fun in it for a long time.'

'So why are you still around?'

Pat reached for a drawer and pulled out the bottle. He topped up his glass and added a tiny measure of water from a small jug that was normally next to a plant on a filing cabinet. 'Because what else would I do with my life if I didn't do this? Everything I've done, everything I've worked for, gone in a moment as soon as I walk out of that door, just to be another old man on a park bench.'

'You've earned that space on the bench. Embrace it.'

Pat raised his glass in salute to the office in front of him. 'This is me, and it's you too. Being a lawyer is your calling, and when the time comes, you'll hang on to it like I am. If there's anything of a younger me in you, it's that. It's not what you do in court but how you see the job. You're just like your father, a fighter, except you're in a suit. Find the fun, like your father did.'

'I don't think he sees me that way.'

'He does, deep down.'

Before Dan could ask any more about it, Pat said, 'How was court today?'

'We're getting nowhere. Carter is sticking to his story and the prosecution are slowly building a case against him.'

'Why should you care? Do the case and cash the cheque.'

'Because something about it isn't right. I can't work out what, but it feels like we're only getting half a truth.'

'Isn't that always the way?' Pat took a sip and closed his eyes for a moment. 'The prosecution presents a version. We do the same. The truth is usually somewhere in the middle.'

Before Dan could respond, there was a bang on the front door.

Pat raised his eyebrows. 'It might be your visitor. She must have seen your car.'

Dan left Pat's room and went to answer the door.

There were no security cameras, no peephole. Just an old wooden door.

He opened the door slowly. When he saw who it was, he was surprised. It was Sara Carter, Robert Carter's wife. He recognised her from the public gallery.

'I need to speak to you.'

Dan let the door swing open fully. As she rushed inside, looking behind her, Dan followed.

'I've been trying to find you.' She was agitated, her eyes darting around, as if worried that someone was following her.

'So I hear. What can I do for you?'

'There's something you've got to know.'

Dan pointed up the stairs towards his office. 'You better go up then.'

Sara followed his direction, trotting up the stairs.

Whatever she had to tell him, she seemed in a rush. He wasn't going to make her wait.

Fifty-nine

Jayne weighed her keys in her hand as she stood outside her apartment door. She'd been jittery about going in ever since she'd thought someone had been inside. She hated that fear. It was a weakness, and she'd come to Highford so that she wouldn't be weak.

She took a deep breath and went inside.

The apartment was empty. She knew that as soon as she entered. That night, there'd been an invisible threat. She hadn't been able to pinpoint how she'd known. It was a sensation, nothing more. A prickle of her skin, or a disturbance in the air that told her she wasn't alone. It wasn't there anymore.

Her keys clattered as she put them on the table in the hallway. She went into the bedroom and threw her jacket on to the floor, checking around the room before unbuttoning her blouse and flopping on to the bed. The clothes felt too strange; buttoned up, straight. Going to court wasn't for her.

She let her head sink into the pillow and closed her eyes. Her thoughts wandered back to the case. It didn't feel like they were making any real progress, with Carter not co-operating, but it made her feel alive, a good change from the routine of serving court papers. The Carter case had awakened an interest, the enjoyment of seeing a case to the end, rather than her usual bit-part in the story.

She sat up and looked around the bedroom. There was a muddy mark on the carpet in the corner that she was sure hadn't been there a few days earlier. Or perhaps she just hadn't noticed? Was she seeing shadows that weren't there?

She couldn't afford to think like that. Her apartment was her sanctuary. She'd chosen it because of the noisy neighbours, who allowed her to fade into the background.

Had that night changed things? Perhaps what she thought was the good thing about her apartment was actually its weakness? It gave her a hiding place, but no one would pay any attention to her when she needed them. There were too many bangs and noises in the building, with drunken shouts, loud music and visitors knocking on doors. Who'd notice another commotion?

She cursed herself and clambered off the bed. She wouldn't let herself become a prisoner to her fear.

She stripped off, shivering slightly, her apartment always too cold even in summer, and went into the bathroom.

The water in the shower took a few seconds to get warm. Before she got under the water, she had a look around the bathroom. It wasn't very welcoming. No plants or small touches that gave any hint that she planned to stay for too long, her flat just a place to eat, sleep and have sex. She should change that.

As she thought about that, she realised that it had been a couple of weeks since she'd had someone in her bed. She missed it. It wasn't about the person, but about being able to use him for what she needed. She hadn't met a man who had a problem with that. No attachments. No emotions. No expectations. She gave them what they wanted: an attractive young woman who didn't allow herself any inhibitions during sex, because it was for her, not them, and she didn't complain when they collected their clothes and sneaked off into the night. She preferred the light to stay off while she waited for the click of the apartment door. They didn't need to know anything about her.

She knew what some of them thought about her. She'd seen the looks exchanged with their friends when she saw them again. The nods, the smirks. Good, let them talk about her, share her secrets. She could tell them how he had been too small or too quick, how she'd had to finish herself off in the bathroom because their huffing and puffing had ended before she'd had time to start enjoying herself.

She climbed into the water and closed her eyes as the water ran over her body. Relaxing, invigorating, she let the water pummel her for a few minutes.

A noise outside.

She stopped.

What was it? A creak of the door? A footstep? A floorboard.

She wiped the condensation from the shower screen and peered out, her arm over her breasts. The bathroom door was open. She hadn't locked it, but she thought she had closed it. She didn't let the door swing open that much, it let out too much steam.

There was another noise. A knock. Someone moving.

She pulled back the shower screen and stepped out. She held a towel over her body and ran to the door. As she looked into the bedroom, she tried to see whether anything had moved.

'Hello?' She hated the tremble in her voice.

No reply.

She listened out, the towel held tightly to her body, her legs crossed, impulsive in the way she protected herself.

A click.

She yelped. Her apartment door?

She waited for a few moments to see if anyone appeared, but the apartment stayed still. She wanted to get dressed, but she needed to know. She tiptoed through the bedroom and put her head round the door to give herself a view of the hall.

No one there.

Her head hung down, her hair dripping water on to the floor. As she looked behind her, she saw that her feet had made wet footprints on the carpet. There were no other marks there, like mud brought in from outside.

She was thinking about it too much, making leaps of fact from the bangs and noises of an old house occupied by drunks and drug-users. She had to stay in control.

Then she saw it. One hand went to her mouth, her other clamping the towel even closer.

Her spare front door key. The one she used was on the same key ring as her car key, but her spare was always left hanging on a hook by the front door. She couldn't remember the last time she'd used it, but now it was on the table in the hallway, next to where she'd put her usual set when she'd come in. She'd have noticed it when she came in, she was sure, and couldn't remember the last time that she'd used it.

Someone had been in there and left it behind.

She had to get out.

Sixty

Sara Carter followed Dan into his office.

She slumped on to the knackered old brown sofa that he used when he was between jobs on an all-night duty solicitor roster, the arms worn and shiny, the cushions sagging.

'I saw you at the trial, watching,' Dan said. 'And now you're hanging around, looking for me.'

'You saw me?'

'Outside here, not long after Jayne had been to see you. I recognised you when I saw you in court. You looked like you wanted to tell me something, but were stopping yourself. Now you're here.' He held out his hands. 'So what is it?'

'Robbie looks awful. I've never seen him like that before. When the trial started, I wanted to see him suffering, because of what he did to me. No, not just to me. To us. Our daughter. How could he? But now I've seen it.' She blew out a breath. 'I can't stand it.'

'What about what he did to Mary?'

'Did he do that?'

'That's what the prosecution say.'

'I need to know. It's important.'

'He says not. It's the best I can do.'

'They've got it wrong.'

'Got what wrong?'

'He's not some mad stalker. Not Robbie. Deep down, he's a decent guy.'

'Perhaps you're the last one to see what he's really like? He's been warned off before.'

'Yes, and he learned his lesson, said he'd never do it again. I believed him.'

Dan wanted to reach out and take her hands, look her in the eyes and tell her to take a look at what he did. Dan had represented countless men who'd said they'd never do it again, but they always did. Instead, he said, 'And here we are again, Robbie accused of stalking someone else.'

'No, that's wrong.' Her voice became strident. 'This Mary, the girl who was murdered. He wasn't stalking her. I know that.'

'How do you know?'

She bent forward and reached into the small rucksack she was carrying. She pulled out an envelope. She hesitated for a moment before pursing her lips and holding out the envelope. 'I found this.'

Dan took it from her. 'What is it?'

'Love notes from Mary. Photographs of Robbie and Mary together.'

Dan spilled the contents on to his desk. There were three photographs, along with other scraps of paper, some of which bore handwritten scrawls. His thoughts scrambled to make sense of what he was seeing. It changed everything. It gave him something more than the unreliable testimony of a local drunk.

He picked up some of the pieces of paper. *Look gorgeous babe* was written on the back of a beer mat with one side torn off, something spontaneous fashioned out of whatever Mary had to hand. On a small piece of paper torn from a notebook were the words *I want you later.*

'I didn't think people did this anymore,' Dan said, almost to himself, and then to Sara, 'I thought it was all messaging apps or social networking sites.'

'It must have been when they were in the same pub together, because she didn't want to be caught texting him. Or perhaps Robbie didn't want anything on his phone. She probably slipped them to him when she was passing. Their little secret.' She pulled a face. 'It makes me feel sick.'

Dan picked up the photographs. There were three, all taken with Mary holding the camera at arms length. One taken in the bedroom in which she died; Dan recognised it from the crime scene photographs. Their bare shoulders and the flush to their cheeks left no doubt that they'd just had sex, with Mary's broad grin providing evidence that she'd enjoyed it. Another showed them both in the country somewhere, Mary's bright smile, all too familiar from the press stories, dominating the picture. In the last one, they were huddled together, both in woolly hats, Carter holding a sparkler in front of the camera, Mary with her head back, laughing.

'Bonfire Night,' Sara said, her jaw clenching. 'Two weeks before she died. I wanted us to go to the bonfire in the park, because there were small fairground rides for Tammy to go on and she was old enough to find it exciting, maybe not too scary. But he didn't come home. Said he'd got too busy at work, had to do some overtime, and got angry when I questioned him, accused me of getting on his back all the time. Yeah, I know now, all bullshit. He was with her. She knew he had a daughter, and had me, and still she did that. How could she?'

'He was in love with her,' Dan said, almost to himself, but regretted it as soon as he had, when he saw the tears in Sara's eyes.

'No, he wasn't.' She wiped her eye with the back of her hand. 'He was in love with the excitement of it, just like the woman from before. Someone new. Someone without a child to spoil his nights. Someone who didn't bear the scars of having his baby. The stretchmarks. The tiredness. But he's supposed to love those things, because those come from having Tammy, and we had her because we loved each other. Or so I thought. The difference between Mary and the one before is that she didn't tell him to get lost. Instead, she invited him into her bed, and away from mine.'

'Where did you find this?' Dan lifted the envelope.

'In the small bedroom. He's got it kitted out as his gaming room, with a TV and a beer fridge, and he escapes there sometimes.' She wiped her eye again. 'I thought it would stop him feeling trapped. He could hide away and do his own thing, but it didn't work. When he got locked up and I heard what he'd done, I cleared out the room. He's probably never coming back. The envelope was at the back of a drawer in the computer desk.' She curled her lip in disgust. 'Perhaps he got it out sometimes, to think about her while I was in bed, alone again.'

Dan gave her a look of regret. He liked her. She was a young woman trying to make the best of a life that wasn't treating her too well, when all she'd done wrong was trust someone who wasn't deserving of it. But his job wasn't to look after her. Robert Carter was his client and he was the one who mattered right then.

He looked again at the photographs. What should he do with them?

He could show them to the prosecution, try to persuade them that the case had become weak and hope that they'd offer something, anything, to make it go away.

He discounted that idea. The prosecution wouldn't cave in on a case where there had been so much media scrutiny, with the jury sworn in and hearing the evidence. He could just keep them back and use them later to rubbish the prosecution case, the surprise exhibit, the rabbit from the hat, hoping that it would make the prosecution look like a shambles. But what would the jury think? It would stop Carter being a stalker, but would it make his explanation any more credible? He could show that Carter loved Mary, but love creates passions that are sometimes hard to control. Like Jayne had said, it turns a murder no one understands into one that every one can understand: a crime of passion, lovers' tiff, as old as human relationships, and expressed with hate and blood. It would muddy the prosecution case for a while, but it would soon become clear again, and then even clearer than before.

One thing bothered him though.

'Why now?' he asked.

Sara looked down. 'Tammy.'

'I don't understand.'

'I wasn't going to say anything. Let the bastard suffer, that's what I thought. I hated him, I was hurting, but it isn't just about me. What about Tammy? It's made her miserable. She misses her daddy, asks about him, and I don't know what to say. But I know other people will fill in the gaps for her as she gets older. How her daddy's a killer, a murderer, a beast. The other parents at the nursery gate avoid me, they don't want their children to play with Tammy. I wanted to know the truth because I owed it to her, so I went to court. And not just that. I wanted him to see me and be reminded of how much he's hurt me, and hope that he'll think about Tammy too and tell the truth, whatever that is.'

'And?'

'He's shrunk somehow. He looks broken, like there's no life in him. Even when he looked over, it was as if he couldn't see me any more. He's lost weight too. I can't believe he's the same man. It sounds stupid, but I feel sorry for him. And then I heard what the prosecution were saying. That just isn't right, all that about him being a stalker. I know it's wrong.'

'And you wanted to put it right?'

'Yes. I mean no. It's not as simple as that.'

Dan rubbed his eyes. It had been a long day. 'You're going have to explain.'

'It's about Tammy again. I listened to what that barrister was saying, and I saw the lady from the press writing it all down, so I knew it would be in the paper. All of Tammy's friends' parents will see it. And with the Internet, it never goes away. When Tammy's older, she'll want to find out about her father, and an Internet search will bring all of these articles up. Is that how I want Tammy to see her father? To see herself, as part of his bloodline? Something unhinged, dangerous? No, no way. I can do something to stop that.'

'Why didn't you just go to the papers and sell the pictures?'

'Do I look that cheap?' Anger flashed in her eyes. 'I am doing this for Tammy, so that her father doesn't go down in history as some oddball stalker who killed his victim.'

Dan glanced back towards the pieces of paper on his desk. One thing was troubling him.

'You said you've come to me because of what you saw at the trial.'

Sara nodded.

'So why have you been following me around? I saw you near the office. That was before you saw Robbie in court.'

'I didn't know what to do. I didn't know all the details of the case, but I hung on to the pictures because they were about Mary, so they had to be important. I didn't want to take them to the police, because what if it made it worse for him? Tammy might blame me when she's older. And there were those men who came. They were threatening. I was scared, I don't mind admitting.'

'And now?'

'I've got to do it, for Robbie, and for Tammy. He's a lot of bad things, but he's not the man they say he is.'

'Have the police ever asked you about Robbie and Mary?'

'Yes. Right back when he was arrested.'

'What did you tell them?'

'That I'd never heard of her, but that was before I found those,' and she pointed to the contents of the envelope.

'Will you give evidence?'

'Do I have to?'

'I don't know yet, I need to decide what to do with what you've told me, but if I'm going to use these, I'll need you.'

A pause, and then she nodded. 'If I have to. He's not a bad man. He's a cheating pig, but he's not a violent man.'

'Is he capable of murder?'

'He never loses his temper. Not properly.' She pointed to the photographs. 'And we were once like that too. Mary was nothing new.'

Dan thanked her. He saw his evening slip away, as he knew he needed Carter's QC, Hannah Taberner, to see them, so she could decide how to play the new evidence. And Jayne too.

It was time to start planning the trial proper.

Sixty-one

Jayne was outside Dan's apartment building. He wasn't answering. There were no lights visible. His car wasn't in the car park.

She'd been driving around, wanting to stay away from her apartment until she worked out what to do. Her hair had dried into tangles as she hadn't hung around long enough to dry it. She'd grabbed the first jumper she could find and thrown on jeans and her pumps. She'd been driving for an hour and still hadn't come up with any answers.

She ran back to her car and set off quickly, her wheels rumbling across the cobbles before she turned down the hill and towards Dan's office.

The parked cars seemed to rush by as she took short cuts along the narrow terraced streets. The dark stone buildings were replaced by the neon signs of taxi offices and kebab shops as she got closer, and as she turned into the side street that Dan's office overlooked, she saw him in the first floor window. He was talking to someone. Pat Molloy?

She left her car outside an empty furniture shop and rushed to Dan's office building, banging on the heavy wooden door as she got there. She stepped back so that he could see it was her, and he gave her the thumbs up as he turned to see who was making the noise.

Her breaths calmed as she heard the footsteps on the other side of the door.

As he opened it, he said, 'You're just in time,' smiling, breathless from the rush to the door.

'For what?'

'Chinese. We've just ordered and there should be enough for you. Come in. You okay with chicken?'

'Yes, fine, thank you,' she said, as she went inside. She followed Dan cautiously as he went upstairs, unsure about who *we* meant.

'Go through,' Dan said, as he rummaged through cupboards.

Jayne kept on towards Dan's office at the front. As she went in, Robert Carter's QC, Hannah, was wrestling with a corkscrew, which was jammed hard into a bottle of red wine that she had clenched between her thighs.

Hannah looked up. 'These are absolute buggers. Give me screw tops any day,' and then gasped with delight as the cork came free. To Jayne, her voice seemed as rich as the red wine that she poured into the two wine glasses on Dan's desk.

Jayne pulled her jacket around herself, glancing down at the hole in her pumps and her ragged cuffs.

'You here to help?' Hannah said, and then shouted, 'Dan, have you found an extra glass? This sweetie looks thirsty.'

That made Jayne smile, despite her nervousness.

Dan appeared in the room with an assortment of plates and a straight glass. 'This okay?'

'If you don't mind me gatecrashing the party, that is,' Jayne said.

'You're part of Carter's team.'

'You should have the funny glass, Dan,' Hannah said, as she passed Jayne a wine glass.

'Has something happened? It feels like a celebration.'

'Not a celebration,' Dan said, holding his glass out for Hannah to fill. 'A strategy meeting. We've discovered something.' He passed one of the photographs to Jayne.

Jayne gasped as she looked at it. It was the photograph of Carter and Mary in bed. 'Does this show what I think it does?'

'Carter and Mary were lovers.'

'I know Henry hinted at that, but this, well, this makes it all different, doesn't it?'

'It looks that way. Carter's wife found them in his desk.'

'Wow,' was all she could say.

'Exactly, my dear,' Hannah said. 'It changes the whole case.'

'So no weird stalker?' Jayne said, as she sat down on the sofa. She looked again at the photograph. Carter and Mary looked so happy together. She could see the weight Carter had lost in prison. At court, his cheeks looked gaunt and pale, the skin under his eyes dark, his gaze distant. In the photograph, he glowed, looked happy and healthy. He looked alive.

Dan sat down on a chair by the window and put his head back. 'So what do we do?'

His question was directed at Hannah, and for a moment Jayne saw how far Dan's world was from her own life. She felt a rush of embarrassment that she had turned to him when she was in trouble. This was his life. In the company of another lawyer, planning, theorising: a professional person who fed her cases because he felt sorry for her.

Jayne put her glass down. 'I can't stay.'

'Why not?' Dan said.

'This is for lawyers. You're planning the case. It's nothing to do with me.'

Hannah sat forward. 'Tosh. You're helping Dan at court, so you're part of the bloody team.'

'And we've got food,' Dan said, just as there was a knock on the door. 'I'm sure they just microwave it. It's always too quick.'

'As long as it doesn't spoil the wine,' Hannah said, and raised her glass.

As Dan went downstairs, Hannah said, 'What do you think about this?' and nodded towards the photograph Jayne was still holding.

She thought about what to say. A QC was asking her opinion and she didn't want to appear foolish.

'It strengthens our case,' Jayne said, eventually.

'How?'

'We had a drunk who'd seen them together, but who'd believe him? He'll make us look desperate, like we'd found someone who'd say anything for a bottle of cider.'

'He told the detective the same though. That's one reason why he might be believed.'

'But there's a reason why he might say just about anything. He might have got the wrong person, maybe it was another couple he'd seen and his addled brain had made an incorrect identification. Carter's story is already ridiculous. Relying on some drunk, even if we can get him to court, makes him look desperate too. And the drunk could only testify to one night of their relationship. This makes it a serious thing.'

'You see, being a lawyer is quite easy,' Hannah said, grinning. 'We don't do anything special. There are no magical thought processes. Your opinion is as good as mine. The only difference is that Dan and I know the rules, what we can ask and what we can't, and how to do it. You learn those things, in the same way that a decorator learns how to hang wallpaper, but your opinion about which wallpaper looks good and which doesn't is as valid as the decorator's.' She raised her glass. 'So stay and join in.'

Dan came in with two bags of food and filled the office instantly with spicy aromas. He laid out the cartons along the desk and handed Jayne a plate. 'Dig in.'

There were chopsticks on the desk too, wrapped in cellophane, and Hannah reached for a packet, tearing at the wrapper with her teeth. Jayne grabbed a spoon instead and began to fill a plate, her stomach reminding her how hungry she was.

The room fell silent for a few minutes as everyone ate. As Jayne went back to fill her plate again, Hannah said, 'There is one problem with this new information.'

'What's that?' Dan asked.

'It's not just the prosecution who claim there was no relationship between Carter and Mary.' She lifted a piece of chicken into her mouth. 'Carter says the same.'

'That's a conversation for the morning,' he said.

'But what do we gain by using this evidence?' Hannah said. 'Let's think about this. He becomes a liar, for a start.'

'So we have to explain that first of all.'

'No, he has to explain it. Or, do we even need to?'

'What do you mean?'

'Does explaining it make the case better or worse? We make him a liar. We make it a crime of passion. We make it easy for the jury to understand.'

'I used to think that,' Jayne said. 'But if we know it's the truth, we shouldn't be scared of it.'

Hannah raised her eyebrows.

Jayne knew what Hannah's expression meant, that truth didn't have to come first in a courtroom.

'She's right,' Dan said, chewing. 'If Carter is going to be convicted, I'd rather he went to jail because of the truth, not because of a lie we couldn't persuade him to renounce. And there's his own legacy to think about.'

'Legacy?' Hannah said, reaching for some rice before spooning it on to her plate. 'What the hell are you talking about?'

'What his wife said, the reason she came forward. His daughter. We can point that out to Carter. How does he want his daughter to remember him? A cheat? There's no doubt about that, and it will be hard enough for her to get over that – the thought that her father was prepared to sacrifice her for Mary. But some kind of psychopath, a sexual predator who followed a pretty young woman home and stabbed her in her bed? How can his daughter ever cope with that? Will it affect how she sees herself, worry if there is some of that in her?'

'You can't rescue everyone,' Hannah said.

'Why not? Why can't I try to do the right thing? Because I'm a lawyer? A lot of lawyers I know went into the law because of thoughts like that.'

'But then life wises them up,' Hannah said.

'No, money changes them.'

Jayne detected a barb in his tone. Hannah took a drink of wine before she said, 'All right, we'll do it your way. But we need more than one strategy, because we don't know what he's going to say. If he's going to tell us a new version of the truth, there are two possibilities. He might admit that he was involved with

Mary, and the rest of his story stays the same. That's the best outcome.'

'And the worst?' Dan said.

'He breaks down when confronted with the photographs and admits killing her, that they argued about whatever lovers argue about, and he lost his temper. He grabbed something, a knife, scissors, anything, and, in a fit of rage, he stabbed her.'

'He might have been defending himself,' Jayne said.

'She was lying down when she was killed,' Hannah told her. 'The blood spray confirmed that, all over the bottom sheet. And if she was lying down, he'll have a tough job persuading anyone it was self-defence. Remember what we know about Mary: sweet, caring, friendly, nice. Compare that with what we know about Robert Carter: lying, cheating, deceitful.'

'It will explain one thing,' Jayne said.

'Go on,' Dan said.

'When she was found, Mary was under the sheet, and it was draped over her head, her legs sticking out. Like you said, the blood spray was on the bottom sheet, but not the top. There were no stab holes. Whoever killed her covered her up. Why would anyone do that?'

Dan and Hannah exchanged glances.

'Only someone who cared for Mary would do that,' Jayne continued. 'If it was someone random, they'd just leave, wouldn't care about how Mary was found. If it was someone who cared for her, in whatever way, once the rage had gone there'd be shame, remorse even. The last thing they'd want to see is Mary's face. They'd cover her so that they didn't have to look at what they'd done. Some random psychopath wouldn't do that.'

'So it's more likely that someone would do that if they were close to Mary?' Hannah said.

'That's my guess.'

'Like a lover?'

Jayne shrugged.

'Or a friend,' Dan said.

Hannah smiled. 'We're back to Lucy.'

'That's the only hope we have. If we put Carter under pressure and he admits killing her in a rage, all we can do is make him change his plea to guilty.'

'He'll go to prison for life,' Jayne said.

'No, he'll get a sentence for life,' Dan said. 'He'll be out in fifteen years if he admits killing her in a jealous rage or in some argument. If he's a lone psychopath who follows women and murders them in their bed, he might never get out.'

'But if he stabs someone in a jealous rage, he'll probably do it again, even after he's released,' Jayne said. 'It's a different type of murder, less random, but the controlling, the jealousy, is just as dangerous.'

'He might learn his lesson.'

'Does that ever happen? Really?'

'If we go after Lucy, what do we think might have happened?' Hannah said. 'Carter has spent the last five months not admitting the truth. He won't tell us what happened unless we guess correctly.'

'A sex game?' Dan said.

'How?'

'Lucy is very upfront about sex. One of the other housemates described her as being loud, almost as if she wanted everyone to hear her, so that everyone knew what a good time she was having. She and Peter were very open. Did they all end up back at the house and had a party? A group thing? Did it get out of hand? Perhaps Mary wasn't really going along with it, and a wild night turned into rape and murder, Carter being egged on by Lucy and Peter. It would explain Lucy's father maintaining a close interest in the case.'

'You've thought of all of this before,' Hannah said, surprised.

'It was a theory we were working on, but we never found enough evidence. And Carter wasn't interested in giving a different account. But we didn't have this proof before.'

'And there's the other possibility,' Jayne said.

Hannah turned to her. 'Go on.'

'All those times Mary had looked down on them for behaving like they did, and what did they find when they sneaked back? Little Miss Goody Two Shoes is sleeping with a married man. Is that when some kind of assault took place? Were Lucy and Peter going to attack her, rape her, and then they stabbed her when she screamed?'

'But Mary was lying down. She'd be too vulnerable. She'd get up, wrap a sheet around herself, not lie there and let happen.'

'Unless she was cowering because they'd surprised her. Or was she being held down, Lucy egging on Peter?'

'It does make some sense,' Dan said. 'And just in the nick of time.'

'What do you mean?' Jayne asked.

'She's given her evidence for the prosecution. Tomorrow, it's our turn.'

'What happens next?'

'We find our witnesses. Make sure they're ready for tomorrow.'

'Will they be giving evidence tomorrow?'

'No, but I want them at court, so we can show that we have them. This is a surprise tactic and the judge will get on our case. If we don't have the evidence to back it up, we'll be in trouble.'

'He's right about that,' Hannah said. 'I'll send you in alone if there's blood to be shed.'

'And keep them safe. We don't know what Lucy's father is up to, but remember what happened to Shelley.'

'Henry too?' Jayne said, and pointed at the photographs. 'Do you still need him? You can show they were lovers without him.'

'If Carter won't change his story, Henry is the only person who backs him up that they were happy on the night,' Hannah told her. 'We just pretend we never saw those photographs.' She looked at Dan. 'One other thing: I think you should examine Lucy.'

Dan was confused. 'Why's that?'

'Because if we're going to launch a surprise attack, that's the best way. You're the junior, there to ask questions from the routine witnesses. Simon Parkin will switch off when you get to your feet, thinking that we're not challenging her.'

'Will that make any difference? Lucy won't understand the distinction.'

'In this case, we need every difference we can get, no matter how small.'

'And me?' Jayne asked.

'What do you mean?'

'What about my safety?'

Dan smiled. 'You're the toughest person involved in this case. You'll be fine.'

Jayne blushed. 'Can I stay with you again?'

Dan paused for a moment as Hannah raised her glass to her mouth to conceal her grin.

'Yes, do that.'

Jayne was pleased. It meant that she didn't have to go back to her own apartment. That was all that mattered.

Sixty-two

Jayne found a table by the window in a small pub on the main street, on the lookout for Henry, trying to make sure the witnesses were ready for the next day. She'd never met Henry before, but knew of his crowd. They were usually at the end of the precinct, occupying benches near the only department store in Highford. The pub was on the corner of two streets and it gave her the best view in town, used by the people-watchers during the day, those with rheumy stares and broken veins like tiny scratches across their cheeks. At night during the week, it provided a view of an empty precinct and the occasional person wandering home.

There were only three other people in there, all clustered around the bar. Jayne tuned out of the conversation; it was three middle-aged men starting to slur about their favourite historical generals, just pub-bore chatter that she tried to avoid.

For an hour, she watched the traffic lights change and nursed two beers, always hoping to spot the weave and stagger of Henry's group. There was no sign.

As she drained her second beer, the talk at the bar turned to famous women and what they'd do to them if they ever got the chance. She took that as her cue to leave.

Mickey was her next stop, but still she needed to find Henry. On the way to Mickey's, she could drive past where Henry had seen Carter and Mary; that might be where he spends his evenings.

It wasn't a long drive, and pretty soon the rasp of her exhaust was echoing between the tight terraced streets. She was close to Mickey's house when she saw a small cluster of people in a small park. She pulled into the side of the road and opened her window, to work out the ages of those in there. She didn't want to walk into a dark secluded spot to interrupt a group of teenagers doing whatever they got up to in the shadows.

Voices drifted towards her, some laughter, male and female, but it was older, hoarse and worn out.

She strained to see into the park, but all she could make out was a shadowy knot. Just then, there was a small burst of flame and pink faces leaned into it until their cigarettes glowed red. She recognised the faces of Henry's group.

The gate creaked loudly as she went into the small playground. Everyone in there fell silent. 'Henry?'

A pause, and then someone said, 'Who is it?'

'I'm Jayne, from Dan Grant's office.'

Another pause and then, 'Over here.' The voice came from a grey outline sitting on a swing.

As she got close, he leaned down to pick up a can of beer. Not to drink from, she thought, but to make sure she didn't kick it over.

'What do you want?'

Even from a few feet away, the smell of strong, cheap lager was overpowering, the faint reach of the streetlight catching the moistness of his bottom lip and the sweaty sheen on his face.

'We need you at court tomorrow.'

'Why? What have I done?'

'It's about Mary, the girl who died. You saw her, with Robert Carter. Remember?'

'I've changed my mind.'

'What do you mean, you've changed your mind?'

'I didn't see them. I made it up. Ask everyone. I'm full of it.'

Jayne closed her eyes for a moment. 'Who's got to you?'

A pause and then, 'No one's got to me. I just don't want to go to court.'

'We could get a witness summons.'

'Good. Do that.' He belched. 'Now leave me alone.'

'Henry, don't do this.'

He shook his head. 'No can do.'

Some of the others stepped in front of Henry, blocking her view of him. The swing began to creak slowly. That told her the meeting was over.

She turned and walked quickly out of the park. The group stayed silent until she was in her car and her engine had turned over.

She was scowling as she put her car into gear, ready to carry on with her journey to Mickey's house.

In the dark, Mickey's street was a line of closed curtains bathed in flickering lights from televisions.

Jayne tapped on his door. There was a shout from inside, his mother, asking for Mickey to get the door. She stepped back at the rumble of footsteps and, as the door opened, she was bathed in the light from the bright hallway. It was Mickey, although only the curls of his hair were visible, his face in shadow.

He didn't say anything, no invitation to go inside, so Jayne said, 'We need you at court tomorrow.'

'Me? Why?'

'To give evidence about what you saw on the night that Mary was killed.'

He stayed silent for a few seconds before saying, 'Come in.'

She brushed past him and along the hallway. As she went past the first door, the same female voice from before shouted out, 'Hello, love.'

Jayne turned to look in the room and Mickey's mother was sitting just a couple of feet from the television, her hands across a walking stick.

'Hello again,' Jayne said. 'How are you?'

'Just grand, love, just grand. You can't keep away from my Mickey,' and she chuckled to herself. 'Don't keep him up late.'

'Ignore her,' Mickey said, as Jayne followed him into the back room. Mickey went to the kettle to fill it, but Jayne told him not to bother. She had her mind set on something stronger.

'About tomorrow then,' Mickey said.

'I'll collect you at half nine, and then we're going to drive around until I get the word that you're needed at court.'

'Drive around? Why not just tell me to be there?'

'Because we don't know if there's any danger involved.' When Mickey paled, Jayne said, 'You knew Shelley, Robert Carter's lawyer, and you heard she was murdered.'

'I might get killed for doing this?' he said, and put the kettle down. 'No, no, no. I can't have that. What about Ma? What about me?'

'You'll be fine, I'll be here to look after you.'

'But afterwards? Once the case is finished, where will you be?'

Jayne heard echoes of her own conversations with Dan following her acquittal. 'Do this for me, please. That's all I ask.'

Mickey nodded slowly, her words calming him. 'All right, I will. But stay with me once you come for me.'

'I'll do that for you.'

She left Mickey in the back room and left the house quietly. Once outside, she let out a long sigh. The defence was nearly ready. They'd done all they could.

Sixty-three

Dan and Hannah waited in the interview room in the bowels of the Crown Court. They were both in their tabs and gowns, ready to go into court, although Hannah's wig was still in its green oval tin. Dan was leaning against the wall. Hannah was sitting on a wooden chair, her legs crossed.

'How do you think this will go?' Dan asked.

'Whichever way the client wants it to go. Don't get too involved in it.'

'There's something we know to be untrue, and it might cause him to be found guilty. I can't have that. It would be an injustice.'

'Are you sure that's it?' Hannah said, an eyebrow raised. 'Or is it that you just don't like losing?'

Dan was surprised. 'Do you think that's what it is?'

'You're a man, Daniel. You think life is a competition. If Mr Carter sticks to his version and he's convicted, who could argue with the decision? The evidence against him is good. If it lands him with a life sentence, that's the system working. If we get him to spill the truth, what if it's worse? Poor Shelley never told you what the conflict was, did she?'

'No, but it's obvious. Lucy Ayres was being dragged into the case and Shelley was being put under pressure not to pursue that part of it. She did the right thing: transferred it to someone who could represent Carter properly, who wouldn't be intimidated by Lucy's father.'

'But she didn't exactly make it easy for you to discover the truth, if that's what it is.'

'She had a meeting with Conrad and Dominic after she'd done the transfer, a meal for three at the Wild Manor. I'm guessing that they laid out what the risks were.'

'Let's see what the poor chap has to say then. We'll tread carefully though.'

They had to wait for a few more minutes until Carter was led along the corridor, just the steady tick of the white plastic wall-clock to fill the silence. The sound of footsteps outside the room was joined by the unclicking of handcuffs, and then Carter entered.

'Sit down,' Dan said.

Carter sat at the table in the centre of the room, opposite Hannah, his hands clasped together on the desktop.

'How do you think the trial is going?' Carter asked.

Dan leaned against the wall. 'How do *you* think it's going?'

'They're making me out to be a bad person.'

'It's a murder trial. What were you expecting?'

Carter shrugged, but didn't answer.

'I spoke to your wife last night,' Dan said.

Carter's nostrils flared. 'I told you not to.'

'She came to me, and she was at the trial yesterday.'

He closed his eyes for a moment. 'How is she?'

'Torn. When she listens to what they're saying about you, she doesn't recognise you. She wonders if she knows you at all, but you're still her husband. She hates you and loves you in equal measure.'

Carter swallowed. 'What about Tammy?' His voice came out as a croak. 'Did you see her?'

'No, not last night, but she misses you. She wants to see you.'

'Not in here. Not like this.'

'Yes, that's what Sara said. If you want to see Tammy again, you need to get out of here.'

'That's why you're here, isn't it,' he said, sitting back, his tone recovering some composure. 'To be my lawyer, to get me out of here.'

'It is, you're right,' Dan said. 'But you'll be giving evidence soon, not me, so we need to check a few things.'

'Like what?'

Dan exchanged quick glances with Hannah, who nodded.

'You and Mary.'

'What is there to say? We were friends. I walked her home. We had coffee. I'm married. She wasn't like that.'

'You seem to know her well, bearing in mind it was a one-off.'

Carter didn't respond.

'What keeps your wife going is that she knows something about you that others don't, which makes her think that what they say might not be true.'

'What would that be?'

Dan bent down to reach into his case and pulled out a brown envelope. He'd copied the photographs of Carter and Mary together, and the love notes; he couldn't risk Carter destroying them in a tantrum. He took them from the envelope and put them on the table in front of Carter, slowly and deliberately, piece by piece, like a croupier in a casino, letting Carter look at them as they were placed in front of him.

Carter paled. He stared at the pieces of paper for a few seconds, then at Dan, then Hannah, and then back to the papers again.

The atmosphere in the room changed.

'We've got the originals,' Dan said.

Carter sat back quickly, made his chair rock, and put his hands over his face. 'No, no, no, no, no.' The words came out muffled but Dan could hear his despair.

Hannah raised her eyebrows.

Carter kept his hands there for a few more seconds before he dropped them to the desk. This time his hands weren't clasped but resting on the desk. His shoulders were less tense, his eyes red. He reached out for the three pictures of Mary and him together, looked at them one by one, and a tear ran down his face.

'No one was supposed to know,' he said, eventually. He wiped the tears away with the back of his hand.

'Why?' Dan said.

'This will change everything for Mary. She can't come back, but memories of her will stay forever. What will they say about her now? She was a home wrecker? A whore? She doesn't deserve that.'

'What about your daughter? What about her memories of you? A stalker? A murderer?'

'I don't matter.'

'I wasn't talking about you. I was talking about your daughter.'

A few seconds of silence, and then, 'I love Tammy, but I can't do it to Mary.'

Hannah sat up and said, 'Did you love Mary?'

'Like no one else I've ever loved.'

'What would Mary want?' Hannah said. 'Her parents are sitting through this trial, thinking that she was murdered by you, someone fixated on her. Wouldn't they prefer the truth, whatever that may be? Isn't that what Mary would have wanted, for her parents to know how she died?' A pause, and then, 'If nothing else, do it for Mary.'

Carter started to nod. The silence grew as he stared at the desk. When he lifted his head, his gaze was stronger, more resolute.

'We fell in love.'

'Where did you meet?' asked Dan.

'Like I told you, in the Wharf. We hit it off, couldn't stop talking and laughing.'

'Is that when you got together?'

'No, not then, but I wanted to.'

'Did she know you were married?'

'Yes. I was wearing a ring, and she asked me about Sara. I told her the truth, that I was married but we'd got married for the wrong reason: habit. We stayed together because it was easy, and the longer you're together the harder it is to get away. Then Tammy came along, and that was it; I was tied.'

Dan leaned forward. 'The jury will hate you if you say that.'

'You said tell the truth.'

'You should, but don't play the *my wife doesn't understand me* card. They'll understand love, but they won't let you rubbish your wife.'

'My love-life isn't on trial.'

'Oh, it is,' Dan said, his eyes wide. 'Everything about you is on trial. The people who decide your fate are sitting in that jury box, judging you. They'll decide if they like you, whether you deserve to be punished, whether they can trust you. Making them like you will be hard, but making them understand you might do as a half-way point.'

'How did you stay in touch?' Hannah said. 'Exchange numbers at the end of the night?'

'I sent her a message on Facebook. I looked for her profile and told her that I'd enjoyed the chat, would like to do it again.'

'What did she say?' Dan said.

'She said the same but didn't want to upset my marriage. Meet for coffee, I said. No harm done.'

'And did you?'

Carter nodded. 'We ended up in bed. Her friends were all at work and Mary had a day off.' He exhaled. 'Don't you see? Everyone's opinion of Mary will change when they hear this. I can't do it.'

'And you're prepared to sacrifice yourself for that?' Dan said.

'I would do anything for Mary. She was no home-wrecker. That was me, all me. I could have stopped it, if I wanted to, but I couldn't help myself. Nor could Mary. We were in love, and for me it felt like it was the first time. Real love, I mean, something deep, so that all I could think about was Mary.'

'Do you still have the messages?'

He shook his head. 'We deleted everything so that no one would know. Mary was adamant about that.'

'Mary wouldn't want this for you,' Dan said, exasperated, gesturing towards the bare walls. 'Can't you see that? She kept it secret to protect you, and she'd feel the same way now, that you should be free, not keeping silent to protect her reputation.'

Carter swallowed hard.

'Tell me about the night she died,' Hannah cut in. 'That's why we're here. Not because you fell in love.'

Carter took some deep breaths. 'Like I've always said, except I missed out the part about us. It's not a big deal. How can I be sacrificing myself when I'm only lying about one thing? Does it change much, really?'

'Tell the story.'

'I'd gone to the Wharf pub, knowing she'd be there. We couldn't talk properly, because Mary didn't want anyone to know about us, not knowing how they'd react. We texted each other from opposite sides of the pub.'

'Who were you with?' Dan said.

'I was alone. That's why they think I was some crazed loner. I was crazed, and alone, because the woman I wanted was there, beautiful and fun, and she loved me too, but we couldn't be together in public. Mary was adamant that she wouldn't break up my family. Whatever we had, it had to be our secret. It was arranged that Mary would walk home with her friend and do the last half-mile on her own. The streets were well-lit and quiet and Mary was insistent. I would meet her along that road. And I did. I was waiting exactly where I said I was going to be. We walked back to her place and made love.'

'How did she die?'

'I smoke, that's why she died. I went outside and left her in bed. I wanted a cigarette. I sat on the front doorstep, like I've always said. The door was open slightly, so I could get back in. I was in heaven. A starry night, having a ciggie, sitting on her front step.'

'How did she die?' Hannah repeated.

'I panicked.'

Dan sat down on the chair next to Hannah. The room was still.

'The front door had closed when I was smoking,' Carter said. 'I don't know why. I think it might have been a draught from the back door opening, but it meant I was stuck outside. It didn't matter. I'd have my smoke and knock on the door. I didn't go back in straight away though, because I was enjoying the moment. Then I heard Mary scream.'

'And you were still outside when you heard it?' Dan said.

'Like I've always said, I was outside when she screamed. I panicked. I could have knocked on the door, but I knew there must be someone else in there. A fight, an argument, but I didn't know what to do. Do I go in and have whoever it is wonder why I'm there? So I waited. Everything was silent. I knew I had to go in eventually, so I ran to the bottom of the street and up the alley, to use the back door. I knew it was unlocked because we'd come in that way. I ran into the house and there was no one else there. Just Mary.' Carter swallowed and wiped his eyes. 'Just Mary. Dead.'

'Did you cover her up?'

'No, I don't think so. It was a blur.'

'She was found covered up. If it wasn't you, someone was in her room after you.'

'I didn't see anyone. What can I say?'

'Why did you run away?'

'Why do you think? Because they'd think it was me, and because I didn't want anyone to know I'd been there, because how would I explain it to Sara? There were a million thoughts racing through my head and I panicked and I ran. What can I say? I know one thing though: I did not kill Mary. I can look myself in the mirror and say that. I can look you in the eye, look Tammy in the eye, and those twelve people on the jury, and say I am not a murderer. A coward. A cheat. A bad husband. A bad father. All of those things, but I'm no murderer.'

'You're forgetting liar,' Dan said. 'You're still holding back.'

'I've told you everything.' Carter folded his arms.

'Why wouldn't you let me speak to your wife?'

'You know why. People had been round to threaten her. I had to think of her, and Tammy.'

'Those people are linked to Dominic Ayres, Lucy's father, but nothing you've said should worry Lucy, so I can't work out why they would threaten your family.'

'Are we done?'

'What do you have on Lucy, and why won't you talk?'

Carter stayed silent.

'Come on, talk to me,' Dan said.

'I've nothing to say.'

'You're doing this for Sara, to protect her?'

Carter leaned forward and lowered his voice to an angry growl. 'You don't know how I feel. I left Mary to die in there. I tried to save her but ran off like a coward. I betrayed my wife and daughter. All of this is swirling around in here,' and he banged the side of his head with his fist, 'so if I can do one little thing to somehow make up for it, to protect Mary's memory, to keep Sara safe, I'll do it.'

'But whatever secrets you're holding back cost the life of my friend,' Dan said, his anger matching Carter's. 'You hold back and they win.'

'It's not about winning. It's about keeping Sara safe. And Tammy. Don't you get it?'

'All I see is you losing, you going to prison for the rest of your life, because there is one thing that will trouble the jury the most.'

'Which is?'

'Someone killed Mary. If it wasn't you, who was it, and why?'

Sixty-four

Jayne was out looking for Henry again.

The day had started with a stretch and a groan on Dan's sofa and a stumble to the shower in baggy knickers, a creased T-shirt of Dan's and socks that had half worked their way off her feet. Yeah, it must have been hard for Dan to resist her as he rushed out, stopping only to leave a note on the coffee table that read *Collect the witnesses. I'll call you when they're needed.*

Business as usual, then. She'd changed into her court suit and blouse and the clock had crept to nine thirty. If she left it too long, Henry would be opening his first can of strong lager. She didn't expect him to stay dry, but she wanted to at least have a chance of controlling him and keeping him functional.

The streets didn't seem as threatening in the daylight as she drove to where she'd been the night before. It was a bad part of town but the mornings were slower than at night. Just long rows of houses, boards covering some of the windows. In others, curtains hung drab and dirty. Wheelie bins cluttered the pavement, all different colours, making the street look like a giant child's playset. There weren't many cars, and the ones that clogged the pavement were dented and scuffed.

She drove past the playground where Henry had been the night before and parked further along. She wished she'd put on her normal clothes, because even though it was late spring the winds blew in hard there, adding to the desolation, the street facing north towards a high hill.

They'd been able to find an address in the file, scribbled on the back of a letter. Henry's door was faded blue wood with glass panels running up the centre, two of them broken. Jayne knocked. The noise bounced back as echoes.

She waited for a few seconds before knocking again, this time louder. No one came to the door.

She stepped back and looked up at the window. The curtains were closed, but that didn't mean anything. She guessed that Henry didn't run an orderly house.

A woman opened the door in the next house along, a cigarette in her hand. Her skinny jeans hung from her hips and her cheeks had a hollowed look that gave away one thing: drugs.

'He went out earlier,' the woman said, her mouth not much more than a dark hole in her face, her voice a whiny drawl.

'Do you know where?'

'No, but he was in a hurry. He doesn't normally get up that early, usually I hear him, and he comes round sometimes for something to eat.'

'Okay, thank you,' Jayne said, and at that moment she realised why people like Henry stayed there. For all of its grime and despair, it was a support network, with people around him who looked out for each other, who didn't judge, all of them doing their best just to get through another day.

That didn't help Jayne though. Henry had beaten her, scurried out so that she couldn't get him to court, and unless she found him in the town centre somewhere, she would let Dan down.

All she could hope for was that Mickey played along. If they lost him too, any plan to shift the blame towards Lucy would be gone.

There were signs of occupation at Mickey's house as Jayne pulled up outside, a glowing lamp visible through the net curtains. At least someone was in.

She'd tried calling Dan, but his phone was switched off.

She knocked on Mickey's door and didn't have to wait long for an answer, as the sound of feet shuffling to the door was followed by the rattle of the lock. It was Mickey's mother, who smiled and said, 'Hello, love. He's been waiting for you.'

Jayne tried to hide her relief. She didn't want to arrive at court with both witnesses missing. He followed Mickey's mother along the hallway and into the room at the back. She gestured for Jayne to sit down and then shouted up the stairs, 'Mickey? Your lady-friend is here,' and then, 'do you want a drink before you go?'

'No, but thank you anyway.' Jayne looked round the room as she waited. The fireplace was old, with cheap brown glazed tiles that surrounded a gas fire with fake coals, which had undoubtedly replaced a grander fire and mantle that a new owner would want to put back in. Glass bells lined one shelf, and on another there were photographs of Mickey and his mother together. On holiday. At Christmas. When Mickey was younger and slimmer. There were pictures of young children on a bright foreign beach grinning under sun hats.

'Your grandchildren?' Jayne said, pointing to the photographs.

'Yes, the little darlings,' she said, and her eyes glazed over. 'I don't see them much, not after the split. I've tried calling, but she puts the phone down.'

'What about Mickey? Does he see them?'

'Not at all. He's been told to stay away, and he does, but it breaks my heart. His too.'

'I'm sorry to hear that.'

'We're doing our best. One day at a time.'

'When I was here before, you said the previous lawyer was shouting. Can you remember what about?'

'I didn't catch all of it, but she was angry. You seem so much calmer. I like you.'

Before Jayne could respond, Mickey came down the stairs, his nervousness audible in the slow drag of his footsteps. When he came into the room, he was wearing a navy suit with an unbuttoned white shirt underneath. Jayne was surprised when she saw how a slight shimmer of stubble made him look quite handsome.

'Is this all right?' he said, looking down at himself.

'You look fine,' Jayne said, smiling.

Mickey's mother shuffled over to him and smoothed down his jacket. 'You look more than fine. You'll do that poor girl proud. Tell them what you know. It's important.'

He looked at Jayne and said, 'Is it usual to be nervous?'

'Yes, it's natural, but you won't be giving evidence today. It's all about showing that we have you. Let Dan take care of it all.'

'But what if I mess it up or if I've got it wrong?'

'Have you got it wrong?'

'I know what I saw.'

'Just stick with that and you'll be fine. I'll be with you.'

He took a deep breath and turned to his mother. 'Will you be all right here, on your own? I might be gone all day.'

'Don't you worry about me. Now go. We'll talk later.'

Jayne headed to the door, keen to get Mickey out of the house, but she had to wait as he hugged his mother. She tried not to roll her eyes with impatience.

Mickey squeezed past her to get to the door, too close to her in the narrow confines of the hallway. His cologne was strong, as if he wasn't used to putting it on and had been generous in his spraying.

'After you,' he said, as he opened the door.

Jayne stepped into the street, allowing Mickey the unnecessary chivalry, and walked over to her car.

Once he'd settled in his seat, Mickey said, 'Are we going to court straight away?' There was a sheen of perspiration on his forehead.

'Not quite yet. There's one other witness to look for.'

He put his hands on his knees, his posture rigid. 'How long will it take?'

'We've plenty of time.'

Mickey looked out of the window.

As she set off, he kept his attention away from her.

She noticed his hands were gripping his knees, his fingers white.

Sixty-five

'I don't know who did it,' Carter said, sitting back, his arms folded. 'I heard her scream and that was it.'

'No shouts, no other noises?' Dan asked.

'No, nothing. When I got into the house, there was just Mary.'

'What did you do?'

'I held her, tried to see if there was any life there, but there was nothing. I didn't know what to do. I could have rung the police, but then I'd have to say why I was there, and how would that look?'

'It was always going to come back to you. Forensic traces. Eye-witnesses.'

'I wasn't thinking clearly. The woman I loved was dead. I was distraught, I was panicking, I was confused. I just had to get away. If I'd known then what I know now, I'd have stayed, just so that she wasn't alone all night. That's what I hate about myself. I left her when she needed me. Instead, I ran home like a coward. I ran a bath to get rid of the blood. I washed my clothes. I sat in my bath and cried.'

'That doesn't look good,' Dan told him.

'I know, but it happened. None of this is good.'

'How well did you know Lucy?' Hannah said.

'Not very well. Mostly from what Mary told me.'

'Which was what?'

'That she was an attention-seeker, but everyone knows that from the papers.'

'How did Mary get on with her?'

He shrugged. 'Housemates, weren't they. You've got to rub along.'

'Was Lucy there?'

'Leave Lucy out of it.'

'We're wondering if that's what happened on the night,' Dan said, glancing at Hannah. 'Did she come in and find Mary upstairs? Did Mary think it was you coming back upstairs and say something? Was it something sexy that didn't seem like the Mary that Lucy knew?'

Carter looked to Hannah and then back at Dan. 'Lucy wasn't there.'

'You sure about that? We've got a witness who puts Lucy at the scene right after she screamed, with her boyfriend.'

Carter opened his mouth as if to say something, then stopped and shook his head instead. 'I didn't see her. Why would she stab Mary? And why run away? They wouldn't have known I was there?'

'A witness saw them leaving just after she screamed.'

'I'm not blaming Lucy.'

'If the jurors are to believe your story, they've got to have an idea of who else could have done it. Jurors like a puzzle, provided they can solve it. If we're going to make this case work, we have to blame Lucy.'

'No, I can't have that.'

'What does that mean? Why are you trying to protect Lucy? Her father's taking a real interest in this case, which makes me think Lucy's worried about something.'

'What like?'

'That's what I'm wondering. If you didn't see her, Lucy must know that you can't incriminate her, so is there something else?'

'What do you mean?'

'If you didn't see who was inside, we could still accuse Lucy, because we've got a witness who saw her, but you won't go with that. Is she going to come out fighting with something you haven't told us about?'

'I don't know what you mean.'

'Is there something she knows that we haven't heard yet?'

'What like?'

'We've heard a lot about Lucy and I can imagine something different happening. A sex game gone wrong, perhaps?'

Carter sat back and folded his arms, his jaw clenched, his stare hard. 'What the hell do you mean?'

'Was Lucy there all the time? All of you getting drunk or stoned? Did Lucy have little digs at Mary. Like you say, prim and proper. You're enjoying it, because this is all so different from the boring marriage you're locked into. Not just one good looking young woman but two, and one of them, Lucy, wants to spice things up a bit. Wouldn't you like that, two women?'

'I wanted Mary, nothing more.'

'You sure? Was Lucy trying to see how far Mary would go? You got carried away? Mary didn't want to, but you were too far gone to see it?'

'No!'

'Did she scream because you raped her, wound up by Lucy cheering you on?'

Carter stood up, knocking his chair up. 'Stop this.'

Dan went forward to the desk, putting his fists on the top, leaning forward. 'You sure that isn't how it happened, with her scream bringing you to your senses? Both of you panicking, so one of you stabbed her.'

'No.'

'Which one was it? You or Lucy?'

Carter shot forward and gripped Dan by the throat. 'I've told you what happened.'

Hannah reached out and put her hand on Carter's arm. 'Come on, boys, let's all calm down.' Her voice was stern, her fingers tightening around Carter's forearm.

Carter looked across at her and relaxed his grip.

'Sit down,' Hannah said to Carter, who did as he was told, glaring at Dan.

'I lied,' Carter said. 'But only about my relationship with Mary. Nothing more.'

'And you're going to say that in court?' Hannah said.

He nodded. 'Yes. That's my story.'

Dan banged on the door, three thumps with his clenched fist. A guard appeared quickly and held up the cuffs. 'I heard a noise.'

'A professional disagreement,' Hannah said.

Dan stayed silent as Carter left the room, glaring at Dan as he went, pausing only to let the cuffs wrap around his wrists.

When the door closed, Hannah said, 'What the hell was all that about?'

'I was testing him to see if he cracked when he lost it.'

'Rubbish. You're the one who lost it.'

'A friend of mine lost her life because of this case. Another has been so scared that she's sleeping on my sofa. I want to know the truth.'

'I knew Shelley too, remember. But stay in control. It's his case, not yours.'

Dan let his breathing calm down, his hands on his hips. 'Okay, I've got it.'

With that, Hannah collected her bag and headed for the door. Dan paused for a moment before he followed her. He remembered Dominic Ayres. The visit to his father. Jayne's intruders. Shelley's murder. However the case went, he wondered what the hell he had started, and how it would end.

Sixty-six

Jayne's phone rang. It was Dan. She pulled over to the side of the road.

'How's it going?' she said, as she answered.

'Carter's confirmed what we know, that he was having an affair with Mary.'

'What did he say about Lucy?'

'Nothing. It's almost like he's defending her, and if he's lying, he's missed his chance to use her to deflect attention.'

'Has the trial restarted?'

'We're about to go in.'

'What are you going to do about Lucy?'

'I don't know. I'm hoping Carter will see sense, but he won't budge.'

'Can we still use the witnesses? Is there any point?'

'Have you got them?'

'Mickey's here, but I can't find Henry. Is he that important?'

'We need everything we can bring. I've given him the hard word and he might change his mind. Just keep driving around. The museum steps are always a good place to start, or the benches at the end of the precinct. As long as he appears in the court corridor at some point, that's all that matters.'

'But if Carter won't go after Lucy, what's the point?'

'I've one last chance. Get them here.'

As Jayne hung up, dropping her phone into the driver door, Mickey said, 'Where are we going first?'

'The town-drunk hotspots,' Jayne said, and laughed. 'Yes, I know, not too glamorous, but there's another witness to find.'

As Jayne threaded her way through the tight streets that skirted the precinct, Mickey peered through the windscreen and said, 'What does he look like?'

'I've only seen him in the dark but I'd say small, messy, red-faced, curly grey hair. Usually with a can in his hand.'

'Sounds like he's wasted his life.'

'Or life has wasted him.'

They did the short one-way circuit but she couldn't see any of the local drunks. The streets were virtually empty. Those who were working had already started, and those who'd fill the pubs, bars and cafes later in the day were yet to arrive. The town museum was at the opposite end of the precinct to Henry's favourite bench by the department store, but they were both empty of drinkers.

'Is there anywhere else we can try?' Jayne said.

'How would I know? I'm not some kind of drunk.'

'You've lived here longer than me.'

A pause, and then, 'Why, where are you from?'

'You wouldn't know it,' she said, her eyes narrowing, trying to cut off the question.

'I noticed you didn't have any family pictures in your flat.'

She turned to look at him. 'You weren't in my flat long enough to notice that.'

'I'm very observant. What's happening at court?'

'Not much, but we're hoping you'll make the difference.'

'Will the prosecution come after me?'

'Why should they?'

'Because I'm helping the murderer. The trial will become about me, make me out to be someone bad.'

'You're not on trial.'

Mickey turned to look out of the window again.

'Mickey?'

He didn't answer, didn't look round.

She rolled her eyes. It was turning into a great old morning.

Sixty-seven

The court corridor was busy with those interested in Carter's case. Mary's parents glared at Dan and Hannah as they went past, Murdoch with them. Dan gave them a nod of respect before he looked away. They were about to expose a side of Mary that her parents might not like. Dan wanted to go to them and say that the truth is what matters, nothing else, but he knew he'd get a frosty reception. He didn't blame them for that.

The door into the courtroom was heavy and old, and it clattered as Dan let it close. Simon Parkin, the prosecutor, looked up and folded his newspaper. It was affected nonchalance.

'Another day of fun,' he said, as Hannah put her papers on the desk, her wig resting on top.

'Dan's going to examine Lucy.'

'Fine. Then we can get to the good stuff.'

'Which is?'

'Your client, eventually. You know what they say, that the best part of the defence case is the end of the prosecution case, because once your client gets in the box, it all goes wrong.'

Dan looked towards the public gallery and saw Sara Carter, sitting in her usual place, alone, at the end of a row of seats.

'Excuse me,' Dan said, and went to the back of the courtroom.

He gestured with a tilt of his head that Sara should come forward. When she joined him at the rail, he whispered, 'He's admitted what's obvious from the photographs, but there's more to it than that.'

'What do you mean?'

'It involves Lucy but he won't say.'

'Why not?'

'Honest answer? I think he's scared, because I can't work out why he wants to protect her. He was involved with Mary, not Lucy. I think he's protecting you.'

'What, because of those men who came to see me?'

'That's my guess.'

'He's got to do the right thing.'

'Have you any photographs of Tammy?'

Sara rummaged in her bag and pulled out a black purse. In the window meant for driving licences, there was a picture of a little girl. 'This one.'

'Give it to me.'

Sara did as she was asked.

Dan winked at her and went towards the dock, pausing only to glance back at Dominic Ayres, who was sitting in his usual place. He waited by the glass dock until he heard the rattle of keys and two white-shirted security guards appeared in the dock, Carter between them.

Dan crooked his finger. Carter leaned towards the glass, putting his ear to the one of the small gaps.

'Look at the back. Sara is here and she wants you to tell the truth.'

Carter followed the jab of Dan's finger, his chin jutting out when he saw her.

'Do it for her. Nothing can hurt her any more than you have already.'

Carter looked towards Dominic and then back to Sara. 'Yes, it can, because I might not be there to protect her. Don't you understand?'

Dan slapped the photograph of Tammy against the glass. 'What about her?'

Carter's eyes welled up with tears when he saw it.

'Wouldn't you do anything for her?'

'Of course I would.' Spittle hit the glass. He looked down for a moment, took some deep breaths as if composing himself. When he looked up, he said, 'I'm protecting her. Don't you get it?'

'No, you're not. Do you know why Sara gave me the photographs of you and Mary? It's not because she loves you. Not after what you did. No, it's because one day this will all be over, Tammy will get older without you, and she'll find out that you're in prison for murdering a young woman. However you think you're protecting her now, it won't last, and Tammy will wonder what kind of monster her father is. How will she live with that? How is that protecting her?'

Carter stepped away and sat down. He put his head in his hands, his fingers gripping his hair.

Dan slapped on the glass. 'Can I do it my way?'

There was a knock on the door at the front of court, and the court assistant ordered everyone to rise for the judge.

'Robert?'

Carter looked back at the public gallery. To Dominic. To Sara. To the photograph Dan had placed against the glass once more. He stood as the judge entered and, just before Dan took his place behind Hannah, he took a deep breath and said, 'Yes. Do it your way.'

*

'I can't do this,' Mickey said, his voice agitated.

Jayne looked across as she drove. 'Why not?'

'It will all come back to me, I know it.'

'Mickey, calm down. It'll be fine.'

'You can't know that.'

'Let's sort out this other witness first, then we can talk.' When Jayne glanced across, his jaw was clenched.

Jayne drove in silence for a few minutes, looking around for Henry all the time. There was a blue Toyota behind her that seemed to be following the same route. As she started on yet another loop of the town centre one-way circuit, she said, 'Tell me about you.'

'What do you mean?'

'What's your life involve? Tell me your story.'

'Why do you want to know?'

'It might relax you.'

'There isn't much to tell. I got married, had a couple of children, tried to do the right thing.'

'What about a job?'

'I told you before, I'm an actor. Or at least, I'm supposed to be. Had a few television spots, adverts and things, but there are long lay-offs.'

'What made you want to be an actor?'

'You get to be someone else for a while.' He paused. 'No, it's more than that. You get to know someone else, even if it's only a character.'

'And now you're back in Highford.'

'Yeah, I came home when I split from my wife. It's been a funny old year.' He turned towards her. 'Why the interest in me?'

'I'm making conversation.'

'How do I know that this isn't some kind of a trap?'

'How do you mean?'

'You're making sure I'm at court so that you can accuse me of something, except you're not telling me, knowing that I might not come.'

'Why would we blame you?'

She glanced in the mirror again. The Toyota was still there. Always a car between, except her route wasn't a usual one. She was touring the town centre, looking for a drunk.

Mickey turned away.

'Come on, don't go quiet on me,' she said. 'Why would we blame you?'

Mickey wiped his eyes and let out a long breath.

'Mickey? What's wrong?'

'I'm nervous, that's all.'

'Trust me, this is no trick.'

'How do I know that? To trust you, I've got to know you, but that's impossible – I can't find out anything about you.'

'Why have you been looking?' Her fingers were tighter around the steering wheel, nervous flutters in her chest.

'If I meet people, I like to know about them. There's nothing wrong with that. You came to my house, wanted to know all about me. Why shouldn't that go both ways?'

'And what have you found out?'

'Nothing. That's what I mean. It's as if you don't exist. Just the usual social media, but no pictures of you or your family. How do you get customers?'

'I rely on referrals.'

'But you could make it bigger. It's almost as if you're in hiding.'

She swallowed. There it was, her secret. What could he possibly know? Stay calm, she told herself.

When she turned to steal another look at him, he stared into her eyes, as if he was looking for something, his gaze piercing, but as quickly as she noticed, it was gone.

'You shouldn't have been looking.'

'Why?'

'Because I say so, that's all.' She tossed her hair and sat up as she drove, to regain her composure. 'Why did you fall out with Shelley Greenwood?'

'I got scared, wanted to back out.'

'What were you scared of? Or who?'

'It was nothing. I had a visit, that's all.' He raised his hand. 'And before you say anything, I don't know who it was, except that it was some guy in a suit. Thickset. Told me not to give evidence or something might happen to me.'

'But you're doing it anyway.'

'I felt guilty, trying to back out. Mary deserved more than that.'

They descended into silence once more. Jayne checked her mirror again. The blue Toyota was still there, one car back.

'I'm pulling off the road,' she said, her eyes on her mirror all the time. 'There must be some old buildings where people hang out.' She didn't want to frighten Mickey but she needed to know whether the Toyota would stay with them.

They passed an area where the shops thinned out and the canal began its curve around the town. 'Try some of the old buildings down there,' Mickey said, pointing towards the canal. 'Whenever I've walked down there, I've come across groups of drinkers.'

Jayne turned into a walled yard, with cobbles that drummed against her tyres. There was an office at one side and a car repair shop on the other, but Mickey pointed straight ahead. 'Keep on going straight, I know this place.'

Jayne followed his direction and soon the car was beyond the cobbles and pitching and rolling over uneven ground, over clumps of long grass that sprouted through concrete patches, her tyres hitting the occasional brick. It was as if they were slowly leaving the town behind, hitting the crumbling edges.

'Where the hell are we going?'

There was a three-storey stone building ahead, it's windows gone, bricked up and painted white. The eaves were visible in places where some of the tiles had been stripped away, and the guttering and drainpipes were missing. The building looked isolated. The canal curved around it, and whatever had been on the other side was long-since demolished.

'I used to come here,' he said. 'The Empire Theatre. My first acting gigs were here, but it closed down a long time ago.'

She climbed out of her car.

The day hadn't warmed up yet but it was a relief to be in the fresh air. Despite Mickey's attempt to look smart for his court appearance, he smelled of stale sweat with just the over-sweetness of cheap cologne to mask it. She couldn't place the brand, but it was familiar. Probably one of the copies sold on the market.

'They hang around here? There's no sign of anyone.'

'I just wanted one last look, before we go to court.'

'There's no time for a nostalgia trip, you need to be in court. You can't be getting dirty looking around this place.'

'Indulge me.' Mickey went to a steel panel that covered what was once a door. He pulled on it, grunting with effort, until it scraped on the ground, pushing dirt as it went. 'Things will change when I get to court. I want to have a look,' and he eased himself into the gap.

'Come on, stop messing around.'

'I used to love this place,' he said, leaving only the echo of his footsteps as he disappeared from view.

'Mickey, come outside.'

'In a minute.' His voice was more distant.

Jayne closed her eyes and cursed him. Dan was expecting her to produce two witnesses at court. One she couldn't find, and the other had taken it upon himself to turn into an urban explorer.

She had a small torch in the glove compartment. She grabbed it and got out of her car. When she went to the gap where Mickey had gone and peered through, all she could see was darkness.

'Mickey?'

No reply.

'Fuck!'

She closed her eyes for a moment and took a deep breath. Every fibre of her instinct told her not to go in there, but she had a job to do and she was going to do it.

As she squeezed into the entrance where Mickey had gone, all the daylight disappeared as if she'd clicked off the switch, so that all she was left with was the loud scrapes of small stones under her shoes, the smell of damp furniture, and an all-consuming darkness.

Sixty-eight

The jurors watched expectantly as Lucy strode towards the witness box. She clasped her hands in front of her and looked towards Hannah. Her eyes flickered with surprise when Dan got to his feet.

The prosecutor's examination of Lucy had been soft and caring, respect for a young woman who'd lost a friend and been faced with the aftermath of something horrific.

Dan's tone was the same when he said, 'Good morning, Miss Ayres.' Gentle. Soft. The rough stuff would come later.

Dan's job was different to the prosecutor's. All Dan had to do was present a believable alternative truth, find those answers that can be twisted and stacked into reasonable doubt in the closing speech. When Carter gets in the witness box, the prosecutor looks for the opposite, as his attack begins. It won't be answers from the accused that the prosecutor aims for, but the silences, those uncomfortable moments when the accused wants to avoid a question, knowing that the answer will damn him.

Dan looked back at Carter, who stiffened and straightened in the dock.

'How much time have you spent in the company of Robert Carter?'

Lucy didn't follow Dan's glance back to the dock. 'Not much.' Her voice was firm. There was none of the flirtatiousness he had seen during her visit to his office. 'Just when he bothered us whenever we were out?'

'Whenever?'

'Yes.' Traces of doubt had crept into her voice.

'Every time you left the house, he was there?'

'Well, no, not every time?'

'Outside your office?'

'No.'

'When you went shopping?'

'No.'

'In every pub you went into?'

'No.' She straightened herself and tossed her hair, a flush creeping up her cheeks.

'Whenever you saw him,' Dan said, emphasising the word *whenever*, 'was it in the same few pubs?'

'Yes, mostly.'

'Mostly? Or always?'

Lucy nodded. 'Yes, always.'

'And you don't know if he was there when you weren't?'

'Well, no, because we weren't there.'

'A fair summary would be, therefore, that your group and Robert Carter frequented the same pubs, and if he saw Mary, he would talk to her?'

Lucy didn't answer. Instead, she just pursed her lips.

'Is that a yes?'

After a pause, Lucy said, 'Yes.'

'And was he ever violent?'

Again, a pause. 'No, not that I saw.'

'Mary had never reported to you that he made threats to her?'

'No. He just creeped her out.'

'Explain what you mean.' When Lucy glanced at the prosecutor, Dan added, 'I know you've given us a flavour already, but I want to explore that.'

'If we were in the same pub, he'd come over every time, to talk to Mary. He would hang around too long.'

'So this occurred when he was already there?'

'Yes. Or if he came in after us.'

'But he didn't follow you there?'

'Well, no.'

'And when he spoke with you or your group, how many times did he threaten violence?'

Lucy looked confused. 'Violence?'

'Yes, violence.' Dan's tone had sharpened.

Lucy took a deep breath. 'Never.'

'But you say that Mr Carter *creeped* Mary out. How did she express that?'

'Whenever I asked her why she talked to him, I could tell from how she was, as if she really didn't want to talk about it.'

Dan reached down for the envelope he'd put next to his notes. He'd made fifteen extra copies of the photographs, bundled together, the scrawled notes too. One for each juror, one for the judge, one for Simon Parkin, and one for Lucy.

Dan passed one along the desk to Simon Parkin and allowed him a moment to look at the bundle.

Simon stared at the pictures for a few seconds. His lips were pursed and the back of his neck acquired some colour.

Before Dan could ask any more questions, Simon rose quickly to his feet. 'My Lord, I need to raise a point of law.'

The judge looked over his glasses at Dan and said, 'Very well,' before asking the jury to leave the courtroom.

When the jurors had shuffled out and Lucy had returned to the witness room, Simon leaned across and hissed, 'You can't ambush me like this, you know that. What the hell is going on?'

'No ambush.' Dan leaned in to keep their conversation private. 'You portrayed Carter as some crazed stalker, with no evidence apart from bad vibes and an old complaint to back it up. Now we can prove otherwise, everything you do will make it look as if you're trying to rescue a crumbling case.'

Before Simon could respond, the judge said, 'Mr Parkin, does this need to be in chambers?'

He grasped his gown and said, 'No, My Lord, people should hear this, because I'm being ambushed.'

'In what way?' The judge looked at Dan when he said it.

'Your lordship heard how the case was opened, and it's always been the case that the defendant attacked the victim after a few months of bothering her, stalking her. The defence knew how the case was being presented and raised no objections.'

'And now?'

Simon held the pictures high. 'I've just been served with these.' His lips pursed with anger.

'Let me see them.'

Dan handed a copy to the usher, who took it to the court assistant, who handed it up to the judge, who frowned as he flicked through the bundle. He raised his eyebrows and said to Dan, 'How long have you had these?'

Dan stood and said, 'Since last night, My Lord. The defendant's wife had them. She was going to destroy them, because she was angry with him, but instead contacted me last night. She's been watching the trial and knew the truth was different.' He turned to Simon. 'I'm sure my learned friend will formally admit them into evidence rather than requiring them to be produced by the witness. I can obtain a statement to exhibit them, if he needs it.'

Simon waved his hand to concede the point.

The judge turned back to the prosecutor. 'What are you proposing to do?'

'I've been made to look a fool.'

'Lawyers always make themselves look foolish. They just learn to care less about it. My question is, what do you want me to do about it?'

'I'm sorry, My Lord, I don't follow.'

'If you wanted the jury to leave just so you could moan for a while, save your breath. If you want me to tear a strip off the defence, too late, they've answered the question. They got the pictures last night.' He frowned. 'You chose to open the case like you did, so answer me this: has there ever been any hint that the victim and the defendant were in a relationship? If you knew but gambled on it not coming out, you played your hand and lost.'

Simon was about to say something, when Dan rose to his feet again and said, 'One of the detectives knew. He didn't pass it on because it came from a local drunk, who saw the defendant and victim walking back to her house, "all loved up", in his words. The officer believed it was the night before Mary died.'

'And what say you?'

'The defence case is that it was the night she died, and that the victim was happy with the defendant. If the police are right, however, and it was the night before, it's more than a one-night stand. It was a relationship, and this is consistent with the photographs.'

The judge sat back in his chair and steepled his fingers under his nose. 'But the police knew? Mr Parkin, is that correct?'

Simon reddened further. 'I've been informed very recently that a detective received information about the defendant walking with the victim, that isn't in dispute. But there was no mention of anything like this,' and he waved the pictures in the air.

'Mr Grant?'

'If the detective believes that the witness was referring to the night before, that's the defendant in company with the victim twice.' He raised an eyebrow. 'The prosecution knew. They just didn't understand it.'

The judge turned back to the prosecutor.

'So what do you want, man? Speak up. I can't stop the defence from putting it before the jury. If you're saying you want a new jury so you can start again, I'll listen to your application, but as the police knew something about this, and you did too, I can't see it going your way.'

Dan looked across at Simon, who seemed increasingly uncomfortable. He'd expected a roasting for the defence, but all the heat was going his way.

'If your case is in trouble because the facts have got in the way, that is just how it goes,' the judge said. 'I'm more interested in the truth being heard.' He leaned forward. 'So what is to be?'

'We'll carry on,' Simon said, much of the fight gone from his voice.

The judge turned to Dan. 'Are there any more surprises to come?'

Dan looked back to the dock. Carter was looking at the floor, his fingers gripping his hair, white with tension. He glanced back to the gallery. Dominic Ayres was leaning forwards, his glare intense, his fingers clasped together. Lucy's mother was staring into space, glassy-eyed. Dan thought back to Shelley, all the years they'd known each other. He had to do it for her.

He cleared his throat and said, 'In relation to Miss Ayres, we have evidence that she was at the scene at the time of the victim's scream.'

Simon spluttered and was about to say something. There was a gasp from the public gallery. The judge held up his hand to regain the silence. 'Keep going.'

'It's information from a witness that the police marked as not relevant,' Dan said. 'The witness heard the scream and looked out of his bedroom window. He saw Lucy Ayres and another male leave by the back gate before running down the alley. It fits with the defence case. The defendant will say that the only thing he lied about was his relationship with Mary, and he did that because he is married and was trying to salvage Mary's reputation.'

'How very noble,' the judge said, his weary tone telling Dan that he thought exactly the opposite. 'Are you going to blame Miss Ayres for the crime?'

'We will present a valid alternative explanation to show that the defendant's story can be believed, which will present enough reasonable doubt to allow the jurors to acquit.' He pointed to the photographs. 'Those pictures will show the real Robert Carter. A man in love.'

'You know that I will advise her about self-incrimination?'

'Of course, My Lord. And her silence may say more than any answer.'

'Good, there we are then. Are we done?'

Simon coughed lightly before I spoke. 'My Lord, I would like to take instructions.'

The judge sighed. 'You are owed that much, at least. How long will you need?'

'Thirty minutes.'

'You have it. And, Mr Grant, no more surprises.'

Dan bowed his assent as the judge rose to leave. Once he'd vacated the court, he leaned across to Simon. 'The strongest cases only ever get weaker.'

A bang of a door echoed around the courtroom. As Dan glanced back, Dominic's figure could be seen through the gap in the door as it closed slowly, striding angrily towards the exit.

'You'd better be right about this,' Simon said. 'I don't mind if it turns out that Lucy Ayres had some part in the murder, but if this is just you blowing a lot of smoke, I'll never trust you again.'

Dan didn't respond. He didn't want an argument. More importantly, he hoped he was right too. He'd started something and had no idea how it would end.

Sixty-nine

Jayne clicked on the torch and gasped.

The theatre was huge and crumbling. She was walking along an aisle alongside the stall seats, row after row of blue chairs, the cloth faded and covered in dust, stuffing spilling out on to the floor. The ceiling was high, with a large plaster rose in the middle, gaps in some places where it had come down, and the remnants of electrical flexes swinging in whatever draughts there were, like moss on a Georgia plantation. Dust swirled in the beam.

'Mickey, where are you?'

Something fluttered above her, making her duck instinctively.

There was a pause before she heard him shout back, 'This way. Down here.'

She closed her eyes in frustration. 'But where are you?'

'Keep on coming down.'

She edged forward. The floor was concrete, the carpet long gone, but there were loose stones and pieces of wood scattered everywhere. The air was pungent with damp, making her cover her nose with her sleeve.

They were supposed to be in court, Dan was expecting them. What the hell was he playing at?

Jayne heard something. She stopped to listen out. There was nothing, apart from the echoes of a crumbling building.

There was movement ahead. A dark shadow. 'I'm just here.' It was Mickey.

Jayne quickened her pace. 'Where are you?'

'Up here, on the stage.'

Jayne shone her beam forward. There was a stage ahead, with a high curtain, although mould crept up the cloth and the colour had long since lost its glory.

'Stop messing around,' she said. 'We've got to go.'

She threaded her way through the debris on the floor until she reached the small steps that took her on to the stage. Dust flew as she went up, and once on the stage, she shone her torch around the auditorium.

'Beautiful, isn't it.'

Jayne yelped and turned round. He was right behind her.

'What a waste,' she said, looking around, her hand on her chest. The floor creaked under her feet. 'Is this safe?'

'It's fine.'

'What are we doing here? We're supposed to be at court.'

'I just wanted to stop here, once I saw it, to remind myself.'

'Of what?'

'Of what might have been. This is where I started out. I was young and keen and ambitious, thought I was bigger than the town. And here I am, back where I started, and like this place, less than I once was.'

'We've got to go. Come on.'

'No, because you don't get it. I'll lose everything when I get to court. I don't know if I'm ready.'

'You're still not making sense.'

He put his head back and took some deep breaths, before saying, 'I'm not who you think I am.'

Seventy

Dan put his phone away and went back to staring out of the windows on the Crown Court corridor. Jayne wasn't answering her phone. Or wasn't getting a signal. Whatever the reason, something wasn't right. Hannah had gone to the robing room, seeking its sanctuary. Dan didn't want to go in there. He wanted to keep on chasing Jayne, because without Mickey, they had nothing to back up their claims about Lucy.

The scene below was so ordinary, people going about their day, no concept of the dramas being played out within the court building. Lives changed forever in the courtrooms behind him and ended up as news fodder, a story to fill a dinner table. For the people in the courtrooms, nothing was ever the same again.

Dan was trying to be patient. He checked his watch. The judge had only granted a short delay and the trial would start again soon.

There were footsteps behind him. It was Murdoch, glowering. 'What are you playing at?'

On the other side of the corridor, Simon Parkin was talking to Mary's parents. Her mother glared across at Dan.

'Defending my client.'

'Come off it, Dan. You're playing games and I want to know why you've dragged me into it, with all these quiet chats, making out like we're all fighting for the same thing.

All you've been doing is laying traps. What have you got that you haven't disclosed?'

'I told you I was going after Lucy.'

'But you didn't tell me with what.'

'You told me it would make no difference, that the case would carry on anyway.'

'Who's the witness?'

'A guy called Mickey Ellis. He was in his bedroom, at his computer desk, when he heard the scream. He lives on the street that backs on to the alley and has a good view from his bedroom window. He can see right into Mary's yard. When he heard the scream, he looked out and saw two people leaving quickly. One of them he recognised as the woman living at the house. Lucy Ayres.'

'But we'd already discounted Lucy.'

'How? I'm still waiting for her phone records, remember.'

'I've just spoken to DC Edwards.'

'I thought he was off the investigation.'

'He's off this case, but he's not gone from the squad. I called the squad room and he remembered why we discounted her as a suspect.'

'So she was a suspect?'

'Everyone's a suspect until shown otherwise, you know that. Edwards went to see Lucy at her boyfriend's flat. She was staying there because she couldn't get into her own house, with it being a crime scene. You remember how the press were highlighting her? Edwards was curious about whether we were missing something, so he went round.'

'On his own?'

'He was showing initiative.'

'Or is it because he wanted to keep going round without anyone knowing, to protect her in order to keep her father happy?'

'It doesn't change what he found. Do you know there's a way to check someone's location on an iPhone? It's in *location services*. If you have it turned on, it keeps a history of where you've been. You can delete it or even turn it off, but it's pretty neat, because it doesn't come from the mast, but from the GPS chip inside the phone. When Edwards spoke to her, she reminded him of it.'

Dan didn't like the way this was going. 'And that's from the same detective who withheld information about Henry?'

'He isn't very good at making notes of everything, but one thing shines through: he hasn't lied. He saw the location history, and do you know what it showed? Lucy's phone never left that address.'

'She might have left it behind. Charging up or something.'

'That's desperate stuff.'

'Let me see her phone.'

'I asked Edwards about that. She's got a new phone now. The old one went to some recycling place somewhere.'

'Bloody convenient.'

'Or bloody truthful.'

Dan rubbed his eyes. He'd lost too much sleep for the case to go badly this quickly. 'How come that wherever I look in this case, Edwards appears?'

'Coincidence?'

'Coppers don't like coincidences.'

'You get him in the witness box and see how it looks.'

Dan didn't have to answer that. He could attack Edwards, show that he was a detective who couldn't be trusted, but it would just make him look even more desperate. He needed to know how reliable Mickey was.

'What have you got?' Murdoch said.

'The witness who saw Lucy leaving the house came from the house-to-house you carried out, the one signed off as *nothing relevant*, the one you refused to disclose to me. We went over it ourselves, and guess what, there was something, and you missed it. Or ignored it completely.'

Murdoch frowned. 'Which house?'

'Number 24.'

'Wait there.'

Murdoch stomped towards the courtroom, the door swinging open. Dan followed, curious. He opened the door into the courtroom and peeked inside. Murdoch was snapping at the prosecution caseworker, making her rummage through the crates of paperwork piled up by the desk along the back row, further along from where Jayne had been sitting.

The caseworker produced a folder and rummaged through, eventually jabbing at something written down. Murdoch stared at whatever was there and set off towards the door. Dan stepped into the courtroom, to cut her off.

'Show me.'

Murdoch slammed the folder on to the desk and pointed at something. 'Door-to-door inquiries. Number 24. There's the entry: *Barbara Ellis. She didn't see or hear anything.*'

'What about Mickey?'

'Underneath: *No one else in but son will call if he has anything to report. Wasn't at home the previous night.*'

Dan frowned. 'That doesn't make any sense. He saw Lucy from his bedroom window.'

'It makes complete sense. Your witness is lying. The question is why?'

Dan paced. Something wasn't right.

Murdoch grabbed his arm. 'Who's Mickey Ellis?'

'Does it matter? I might not be calling him now, if he's lied.'

'Stop playing the game. What do you know about him? I haven't heard his name before.'

'He moved back up here from London. He split from his wife and came home. Some out of work actor.'

'You got a date of birth?'

Dan went to his own file and looked through his notes, finding it in a report submitted by Jayne. He scribbled it down and handed it over to Murdoch.

'Give me five minutes,' she said, and bolted out of the courtroom.

It felt too quiet. The court assistant had found something to look at on his computer so that he could pretend he wasn't listening. The prosecution caseworker averted her eyes as she put the papers back in the crate, but didn't offer an opinion.

Dan left the courtroom with much less urgency than Murdoch.

Sara was waiting for him in the corridor.

'How are you?' he said.

'I'm okay.' Her flat tone said otherwise. 'What did Robbie say about the photographs? He can't deny them, right, but did he love her?'

Dan didn't answer, but his regret-filled smile told her what she wanted to know.

She looked up and blinked quickly. Tears ran down her face. She wiped them away with the back of her hand. 'It's about Tammy now. I've got to bring her up on my own, which will be hard. If he stays in prison she'll never really know him. Girls should know their father, and because of this mess she never will.' She took a deep breath. 'I know he loved Mary. I saw everything. I just want to know why I couldn't give him that.'

'Relationships are complicated.'

'No, life with me was complicated, because it meant responsibility and hard work, and all Robbie wanted to do was play around. I just wanted his help.'

'Let's finish this case and see what you both have left. He's had a long time to think about things.'

She put her hand gently on his forearm. 'Thank you. Just tell him I'm thinking about him. If he didn't kill her, that is.'

'You mean if he's found not guilty?'

'No, I don't mean that. I need to know that he's innocent, whatever the verdict.'

'I'll pass it on.'

Sara walked away, towards the canteen at the other end of the corridor, her head down as she passed Mary's parents. She wasn't the guilty one, but Dan could tell she somehow blamed herself, although he wasn't sure why.

He turned back to the window but became conscious of the sound of quick footsteps, Fast clicks on the tiled floor.

He looked back. It was Mary's parents, her mother's eyes screwed up with anger, too close to him. 'What the hell are you doing?' Mary's father was pulling her back, his hand on her arm, but her free hand jabbed a finger in Dan's face. 'Just a game, that's all it is to you.' She banged her chest with the flat of her hand. 'My daughter. That's what this is about.'

Dan shifted his gaze between the two. 'I don't expect you to understand, but I'm just doing my job.'

'Do you think that makes it better? That this is just another day at work for you?'

Dan didn't respond. Whatever he said, it wouldn't be enough.

'What game are you playing now? More smoke? More mirrors? You lawyers make me sick. All of you.'

'Come on, please,' Mary's father said, pulling her again.

'Do as he says.'

Dan's cheek flared red as the sharp sting of her slap echoed along the corridor.

Mary's father pulled his wife back with more effort this time, his arm round her middle. A security guard approached, his stroll increasing to a jog as he saw what had happened.

Dan held his hand up as the guard approached. 'It's all right, it's all fine.'

The guard stood in front of Mary's mother. 'Do you want me to get the police?'

'What for?' Dan said.

'The assault.'

Dan rubbed his cheek, which was still smarting from the blow. 'There was no assault.'

Mary's mother stopped wriggling in her husband's grip and instead slumped down.

'Are you sure?' the guard said. 'I saw it.'

Dan shook his head. 'I've no complaint.'

As he looked back to the view, just to avoid the discomfort of Mary's parents, he was reminded of how her mother was right, it was just another day for him.

He just hoped that Carter was telling the truth. If nothing else, let there be some justice, however it happened.

Murdoch rushed up to him.

'Not you as well.'

'Mickey Ellis. Where is he now?'

'With Jayne.'

'Shit, Dan. What have you done?'

'What's wrong?'

'We need to find a room.'

And with that, Murdoch strode towards one of the interview rooms, yanked on a door handle and waited for Dan to join her.

Seventy-one

'Who are you then?' Jayne was edging forwards on the stage, wary of the drop. Her voice echoed in the space. Dust kicked up, making her nose itch. Light strained to get into the space from the gap where they'd entered. She kept her torch beam directed towards the floor.

Mickey put his hands on his hips as he looked around the shadows of the derelict theatre. He was blinking back tears. 'I am who I say I am, Mickey Ellis. But who I am isn't good.'

'What the hell are you on about? Come on, we've got to go.'

He put out his hand. 'You'll find all this out when I get to court, so you need to know. You want me to tell the truth?'

'Of course I do.'

'The whole truth and nothing but the truth?'

'Stop this.'

'I've lied to you.'

Jayne groaned as she imagined Dan at court, waiting for her to arrive with the star witness in tow. 'What about?'

'Seeing Lucy running from the yard.'

'You better be joking.'

A car drew up outside, just a small rumble on the cobbles.

'I'm not joking, and it's not funny. You've got to know about me first, because you'll judge me when you hear the truth.'

'I'm already judging you. I'm judging that you're messing up my morning, and perhaps the rest of Robert Carter's life. Come on, go.'

Mickey started to pace, his head up, as if surveying his audience, just distant memories lost in the shadows.

'Do you know why I became an actor?'

'Oh, please.'

'I've got to tell you.'

'Okay, I'll play along. All the clichés, like the audience applause, the smell of the greasepaint?'

He shook his head. 'I thought it would help me understand people. For me, it was never about the audience or the story, but about the character. The appearance, the motivations, what drives them. People interest me. I study them. But what acting jobs have I had? Someone looking at a new table in an advert for a furniture shop. Dressed in a suit, pretending to be a lawyer in a commercial for no-win no-fee daytime stuff. What's interesting about that? Where's the motivation, the secret?'

A car door slammed closed somewhere outside.

Jayne grabbed his sleeve. 'Yeah, I get it, your career hasn't worked out. Boo-hoo. Come on, we're going.'

He yanked his arm away. 'No, because you're not getting it, and all of this will come out in court. You'll need to know it. Take you, for example.'

A cold shiver rippled up her spine. 'What about me?'

'You're mysterious.'

'Why does that concern you?'

'That's what you don't get – it does. Things like that always concern me, because I need to understand people.'

'Mickey, please, what has this got to do with anything?'

'Because it all comes back to that night. Don't you see?'

'That night?'

'When Mary died. I hear it all the time. Her scream. So much terror. So loud, so shrill. It replays in my head as if it's on some kind of loop.'

'But what about Lucy? You just said that you didn't see her.'

'It's Mary I see. I see her all the time now, her lifeless face, in my head constantly. Her housemates were away, I knew that, and Lucy? She was never there, certainly not on a weekend. It was then or never.'

'What are you talking about?' Jayne started to back away.

'I saw Mary go out. I was watching, like I always am, for the outline of her body against her curtains, or the pink of her skin through the frosted glass of the bathroom. It was meant to be, it had to be. It was so perfect. I could see everything from my window.'

'Mickey?'

'But that wasn't enough. It never is.'

Seventy-two

'What's going on?' Dan said, as he pushed open the door to a side-room. Murdoch gestured to Simon Parkin in the court corridor, and he and Hannah joined them.

'I want Mr Parkin to hear this,' Murdoch said.

'Hear what?'

'How much do you know about Mickey Ellis?'

Dan was surprised. 'Nothing much. I've never spoken to him, just heard what Jayne told me. He's a bit lonely, split from his wife, but apart from that, she says he seems normal. But I don't need to know him, just what he says, and he seems like a man who notices things.'

'You haven't got the full picture.'

'You better tell me then, because I'm getting bored of this unfolding mystery.'

Murdoch leant against the opposite wall and put her head back, her eyes closed for a moment. When she opened them again, she said, 'I've just had someone check him out on PNC. Did he tell you why he split from his wife?'

'I didn't need to know.'

'Oh yes, you did, because the reason Mickey Ellis split from his wife is that he's a pervert, and a dangerous one.'

Dan felt his whole body cool. His mind was filled with images of Jayne with him. 'Why isn't he locked up then?'

'Because he's no fool, which is why he's so dangerous.' Murdoch went to sit down and let out a long breath. 'He's slipped through a crack in the law. He was arrested in London, but the police there couldn't prove that what he did was unlawful. That didn't make it any less unpleasant for his victims.'

'Criminals are those who commit crimes,' Dan said. 'Are you telling me he didn't commit any crimes?'

'He was arrested, but they couldn't get a charge. His hobby, and that's the best way I can describe it, is going into women's houses and searching them. He'd find a way to get in without causing any damage, and once they were at work, he'd look into their life. Search their drawers. Lie on their bed. Masturbate on their bed. They found footage of it when he was arrested, Ellis wanking on someone's bed, holding something taken from the laundry basket. Just lying there, like he was in his own home, staring at the phone he'd propped up on the bedside cabinet. He filmed the contents of their drawers. He filmed their laundry baskets. Their dirty underwear, for Christ's sake.'

'How come you couldn't get a charge?'

'Because he had a smart lawyer who told him to stay quiet, and a prosecutor who wouldn't put it before a court to see how it turned out.'

'That's unfair,' Simon said. 'If there's no crime, that's it.'

'I don't get it,' Dan said.

'Maybe you're not quite the hotshot you think you are,' Murdoch said. 'Let's go through the crimes. What about trespass?'

Dan pinched the top of his nose as he concentrated. 'No such crime in the context of a house. It applies to outdoor gatherings. An anti-rave thing.'

'Exactly. What about burglary? How would you defend it?'

'Anything damaged?'

'No.'

'Anything stolen?'

'No.'

Dan didn't have to voice the answer, because Murdoch knew it. He could imagine the heated discussions that probably took place with the prosecutor. Burglary is more than just going into someone else's house. It has to be done for a specific reason, like to steal, cause grievous bodily harm or rape. It's no crime to look around someone's house out of curiosity.

'Were the occupants always out?' Dan said.

'At first.'

'What do you mean?'

'I was given the number of the detective in charge and I've just spoken to her. It started out as daytime creeping. When they were at work, so I was told. It was almost as if he just wanted to snoop into their lives, but it became like that wasn't enough, because he started going into the house at night.' She shuddered. 'The detective said that he filmed the women on one of those little cameras. He'd watch them sleep. On one, he was under the bed, because you could make out her legs as she got ready for bed.'

'Jeez, that's creepy.'

'Yeah, just a bit, but guess what, he thought of all the angles on that.'

'How do you mean?'

'He didn't say anything in his interviews. There was plenty of footage but no one could identify who they were. Just ankles walking around a bed, or shadows, the sound of breathing. And never the same house twice.'

'That scuppered a stalking charge then.'

'That's what the prosecution said. No one knew who he was watching.'

'How did you arrest him?'

'He was caught in someone's house, dressed in black, kneeling on the floor, watching her sleep, inches from her. Just about the creepiest thing I ever heard. The poor woman didn't know how long he'd been there.'

'Voyeurism?'

Murdoch shook her head. 'She was in pyjamas and asleep.'

Dan saw the problems straight away. Voyeurism involved watching or recording nudity, – at the least someone dressed in underwear – or doing a private act. 'No crime,' he said.

'Yeah, you've got it. You're thinking just like a defence lawyer, because that's what Ellis's lawyer said too. Mickey stayed quiet but the lawyer couldn't say enough. Most people have been into the back garden in their pyjamas, he said, so pyjamas aren't underwear. And who hasn't fallen asleep in public? On a train, in a park or on a beach? Most people, which meant that sleeping wasn't a private act. If someone had said that they'd been enjoying some solo fun we might have had a chance, but we didn't know who the people were.'

'He slipped through the cracks.'

'No, he didn't slip through,' Murdoch said. 'He had people helping him, to make sure that he slotted right through.'

'Who like?'

'His defence lawyer made sure he knew to say nothing.'

Dan wasn't in the mood to defend lawyers. His thoughts careered around his head, but they weren't quite making sense yet.

'What did the woman in the house do? The one that Mickey filmed sleeping? What was it that got him arrested?'

Murdoch allowed herself a small smile. 'She hit him with a lamp. Very hard. He was still groggy when the police arrived.'

'Was Mickey ever a suspect in this case?'

'No, and why would he be? We focused on sex attackers from the register at first, but he isn't on it because he's never been convicted of anything. No one round here would know him, because he's been living in London. Then we got your client and no one else mattered. Why should we look for anyone else once we had him? We've got a man whose DNA was found on her, who left a bloody fingerprint on her bedroom wall, who stayed hidden until we caught up with him, who came up with a story that was just bullshit. At least, it was based upon what we knew back then.'

'Back then?'

'He said he had no relationship with Mary, and that Mary had shown no interest in him. We didn't know that she was trying to keep it a secret.'

'And now you know different.'

'Yes, now we do, but don't try and make this our fault.'

'Who's talking fault? For what?' His eyes narrowed. 'What are you trying to say?'

'Isn't it obvious? That Carter might be innocent.'

'He's always said that he is'

'Do you believe it? If you don't, nothing else matters.'

'I don't have to believe it.'

'Stop being a lawyer for a minute. Try being a person and decide whether you believe him.'

Dan nodded slowly, dread creeping through him, because he could see what the answers were, but he wasn't ready to voice them.

'I'm prepared to believe him.'

'But if he is innocent, who else could it be?'

He didn't need to say it. He knew the answer. Mickey Ellis.

'We need to find Jayne.'

Seventy-three

'Mickey, what the hell are you talking about?' Jayne was backing away, her feet scraping on the grit on the stage.

'I had to know her, that's all. It's how I am. I'd seen the Mary everyone else saw, bright and bubbly and lovely, and I fell in love with her, like everyone did. But I didn't want to see the Mary everyone else saw. I wanted the secret Mary, the dark Mary. I wanted her shadow.'

'What the fuck are you talking about?'

'We have shadows, all of us, our secret ways, the way we are when we're alone. The brighter you are, the darker the shadow. That's all I wanted to see.'

'You sound like some crazed stalker.'

'No, no, that's not how it is.' He stepped towards her. 'She couldn't know, that was the point, because then she'd act differently. How would I get the real Mary?'

'This is sick.'

He flapped his hand at her, frustration in his voice. 'I knew you'd see it that way. Everyone does, but you haven't seen the things that I have. I knew her better than most. I could see Mary when she was in her bedroom. Sometimes, I'd sit in my room with the light off so I could watch her properly. I didn't mean to hurt anyone.'

'What do you mean, hurt anyone?'

'Just that. I wanted to know her, that's all. If I'm going to court, you need to hear this.'

Jayne wanted to run but she was transfixed. 'And how did you get to know her?'

'I sneaked in.'

'What?'

'I hadn't been in there before, because I could watch the house from my bedroom and there was always someone else in. That weekend was different because the other housemates had gone away. I knew that from their Internet postings, because people display their lives now, and there was the countdown to the weekend away. That made it easy for me. I knew Lucy wouldn't be there, because I watched her go out with her boyfriend and she had a bag with her, and I saw Mary go out, dressed for a night out. I waited for it to go dark and once I was in her yard, I clambered on to the kitchen roof. It was easy to get into the bathroom from there because the window was always half open. I just lifted the sash and I was in.'

Jayne backed to the edge of the stage. There was the sound of someone outside the theatre, the metal screen being moved, scraping across stone. Someone wanting to know who was inside. Someone who'd raise the alarm.

'What happened in the house?' Jayne swung her torch into the gloom to see who was there, but she couldn't see anyone.

'I didn't bother with the other rooms. It was Mary I wanted, that's all. Those shadows. There wasn't much to find. Her laptop was password-protected and there was nothing much in her drawers. There were some love notes, scrawled on café receipts and cinema tickets, but they weren't written by her.'

'What happened to Mary?'

'I'm telling you.' There were traces of anger in his voice.

'Okay, Mickey, stay calm. I just need to know what's going to come out in court.'

'I had to know her, so I waited under the bed. I didn't know when she'd be back so I couldn't relax on the bed. I moved some things to make space. I didn't think she'd notice. I thought she'd come home and be sleepy from drink, and I'd get to see the side the booze had uncovered. I'd hear her, and it would be the real her, because she wouldn't know I was there.'

'You fucking creep.'

He put his hands over his face for a few seconds.

'He came back with her,' he said, his voice muffled at first before he dropped his hands. 'Both of them, laughing and kissing, and for a moment I got her, her passion coming out, but it was all for him. You can guess the rest. I had to lie underneath them and listen. I heard everything, and I thought at least it was another secret I had of hers, how she was with men, but it wasn't like that. I wanted her, just her, not the person she showed to him. I had to get out. I felt dirty, like she'd violated me.'

'She'd violated you? You want me to feel sorry for you?'

'But I just wanted to know her. Don't you get that? Haven't you been listening properly? The real her.'

'This is why your wife kicked you out. This is why you haven't got a job, because you were arrested. This is your hobby. The people who know you don't like what you did, so you ended up back at your mother's house.'

'Opposite Mary. It was fate.'

'You're being pathetic, looking for blame elsewhere.'

'Stop it.'

'Why? Too close to the truth? And why are we here? Why did you spin us the lines about Lucy? All you did was draw attention to yourself.'

'I loved Mary.'

'What bullshit. You didn't love her. You prized her, like a possession, something to look at. How could you love her when you didn't even know her?'

He took deep breaths, as if he was struggling to breath.

'Mickey?'

He moved towards Jayne and said, 'I was there when she died.'

Seventy-four

Dan threw his phone on to the desk. 'She's not answering,' he said, and then to Murdoch, 'you either drive me, sirens and lights, or stop me for speeding, but I'm going.'

'Where?'

'Highford, where Jayne is.'

'How do you know she's there?'

'Because that was the point of today, to make sure I had witnesses in court. She was going to collect Mickey Ellis.'

'If she's driving, she might not answer the phone.'

'Won't you do something?'

'What like? Set up roadblocks on the edge of Highford because someone driving on the motorway didn't answer her phone?'

Dan slammed his hand on the desk. 'You said that Mickey is dangerous, dammit. You said what he's told us can't be true. This is about a woman murdered in her bed, a story told to us by someone who creeps around bedrooms. Perhaps I'm reading too much into this, but doesn't that make him seem even more dangerous? And someone that I know is with him isn't answering her phone.'

'Dan, you've got to understand –'

'I don't have to understand anything. It's your call, Murdoch, but remember this conversation, because you might have to recall it later, to dig yourself out of the shit.'

He thumped the door open and ran along the corridor. People turned to watch him as he hit the external door at speed, rushing into the square in front of the courthouse.

There was a shout behind him. 'Wait!' It was Murdoch.

Dan turned.

'Let me make a call. Don't go over there, you might make it worse.'

'How?'

'This isn't about you rescuing her to ease your conscience.'

'What are you talking about? I just want to help Jayne.'

'You feel responsible, because she's doing this on your behalf. She doesn't need her knight on horseback to rescue her. She needs us to find her. You don't know where she is or what might be happening. Stay here. Do your job, and let us do ours.'

He looked around and wondered what he would do if he got to his car, how he could help Jayne, and he knew she was right.

Murdoch pulled her phone from her pocket. 'Do you know what car she drives?'

'A blue Fiat with a dodgy exhaust.'

'Registration number?'

'I've no idea. I'd know it if I saw it though, because the passenger door is crumpled where someone drove into her.'

'We need more than that,' she said, as she dialled a number.

'I can give you her address,' and he did, when something occurred to him. 'I've just remembered something. On the same day Jayne spoke to him for the first time, he turned up at her apartment and frightened her.'

'What do you mean, frightened her?'

'Rushed her when she opened the door. He apologised and said he thought she was going for him, and she accepted it, but it freaked her out. And another time, she thought someone was in her apartment, waiting for her.'

'Had she given him her address?'

'He said he'd tracked her down through social media.'

'Has Mickey disclosed anything that might tell us where he might have gone, like a favourite place?'

'Nothing that Jayne's told me. You should know more than me, but you focused on Carter and stopped looking.'

'Don't pin this shit on me. Carter lied to us, you know that now. If he'd told us what he's saying now, or had produced those letters, we might have kept on looking. His story made no sense, and when that happens, it's usually hiding guilt.'

Whoever she'd dialled had answered. 'It's Tracy. We're looking for a young woman in an old Fiat. She might be in danger.' A pause and then, 'Has anything been reported in the last hour? I want to know everything.'

Dan closed his eyes as he waited, his stomach rolling, dreading the news.

'Got it, thanks.' She turned to Dan. 'Not much so far, it's a quiet day. A road accident by a school, but not a Fiat. Two break-ins, and three shoplifters. Nothing else.'

He let out a long breath but he knew it meant nothing. She should have called. Something was wrong, every instinct told him that. All he could do was wait.

Seventy-five

'You killed her?'

'I didn't kill her. I said I was there. Aren't you listening?'

'You were there. Under her bed. Lying in wait.'

'I did not murder Mary. I loved her.'

'How could you love her? You didn't know her.'

His fingers gripped his hair as he screeched, loud in the space. 'You don't have to know. Sometimes, you've just got to feel it.'

'Do you love me?'

A pause. 'What do you mean?'

'Someone was in my flat. The lights were tampered with. Was that you, waiting for me?'

Mickey fell silent.

'It was you, wasn't it? You took my key when you burst in that time, and once you had it, you sneaked in. You were waiting for me.'

'It wasn't like that.'

'What was it like?' Jayne stepped closer and jabbed him in the chest, her torch beam jolting. 'Was it just a need to see me naked? You wanted to know what noise I make when I masturbate? Is that it?'

'You make it sound seedy.'

'It is fucking seedy, don't you get it? You want to see me naked, is that what you want? Why didn't you just ask for a picture?'

'It's not like that.'

'It's exactly like that.' She pushed at him. 'Here, I'll get undressed now, if you want.'

'No, no, don't.'

'Why not? This is what turns you on.' She made a show of undoing her buttons on her shirt, shining her torch on to her chest. 'Enjoying the show, Mickey?'

'Stop it.'

One more button.

'Enough yet?'

'Stop it!'

She grabbed his hand and started to place it in her blouse. 'Enjoying yourself?'

He pulled himself away and stumbled backwards, his arms wheeling, until he tripped on a loose brick and went to the floor, dust flying as he landed.

'Why did you do that?'

'You're pathetic. I'm going.'

'No, stop, you've got to listen.'

'Why should I?' She turned to go, feeling her way to the edge of the stage, ready to work her way towards the sliver of daylight straining into the theatre.

'For Robert Carter.'

That made her stop.

She turned around. He was trying to haul himself up, grunting, holding one arm as if he'd injured it falling over. She stepped closer.

'This had better be good.'

'I didn't kill Mary.' He looked up at her as she stood over him. 'If you want to hear it, you've got to listen to me. This is the problem, you see, that people won't believe me, because they won't like me.'

'Who killed her?'

'I didn't see it happen.'

'You need to start talking.'

He rolled over to a sitting position.

'They'd finished. Carter wanted a cigarette.' His words came out in short bursts between sharp breaths. 'I'd listened to them talking. All love stuff. I hated her for it, it felt as if she'd cheated on me.' He held his hand up. 'Save your breath, I know what you'll say. That's how I felt. It's just how it was. All I wanted to do was get out, get away. I didn't want to listen to her anymore. Mary was saying how guilty she felt because he was married, how it wasn't really her, that she wasn't like that. Carter was getting stressed about it, telling her how she was spoiling it, that he didn't want to think of home, so he went outside for a smoke. Mary lay there for a while, and I was thinking that he would go home and she'd go to sleep and I could leave, but I couldn't wait that long. Mary went to the toilet, and when I heard the bathroom lock click, I sneaked out from under the bed. I had to get out. I couldn't stand listening to them anymore. Except just as I got on the landing, someone came in through the back door. I ducked into the bedroom next door, and I heard them arguing with Carter.'

'Them?'

'Lucy and Peter.'

'Where were they arguing?'

'By the front door. He must have stepped inside, because Lucy was asking what he was doing there, sounding really angry. Get the fuck out, all that kind of thing. He didn't say much back, but Lucy was really going at him. That's when Mary came out of the toilet.'

'What happened?'

'She was naked, I could see her through the crack in the door, and it was as if she'd thrown a firecracker down the stairs. Lucy ran upstairs, laughing, but it was nasty, mocking, saying how little Miss Perfect wasn't so perfect. I thought they were going to start fighting, because Lucy pushed her, hitting her shoulder, but Mary couldn't defend herself because she was naked and trying to cover herself up.'

'Where was Carter?'

'He was shouting upstairs at first, telling Lucy to leave her alone, that she didn't understand. Lucy's boyfriend was telling him to go, that he wasn't supposed to be there. He told him to go home to his wife. That must have scared him, because I heard the front door slam, as if he'd run out in a panic. Once he'd gone, the boyfriend came upstairs.'

'And you mean Peter?'

'Yes, him. Then it got nasty.'

'How?'

'Mary was trying to get into her room but Lucy was taunting her, spitting about all the things she reckoned Mary had said in the past. It sounded like Lucy saw this as payback somehow.'

'What was Mary doing?'

'Shouting, asking Lucy to leave her alone. She was on the landing, still naked, but she was angry, saying that it was none of her business, but then, well . . .' He exhaled sharply. 'Things got really bad.'

Jayne turned round, hearing a noise in the theatre somewhere. Like someone walking into one of the chairs.

'Hello?'

No one answered.

She shone her torch into the stalls, but there was no one there.

'Tell me, quickly. Bad? How?'

'Lucy grabbed Mary, had her round the arm, was pulling her around. She said to Peter that maybe he'd like a go, because she was that sort of girl now. Lucy pushed her into the room and I didn't see what happened next, but I could hear it. Lucy shouting at her, calling her a slut, a hypocrite, a home-wrecker, screaming at Peter to fuck her. That's what she was shouting. "*Fuck her, fuck her, show her.*"'

'What was Mary doing?'

'Shouting back. "*No, no, no*". There were several loud bangs, as if they were fighting, the bed knocking. And then there was that scream. But it stopped, just like that,' and he clicked his fingers. 'Someone cut her off.'

'That's when she was stabbed.'

He nodded. 'I'm guessing so.'

'And you were in the next room?'

He didn't answer.

'You make me sick.'

'I didn't kill her.'

'But you could have helped, don't you get it? You were too cowardly, just like Carter. Mary was going to be raped by Peter and you were going to stay quivering in that bedroom as it happened, too scared of your sordid little secret to do anything. And Robert Carter had run home like a scared little boy, leaving Mary to fend for herself, more worried about his wife finding out. That's why she died, because the only two people who could have helped her chose not to, and when she tried to scream for help, she was killed.'

Jayne moved away and paced in a tight circle.

'Carter didn't go home. Not straight away. He came back. I was going to sneak out but I heard him come in through the back door. He ran in, shouting for her, but he went quiet when he went into the room. He was with her for a few minutes, sobbing, until he ran out. I stayed where I was, and when I came out I saw her. She was naked still but covered in blood. I couldn't leave her like that. I covered her over, to be respectful.'

There was another noise in the theatre. Like scrapes on grit. Closer this time.

'Hello?'

No response.

'I should have helped, I know that, but I was scared.' Mickey said. 'I didn't know she was going to be killed, though. I thought they were fighting, that's all.'

'Shush, be quiet.'

'You want to hear this.'

Jayne whirled round. 'Why didn't you come forward before?'

'I did, when that other lawyer came to see me. I told her what I told you.'

'What, the revised version, that you were at home looking out of your window?'

'I was just trying to point towards the real killers. I didn't want to get involved, that's all, but Mary shouldn't have died and Robert Carter shouldn't be in prison. No matter what you think of me or Robert Carter, we did not murder Mary

Kendricks. And yes, I'm a coward, but I can't stand by and watch this happen.'

Jayne closed her eyes and sighed. He was right. It was about Robert Carter and getting to court. They could deal with the other kind of blame later.

'Why did Shelley shout at you?'

'Because I got scared. I wanted to back out.'

'Why?'

'I had a visit. Two men in suits. They were really scary, and made it plain that if I gave evidence, something would happen to me. Or worse, to my mum.'

'And when I called round?'

'I knew I should have stayed strong. Like you said, I'd been a coward and told Shelley I was backing out. If I stayed quiet with you, I'd be a coward again.'

'Except you couldn't say that you were in the house.'

'I had to leave my home in London because of what I did. I couldn't leave this one too.'

'You could always try not going into women's houses.'

He shrugged.

'Let's get to court. Let's at least save Robert Carter.'

Mickey stood up and dusted himself down.

Jayne went towards the edge of the stage, until a voice said, 'Stop there.'

Her mind whirred through recent memories, trying to work out where she'd heard that voice before. Then it came back to her. A hand round her neck. An alley in Manchester. Peter.

'It's over, Peter,' she said, trying to keep her voice steady.

'It is.'

Quick movement, the rumble of feet across the stage, and something struck her on her cheek. A fist, hard and powerful.

The theatre faded, the ceiling swirled above her as Jayne fell backwards, dazed, the torch beam sweeping overhead until it clattered to the ground behind her.

The world went black as the back of her head crashed against the stage.

Seventy-six

Dan tugged on his lip, a nervous tic. His phone was in his hand, his eyes on the window, looking out for Jayne approaching the building. Every time he'd called her, there'd been no response.

Murdoch was on the other side of the corridor, deep in conversation with Simon Parkin.

Dan held out his hands in query. Murdoch held up her phone and shook her head.

The loud clicks of leather soles entered the corridor, rising high above the whispers of conversation. It was Hannah coming from the robing room. 'Any news?' she said.

'No, nothing. What do we do?'

Hannah grimaced. 'We've got our client's instructions now. More than that, we've told the judge what our case will be, that we're going after Lucy. We can't back down from that. And what if we don't, because we think we're missing our star witness, and he walks through the door?'

'What, the stalker star witness?'

'Remember, we're not telling a different story. We're just spreading the doubt around. We could get lucky and the jury might think that he did it.'

The speakers in the corridor buzzed, followed by the announcement, 'Could all interested parties in the case of Robert Carter please return to courtroom number one.'

'Looks like we're stuck with whatever we've got,' Dan said, and set off towards the courtroom.

As he got to the doors, Dominic Ayres stepped towards him, blocking his path. He got in close so that no one could hear him apart from Dan. 'Tread carefully, Mr Grant.'

'What is that supposed to mean?'

'Just be careful of this path. Actions create consequences.' His eyes were dark, tension lines across his face.

Dan got closer, almost nose-to-nose, his jaw clenched. 'Don't you realise that every time you tell me to do something, I want to do the opposite?'

'That would be very foolish.'

'We'll see,' he said, and banged the courtroom door open.

The door closed slowly, the atmosphere calmer inside, more hushed. He turned to Hannah. 'I'm sorry about that. A fight with the father of the next witness isn't a good move.'

Hannah patted his back and winked. 'You've had a rough morning. I didn't see anything.'

The court assistant stood up. 'Are you ready to proceed?'

'Almost,' Dan said.

'The Judge wants to restart in five minutes.'

He checked his phone again. Still nothing.

'Yes, fine, we're ready then.'

*

The sounds came back slowly. Fluttering wings, water running down walls, the little scratches of rats running around under the stage. Jayne tried to take deep breaths but her jaw hurt. She felt sick, her heart beating too fast, her mouth dry.

She opened her eyes when she heard rumbles and thumps by her. Two men fighting. Angry shouts and grunts. Someone pushed against a wall. Glass smashed.

She lifted her head.

Peter was standing, his feet apart, his arms down, staring at the floor. He was holding something in his hand. It glinted in the faint strains of daylight. It was a long piece of glass. He was wrapping something around one end. A handkerchief.

She grimaced as she rolled over on to her front. Pain flashed across her forehead as she pulled herself on to all fours. She tried to keep her movements silent. There was someone on the floor, groaning in pain. Mickey, she presumed. It was hard to see properly. It was still dark and she saw flashes of light whenever she moved. She didn't know where her torch had gone.

Peter knelt down over Mickey.

She was still dizzy from his attack, her face clammy with blood. She couldn't stay there, Peter would kill her. He'd heard Mickey's story and knew the truth would come out. He was desperate, scared.

She sucked in air and counted to three. It was now or never.

She rushed forward, screaming. Peter turned. She aimed a kick at his head, her foot travelling through the air with the force of a hammer-swing.

Her foot thudded into the underneath of his jaw. His teeth clattered together, his head pushed back and he reeled onto the floor.

She didn't wait to see how injured he was. She ran.

In the darkness, the floor took a long time to arrive as Jayne jumped from the stage, not knowing where the steps were. She fell as she landed, lurching forward into one of the front row seats, but didn't wait to be caught. Behind her, Peter was yelling in pain.

She scrambled to her feet and headed for where she thought the wall would be, using the row of seats to guide her, her hand slapping against each one. She stumbled a couple of times, loose stones everywhere, but didn't go to ground. Get to the wall, follow it to the exit, visible as a glow of light at the other end of the theatre.

Peter got to his feet, his movements audible in the space. She looked back and stumbled over a seat, shrieking as she went down.

He was running, his footsteps loud on the stage.

She had to keep going.

She was up again quickly, needing to keep ahead of him. Her feet skidded at whatever was on the ground but she wasn't going to stop. He was keeping pace with her.

She slammed into the wall, as it appeared sooner than she expected, and for a second her dizziness returned. There was no time to nurse herself. She ran along the aisle, her hands scuttling along the wall as she went, feeling her way out.

There was a noise behind her. The sound of his feet landing. She looked back. He was off the stage.

The seats rushed past her as she headed for the glow ahead, getting closer with every second, but Peter was gaining, the sound of his footsteps getting louder. Cobwebs brushed her face, sticking in the blood, metallic on her lips.

She bolted through the gap where there had once been a door and blinked at the light that streamed through the metal panel that had been pushed to one side. Peter was close, but she could make it. She sprinted towards it and slammed her shoulder into the metal, pushing it open against the small stones underneath.

She was outside.

She winced and shielded her eyes. As she became accustomed to the light, she noticed her blood-soaked hands from where she'd held her temple.

Her car was ahead. She bent over and sucked in deep breaths. There were shouts behind her and the sound of Peter pushing against the metal panel.

He emerged into the sunlight behind her. Jayne glanced backwards. Just get to her car, she thought, and pray it started first time.

She ran again, rummaging in her pockets for her car keys, but they spilled to the floor when she pulled them out and skittered under the car.

She looked around. Behind her was a long open yard. Although she could attract attention, he'd catch her too quickly. He was leaner and fitter than she was, and he had a weapon.

Reason with him, she thought.

'Put the glass down.' Her voice was slow and calm. She'd been there with Jimmy, knew how to stop him from blowing up when he'd come in too drunk and angry. 'We can sort this out.'

Peter's shoulders were tense, his clothes dirty, his jacket torn at the arm. He grinned at her, blood staining his teeth, and ran at her.

She turned as if to run across the yard, but he was already too close. She went the other way and bolted for the fence alongside the canal.

It was eight feet high but she jumped at it, her foot pushing up the wooden slats, her hands across the top, hauling herself upwards.

He went after her. His shoes skidded on the cobbles.

She was almost over when her jacket snagged on the wood. It stopped her from dropping down on the other side, her legs sticking out behind her. She looked back, desperate to get over. He was right on her, his teeth bared, his arm swinging, the jagged piece of glass in his hand.

She kicked backwards, caught him in his chest, knocking the air from his lungs and propelling him backwards. His arm flailed as he went, but he made one deliberate slash at her leg before his head hit the floor with a crack.

She cried out in pain as the glass cut across her leg, slicing through the trousers she was wearing for court and opening a deep gash. Peter groaned, dazed, before she was able to use her weight to force her jacket to tear and drop to the ground on the other side.

The pain was intense, like burning, as she got to her feet. The cut was deep, she knew that, and her trousers were sticking to the blood. She balled her fists to beat back the pain and looked both ways along the towpath. It was a long way to an escape route in either direction. She looked towards the canal. There was a bridge further down, just fifty yards away, a low metal bridge. On the other side, a path disappeared between two buildings. There were bright lights ahead. A fast food place. A garage.

She set off limping, grimacing and gritting her teeth with pain every time she put weight on her leg. She couldn't go at any speed, but at least he wasn't following.

The steps on to the bridge made her cry out, her left leg almost useless. She was starting to feel faint and cold, like someone was turning up the brightness control towards whiteout.

The canal bridge was only made for pedestrians, and was narrow with metal sides. It made her footsteps echo more, but it was the only way she could go. Her leg dragged but she forced herself to go on. She didn't look for Peter. Just keep going was her only thought.

Every step got harder. The other side of the bridge seemed to get further away. Her eyes lost their focus.

As she bumped down the steps, Peter was on the other side of the canal, straining as he climbed over the fence.

When she got to the bottom, she fell and went to her knees, panting hard. She tried to focus ahead, to where the street was, but the traffic seemed like it was far into the distance, just a hum. Her breaths were loud in her head, along with the fast pump of her heart.

She looked to where the footpath went between two buildings. It was long and in shadow, no windows overlooking it. If she was caught down there, she was done.

A canal barge appeared on the distant horizon but it was moving slowly. She couldn't wait that long and she couldn't go any further. She was in too much pain, becoming too faint. If she could just hide until the barge arrived, she could dive into the water. They'd rescue her, she'd be safe.

Peter was on the bridge, his steps loud.

Jayne scrambled under the bridge. As she looked for the barge, she could see Peter's shadow on the water, moving slowly, his head down. Perhaps he was too injured and would give up, not knowing where she'd gone.

She looked up.

There were metal supports under the bridge. She could reach them by scrambling up and hiding where her leg wouldn't have to hold her any more. He might think she'd headed for the road and go that way.

She wrapped her arms around the lowest support and swung her good leg up, hooking her foot on to it, using that leg to drag herself up until she was lying on one of the bridge supports. His footsteps were slow, heavy and deliberate, right above her head, making her close her eyes. She put her head against the metal, jagged against her skin, but she needed to stay calm, recover some energy. All she had to do was lie still and hope Peter didn't look under the bridge.

*

Dan looked round as the public gallery started to fill. Sara Carter took up her usual position in the corner, the reporters moving with her, one of them murmuring to her as she sat down. Her bag was on her lap, her knees together, defensive. Dan could guess what the conversation was about: a request for an interview to be printed after Carter's conviction, which would then be sold to one of the nationals.

Lucy's mother came in and sat at the other end. She glared at Dan. Dominic wasn't with her. Mary's parents joined her.

Hannah nodded to him. 'As we were, Daniel.'

He didn't respond, his mind still on Jayne.

Hannah leaned in close and whispered, 'Don't worry about her. There's nothing you can do right now and we need to win this case. That's our job. You've done nothing wrong, you just followed the evidence.'

He exhaled loudly. 'I'll take this slow, give Jayne time to get in touch, but what do we do if we don't have the witness that we said we'd have?'

'Remember, Mickey isn't being called today. He's only coming so that we can show that we have him. We can worry about him later. The judge won't stop us from running our case. He'll just tell the jury we've nothing to back it up with.'

There was the familiar sound of the door to the cells being unlocked, followed by the murmurs of conversation as the guards headed upwards. Carter's cuffs jangled, undone when he emerged into the dock, blinking into the light as always.

He stepped close to the glass and hissed at Dan to join him there.

Dan followed, one eye on the court assistant, who was heading towards the door to collect the judge.

'What is it?'

'What you said before, about going after Lucy. That won't stop Dominic Ayres, will it?'

'I doubt it. Our witness puts Lucy at the scene, coming out of the back yard after the scream. Dominic told me that he won't allow his daughter to be exposed.'

'So whatever happens, if we go after Lucy, Sara is in danger?'

'You can't back out now.'

'No, no, I'm not. There's something you should know.'

A loud knock announced the judge's entrance and everyone stood.

Dan turned to face the front, his finger to his lips to tell Carter to stay quiet.

Once the judge had taken his seat and Dan had given his bow, not much more than a nod of the head, he leant towards the dock. 'Too late now.'

'No, you've got to hear this. Go after Lucy. Go for the truth.'

'Which is what, because we've had too many versions of it?'

'Lucy and Peter were there, in the house.'

The judge looked towards Dan. 'Everything all right, Mr Grant?'

'Yes, My Lord, please forgive me. If I could be allowed one moment . . .'

'You've got until the jury arrive.'

Dan bowed his gratitude and then, 'What do you mean, they were in the house?'

'Just that.' He looked back at the public gallery, to where Sara was sitting. 'If Sara is going to be in danger anyway, I might as well tell the truth. I didn't kill Mary. Peter or Lucy did. Lucy and Mary were arguing upstairs.'

'Which one did it?'

'I don't know. Like I've always said, I was outside. They'd caught us and it all kicked off between Lucy and Mary.'

'What were they doing there?'

'Her damn phone. The battery had run out and she'd left her charger in the house.' He wiped a tear away. 'She'd come back for her damn charger, that's all. I left the house because I was panicking, but I didn't leave. I was going to go home but I couldn't leave her. I tried to go back in when the argument got louder but I was locked out. I didn't know what to do. I was pacing, scared, but then I heard her scream. By the time I ran round to the back, Lucy and Peter had gone.'

'But why didn't you tell the police this?'

'I received a visit the next day, from Lucy's father, along with a couple of goons. They told me they'd kill me if I said anything to the police about Lucy, and then they'd go after Tammy and Sara. They were scary, talking real quiet but I could tell they meant it. I stayed quiet, but I didn't think they'd accuse me of it.'

'Did you tell Shelley this?'

'No, because I was scared still, but she found a witness, just like you had, and tried to get me to open up more. I couldn't though. I was trying to protect Tammy and Sara. I couldn't protect Mary. The least I could do was protect them.'

Before Dan could respond, the jurors were shown back into the courtroom, all staring at the dock as they went in.

As Dan took his place at the lectern, the judge said to the court usher, 'Could you bring Miss Ayres back, please.'

Dan put his phone on to the lectern, all the settings switched to silent, the papers alongside. He closed his eyes for a moment. Now was the time. He had no idea what was about to happen, but this next thirty minutes would decide Carter's fate. And perhaps his own.

*

Jayne held her breath as Peter came down the steps of the bridge. His footsteps echoed under the bridge, loud thuds, jolting her each time, inches from her head.

Once he reached the bottom, the sounds changed to crunches on the gravel packed into the towpath. He stopped. His shadow stretched across the ground. He was turning, surveying.

A tapping noise. The jagged glass on the rail of the bridge steps. He was taunting her.

Jayne rested her head on the iron beam she'd straddled, trying to maintain her balance, praying that she was in the shadows enough.

He turned, slow and deliberate. He'd be able to reach her if he appeared underneath her.

He moved closer. He wasn't going between the buildings, to the bright lights of the main road. Why was he staying there?

Then she saw them.

Bloodspots.

On the ground below her, there was a steady trail of small red spots, leading away from the steps and curling round underneath the bridge, still wet, glistening in the sun. She thought he'd been too hurt to move quickly, but he'd been tracking her.

His arm came into view, then his shoulder. He appeared underneath her. He used the piece of glass to point along the ground, following the bloodspots.

Her heartbeat felt high in her chest, her breaths fast and urgent. The scene below merged with bad memories. Cowering in the bedroom as Jimmy screamed at her. Of soothing him as her own blood ran down from her nose, trying to show that she knew how bad he felt, that she shouldn't get him so angry, because she knew he had a temper. They'd work it out, that's what she always said, that the good outweighed the bad.

She closed her eyes.

Jimmy screaming that one last time. The kitchen knife was in her hand, she'd been cutting vegetables. Or had it been on the side nearby and she'd picked it up? She'd never known the answer, things had moved too quickly. His hand gripping her jaw, spittle on her face. Her hand on the knife handle. His leg pushing between hers, forcing her own apart, the kitchen surface digging into her back.

She opened her eyes. No time for that.

Peter was underneath her. Just a couple of feet away.

Her hands tensed around the iron beam.

The drop of blood took a while to fall.

She felt it before she saw it, pooling on her leg, the pressure of her body on the beam forcing out the blood. She moved her head to look at it, before it stretched out as a long drop and headed towards the floor, right by Peter.

She didn't know whether he saw it, something dark moving at the edge of his vision, or just sensed it, but as it landed on the path he looked at it.

He didn't move straight away. He stared, as if working out what it meant, before turning his head slowly upwards. He grinned when he saw her.

She had no time to plan what to do.

She tightened her arms around the metal bridge support and swung her legs, let the weight of her body travel through the air as if on a swing, gritting her teeth and screeching as the sudden movement made her leg burst with pain.

Her feet connected with his chest and pushed him backwards, stumbling as he went, until he was on the floor, the piece of glass landing with a loud tinkle behind him.

She dropped, and howled in agony as her injured leg hit the ground, all of her weight on it. Adrenaline was driving her onwards, her need to get away from him too great.

She stumbled towards the path, determined to get to the street and make a noise, dragging her injured leg. Peter was gasping for breath; she hoped she'd popped a rib, maybe taken out one of his lungs. Anything to help her get away.

She yelped as his hand grabbed her ankle and yanked her backwards. She fell to the ground, winded. He dragged her, her shirt riding up her body until her stomach scraped along the gravel.

She tried to kick out, but it was no use.

Once she was close enough, he grabbed her shirt and pulled her on to her back. He straddled her chest, breathing hard as he looked down on her. Blood dripped from his mouth on to her face, and she tried to move away but couldn't. She couldn't breathe with his weight pressing down on her.

'Let me go,' she said, but it came out in gasps. It was useless. She was exhausted.

His hands went to her throat and squeezed.

Her eyes bulged and panic rushed through her. He was panting but his eyes were screwed up, his grip tight and strong. She tried to buck underneath him but he was too heavy and she was too weak. Her hands went to his arms, to try and stop him, but she didn't have the strength.

Her chest ached for breath, pushing outwards, her mouth open, but it was futile. Her hands banged on the ground as her survival instincts kicked in and she struggled more, but he had every advantage. He was on top. He was heavier and stronger.

There was a clink. Something under her hand.

She reached out again, her eyes never leaving Peter, although his outline seemed to look darker, and she could no longer hear him.

The same noise, a clink on the stone, except this time she felt what it was.

The piece of glass, the one Peter had dropped. It was still warm from where he'd held it.

She gripped the glass, the handkerchief still around it, and took a deep breath, summoned all the strength she had left. One last chance.

She flailed her arm wildly at him.

Blood flecks fell on to her face as the blade cut across his cheek, slicing it open.

He cried out and his grip slackened as one hand went to his face. Blood spurted through his fingers.

He was groaning in pain and shock as Jayne bucked hard underneath him until his bodyweight shifted. She pushed some more and he fell from her, his eyes wide, his hand still clamped to his cheek.

She jumped on him, straddled him like he had her, her knees pinning his arms down. She held the jagged glass in both hands, angling it downwards, the edges cutting into her fingers, ready to plunge.

Jimmy all over again.

Her mind flashed back to that moment. Jimmy with his leg between hers, pushing her back, his hand round her throat, screaming abuse, his other hand reaching for the buttons on her jeans.

She'd known what was coming. She'd been there before, convinced herself that she'd acquiesced rather than been forced, tried not to think whether there was any difference. So many times, making herself go blank. Too many times. Not anymore.

She looked down at Peter and saw Jimmy in his eyes. His snarl, his fury.

Her hand had gone into Jimmy, thrust forward, just to get him off, to make him stop, not to kill him, but the knife had been in her hand. Now she was gripping a blade again, except this time it was glass and he was underneath her. He was the one with fear in his eyes.

He'd killed people. Would do so again. He'd wanted to kill her.

Her hands gripped the glass tighter.

He wouldn't do it again.

She lifted her hands higher and screamed.

There was a noise behind her, someone on the bridge. She glanced upwards. Mickey running, staggering, shouting, 'Jayne, no, don't do it.'

She looked down.

Peter was crying, snot and tears coating his cheeks.

Jayne hung her head and threw the glass into the canal. She clambered off him, stopping only to kick him in the stomach.

He curled up, his arms over his head.

Mickey appeared next to her, panting. His clothes were torn and dirty and he had a bruise developing under his eye, blood streaming down the side of his face. 'Leave him. Get to court.'

After a few deep breaths, she nodded her agreement.

'Come on, let's go.'

Seventy-seven

The tension in the courtroom was palpable as Lucy re-entered the witness box.

Dan rose to his feet. He pretended to look through his notes to make Lucy more nervous, before he said, 'Miss Ayres, you were just explaining how Robert Carter creeped out your friend.' He emphasised the words *creeped out*.

Lucy didn't answer.

He indicated with a look towards the court usher that he had something to show her. He handed over thirteen copies of the photograph bundles, fanned out. 'One for Miss Ayres, twelve for the jury.'

He waited as the usher passed the bundle of photographs to Lucy and watched as she flicked through, her eyes narrowing. He watched the jurors as they did the same. Their eyes betrayed their surprise. A couple of jurors shifted their attention to the dock, as if they were wondering if they'd read Carter wrong.

Simon Parkin remained impassive. Dan knew what he was doing: making out like there was no real surprise, nothing to worry about.

It wouldn't be enough, but it was a start.

Lucy blushed as she looked through the images. 'I don't understand,' she said, eventually. All the confidence was gone from her voice.

'You agree that's Robert Carter and Mary?'

'Of course.'

'In the second picture, is that Mary's bedroom?'

She turned back to it. 'It looks like it.'

'And the third one, where they're playing with sparklers. Did you go to a bonfire with Mary?'

Lucy thought back on that and said, 'No. We went to a bonfire party and we invited her, but she said she was visiting her parents.'

Dan stayed silent to let that sink in. The conclusion was obvious, that Mary had lied so she could spend time with Carter.

'Going back to your earlier view on what Mary thought of Robert Carter, how he creeped her out.' Dan looked at the jury as he asked, 'Did you get that wrong?'

Lucy swallowed and tossed her hair. 'Well, obviously.'

'And does it surprise you, about Mary?'

'How do you mean?'

Answering a question with a question. She was buying time to think of what to say. 'Robert Carter is married. Mary wasn't his wife. Does it surprise you?'

Lucy paused before she answered. 'It does.'

'Why?'

'Because she wasn't that sort of person.'

'What is *that sort of person*?'

She lifted the bundle when she said, 'Someone who'd sleep with a married man.'

'But you were dear friends.' Dan made no effort to keep the sarcasm from his voice. As Lucy bristled, he asked, 'Or do you accept now that you didn't know her very well at all?'

'I'm surprised, that's all.'

'You've exaggerated your friendship.'

'Mary was dear to me.'

'You and Mary argued constantly. Isn't that the truth?'

'No.' Her tone was more hesitant.

'You've never argued about cleanliness?'

Lucy didn't answer.

'Or attitudes towards sex?'

'No, not as such.'

'What about how you have sex?'

'What do you mean?'

'Noisy, attention-seeking, making sure everyone can hear?'

'Not that I remember,' she said, her cheeks much redder.

'So that is a possibility? That you argued?'

She looked towards Simon Parkin, who was staring at his notepad as he made notes, and then to the public gallery, where her mother was sitting.

'Yes, it's possible,' she said, with a frustrated sigh. 'We shared a house. Arguments happen. That doesn't mean we weren't friends.'

'Tell the court about your arguments about sexual attitudes.'

Lucy looked towards the gallery, towards Mary's parents. 'Mary could get a little snooty about things.'

'What *things*?'

'The men I had staying over.'

'Just that?'

'She used to complain about the noise.' Someone in the public gallery laughed, earning a glare from the judge. 'She was more reserved about it.'

'You remember this now, but couldn't before. Do you also remember now calling her "prim and proper", "a real little madam"?' Dan pretended to look for the quote in his notes, from his conversation with the other housemate, Beth Wilkins. '"An uptight bitch?"'

'I don't think I went that far,' she said, with little conviction.

'"Don't think?"' Dan repeated, looking at the jury as he said it.

Lucy straightened her shoulders and pursed her lips as she tried to work out what was coming next. 'We argued sometimes, I accept that.'

'About how different you were to Mary?'

'Yes.'

'About Mary being a bit more prim and proper?' When Lucy didn't answer, he added, 'Do you want to rethink your earlier answer?'

'I might have said something like that, but I can't remember.'

'And here you are, finding out that the prim and proper little madam, the uptight bitch, was sleeping with a married man. She was having an affair with a married man. Just surprised, or more than that?'

'Shocked.'

'Are you sure?'

'Of course I'm shocked.'

Dan looked towards Hannah, who indicated with a discreet twirl of her finger that it was time to move on to the next part, the whole crux of the defence. Dan glanced back towards the public gallery, thinking of Lucy's mother, but his eyes drifted towards Mary's parents. Her mother was sitting with her lips pursed, staring straight ahead. Mary's fathers' focus was more direct, staring at Carter.

He looked at his notes, pausing, anxious about moving on, because once he started on the next part, there was no turning back.

Hannah looked back at him and held her hands out as if to query the hold-up.

Dan coughed and looked across to the jurors, who were staring at him, expectant, confused, wondering at the delay.

He turned back to Lucy. He tried to keep his voice steady. Never give away your true feelings, he knew that, keep up the performance.

'Miss Ayres, you were there when Mary died, weren't you?'

There were gasps from the public gallery. The jurors' mouths opened, looking from Dan to Lucy and then back again. Lucy reddened and reached out for the edge of the witness box, gripping the brass rail, her fingers white from tension. She looked down and blinked a few times, before slumping on to the small wooden seat in the wooden box.

The judge leaned forward. 'Miss Ayres, are you feeling all right?'

There was no response.

'Miss Ayres?'

She stayed silent, and then slumped to her knees.

The judge turned to the usher and said, 'Please escort the jurors out. It seems there will be another short delay.'

*

Jayne grimaced every time she changed gear, her leg bleeding badly, her trousers stuck to her. Tears streamed down her face. Not from pain, but out of relief she couldn't put into words.

'I'm not a murderer,' she said, almost inaudibly.

Mickey turned to her. 'I don't know what you mean.'

'I wanted to kill him, but I didn't.'

'You were defending yourself.'

'I could have killed him though, I know.' She banged the steering wheel with her hand. 'He tried to kill me and I'd have been justified in doing it, but I didn't.' She wiped her nose with her sleeve. 'I didn't have it in me. I thought I did, but I didn't. I couldn't do it.'

'You were scared, that's all.'

'You wanted my shadow. There, you've got it. I killed someone and I've always wondered if I could do it again, whether it was something in me. How does it feel to know?'

'Don't.'

'Don't what? Despise you for what you are?'

'I'm trying to do the right thing here.'

Jayne looked over, wide-eyed. 'Oh, you're doing it, all right, even if I've got to drag you into the courtroom.'

'I won't back out.'

Jayne was leaning forward against the wheel, grimacing in pain. 'You're a complete shit. A creep, a pervert. You already know you are, but everyone will know that soon. I hope you're ready for that. You helped me back there, but don't begin to think that I owe you anything.'

'I understand. I'm sorry.'

'Are you? Really? How can you have any idea what it's like to know that someone has been creeping around your home, looking through your private things?' She wiped her eyes with the back of her hand. 'You can't understand.'

Mickey looked out of the window, his arms folded.

They were almost there. The rolling fields by the motorway had turned into out-of-town retail parks and then the slow climb into the city centre began, past the grime of the inner city terraced streets and traffic-spoiled shop-fronts, Jayne gritting her teeth all the way.

'I know you hate me right now, but at least let me tell you I'm sorry. I'll try to change.'

'I'm not interested.'

The court building loomed ahead, high grey stone, pillars by the entrance, steps leading to the doors. There was no time to look for a car park. She pulled to the side of the road and stopped.

'We need to get inside.'

Mickey stepped out.

Jayne yelped in pain as she got out of the car, her leg swollen, the movement pulling her blood-sodden trousers from the wound, tearing at her cut.

She limped towards the court steps, Mickey with her.

Someone walked towards them, purposeful, arms swinging, fast and angry. Dominic Ayres. She hadn't noticed him, but he'd been pacing outside, his phone in his hand.

He was about to say something when Mickey put his hand up. 'I'm not interested. I'm not scared anymore.'

Before he could respond, there was movement behind him. It was DI Murdoch, trotting down the steps.

'Jayne, are you okay?' and she went towards Mickey, as if to arrest him, reaching for the cuffs on the back of her trousers.

'I'm fine, leave him. He rescued me.'

Murdoch looked at Mickey and then back to Jayne. 'What's going on?'

'It's Peter,' she said, and started to tell the story.

*

Thirty minutes had passed before Lucy indicated she was well enough to continue. She'd drunk numerous glasses of water before getting to her feet and patted her forehead with tissues passed to her by the usher.

The judge asked her whether she felt well enough to carry on.

'I'm fine, thank you,' she said. 'It was the question, that's all. It was so shocking, to be accused of something like that.'

'Miss Ayres, all counsel are aware that you are not obliged to answer any question that may incriminate you. Do you understand that?'

After a short pause, she nodded. 'I do, and thank you. I'm ready.'

As the usher went to bring the jurors back, Hannah leaned back towards Dan and whispered, 'Don't let up. The jurors might think she was faking it. She was playing for time, that's all, working out what story to spin.'

When the case was ready to proceed once more, Dan repeated the question. 'Miss Ayres, you were there when Mary died, weren't you?'

She looked towards the jury and spoke firmly. 'I wasn't there.'

'Are you sure?'

'Of course I'm sure.'

'As sure as you were about Mary being creeped out by Robert Carter?'

Lucy didn't answer.

'Or as sure as you were about never calling her an uptight bitch?'

'I wasn't there. I was with Peter all night, at his place.'

'Doing what?'

'You really want to know? Watching a film and then we had sex.' She set her mouth in a thin line.

'That's a lie, Miss Ayres.'

'It's the truth.'

'Why did you go into Mary's bedroom the following day?'

'Because something didn't feel right. Call it a sixth sense.'

'A sixth sense,' Dan said, drawing out the words. 'There was no disruption downstairs, was there?'

'It seemed normal.'

'No broken furniture. No smashed windows. Nothing that would indicate that it was anything other than an empty house.'

'It's hard to explain.'

'No, it isn't, Miss Ayres, because when you went into that bedroom, you knew what you'd find, didn't you.'

'What do you mean?'

'You already knew Mary Kendricks was dead, because you were there when Mary Kendricks was murdered.'

'I was not.' Her voice was louder.

'You argued, because there she was, the prim and proper little madam, resting up after sleeping with a married man.'

'That is rubbish.'

'You were there with your boyfriend, Peter, and tempers frayed when you argued?'

'There was no argument. If your client says that, he's lying.'

'And because of this argument, Mary was stabbed.'

'I wasn't there. I had nothing to do with it.'

Dan looked towards the jury. Their attention was fixed on Lucy. 'You were seen, Miss Ayres, running out of the yard, not long after Mary screamed.'

Lucy clenched her jaw and looked to the public gallery. 'That's impossible. I told the police where I was. They checked it out.'

'Miss Ayres, this is your chance to tell the court how it happened. Who killed Mary Kendricks?'

'I don't know, because I wasn't there.'

'Once Mary had been killed, you and Peter ran away and prepared an alibi.'

'Not true.'

'You stayed together the whole of the following day. That's right, isn't it.'

'We were upset. We'd seen Mary's body.'

'And you dealt with that by cuddling and kissing near the crime scene?'

'Everyone behaves differently. You can't plan these things.'

'You stayed together to that so your versions wouldn't fall apart, didn't you.'

'That is rubbish,' she said, tears welling up in her eyes, the closest to true emotion Dan had seen from her. 'We needed each other, that's all.'

There was a noise in the public gallery. The door clattered.

The judge looked to the back of the courtroom and held up his hand. 'Everyone must stay silent or leave.'

Dan turned to look at the public gallery. Dominic was there, standing over his wife, saying something to her. His wife's hand was over her mouth, her eyes wide.

'I said, silence or leave the court. I'll hold you in contempt.'

Dominic ignored him, still talking to his wife, his body language animated.

Dan looked back towards Lucy. She was watching what was happening at the back of the courtroom. She'd paled.

The usher went towards the gallery as the court assistant tannoyed for security to enter the courtroom.

Another noise as the door opened again. This time it was Jayne, bloodied, out of breath, dirty. He didn't care. He almost shouted out when he saw her.

Jayne gestured towards the witness box and nodded, her eyes wide.

Dan turned again to Dominic, aware that something important was happening.

Before he turned back, as a security guard came into the courtroom, Dominic made a gesture towards Lucy. Dan gasped when he saw it, because he understood straight away what it meant. A finger dragged across his throat.

The cutthroat gesture.

Dominic sat down, staring straight ahead, his body rigid. Mary's parents were looking at him, confused. The security guard stepped closer but didn't intervene.

Dan turned back to the witness box. Cutthroat. The defence of the desperate. *It was not me but my accomplice who did it.*

Lucy was still gripping the brass rail, except now she was looking down, gulping breaths. Dan thought she was going to fake another collapse.

The judge peered over his glasses. 'Miss Ayres? Do you feel all right?'

She looked up and nodded and then faced Dan. She'd been given the signal by her father. Dan had seen it.

'Who killed Mary Kendricks?' Dan said.

Lucy looked to the gallery again and back to the jury. Her tongue flicked to her lips.

'Miss Ayres, do you want me to repeat the question?'

She shook her head. 'No, I heard you. I can answer it.' Another glance to the public gallery and then, 'Peter killed Mary.'

There were gasps from the gallery. Carter got to his feet.

'I shouldn't have lied, I was scared, still am. He said he was going to kill me if I told anyone.'

'Where were you when Mary was killed?'

'You've got to understand me first.' She looked around the courtroom, as if she were desperate to be believed. 'I shouldn't have lied, I'm sorry, but I didn't do it.'

'Where were you, Miss Ayres, when Mary was killed?'

She looked down again and swayed. Dan thought she was going to faint, until she said, still looking down, 'in the room with Peter, arguing with Mary. Peter got all excited, I don't know why. Because he was drunk perhaps, but he pinned her down on the bed. Mary was naked and it must have got him worked up, but I was trying to pull him off her, because I thought he was going to rape her. I shouted at him to stop, tried to stop him, but he pushed me away, and then,' and she paused to take a breath. 'Then Mary screamed.'

The courtroom had fallen silent. Everyone was straining hear to every word, rapt, aghast.

Dan didn't need to ask a question. Lucy wanted to get it all out.

'When Mary screamed, Peter panicked. There were some scissors on the table next to her bed. He grabbed them and raised his hand,' and she acted out the motion. 'His eyes were crazy, it was all crazy, but he punched down with them, kept on going until they were all the way in, then again, and once more into her neck.' She wiped her eyes. 'Mary went still, like someone had unplugged her. It cut her scream straight off.' She looked towards the jury, and to Dan, and then to the judge. 'I panicked, I didn't know what to do, so I ran, and Peter followed.'

'And you've kept this quiet all this time?'

'I was scared. You don't know what he's like. He killed that woman too. The lawyer, Shelley.'

Dan felt a jolt. 'What do you mean?'

'Just that. He thought she'd been talking to you and that woman who works for you and he didn't know what had been said. He drove there, as soon as that woman followed him, and threw her off the bridge.' Lucy looked around the room, her eyes pleading. 'If he'll do that to her, what would he have done to me?'

Dan let her words sink in. He wanted to get more from her, because he didn't believe her. He'd seen the sign from her father and knew what it meant, an agreed signal that if the case goes badly, she should make sure that Peter took the blame. Her answers weren't about rescuing Carter but about rescuing herself.

He couldn't think about that. He needed to think about Robert Carter.

'Where was Robert Carter when this was going on?'

Lucy paused to wipe her eyes again, tears streaming down. 'I don't know.' She nodded, as if to reaffirm it. 'He'd left the house. I don't know where he was.'

'Did he play any part in the murder of Mary Kendricks?'

She looked up to the ceiling, her lip trembling. The court-room had fallen silent, everyone poised for her answer. When she looked down again, her stare was resolute. 'No. He wasn't there. It was Peter. All Peter.'

Carter banged on the high glass surround, shouting at Lucy, nothing comprehensible, just howls of anguish. Sobs came from the gallery. Sara Carter. Mary's parents. Lucy's mother. Dominic was straight-faced. The reporters moved towards the doors, knowing they had a story and wanting to be outside when Lucy left court to take photographs.

'No more questions,' Dan said, and sat down. It was all over.

Seventy-eight

Dan walked towards Jayne's car. She was parked outside his office, sitting in the driver's seat, drumming her fingers on the steering wheel.

Three weeks had passed since Peter and Lucy's arrest. According to Murdoch, there'd been concerns that they'd stay quiet, but once they got into the interview rooms, they wouldn't stop talking, each blaming the other for the stabbings. The prosecution had charged them both with murder, but Dan knew it would be a difficult case, because the prosecution would have to prove that each encouraged the other to take part, that they knew Mary would be harmed.

Shelley's murder was easier to solve. Lucy and Peter had travelled to Highford together, CCTV from Manchester city centre showing them running to her car, with ANPR cameras tracking them all the way. Her boss had made a statement explaining how she'd said there was a family emergency. It didn't matter who'd pushed her, because they'd been each other's accomplices.

Lucy had a good lawyer, of course, Conrad Taylor, who'd be keen to put all the blame on to Peter. Mickey's evidence was crucial, although Dan knew there were difficult times ahead for him, now that his secret was out. Highford was a small town with long memories.

More than Mickey, the prosecution had the news footage of Lucy near the scene the day after Mary had died. In court, she'd said how scared she was, but all the footage showed was her in charge, talking to Peter all the time, whispering in his ear, seemingly controlling him.

Dan had spent some time with his father afterwards, and had enjoyed telling him how he'd brought down Dominic Ayres. There'd been a series of drug busts on properties owned by him, where cannabis farms were discovered, small terraced houses filled with plants and foil extraction pipes and hydration systems. The police couldn't prove he'd been involved in their growth, but there'd been a clear enough audit trail to charge him with money laundering as well as witness intimidation, relating to Mickey. He was currently in prison, waiting for his trial, as were Lucy and Peter.

His father had been proud. Like Dan had told him, there was more than one way to win the fight.

As for Robert Carter, he came out of prison to not much of a fanfare. He made the papers, but he was portrayed as the man whose cheating had led to Mary's death, and as the coward who'd stayed quiet and left her to die. Dan found it hard to disagree. Sara wasn't going to have him back but she'd thanked Dan for getting him out, and she wanted Robert to see his daughter.

As he got closer, Jayne pressed the button to lower the passenger window. Dan leaned in. 'You don't have to go,' he said.

'Thank you, but I do. I've needed to do this for a while.'

'Will you be all right?'

'You kept on telling me that I would be, that I don't need to hide. I hope you're right.'

'Are your parents expecting you?'

'No. I'll turn up and see how it goes.'

'And what about Jimmy's family?'

'They'll find out I'm back, it's that kind of area. I'll just have to see what happens when we meet, because we will, I know it.' She smiled. 'I know one other thing too: I can look them in the eye and know that I didn't murder him. I haven't got it in me. What I did was to protect myself, nothing more, and I didn't mean to kill him. I still see the images when I close my eyes, but I know myself better now. That helps.'

He wanted to reach in and hold her, happy that she was feeling good about herself. If anything good had come of this, it was that.

'Are you coming back?'

She shrugged. 'Who knows? If I do, is there still work from you?'

'You're cheaper than an employee.'

'You're all heart,' she said, laughing. 'I should go.'

He wanted to reach in and tell her not to go, that she should stay and they should try to get know each other better, in circumstances where her case wouldn't be a cloud over them both, but he stopped himself. 'Yes, you should.'

'Thanks for everything.'

'My pleasure.'

'You sure?'

'Some of the time.'

Jayne started the engine. 'Anything else before I go?'

Dan wanted to tell her he'd got it wrong about Jimmy's family, that she wouldn't be safe if she went back. They could have some fun, and they'd worked well together. He wasn't used to having someone in his apartment and she'd made it better somehow. Brighter, more fun.

He didn't do any of that. He stepped away from the car and gave her a small wave.

She sighed and then blew Dan a kiss as she put the car into gear and set off, waving as she went.

He watched her go.

As he turned back to his office door, a woman was standing outside, watching him. Mary's mother, her father behind her.

Dan smiled politely as he got close, but it was forced, not sure what was coming.

Mary's mother was holding a handbag in both hands, although there was a handkerchief crushed into her palm.

'Mr Grant,' she said.

'Yes, hello.'

'I just wanted to say sorry for hitting you.' There were tears in her eyes as she said it.

'You were upset, the trial was a tough time for you.'

'I've been feeling bad about it, but the more I've thought about it, the more I realise you did the right thing, because the right people are in prison, even if you did it for the wrong reason.'

'I think of it differently. I was doing the wrong thing, but for the right reason.'

'I don't understand.'

'I defend people, Mrs Kendricks, whatever they've done. I do that because someone has to. Robert Carter didn't kill your daughter, and if I hadn't come along, he might have gone to prison for life and Lucy and Peter would never have been punished, and perhaps they would even done it again. I did the wrong thing in not spotting their real guilt, but what I did, I did it because I was defending my client, whatever people thought about him.'

She frowned. 'I think I understand,' and then, 'how is Robert?'

'He's rebuilding his life. His marriage is over, but he wants to be there for his daughter.'

'I wish Mary hadn't been involved with him.'

'It was done. Life isn't perfect, but they were happy, in their own little way.'

'Thank you,' she said. 'I just wanted you to know I'm sorry.'

'It's forgotten.'

She turned to walk away, pausing to link arms with her husband.

Dan turned back to his office. Margaret was knocking on the window to attract his attention, holding a phone to the glass.

He went inside and closed the door.

'It's the police station,' she said. 'They're on hold for you. Someone wants you down there.'

And so it began again. Another case. Another day.

He smiled to himself. That was why he did it.

Acknowledgements

It is not easy to write a book. It involves many hours of solitude, always trying to find a way through the fog, and of course my family are always in the background. I owe them a lot and the books wouldn't be there without their support.

From The Shadows is my first book with Bonnier Zaffre, and it has been a delight to work with so many talented and enthusiastic people. In particular, my editors Katherine Armstrong and Katie Gordon have provided advice and direction where I needed it, and I am looking forward to a long and fruitful partnership.

I must mention the continued support and belief of my wonderful agent, Sonia Land of Sheil Land Associates. Her advice has been invaluable through the years.

Most of all, without people who read books, there'd be no need for writers. The biggest acknowledgement must go to all those people who have read my previous books and are taking the time to read this one. All I can do is try to write books I hope you enjoy. For as long as you still enjoy them, I'll still write them.

9